I0765423

Copyright 2025 by Erosetti Press
ISBN 978-1-968703-14-1 All Rights Reserved - Inquiries:
erosettipress.com & coaxdreams.com

ErosettiPress.com

INTRODUCING THE DELUXE EDITION

THE VOLUMPTUOUS DETECTIVE

Wanda Wolfe first appeared in the pages of *Kiss Comix* in Spain, drawn in black and white with watercolor crayon greys (three original pages follow this introduction!). From the beginning, Wanda's mix of bawdy humor, erotic excess, and sharp parody of mystery and crime fiction struck a chord with readers far beyond Spain, earning her a devoted international following.

As the series grew, Coax painstakingly hand-colored the stories for digital release—a process that marked the beginning of his road into self-publishing. What emerged was not only a fresh presentation of Wanda's escapades but also an important step in Coax's evolution as an artist and independent creator.

The premise remains gloriously outrageous: Wanda Wolfe, voluptuous private eye, dives headfirst into the most twisted cases. Indecent informants, perverse masterminds, and well-equipped accomplices cross her path, but nothing deters Wanda, who solves every mystery with her singular combination of wit, nerve, and unabashed sexuality. In her adventures, readers will catch sly nods to Agatha Christie's drawing-room mysteries, Cold War agents and spies, pulp thrillers, superhero capers, and even the serialized rhythms of classic TV shows —all filtered through Coax's erotic imagination. She is at once a parody of pulp detectives and a cult erotic heroine in her own right.

This Deluxe Edition brings together all eight Wanda Wolfe comics in a single volume, accompanied by bonus sketches, illustrations, and the opening page of a new story in which Wanda makes a playful cameo. It is the most complete celebration in print yet of Coax's Detective Wanda Wolfe. No case unsolved, no pleasure denied.

DANTE REMY, EDITOR

WORKING PROCESS FOR THE COVER

DETECTIVE
WANDA WOLFE
by COAX
SEXY!
FUNNY!
KINKY!
3 FULL STORIES
ONLY FOR MATURE READERS!
COAXDREAMS

DETECTIVE
WANDA WOLFE
BY COAX
THE HOTTEST COMICS!
No.1
SEXY! FUNNY! KINKY!
3 FULL STORIES
* Only for MATURE readers!
A COAXDREAMS PRODUCTION

EXTREMELY HOT!
DETECTIVE
WANDA
WOLFE
BY COAX
No.1
SEXY!
FUNNY!
KINKY!
3
FULL
STORIES
* Only for MATURE readers!
Erosetti
Press

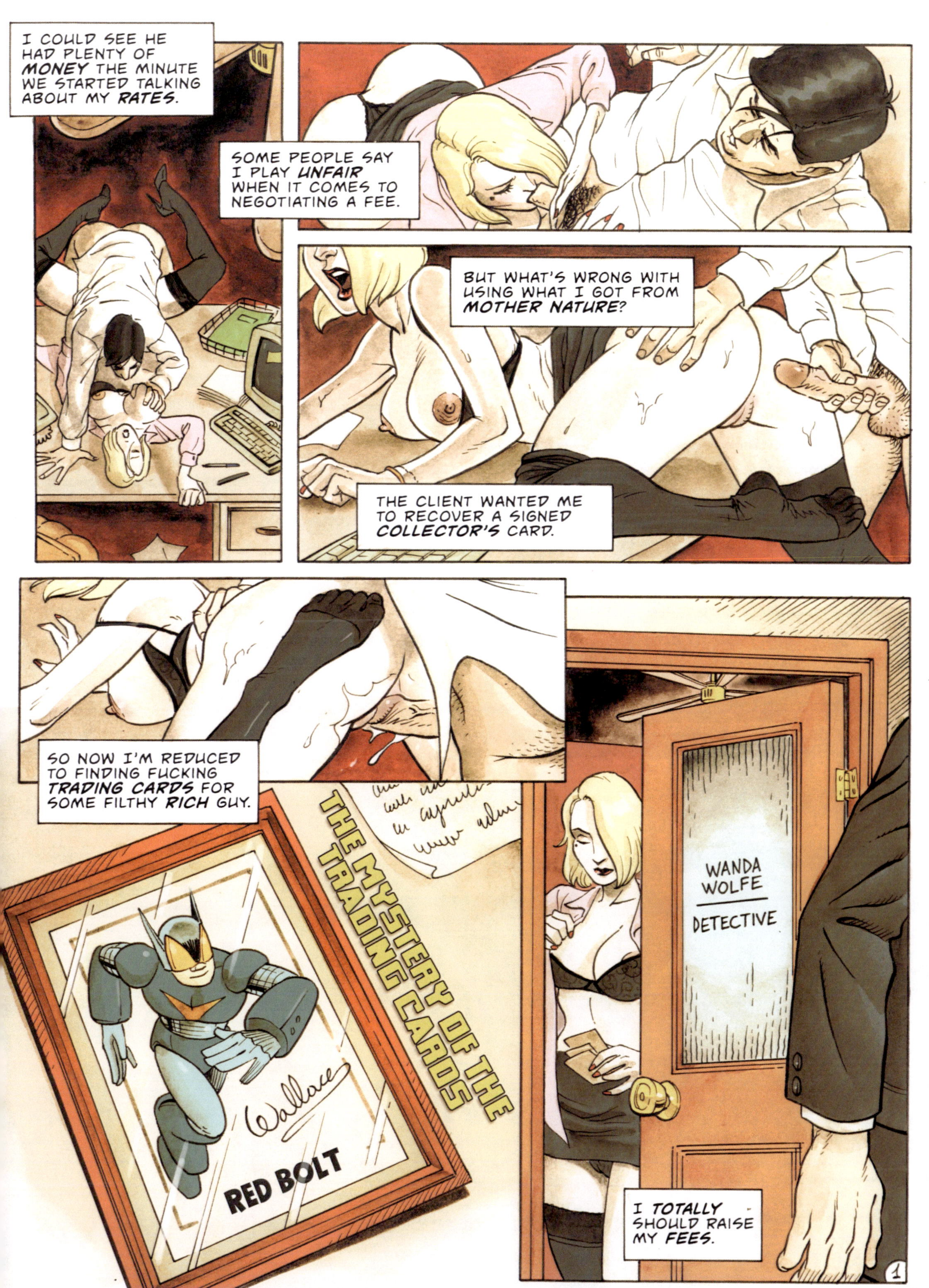

I COULD SEE HE HAD PLENTY OF MONEY THE MINUTE WE STARTED TALKING ABOUT MY RATES.
SOME PEOPLE SAY I PLAY UNFAIR WHEN IT COMES TO NEGOTIATING A FEE.
BUT WHAT'S WRONG WITH USING WHAT I GOT FROM MOTHER NATURE?
THE CLIENT WANTED ME TO RECOVER A SIGNED COLLECTOR'S CARD.
SO NOW I'M REDUCED TO FINDING FUCKING TRADING CARDS FOR SOME FILTHY RICH GUY.
THE MYSTERY OF THE TRADING CARDS
Wallace
RED BOLT
WANDA WOLFE
DETECTIVE
I TOTALLY SHOULD RAISE MY FEES.
1

THE FLEA MARKET SEEMED THE *BEST* PLACE TO START.

BUT IT WAS *ODD*. NOBODY HAD EVER *HEARD* OF THIS COLLECTOR'S SERIES BEFORE.
WERE THEY *LYING*?
OR WAS MY CLIENT WASTING MY *TIME*?

MAYBE I JUST NEEDED SOME MORE *OBLIGING* INFORMANTS.

THE GOOD THING ABOUT DEALING WITH *MEN* IS THAT YOU *ALWAYS* KNOW THEIR PRICE.

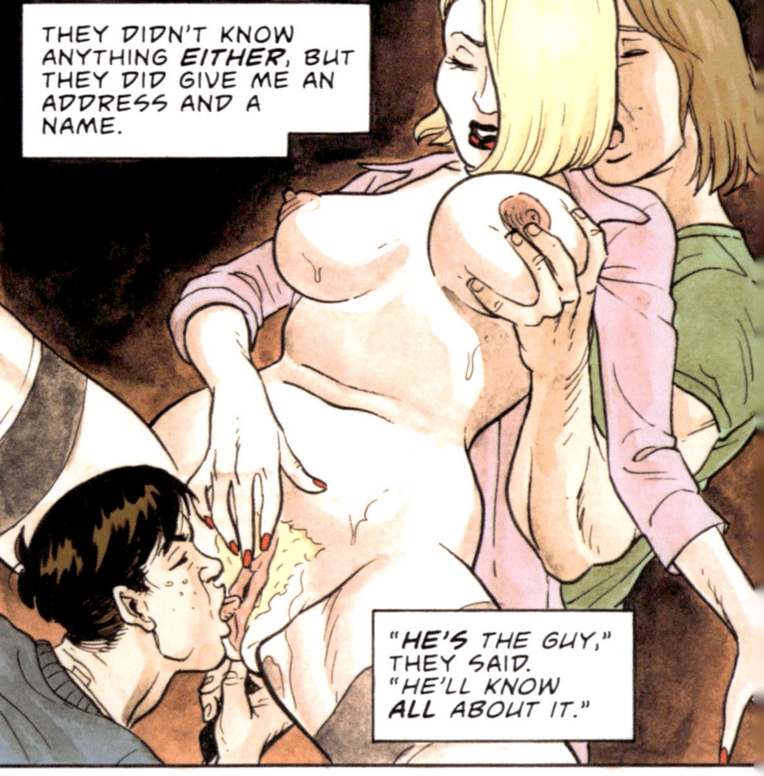

THEY DIDN'T KNOW ANYTHING *EITHER*, BUT THEY DID GIVE ME AN ADDRESS AND A NAME.
"*HE'S* THE GUY," THEY SAID. "HE'LL KNOW *ALL* ABOUT IT."

WE'LL SEE.

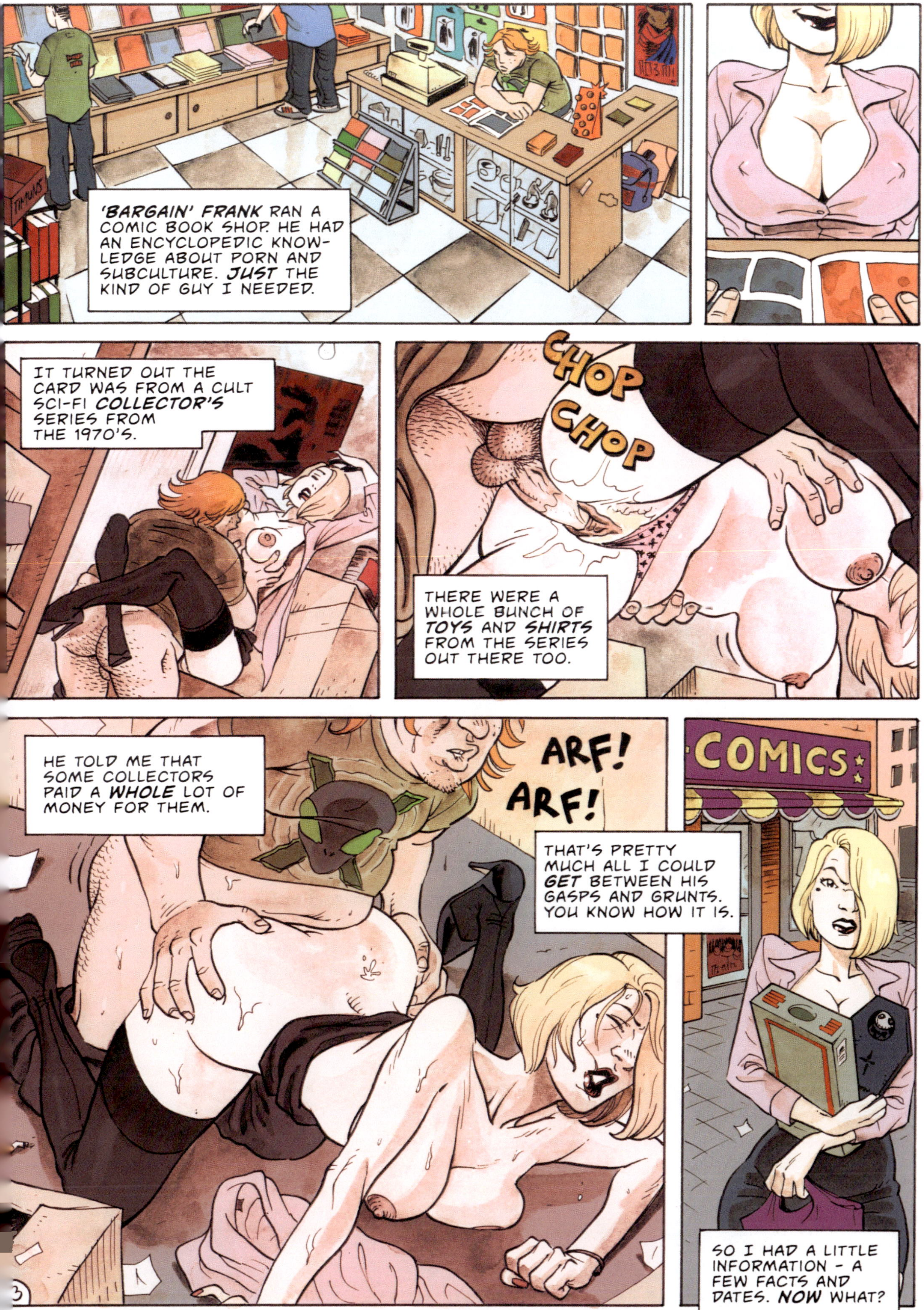

'BARGAIN' FRANK RAN A COMIC BOOK SHOP. HE HAD AN ENCYCLOPEDIC KNOWLEDGE ABOUT PORN AND SUBCULTURE. JUST THE KIND OF GUY I NEEDED.

IT TURNED OUT THE CARD WAS FROM A CULT SCI-FI COLLECTOR'S SERIES FROM THE 1970'S.

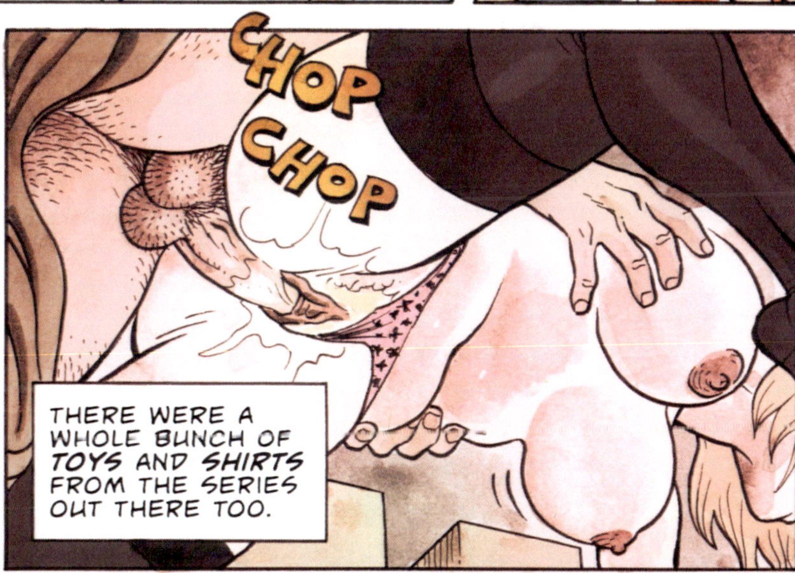

CHOP CHOP
THERE WERE A WHOLE BUNCH OF TOYS AND SHIRTS FROM THE SERIES OUT THERE TOO.

HE TOLD ME THAT SOME COLLECTORS PAID A WHOLE LOT OF MONEY FOR THEM.
ARF! ARF!
THAT'S PRETTY MUCH ALL I COULD GET BETWEEN HIS GASPS AND GRUNTS. YOU KNOW HOW IT IS.
COMICS
SO I HAD A LITTLE INFORMATION - A FEW FACTS AND DATES. NOW WHAT?

FYT
RED BOLT? OH SURE. I REMEMBER THAT FROM WHEN I WAS A KID.
ALEX WAS MY SAVIOUR. HE WAS SOMETHING OF A GEEK, BUT HE'D BEEN ABLE TO HELP ME MANY TIMES BEFORE.
SUCH A SWEETIE.
MY GUESS IS THE THIEF IS A BIG FAN OF THE SERIES. BUT HOW ON EARTH DO WE TRACK HIM DOWN? HE COULD BE ANYONE.
I LIKED TEASING HIM, I'LL ADMIT IT. BUT I NEVER GAVE HIM WHAT HE WANTED.
UH... WITH CULT SERIES LIKE THIS, THE FANS TEND TO GATHER FOR SCREENINGS, MEETINGS, COSPLAY AND STUFF. BUT I DON'T KNOW WHEN...
THANKS, HONEY.
I'M SO WICKED, I KNOW.
THANKS TO ALEX, I NOW KNEW EXACTLY WHAT I WAS LOOKING FOR, IN MY JOB IT'S ALWAYS IMPORTANT TO ASK THE RIGHT QUESTIONS.
ANSWERS COME QUICKLY.

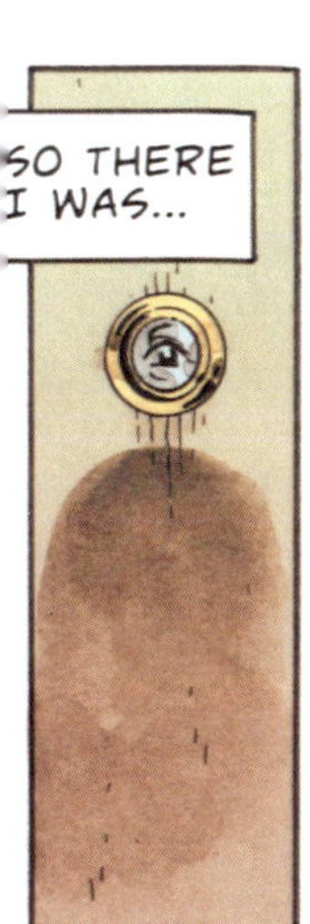

SO THERE I WAS...

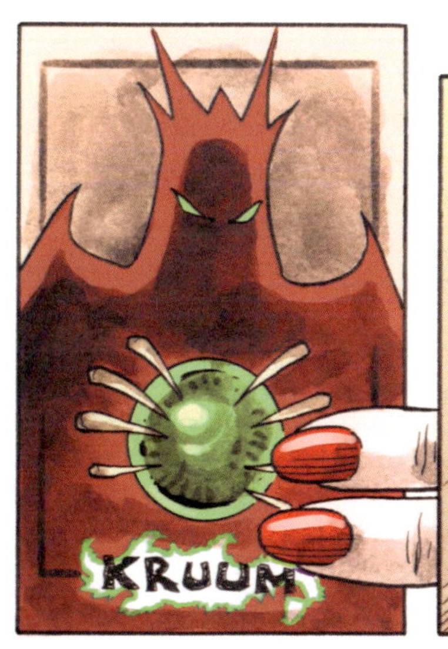

KRUUM

GALACTIC GREETINGS, TO YOU, FRIEND! BEEP!
...
IN THE FUCKING MADHOUSE.

THE PEOPLE THERE WERE COMPLETELY DERANGED.
I DON'T THINK THEY WERE EVEN LOOKING AT MY TITS.
WOULD THIS BE THE RIGHT PLACE TO FIND THE TRADING CARD THIEF?

OHH MY GOD! OF COURSE! IT'S YOU! IT'S 'BARGAIN' FRANK!
WHY HADN'T I REALISED SOONER? HE WAS THE CRAZIEST OF ALL THE CRAZY GUYS, AFTER ALL!

THEN THE FILTHY LITTLE ASSHOLE CALLED ME SOMETHING BAD.

AND THE WHOLE ROOM STOOD UP, ALL OF THEM ANGRY AT ME.

BUT I WAS READY.

5

ASYA
GASP!
OKAY, SO I FELT PRETTY FUCKING RIDICULOUS DRESSED LIKE THAT.
BUT HEY, IT WORKED PERFECTLY.
DON'T LET HIM ESCAPE, MY WARRIORS!
AND IT TURNED OUT TO BE A REALLY MEMORABLE NIGHT.
AAHHH
OOHH!

I RECOVERED MY CLIENT'S SIGNED TRADING CARD...
'BARGAIN' FRANK WAS THROWN OUT OF THE COLLECTOR'S CLUB...
AND I GOT BACK TO MY USUAL JOB ROUTINE.
CHOP
AH!
AH!
FUCK
FUCK
THOUGH I DON'T THINK I'LL EVER FORGET...
MY FABLED WARRIORS OF...
RED BOLT
THE END.

FUCK! FUCK!
AAH! OOH!
GHN! GHMF!
MMMHN! OOOH!
UH! MHF! UUH! OOH!
ARRFFS! GMMFS!
AAAr
HUMAN HEAT
ALVARO 2002
AN INTRIGUING NEW CASE FOR DETECTIVE WANDA WOLFE!

I THINK THE PARTY GOT A LITTLE OUT OF CONTROL LAST NIGHT. LOOKS LIKE AN OPEN AND SHUT CASE.
SORRY, MISS, YOU CAN'T COME IN HERE...
DETECTIVE WANDA WOLFE.
THAT WOMAN WAS THE WIFE OF MY CLIENT.
LET ME SEE THAT FUCKING #*@~# BITCH!
SIR, YOU CAN'T GO INSIDE.
SO YOU FINALLY GOT IT! THE BIGGEST DICK! I HOPE YOU CHOKED ON IT!
JUST RELAX, MAN. IT'S NOT LIKE SHE CAN DO IT AGAIN...
5%&#* ASSHOLE!
SPUT!
UM... OFFICER, WOULD YOU TAKE HIS STATEMENT?
HEH. QUITE A SHOW, DON'T YOU THINK SO, DETECTIVE?
IT WAS EVEN WORSE DURING THE GANG WARS IN CHINATOWN. NOT FOR THE FEINT-HEARTED. I REMEMBER THERE WAS ONE TIME WE...

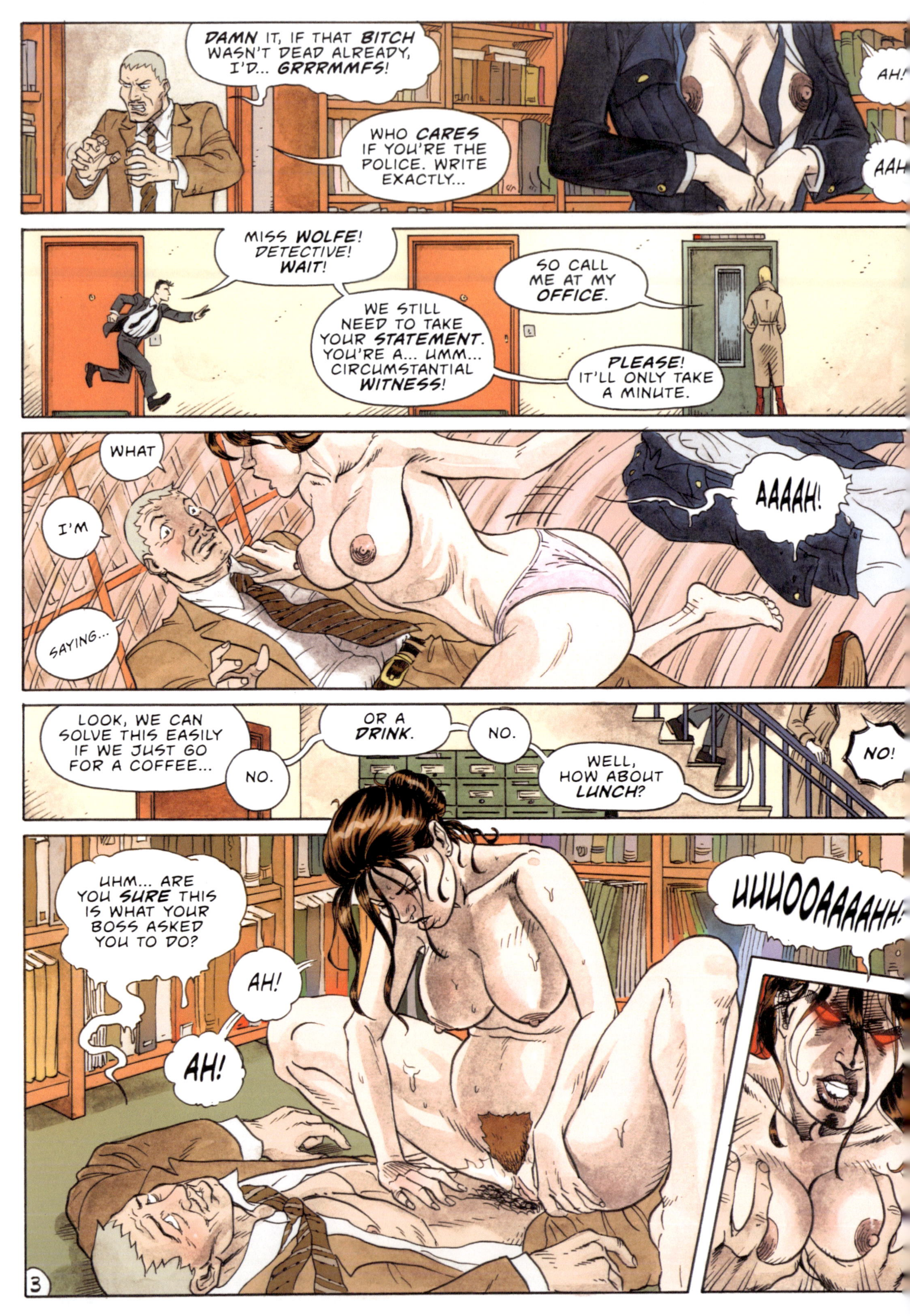

DAMN IT, IF THAT BITCH WASN'T DEAD ALREADY, I'D... GRRRMMFS!
WHO CARES IF YOU'RE THE POLICE. WRITE EXACTLY...
AH!
AAH!
MISS WOLFE! DETECTIVE! WAIT!
WE STILL NEED TO TAKE YOUR STATEMENT. YOU'RE A... UMM... CIRCUMSTANTIAL WITNESS!
SO CALL ME AT MY OFFICE.
PLEASE! IT'LL ONLY TAKE A MINUTE.
WHAT
I'M
SAYING...
AAAAH!
LOOK, WE CAN SOLVE THIS EASILY IF WE JUST GO FOR A COFFEE...
NO.
OR A DRINK.
NO.
WELL, HOW ABOUT LUNCH?
NO!
UHM... ARE YOU SURE THIS IS WHAT YOUR BOSS ASKED YOU TO DO?
AH!
AH!
UUUOOAAAAHH!

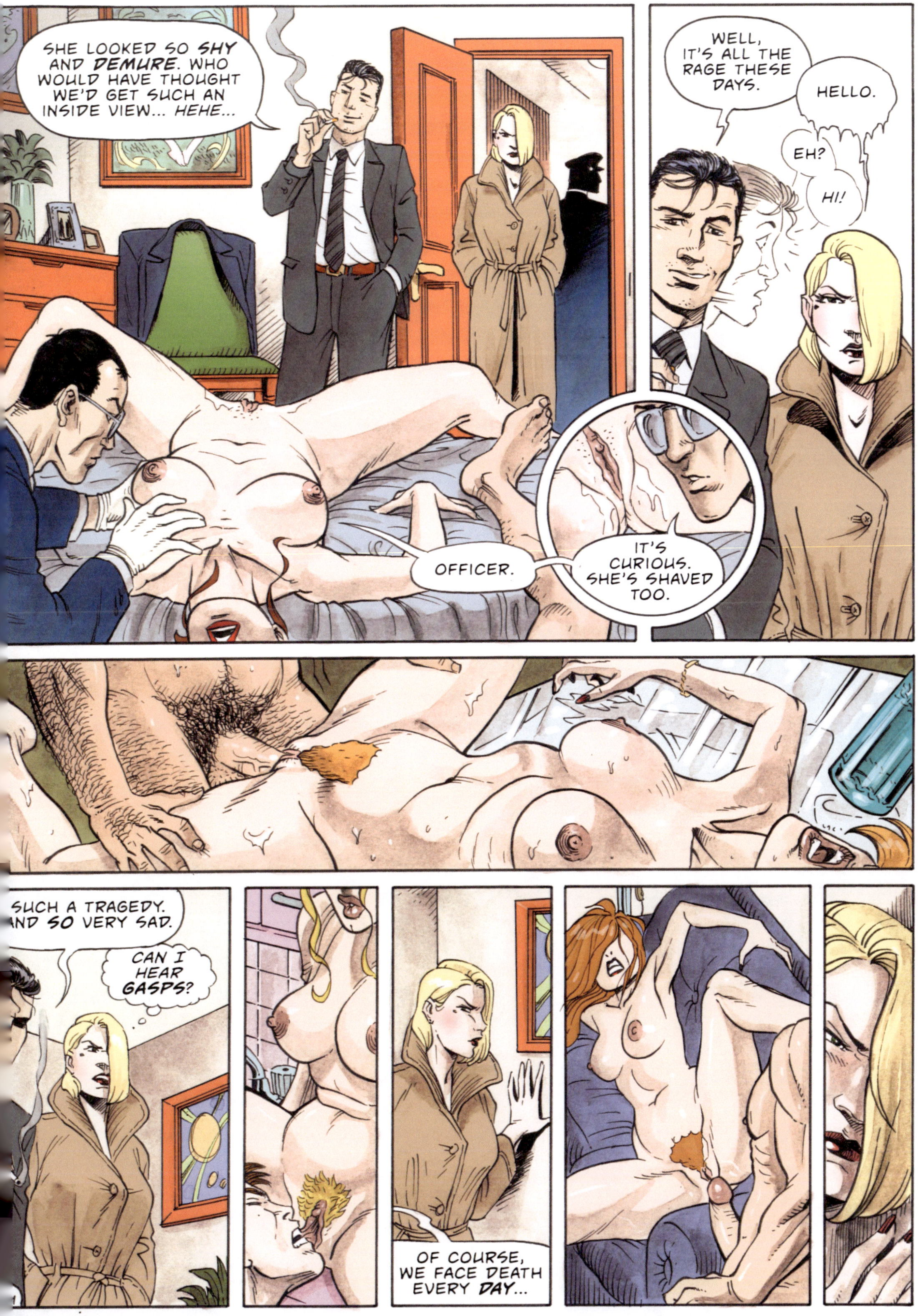

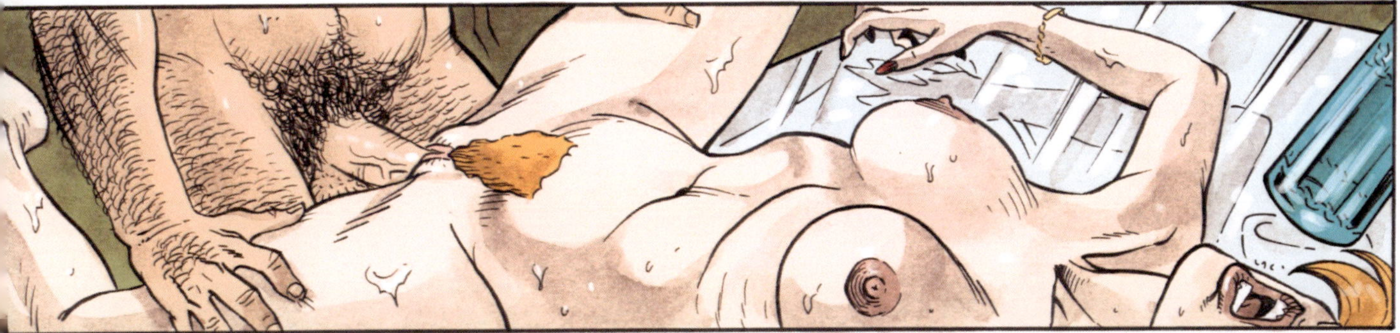

SHE LOOKED SO SHY AND DEMURE. WHO WOULD HAVE THOUGHT WE'D GET SUCH AN INSIDE VIEW... HEHE...
WELL, IT'S ALL THE RAGE THESE DAYS.
HELLO.
EH?
HI!
OFFICER.
IT'S CURIOUS. SHE'S SHAVED TOO.

SUCH A TRAGEDY. AND SO VERY SAD.
CAN I HEAR GASPS?

OF COURSE, WE FACE DEATH EVERY DAY...

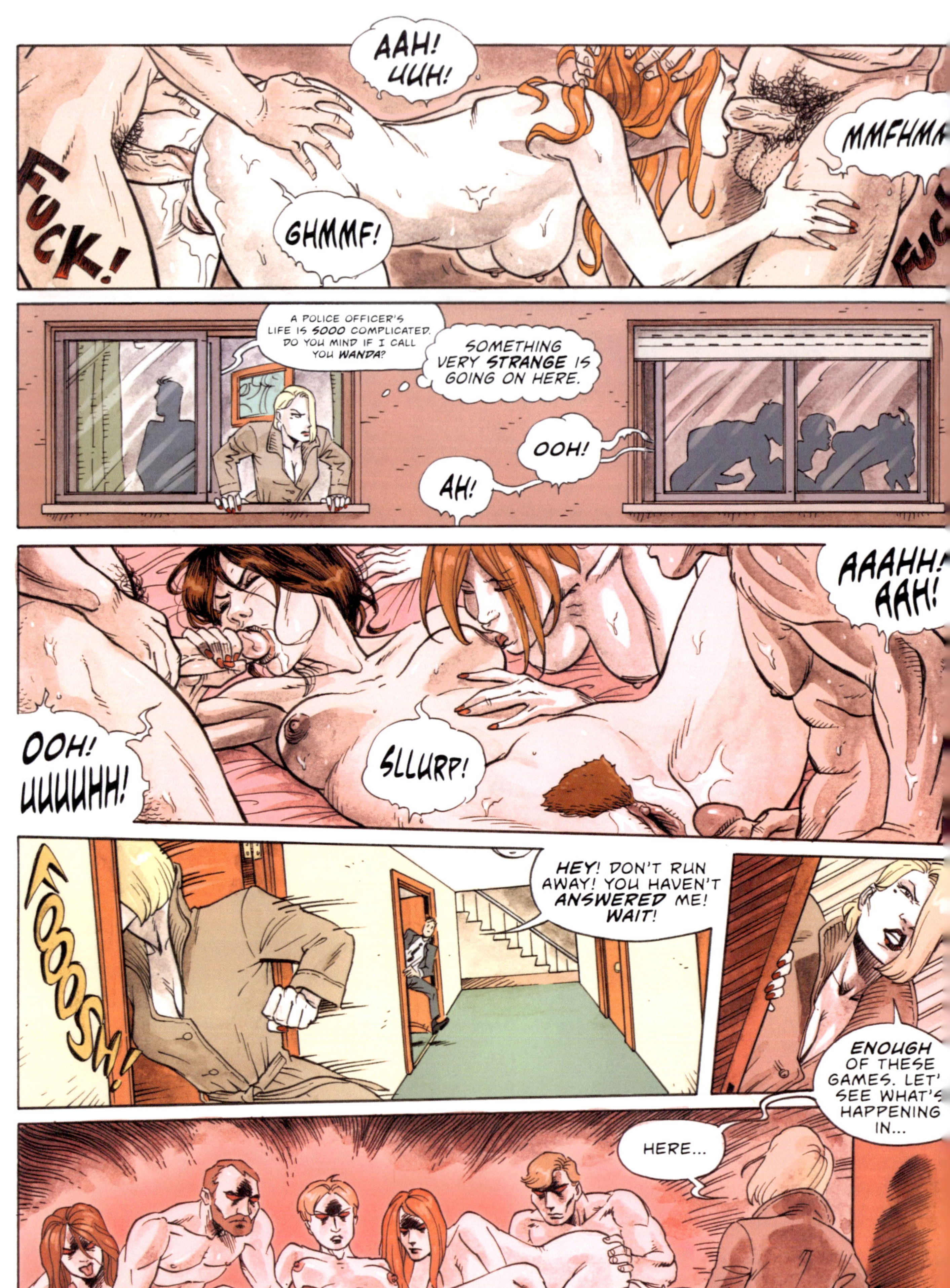
AAH! UUH!
MMFHMM
FUCK!
GHMMF!
FUCK!
A POLICE OFFICER'S LIFE IS SOOO COMPLICATED. DO YOU MIND IF I CALL YOU WANDA?
SOMETHING VERY STRANGE IS GOING ON HERE.
OOH!
AH!
AAAHH! AAH!
OOH! UUUUHH!
SLLURP!
FOOOSH!
HEY! DON'T RUN AWAY! YOU HAVEN'T ANSWERED ME! WAIT!
ENOUGH OF THESE GAMES. LET' SEE WHAT'S HAPPENING IN...
HERE...

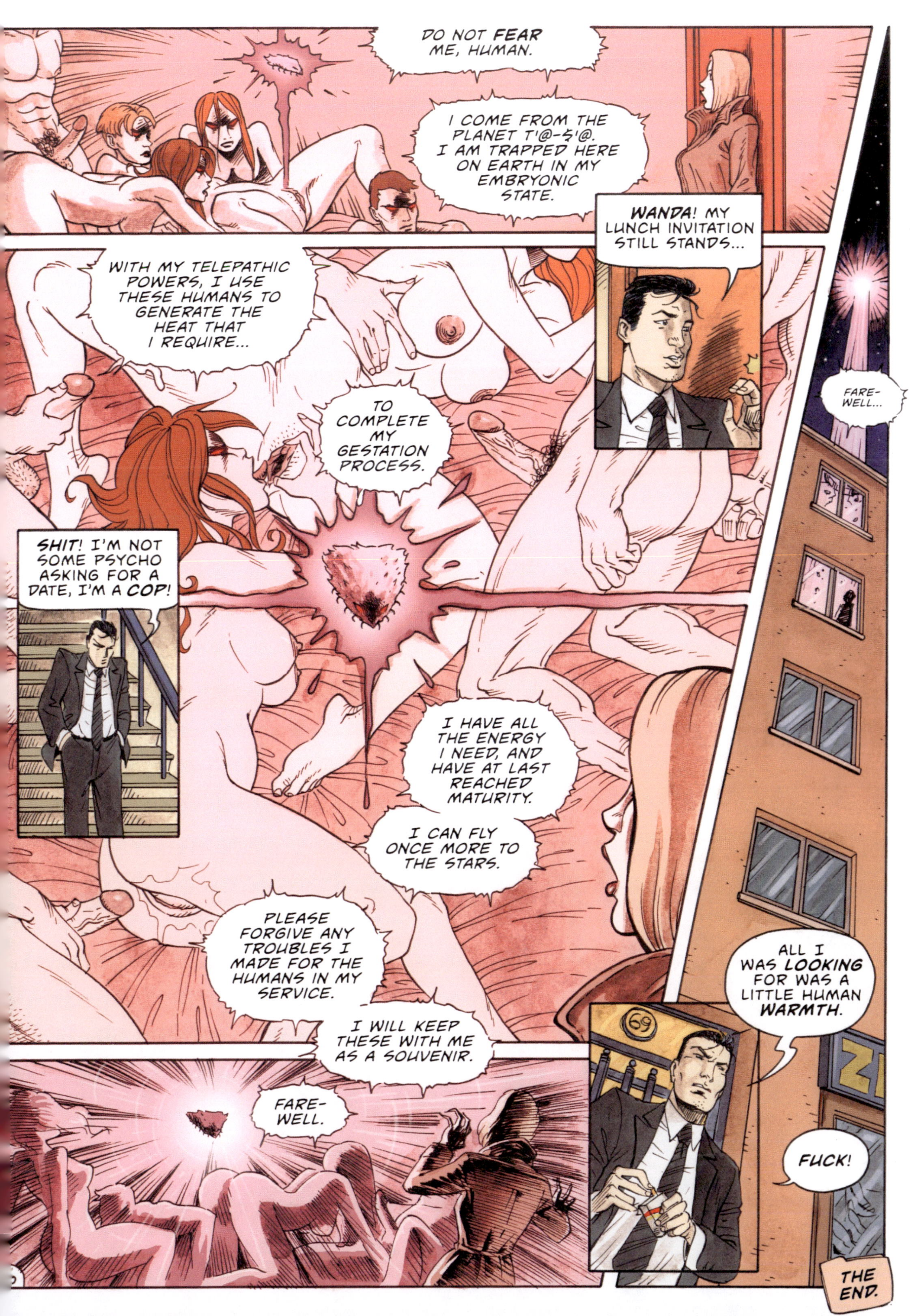
DO NOT FEAR ME, HUMAN.
I COME FROM THE PLANET T'@-$'@. I AM TRAPPED HERE ON EARTH IN MY EMBRYONIC STATE.
WANDA! MY LUNCH INVITATION STILL STANDS...
WITH MY TELEPATHIC POWERS, I USE THESE HUMANS TO GENERATE THE HEAT THAT I REQUIRE...
TO COMPLETE MY GESTATION PROCESS.
FARE-WELL...
SHIT! I'M NOT SOME PSYCHO ASKING FOR A DATE, I'M A COP!
I HAVE ALL THE ENERGY I NEED, AND HAVE AT LAST REACHED MATURITY.
I CAN FLY ONCE MORE TO THE STARS.
PLEASE FORGIVE ANY TROUBLES I MADE FOR THE HUMANS IN MY SERVICE.
I WILL KEEP THESE WITH ME AS A SOUVENIR.
ALL I WAS LOOKING FOR WAS A LITTLE HUMAN WARMTH.
FARE-WELL.
FUCK!
THE END.

The original uncolored first page of "Mission Incredible" appearing In Kiss Comix No. 131.

IT WAS A CASE BETTER SUITED TO 007, SUPER-SPY, NOT TO ME.
I HAD TO GET THROUGH THEIR SECURITY AND RECOVER A STOLEN TOTEM.
I COULD SMELL THE PROBLEMS STRAIGHT AWAY.
SOMEONE ELSE WANTING THE REWARD HAD GOT THERE FIRST AND DEALT WITH THE SECURITY GUARDS.
THEY WERE CLEARLY A SKILLFUL ENEMY: FAST, SILENT AND GOOD WITH KNOTS.
NOT TO MENTION CREATIVE AND A BIT SADISTIC.
THEY WERE OBVIOUSLY DANGEROUS.
BUT AT LAST...
MMF!
HHHPP! MMH!
GMMFS!
1

THE REINFORCED SECURITY BOX!
THERE IT WAS, AWAITING MY ARRIVAL.
THE VALUABLE TOTEM, DEIFIED BY THE ANCIENTS, SYMBOL OF THE GOD'S POWERS.
IT WAS ALL BUT BEGGING ME TO TAKE IT.
POR ALVARO
MISSION : INCREDIBLE
AND I PLANNED TO DO JUST THAT: GRAB IT AND GET OUT FAST, BEFORE TROUBLE SHOWED UP.
BUT I WOULDN'T BE THAT LUCKY.

FSSS!
I HEARD IT JUST IN TIME.
IN SITUATIONS LIKE THIS I HAVE ALMOST A SIXTH SENSE. MY NIPPLES GET AS HARD AS STONE AND I JUST... SENSE THE DANGER.
WE FELL TO THE FLOOR, STRUGGLING LIKE BITCHES.
WHAT A FIGHT! ROLLING, RUBBING AND SCRATCHING. FLUIDS EXUDING.
THE LATEX OVER OUR SKIN CLUNG TO THE SWEAT, AND WITH ALL THE TOUCHING... I WAS GETTING HORNY.
THE LAST THING I NEEDED RIGHT AT THAT MOMENT WAS A BUNCH OF ORGASMS.
I NEEDED TO GET LOOSE FROM HER...
3

I PULLED OFF THE LATEX SUIT, STILL FIGHTING WITH HER.

AND I WAS SURE I HAD THE UPPER HAND.

SHE HAD SIMPLY PRETENDED TO BE BEATEN.

JUST...

BEFORE I REALISED...

MY MIS-TAKE.

AND MY NAKED BODY GAVE HER EVERY CHANCE SHE NEEDED TO USE HER NINJA-GEISHA SECRET SKILLS OVER MY HYPER-SENSITIVE SKIN.

HER TONGUE WAS HER DEADLIEST WEAPON.

LICKING, SUCKING AND RUBBING, STIMULATING ME IN PLACES I NEVER REALISED WERE SO SENSITIVE.

AND HER HAIR WAS WORSE, SLIDING SOFTLY OVER MY VAGINA... OVER MY CLIT... UUOOH!

4

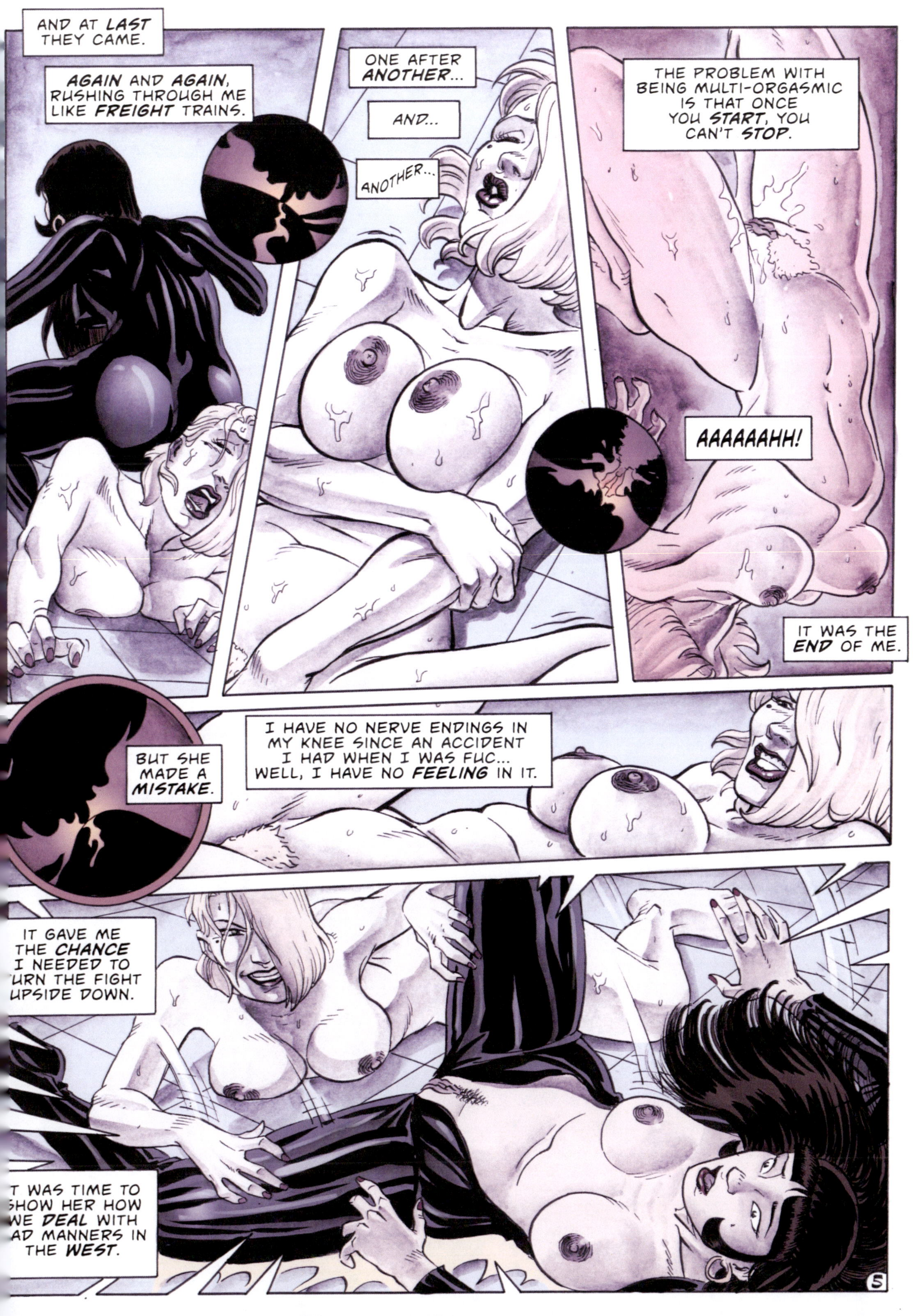

AND AT LAST THEY CAME.
AGAIN AND AGAIN, RUSHING THROUGH ME LIKE FREIGHT TRAINS.
ONE AFTER ANOTHER...
AND...
ANOTHER...
THE PROBLEM WITH BEING MULTI-ORGASMIC IS THAT ONCE YOU START, YOU CAN'T STOP.
AAAAAAHH!
IT WAS THE END OF ME.
BUT SHE MADE A MISTAKE.
I HAVE NO NERVE ENDINGS IN MY KNEE SINCE AN ACCIDENT I HAD WHEN I WAS FUC... WELL, I HAVE NO FEELING IN IT.
IT GAVE ME THE CHANCE I NEEDED TO TURN THE FIGHT UPSIDE DOWN.
IT WAS TIME TO SHOW HER HOW WE DEAL WITH BAD MANNERS IN THE WEST.
5

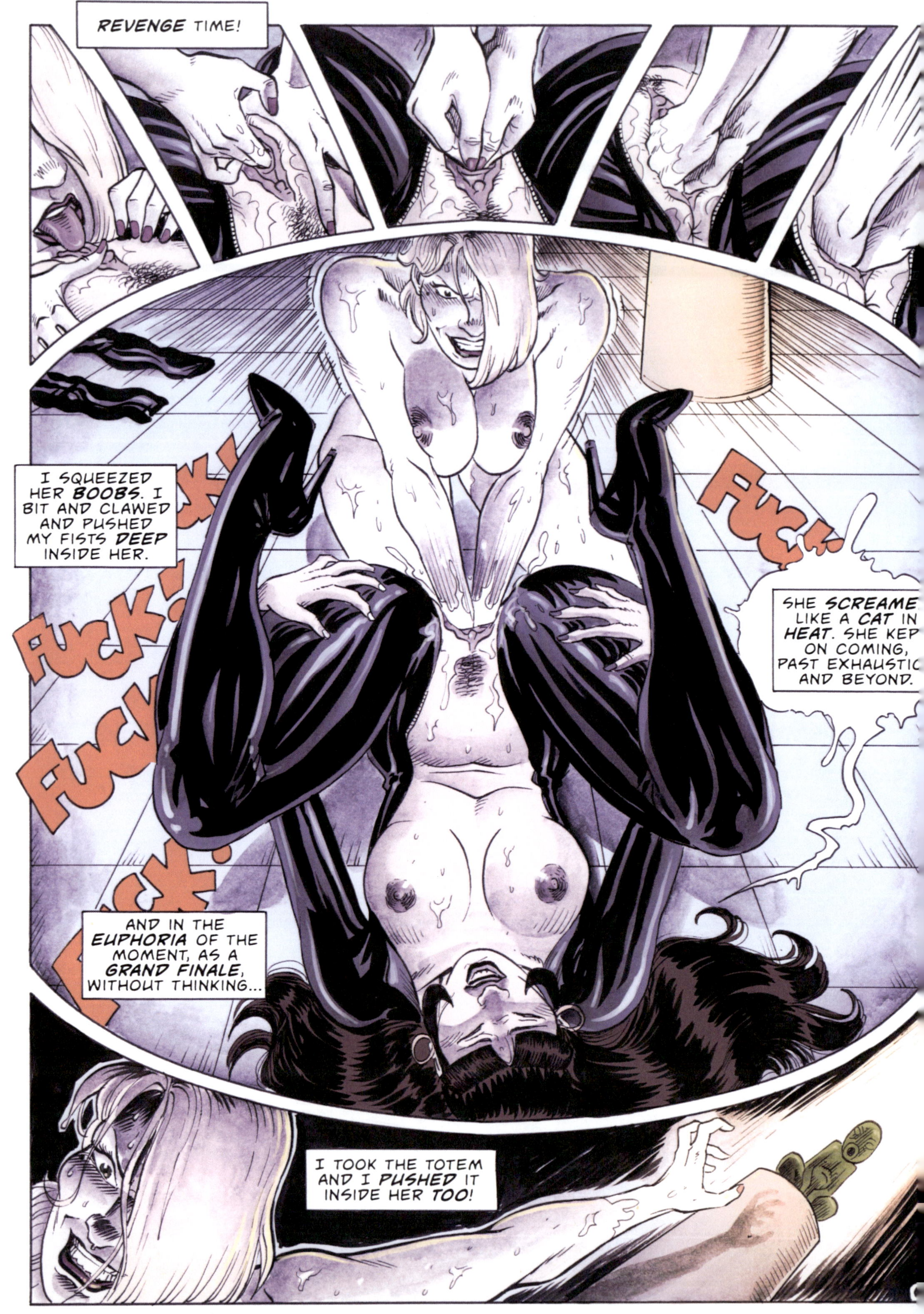
REVENGE TIME!
I SQUEEZED HER BOOBS. I BIT AND CLAWED AND PUSHED MY FISTS DEEP INSIDE HER.
FUCK! FUCK! FUCK! FUCK!
FUCK!
SHE SCREAME LIKE A CAT IN HEAT. SHE KEP ON COMING, PAST EXHAUSTIC AND BEYOND.
AND IN THE EUPHORIA OF THE MOMENT, AS A GRAND FINALE, WITHOUT THINKING...
I TOOK THE TOTEM AND I PUSHED IT INSIDE HER TOO!

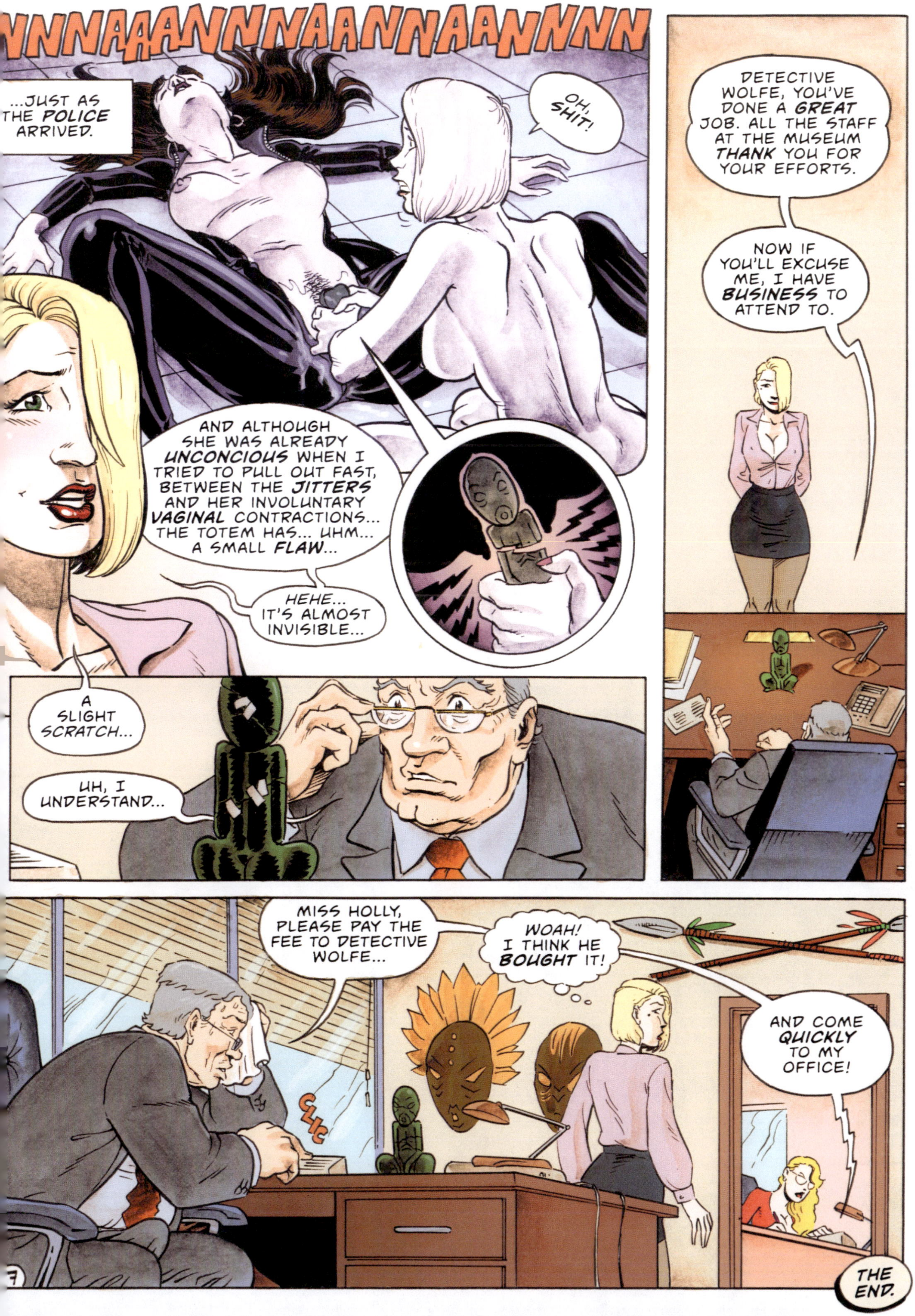

NNNAAANNNAANNAANNNN
...JUST AS THE POLICE ARRIVED.
OH, SHIT!
DETECTIVE WOLFE, YOU'VE DONE A GREAT JOB. ALL THE STAFF AT THE MUSEUM THANK YOU FOR YOUR EFFORTS.
NOW IF YOU'LL EXCUSE ME, I HAVE BUSINESS TO ATTEND TO.
AND ALTHOUGH SHE WAS ALREADY UNCONCIOUS WHEN I TRIED TO PULL OUT FAST, BETWEEN THE JITTERS AND HER INVOLUNTARY VAGINAL CONTRACTIONS... THE TOTEM HAS... UHM... A SMALL FLAW...
HEHE... IT'S ALMOST INVISIBLE...
A SLIGHT SCRATCH...
UH, I UNDERSTAND...
MISS HOLLY, PLEASE PAY THE FEE TO DETECTIVE WOLFE...
WOAH! I THINK HE BOUGHT IT!
AND COME QUICKLY TO MY OFFICE!
CLIC
THE END.

WORKING PROCESS FOR THE COVER
DETECTIVE
WANDA
WOLFE
BY COAX
THE HOTTEST COMICS!
3
FULL
STORIES
* Only for MATURE readers!
A COAXDREAMS
PRODUCTION
SKETCH
FLATS
FINAL

DETECTIVE
WANDA
WOLFE
BY COAX
Erosetti
Press
No.2
3
FULL
STORIES
* Only for MATURE readers!

AHH VINCENT. GOOD OLD TIRELESS, INSATIABLE VINCENT. SO MANY GOOD TIMES. YOU REALLY KNEW HOW TO ENJOY LIFE, THOUGH WE BOTH KNEW SOME DAY IT WOULD END. BUT NOT SO SOON. NOT THIS WAY...
...AS WE STAND HERE IN FRONT OF A DISGUSTING CASE OF... MURDER!!
LORD VENOM - ASSOCIATE - AND HIS WIFE
MR. DE GUILTY - ASSOCIATE - AND HIS WIFE
CHAMBER-MAIDS
MDME. BLACK - THE WIDOW -
THE BUTLER
ORGY & DEATH
A NEW AND ENTHRALLING CASE FOR DETECTIVE WANDA WOLFE!
AHEM THOUGH PERHAPS WE SHOULD START FROM THE BEGINNING. IT WAS A DEADLY NIGHT. A VERY RESTLESS NIGHT FOR EVERY LAST ONE OF YOU...
1

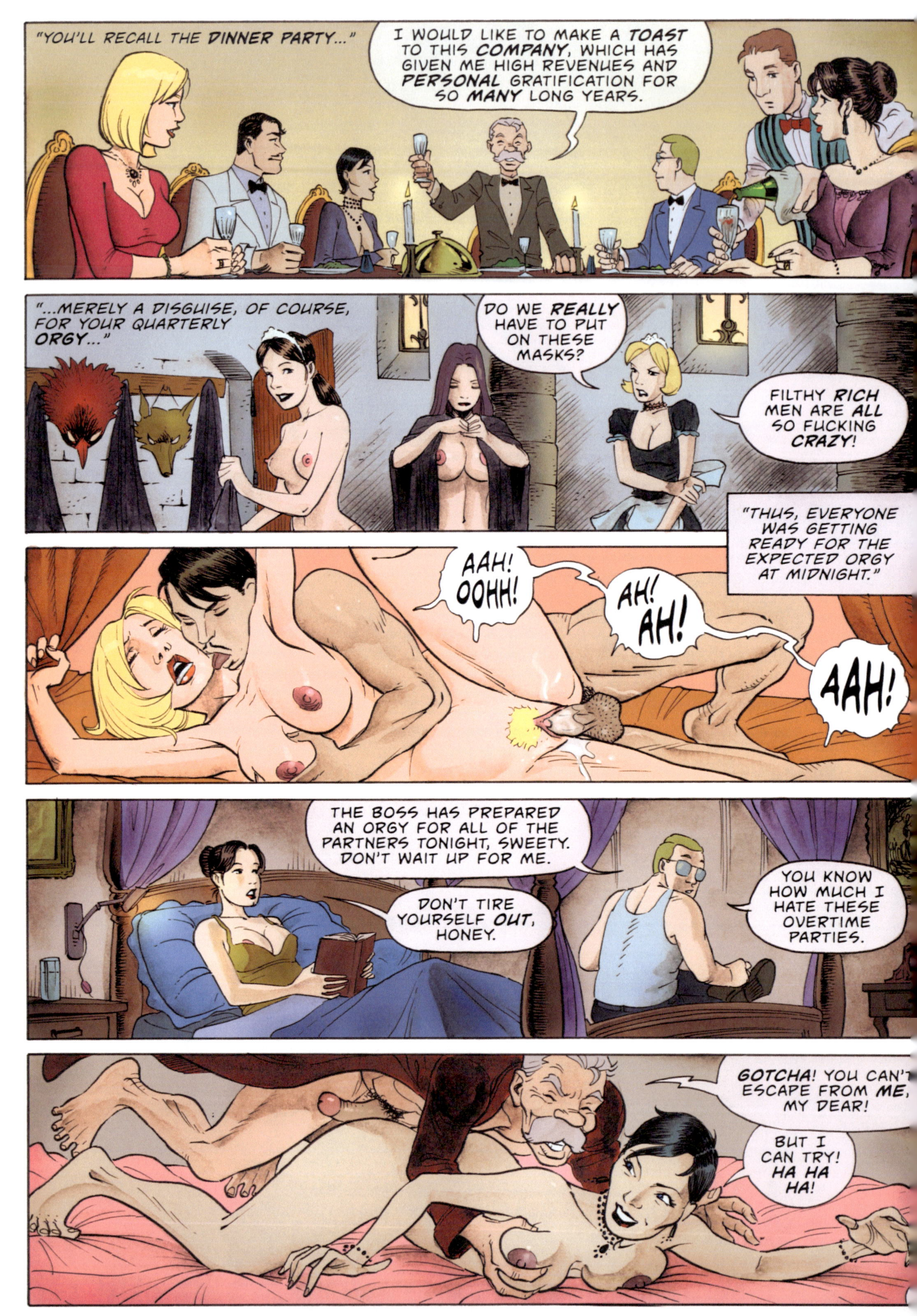
"YOU'LL RECALL THE DINNER PARTY..."
I WOULD LIKE TO MAKE A TOAST TO THIS COMPANY, WHICH HAS GIVEN ME HIGH REVENUES AND PERSONAL GRATIFICATION FOR SO MANY LONG YEARS.
"...MERELY A DISGUISE, OF COURSE, FOR YOUR QUARTERLY ORGY..."
DO WE REALLY HAVE TO PUT ON THESE MASKS?
FILTHY RICH MEN ARE ALL SO FUCKING CRAZY!
"THUS, EVERYONE WAS GETTING READY FOR THE EXPECTED ORGY AT MIDNIGHT."
AAH! OOHH!
AH! AH!
AAH!
THE BOSS HAS PREPARED AN ORGY FOR ALL OF THE PARTNERS TONIGHT, SWEETY. DON'T WAIT UP FOR ME.
DON'T TIRE YOURSELF OUT, HONEY.
YOU KNOW HOW MUCH I HATE THESE OVERTIME PARTIES.
GOTCHA! YOU CAN'T ESCAPE FROM ME, MY DEAR!
BUT I CAN TRY! HA HA HA!

"LORD VENOM WAS THE FIRST TO LEAVE HIS BELOVED'S BED. HE HAD SOME PLANS BEFORE THE ORGY BEGAN."

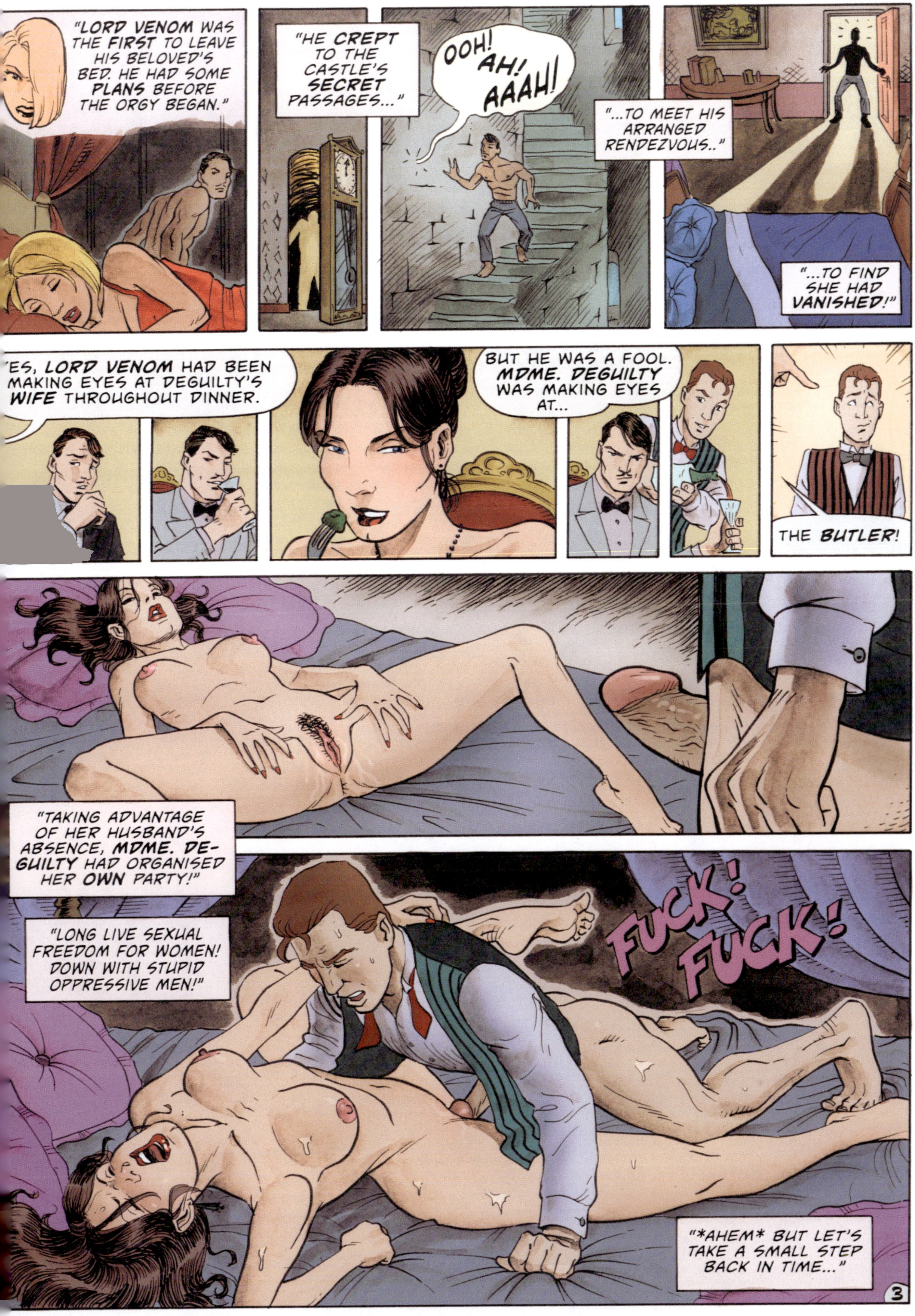

"HE CREPT TO THE CASTLE'S SECRET PASSAGES..."
OOH! AH! AAAH!
"...TO MEET HIS ARRANGED RENDEZVOUS.."
"...TO FIND SHE HAD VANISHED!"

ES, LORD VENOM HAD BEEN MAKING EYES AT DEGUILTY'S WIFE THROUGHOUT DINNER.

BUT HE WAS A FOOL. MDME. DEGUILTY WAS MAKING EYES AT...

THE BUTLER!

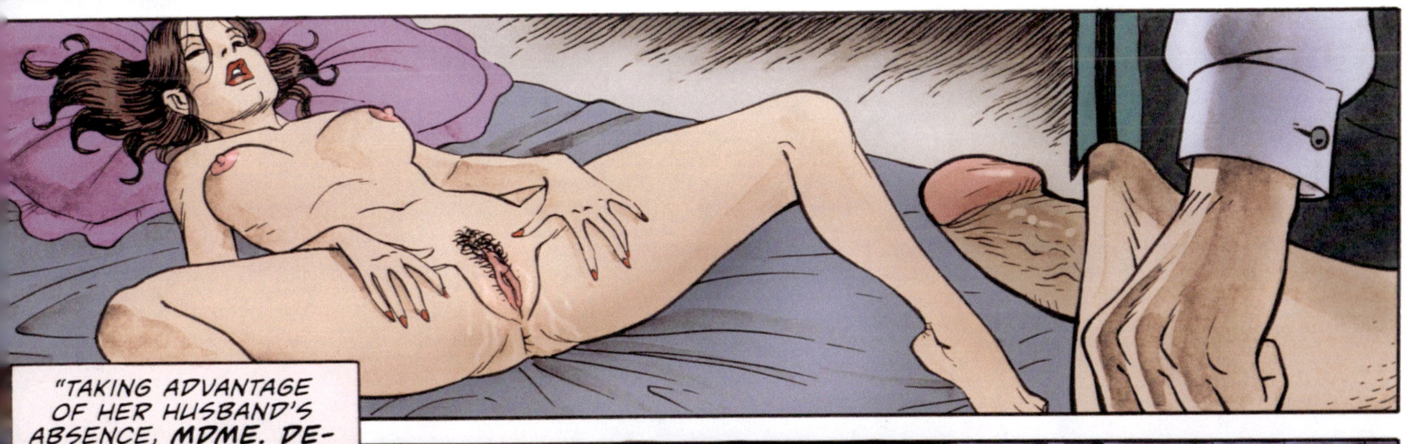
"TAKING ADVANTAGE OF HER HUSBAND'S ABSENCE, MDME. DE-GUILTY HAD ORGANISED HER OWN PARTY!"
"LONG LIVE SEXUAL FREEDOM FOR WOMEN! DOWN WITH STUPID OPPRESSIVE MEN!"
FUCK! FUCK!
"*AHEM* BUT LET'S TAKE A SMALL STEP BACK IN TIME..."

3

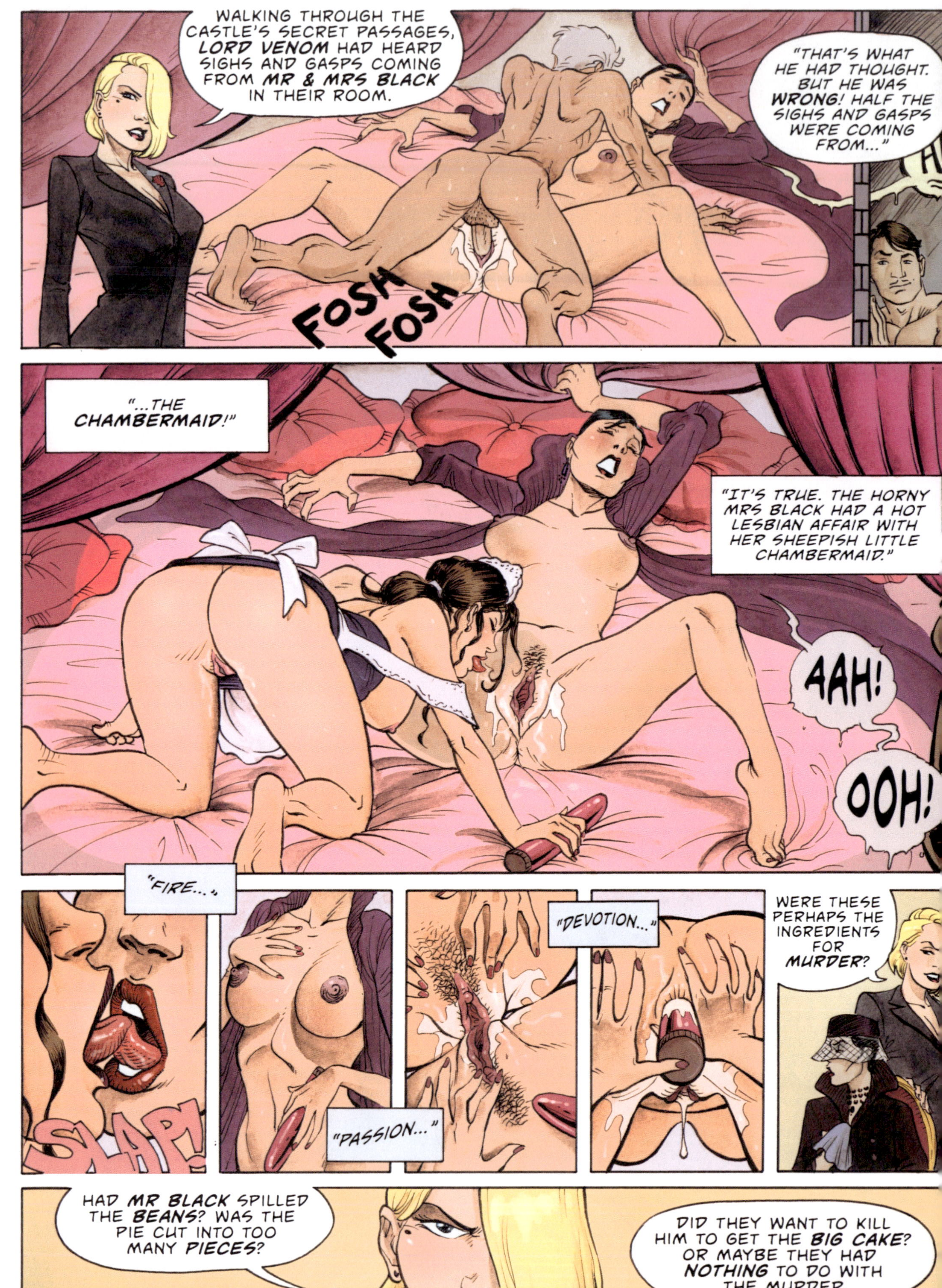

WALKING THROUGH THE CASTLE'S SECRET PASSAGES, LORD VENOM HAD HEARD SIGHS AND GASPS COMING FROM MR & MRS BLACK IN THEIR ROOM.
"THAT'S WHAT HE HAD THOUGHT. BUT HE WAS WRONG! HALF THE SIGHS AND GASPS WERE COMING FROM..."
FOSH FOSH
"...THE CHAMBERMAID!"
"IT'S TRUE. THE HORNY MRS BLACK HAD A HOT LESBIAN AFFAIR WITH HER SHEEPISH LITTLE CHAMBERMAID."
AAH!
OOH!
"FIRE..."
"PASSION..."
"DEVOTION..."
SLAP!
WERE THESE PERHAPS THE INGREDIENTS FOR MURDER?
HAD MR BLACK SPILLED THE BEANS? WAS THE PIE CUT INTO TOO MANY PIECES?
DID THEY WANT TO KILL HIM TO GET THE BIG CAKE? OR MAYBE THEY HAD NOTHING TO DO WITH THE MURDER...

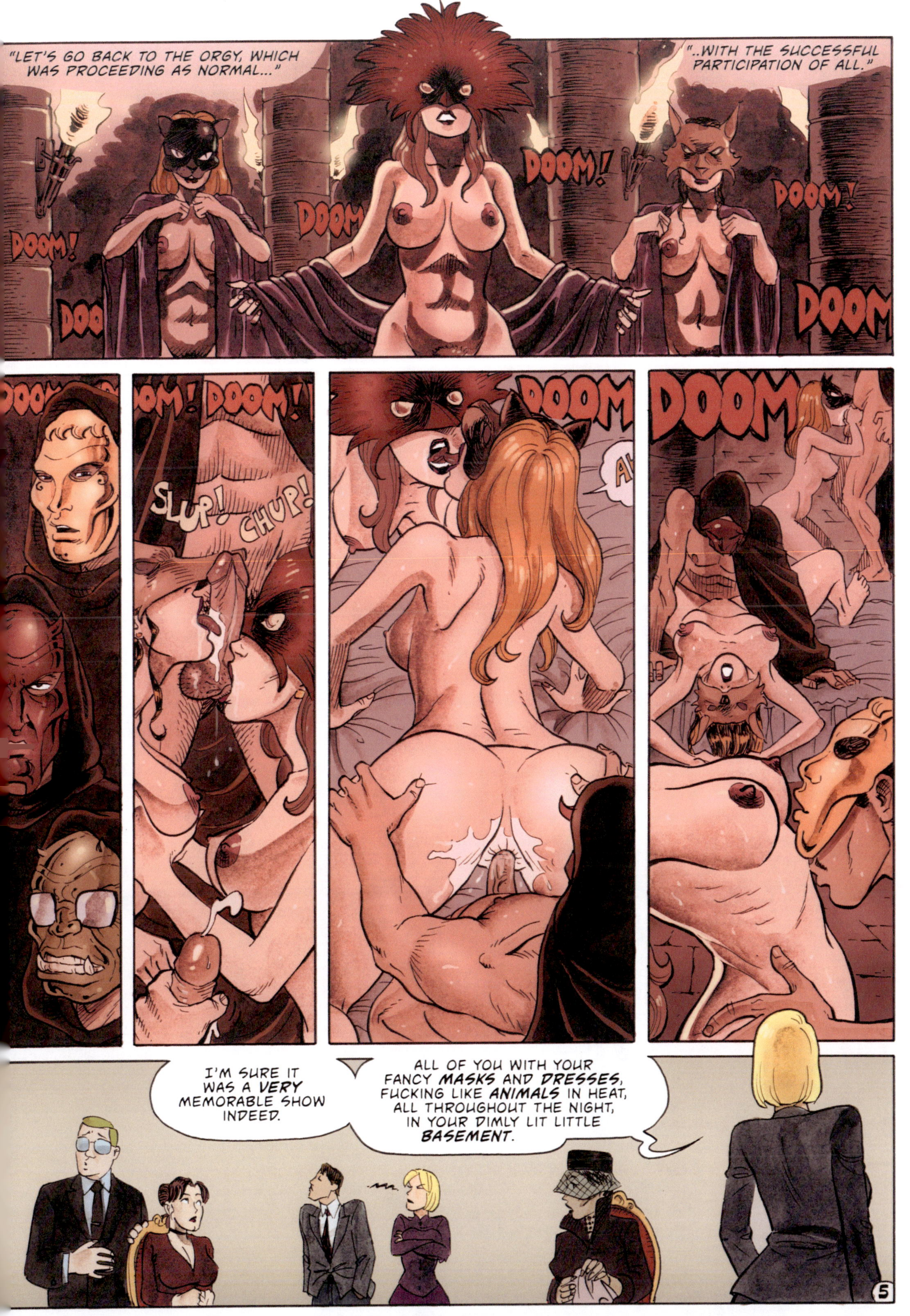

"LET'S GO BACK TO THE ORGY, WHICH WAS PROCEEDING AS NORMAL..."
"..WITH THE SUCCESSFUL PARTICIPATION OF ALL."
DOOM!
DOOM
DOOM!
DOO
DOOM!
DOOM
DOOM!
DOOM
DOOM! DOOM!
SLUP! CHUP!
DOOM
DOOM
AH
I'M SURE IT WAS A VERY MEMORABLE SHOW INDEED.
ALL OF YOU WITH YOUR FANCY MASKS AND DRESSES, FUCKING LIKE ANIMALS IN HEAT, ALL THROUGHOUT THE NIGHT, IN YOUR DIMLY LIT LITTLE BASEMENT.

5

"SECRETLY, ONE OF THE PARTICIPANTS WAS ABLE TO LEAVE THE PARTY WITHOUT BEING NOTICED."
"MR BLACK?"
"DEGUILTY?"
"NO! IT WAS THE BUTLER AGAIN!"
"AFTER HE HA LEFT MR DEGUILT SATISFIE HE HAD THE REPLACE MR BLAC IN THE OR SO THAT BLACK COU GO SATISF

"...MRS VENOM!"

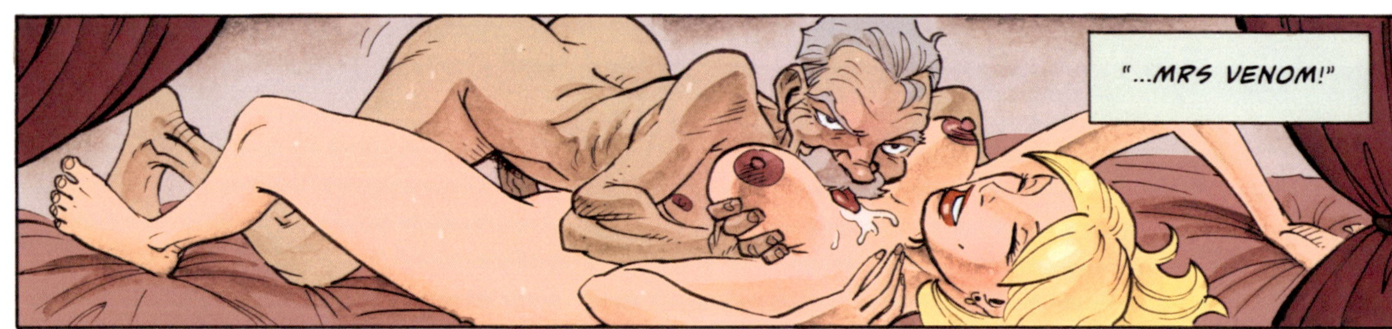

THAT WAY, MR BLACK WAS ABLE TO SATISFY HER WITHOUT RAISING THE SUSPICIONS OF HER NAIVE PARTNERS, WHO...

WOW... THAT DETECTIVE IS SO HOT! MMMM...
ALL THAT EXPOSITION IS REALLY TURNING ME ON... OOH...

WE'RE JUST
MISSING THE
FINAL PIECE
OF THIS
RIDDLE.

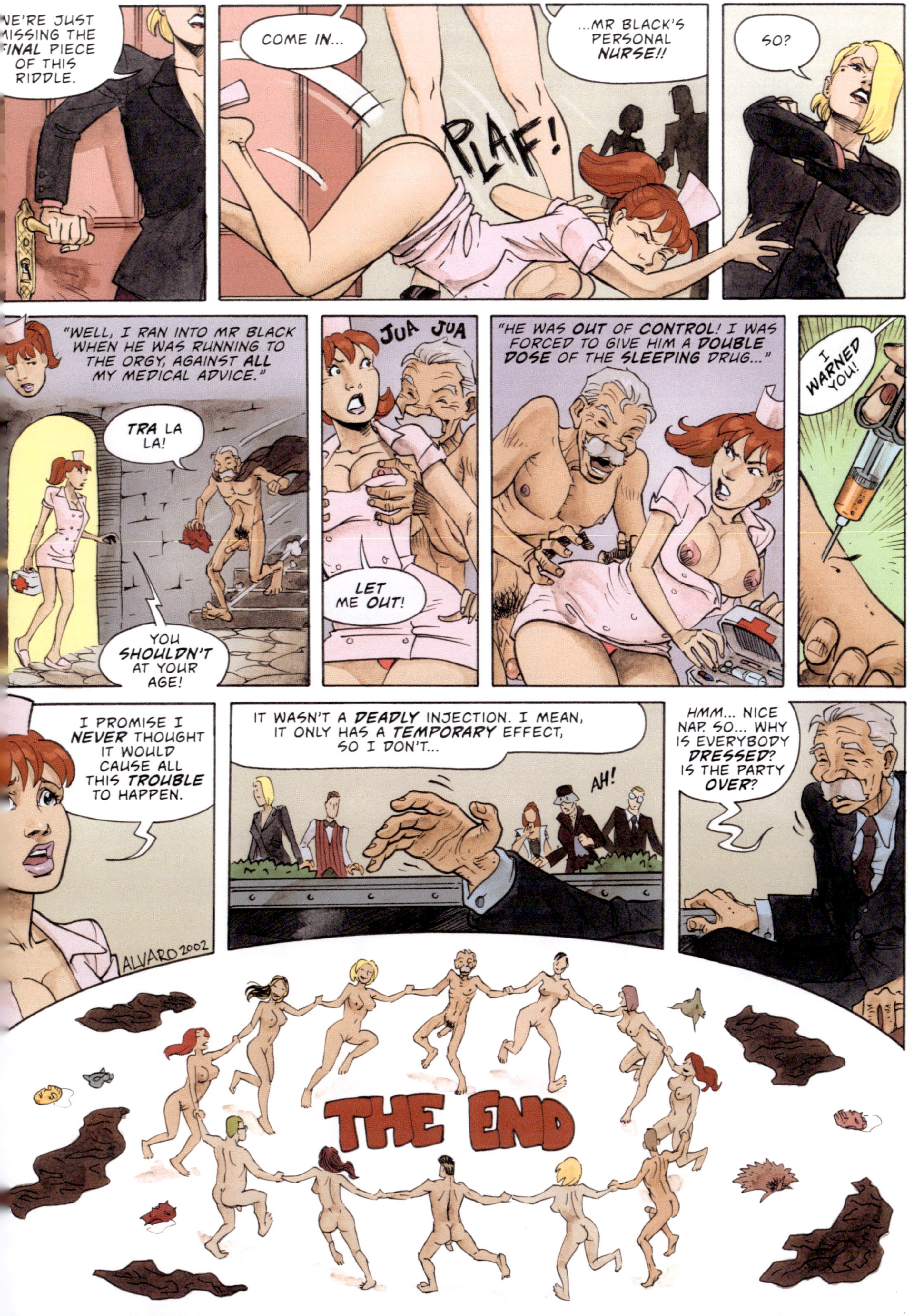

COME IN...
...MR BLACK'S
PERSONAL
NURSE!!
PLAF!

SO?

"WELL, I RAN INTO MR BLACK
WHEN HE WAS RUNNING TO
THE ORGY, AGAINST ALL
MY MEDICAL ADVICE."
TRA LA
LA!
YOU
SHOULDN'T
AT YOUR
AGE!

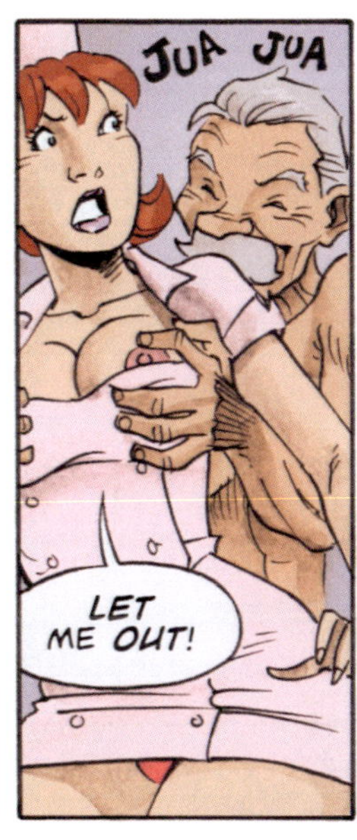
JUA JUA
LET
ME OUT!

"HE WAS OUT OF CONTROL! I WAS
FORCED TO GIVE HIM A DOUBLE
DOSE OF THE SLEEPING DRUG..."

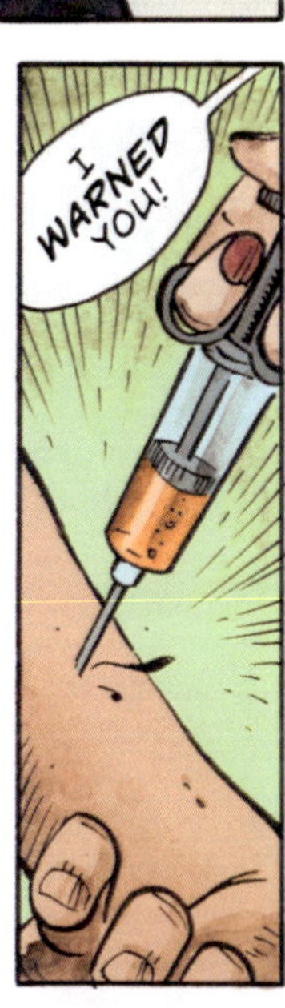
I
WARNED
YOU!

I PROMISE I
NEVER THOUGHT
IT WOULD
CAUSE ALL
THIS TROUBLE
TO HAPPEN.

IT WASN'T A DEADLY INJECTION. I MEAN,
IT ONLY HAS A TEMPORARY EFFECT,
SO I DON'T...

AH!

HMM... NICE
NAP. SO... WHY
IS EVERYBODY
DRESSED? IS THE PARTY
OVER?

ALVARO 2002

THE END

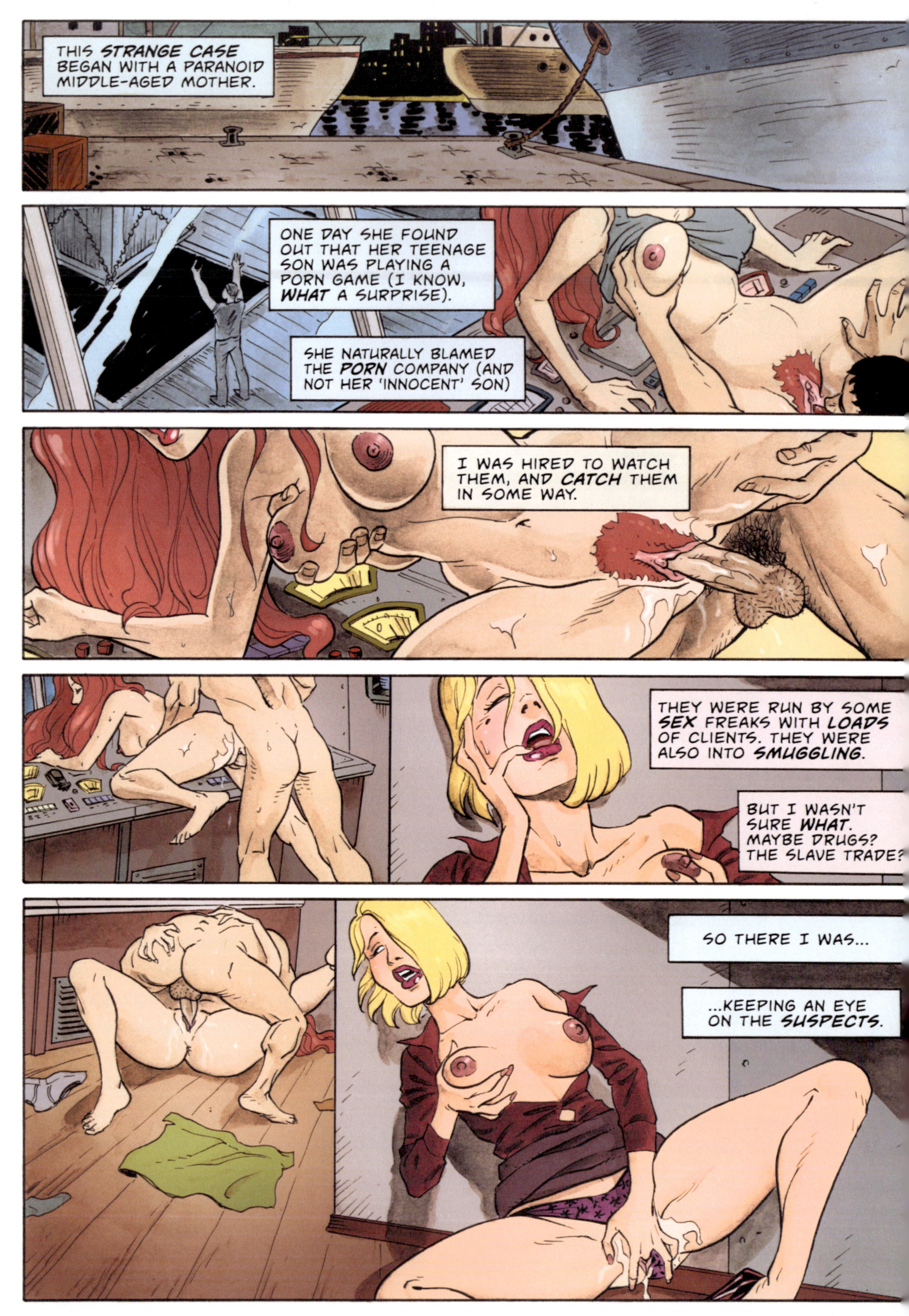
THIS STRANGE CASE BEGAN WITH A PARANOID MIDDLE-AGED MOTHER.

ONE DAY SHE FOUND OUT THAT HER TEENAGE SON WAS PLAYING A PORN GAME (I KNOW, WHAT A SURPRISE).

SHE NATURALLY BLAMED THE PORN COMPANY (AND NOT HER 'INNOCENT' SON)

I WAS HIRED TO WATCH THEM, AND CATCH THEM IN SOME WAY.

THEY WERE RUN BY SOME SEX FREAKS WITH LOADS OF CLIENTS. THEY WERE ALSO INTO SMUGGLING.

BUT I WASN'T SURE WHAT. MAYBE DRUGS? THE SLAVE TRADE?

SO THERE I WAS...

...KEEPING AN EYE ON THE SUSPECTS.

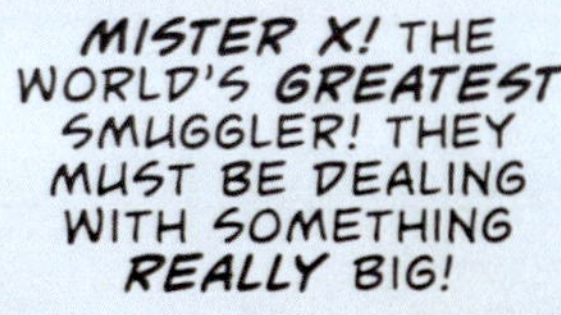

OOH!
YEESS!!
AAH!

UHN!
TAKE THIS!
UHN!
AH!
FUCK!
FUCK!
BONDS
ALVARO 2001
A NEW CASE
~ FOR ~
DETECTIVE
WANDA WOLFE

MISTER X! THE WORLD'S GREATEST SMUGGLER! THEY MUST BE DEALING WITH SOMETHING REALLY BIG!

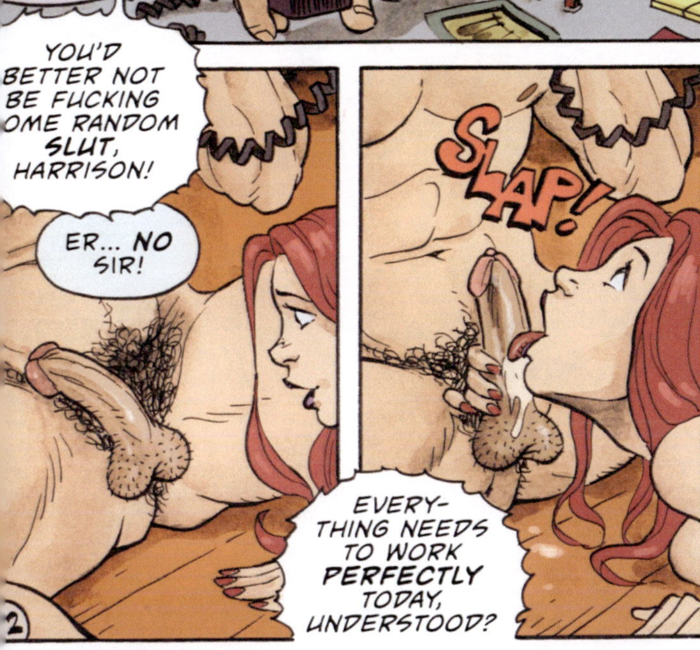

HARRISON! PICK UP THE DAMN RECEIVER!
UF!
UF!
YOU'D BETTER NOT BE FUCKING OME RANDOM SLUT, HARRISON!
ER... NO SIR!
EVERY-THING NEEDS TO WORK PERFECTLY TODAY, UNDERSTOOD?
SLAP!

MISTER X IS COMING TO CHECK THE WARES. OVER AND OUT!
CHUP!
CHUP!

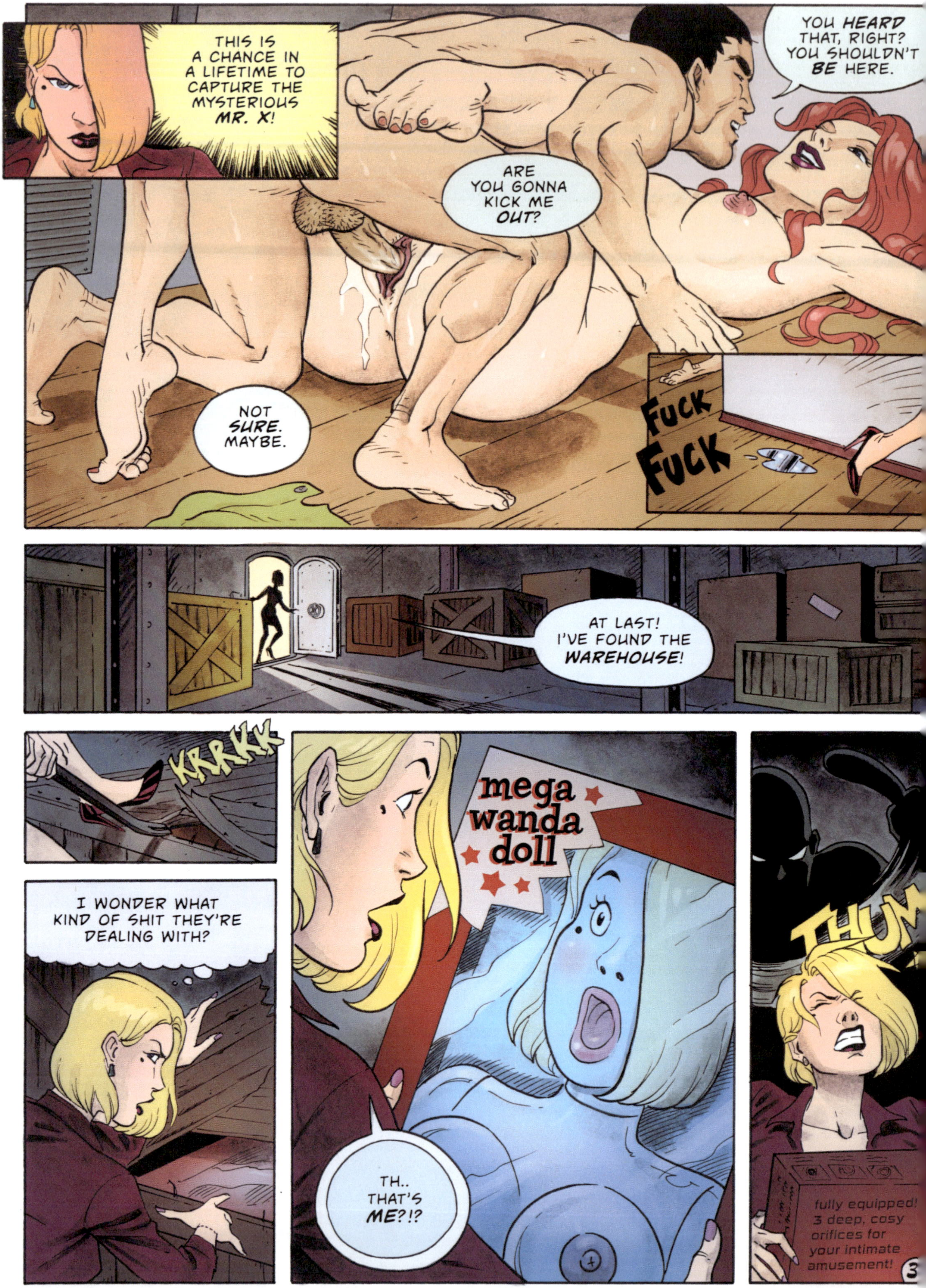

THIS IS A CHANCE IN A LIFETIME TO CAPTURE THE MYSTERIOUS MR. X!
YOU HEARD THAT, RIGHT? YOU SHOULDN'T BE HERE.
ARE YOU GONNA KICK ME OUT?
NOT SURE. MAYBE.
FUCK FUCK

AT LAST! I'VE FOUND THE WAREHOUSE!

KRRKK

I WONDER WHAT KIND OF SHIT THEY'RE DEALING WITH?

mega wanda doll
TH.. THAT'S ME?!?

THUM
fully equipped! 3 deep, cosy orifices for your intimate amusement!

5

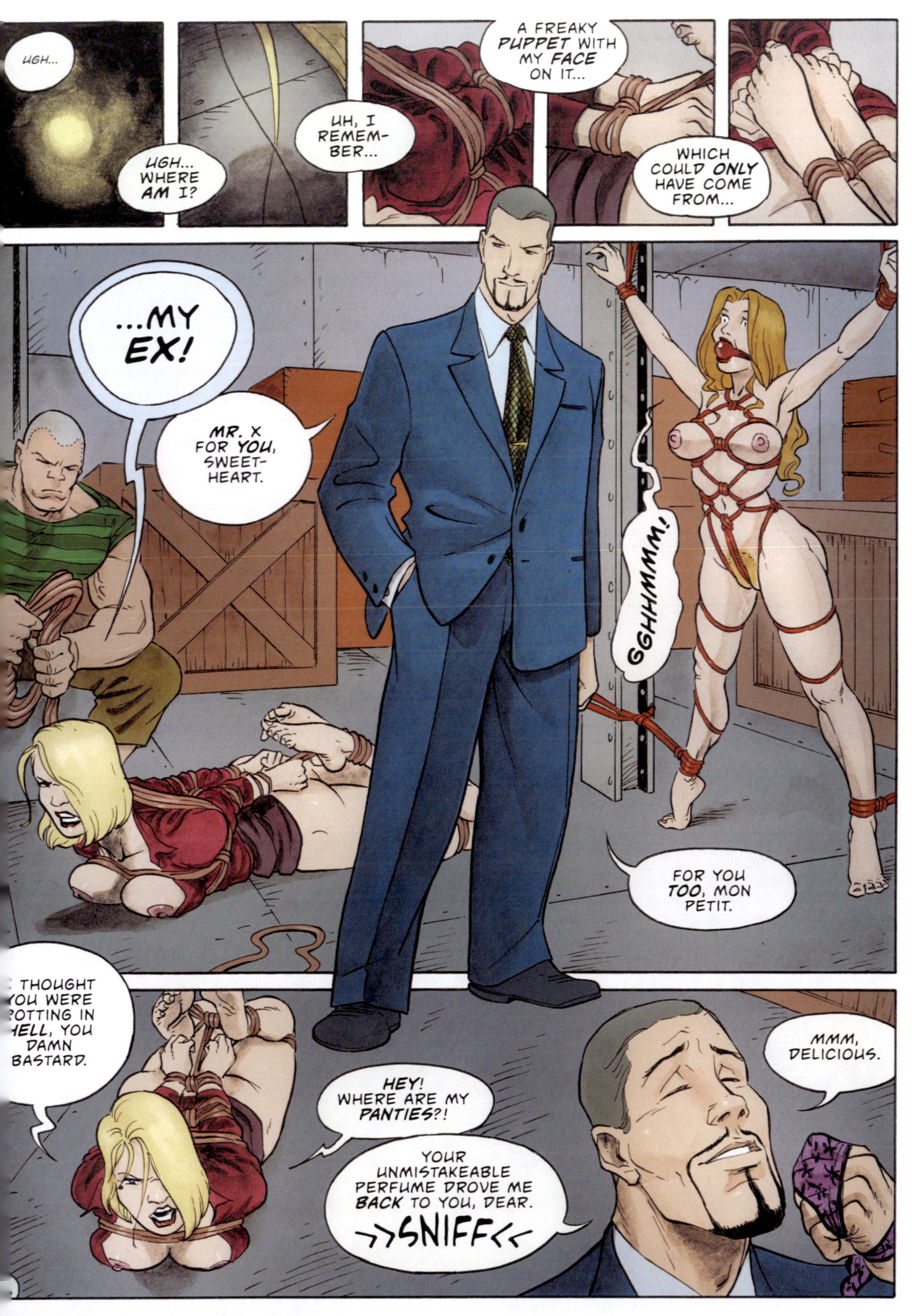

UGH...
UGH... WHERE AM I?
UH, I REMEMBER...
A FREAKY PUPPET WITH MY FACE ON IT...
WHICH COULD ONLY HAVE COME FROM...
...MY EX!
MR. X FOR YOU, SWEETHEART.
GGHHMMM!
FOR YOU TOO, MON PETIT.
I THOUGHT YOU WERE ROTTING IN HELL, YOU DAMN BASTARD.
HEY! WHERE ARE MY PANTIES?!
YOUR UNMISTAKEABLE PERFUME DROVE ME BACK TO YOU, DEAR. >>SNIFF<<
MMM, DELICIOUS.

WHAT A PLEASURE TO HAVE SO MANY GUESTS.
GHHMM!
YOU'VE LIVENED UP THE MOST BORING OPER-ATION.

YOU'LL WONDER ABOUT THE WARE.

WITH THE BRAND NEW MEGA-WANDA DOLL YOU'LL BECOME A BEST-SELLER IN SEX SHOPS WORLDWIDE.
FOR THE DELUXE VERSION I'D LIKE TO INCLUDE YOUR GROANS AND SIGHS.
mega wanda doll

YOU'LL SHARE THE BENEFITS, OF COURSE.
THINK IT OVER, SWEETHEART.
NEVER!
NO WAY!
NOT IN MILLION YEARS
NO!

SIGH. WHY ARE YOU SO UNKIND TO ME?

WELL, IT'S TIME TO LEAVE NOW.
I'LL GET MY REVENGE FOR THIS, MOTHER-FUCKER!
YOU'LL REGRET THIS, YOU SON OF A BITCH! #@*&>!
OH, I FOR-GOT.
TO MAKE THE JOURNEY A LITTLE MORE ENJOYABLE...

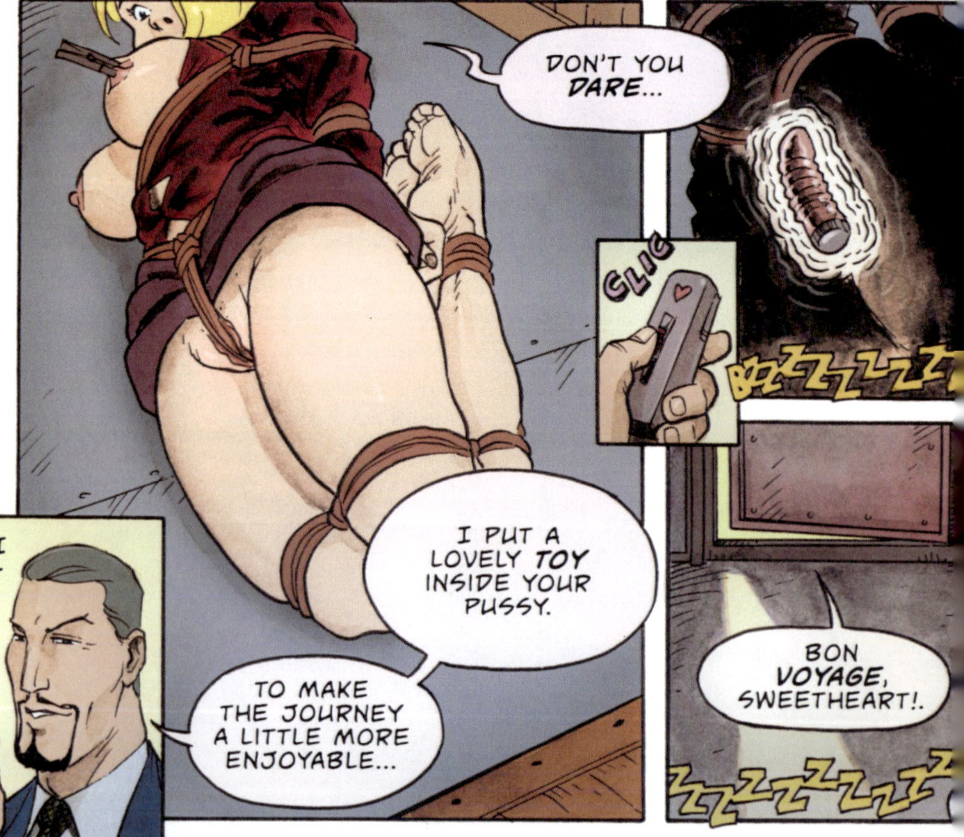

DON'T YOU DARE...
CLIC
I PUT A LOVELY TOY INSIDE YOUR PUSSY.
BON VOYAGE, SWEETHEART!.

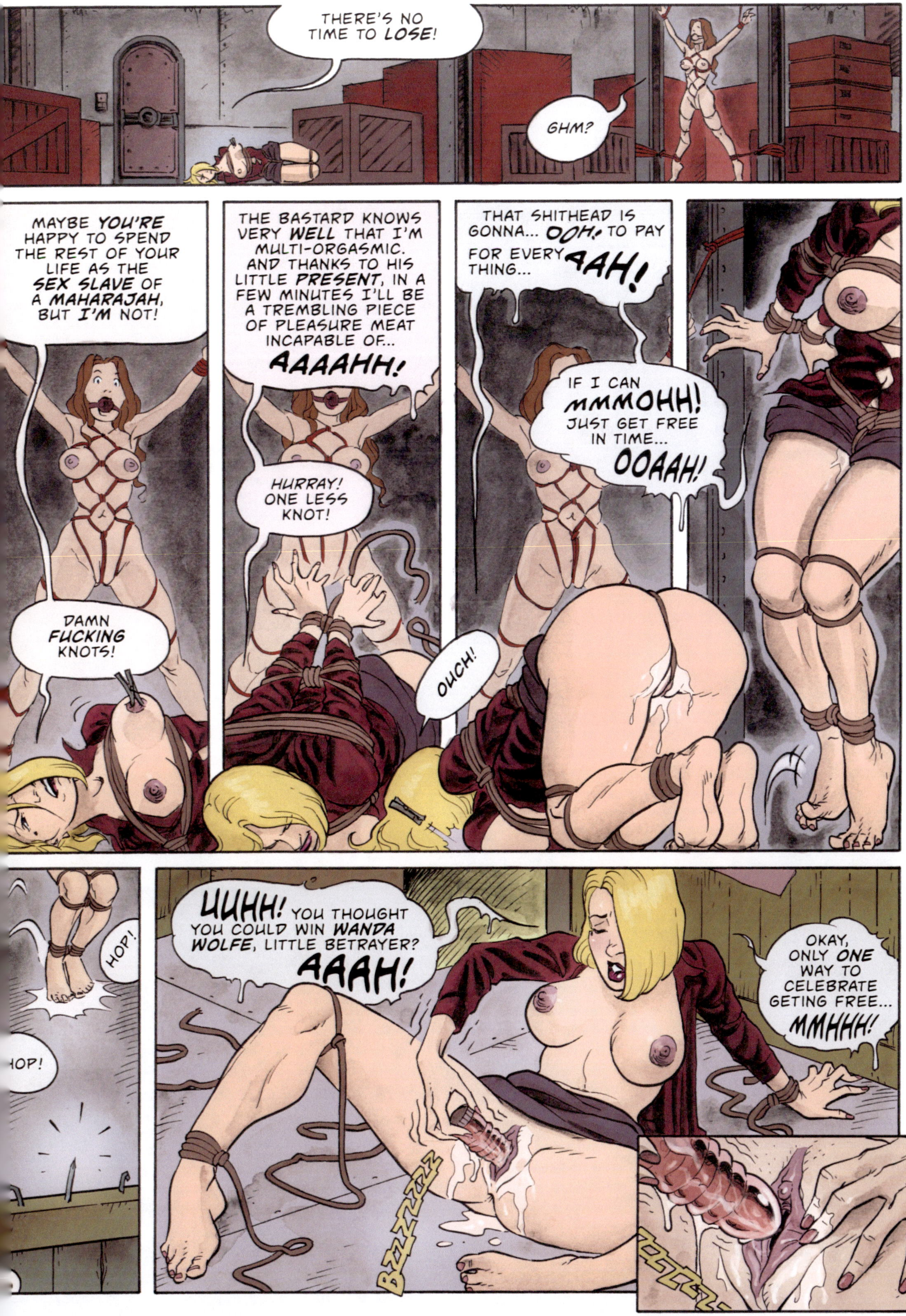

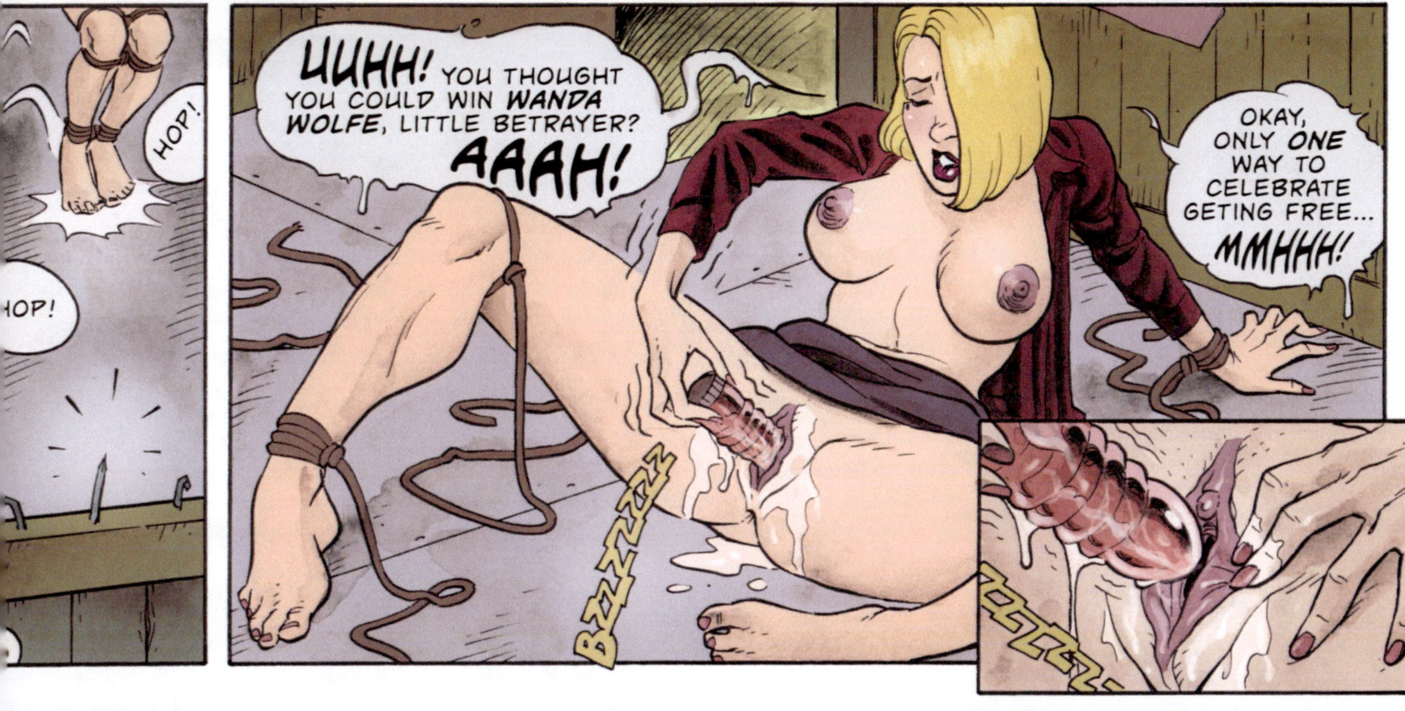

THERE'S NO TIME TO LOSE!
GHM?
MAYBE YOU'RE HAPPY TO SPEND THE REST OF YOUR LIFE AS THE SEX SLAVE OF A MAHARAJAH, BUT I'M NOT!
DAMN FUCKING KNOTS!
THE BASTARD KNOWS VERY WELL THAT I'M MULTI-ORGASMIC. AND THANKS TO HIS LITTLE PRESENT, IN A FEW MINUTES I'LL BE A TREMBLING PIECE OF PLEASURE MEAT INCAPABLE OF... AAAAHH!
HURRAY! ONE LESS KNOT!
OUCH!
THAT SHITHEAD IS GONNA... OOH! TO PAY FOR EVERY THING... AAH!
IF I CAN MMMOHH! JUST GET FREE IN TIME... OOAAH!
HOP!
HOP!
UUHH! YOU THOUGHT YOU COULD WIN WANDA WOLFE, LITTLE BETRAYER? AAAH!
OKAY, ONLY ONE WAY TO CELEBRATE GETING FREE... MMHHH!
BZZZZZ
BZZZZZ

LISTEN, FROM RIGHT NOW THIS FUCKIN' SHIP IS UNDER MY COMMAND!

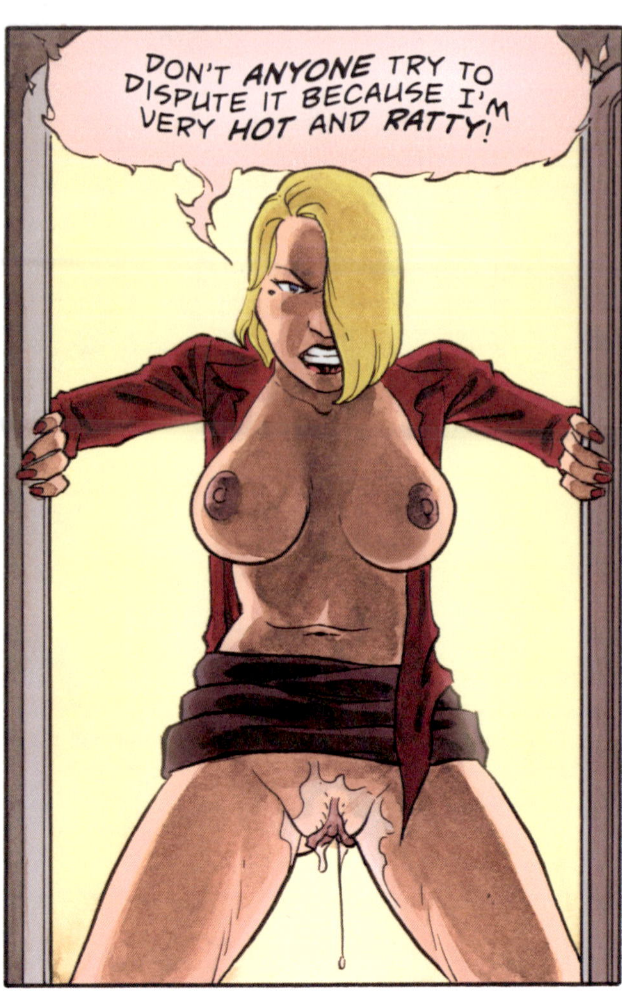

DON'T ANYONE TRY TO DISPUTE IT BECAUSE I'M VERY HOT AND RATTY!

AH!
UH!
OH!
THEY DIDN'T MAKE IT EASY.

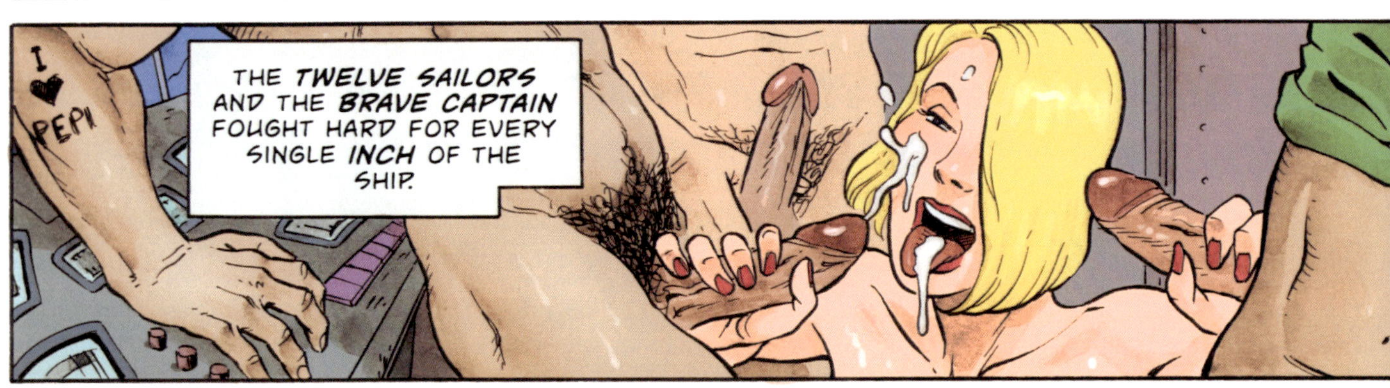

THE TWELVE SAILORS AND THE BRAVE CAPTAIN FOUGHT HARD FOR EVERY SINGLE INCH OF THE SHIP.
I ♥ PEPI

MY COWARD EX RAN AWAY RATHER THAN FACE MY FURY.
SHIT!
AND THE WARE...

mega wanda doll
WELL, I DECIDED TO GIVE THAT TO THE LOCAL AUTHORITIES.
ENI

SO THERE'S NO OBJECTION THEN, GENTLE-MEN?
NO, NO.
OF COURSE NOT.

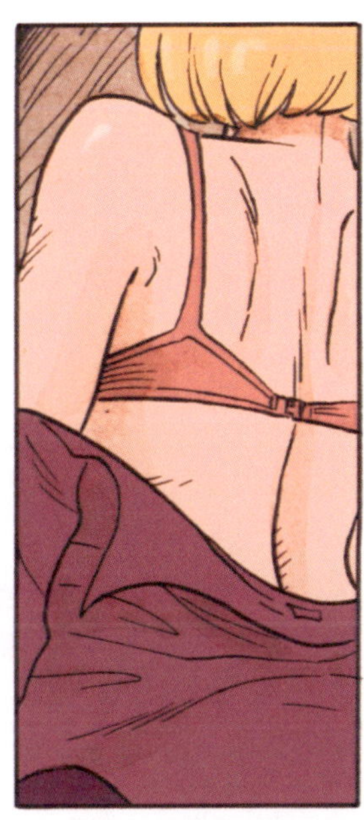
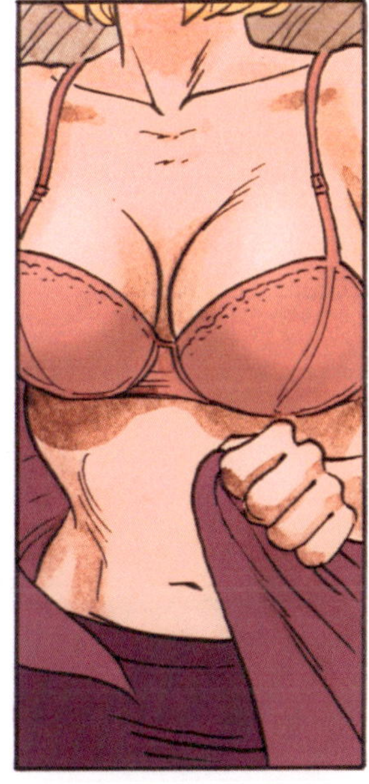

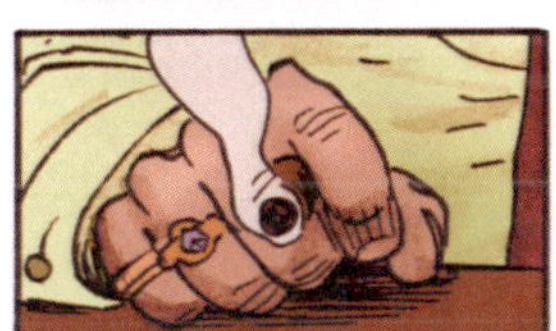

THEN I BET MY BLOUSE FOR 150 DOLLARS, GENTLEMEN.
HOLY COW!
CAN I COMMENT ON YOUR ANATOMY?
NO.
UH.
GULP.
GAMBLERS
A NEW ADVENTURE OF THE DETECTIVE WANDA WOLFE

MMMF!

WHAT THE FUCK?

JUST TELL ME.

I KNOW WHAT YOU WERE THINKING.

PERFECTLY WELL.

I KNOW THE GUYS ALL LIKE YOU.

YES, YOU'VE GOT MONEY, POWER... BUT ALL THAT POWER JUST MAKES YOU USELESS FOR... OTHER THINGS.

NULL.

KAPUT.

GO AHEAD. WATCH. TOUCH. WE BOTH KNOW YOU'RE OUT OF THE GAME.

NEVER!
MMMH. I KNEW I COULD WAKE UP THE BEAST.
AND YOU'LL REGRET IT, BITCH!.
FLASH!
YOU'RE SIMPLY THE BEST!
UCK UCK UCK
GMF!
UGH!
BETTER THAN ALL THE REST. BETTER THAN ANYONE. ANYONE I'VE EVER MET.
OOH! YES! YES! I'M OVER-WHELMED!
UH... OF C-COURSE I GO AHEAD.. WITH 200 DOLLARS...

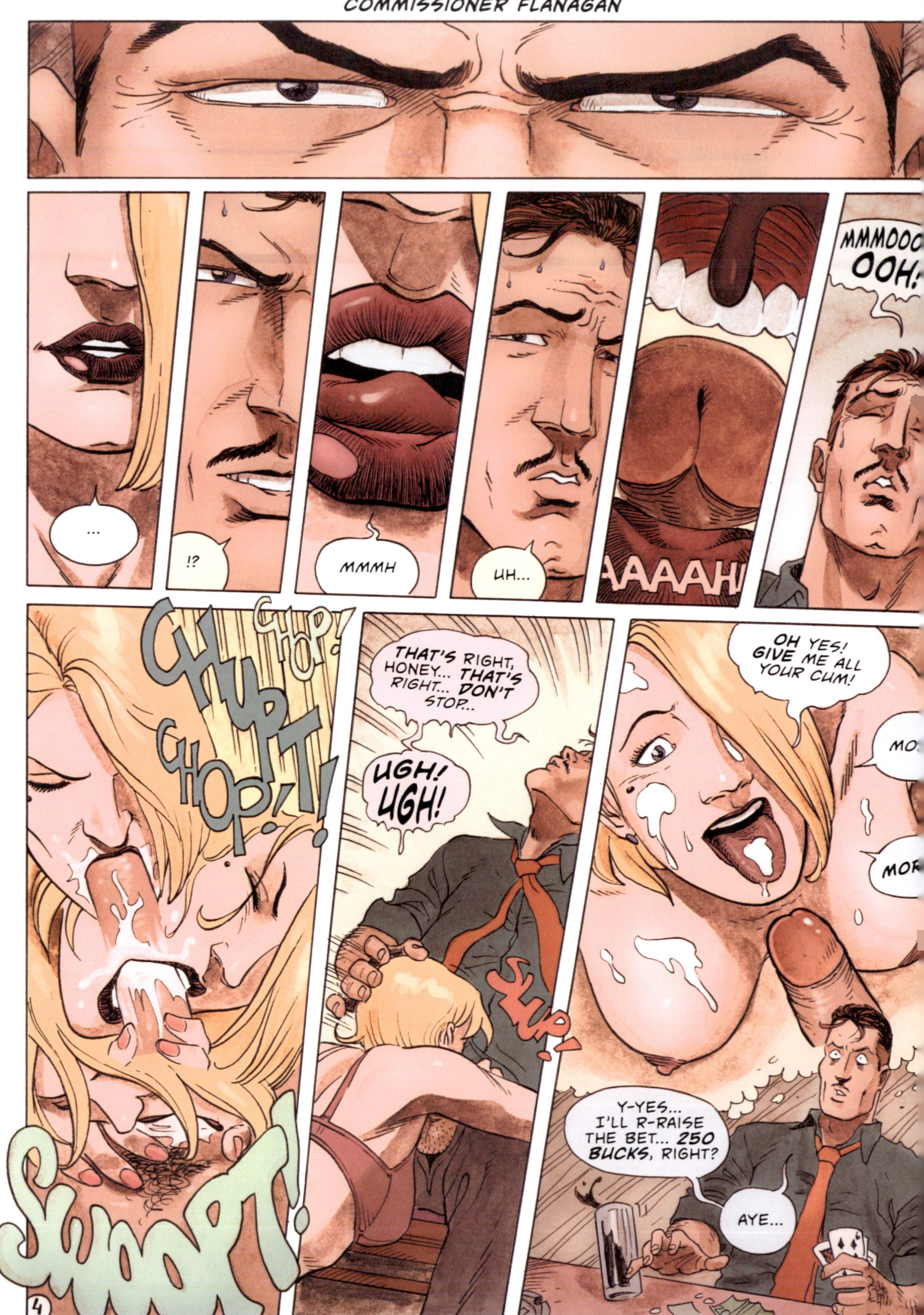
...
!?
MMMH
UH...
AAAAH!
MMMOOO OOH!
CHOP! CHOP! CHOP!T! CHOP!T!
SwooPT!
THAT'S RIGHT, HONEY... THAT'S RIGHT... DON'T STOP...
UGH! UGH!
SLIP!
OH YES! GIVE ME ALL YOUR CUM!
MO.
MOR
Y-YES... I'LL R-RAISE THE BET... 250 BUCKS, RIGHT?
AYE...

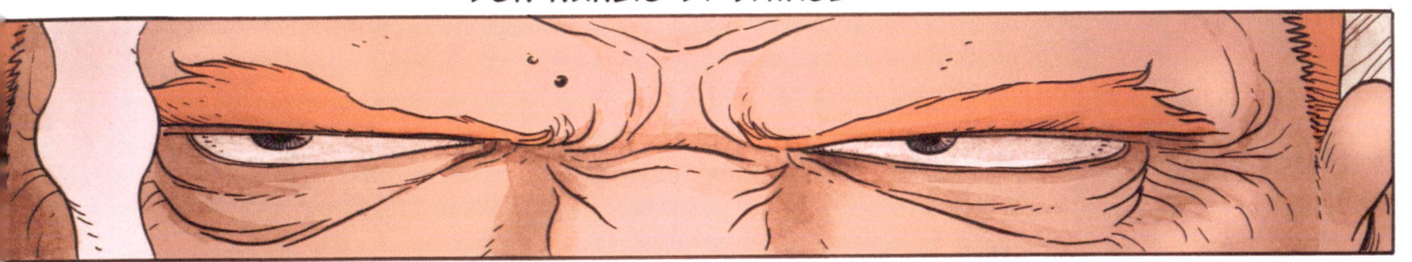

WHAT HAVE WE HERE?

I DIDN'T EXPECT IT FROM YOU.

SO YOU'RE HAVING NAUGHTY THOUGHTS.

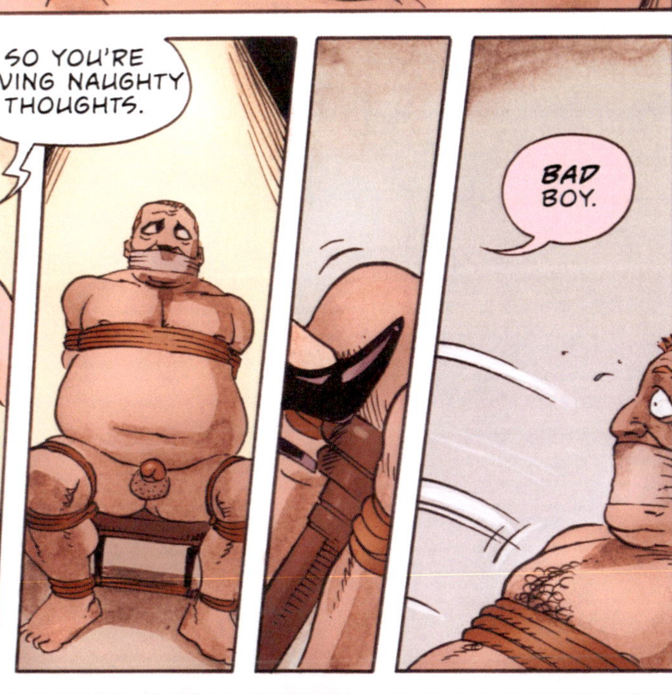
BAD BOY.

I THINK YOU'D AGREE THAT YOU DESERVE PUNISHMENT FOR THIS AFFRONT.
AND SOME KIND OF SATISFACTION TO COMPENSATE.
MMGH!

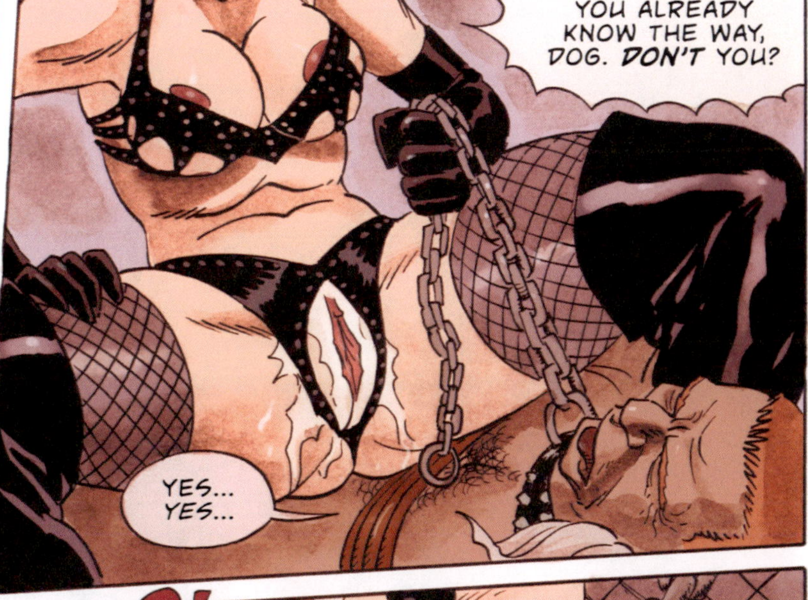
YOU ALREADY KNOW THE WAY, DOG. DON'T YOU?
YES... YES...

SLUP!
SLAP!
THAT'S HOW I LIKE IT.

COUNT THEM OUT LOUD, YOU FILTHY WORM!
TWO!
THREE!
T-THREE HUNDRED DOLLARS... AND CALL YOUR BE
ZISST!

GOOD.

WONDERFUL! MY LUCK HAS CHANGED AT LAST!
AND NOW, GENTLEMEN, IF YOU'LL EXCUSE ME, I'LL WITHDRAW.

WANDA...
GULLIBLE IDIOTS.
GIVE A LITTLE BIT... GIVE A LITTLE BIT OF YOUR LOVE TO ME
GIVE A LITTLE BIT...
END

WORKING PROCESS FOR THE COVER
SKETCH  
DETECTIVE
WANDA
WOLFE
BY COAX
THE HOTTEST COMICS!
No.2
3 FULL STORIES
* Only for MATURE readers!
A COAXDREAMS PRODUCTION
ROUGH COLOR 
FINAL
WANDA WOLFE

DETECTIVE
WANDA
WOLFE
BY COAX
No. 3
Erosetti Press
3 FULL STORIES
Only for MATURE readers!

conX2014

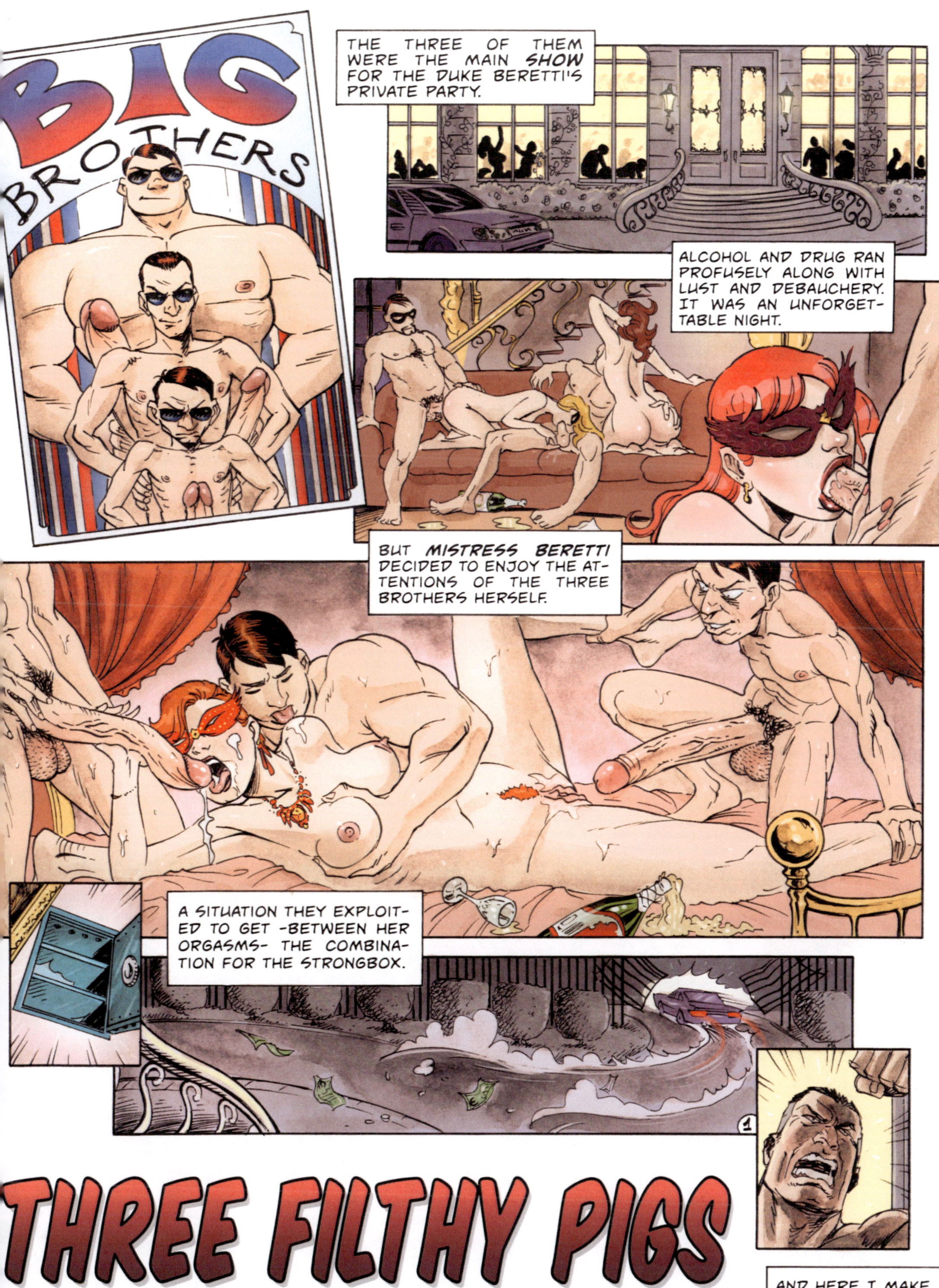

BIG BROTHERS
THE THREE OF THEM WERE THE MAIN SHOW FOR THE DUKE BERETTI'S PRIVATE PARTY.
ALCOHOL AND DRUG RAN PROFUSELY ALONG WITH LUST AND DEBAUCHERY. IT WAS AN UNFORGETTABLE NIGHT.
BUT MISTRESS BERETTI DECIDED TO ENJOY THE ATTENTIONS OF THE THREE BROTHERS HERSELF.
A SITUATION THEY EXPLOITED TO GET -BETWEEN HER ORGASMS- THE COMBINATION FOR THE STRONGBOX.
1
THREE FILTHY PIGS
A NEW AND BIZARRE CASE FOR THE ALWAYS SEDUCTIVE WANDA WOLFE.
LVARO 2002
AND HERE I MAKE MY ENTRANCE, TO UNDO THE MESS...

IT'S ABOUT TIME THAT SOMEONE CAME TO TAKE CARE OF THOSE DEPRAVED BOYS!
YES, THEY ARE FILTHY ANIMALS AND I HOPE THEY HEAR ME!
HEY, I DON'T...
HA HA HA! YOU ARE EVIL...
SENDING THE POOR BOY TO BUY BUTTER AND SANDWICHES!
HA HA HA!
IT'S WHAT I WANTED...
...AND YOU WANTED A HOT DOG, DIDN'T YOU?
DON'T WORRY, HONEY, I DIDN'T FORGET ABOUT YOU. MMMH...
GHM
GHM!
TAKE IT, BABY! WHAAHA HA HA!
AAH!
FUCK! FUCK!
IT'S WRONG TO SPY!
BUMP!
WHAT IS THAT?
WELL...

THAT'S IT!
I LIKE TO LOOK A NICE FINISH.
PUT AWAY THAT JACKKNIFE BEFORE YOU HURT SOMEONE, PEAHEAD!

HEY, GUYS, WE'RE STILL HUNGRY...
PLEASE, BRO, LET ME JOIN. I'VE BEEN GOOD. I WENT TO THE MARKET!
...AND YOU LEFT THE DOOR OPEN!
SO YOU STAY HERE WATCHING MISS SNOPPER.
GET OVER IT. WE'LL DEAL WITH IT LATER.

OH, PLEAAASE. WHY CAN'T I JOIN TO YOUR PARTY?
BECAUSE THE GIRLS FIND YOU DISGUSTING, STUPID!
AND DON'T TALK BACK TO ME!

COME ON, LISTEN TO YOUR BROTHER AND DON'T INFURIATE HIM.

HEY, SWEETS! HERE WE GO AGAIN!
NNNNECC

DID YOU MISS ME, HONEY?
HMMPH, SO BORING.

3

AAAH! GO ON, GO ON! OOOOH! FASTER! UUUH! UH! UH! WRECK MY PUSS
ZZZZ

GHN! TRY WITH YOUR FIST... SLUPF! OUHH!
FOSH! FOSH!

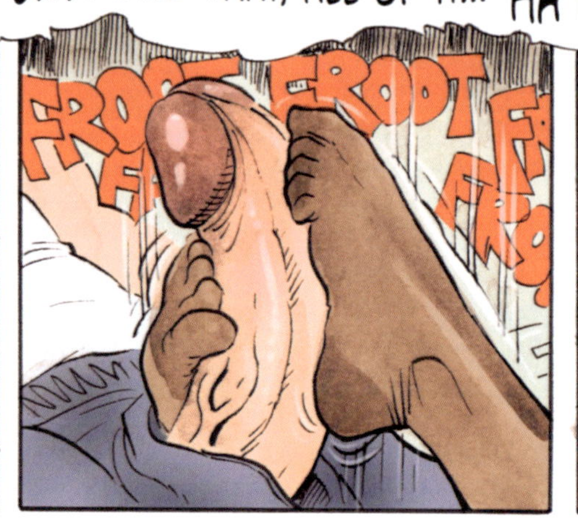
JUST LIKE THAT, ALL OF IT... HA HA H
FROOT FROOT FROO FRO

UUUOOH! W-WHAT? BOTH AT THE SAME TIME?! GNF! STOP, IT'S TOO MUCH... OOOO
UH!

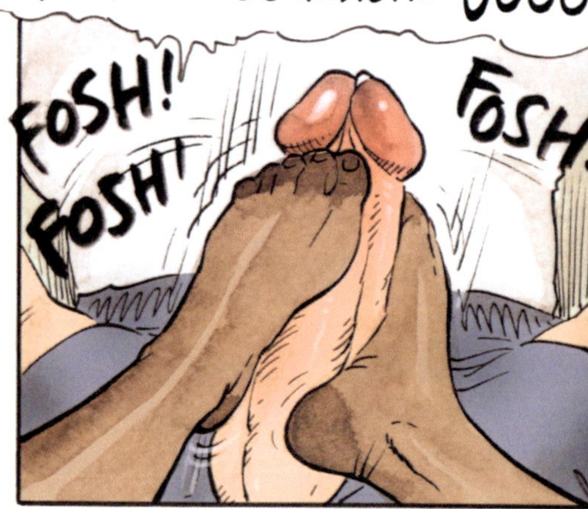
FOSH! FOSH! FOSH!

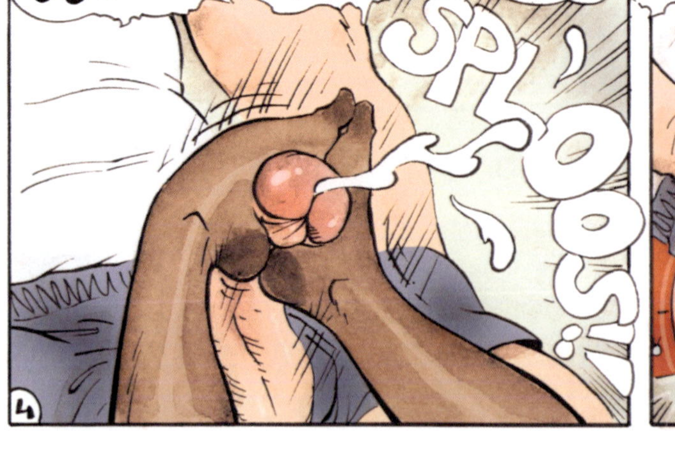
OOOAAH! AAAAAAH! OH! AH! YOU REALLY WANTED IT... OOH! UUUUH
SPLOOSH!

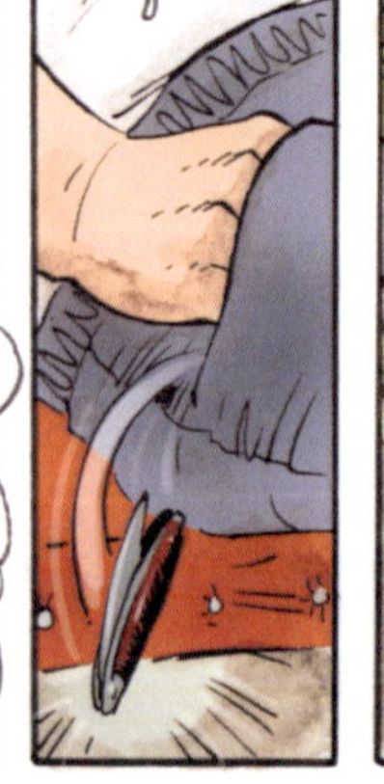

ZZZZZIIIPP

4

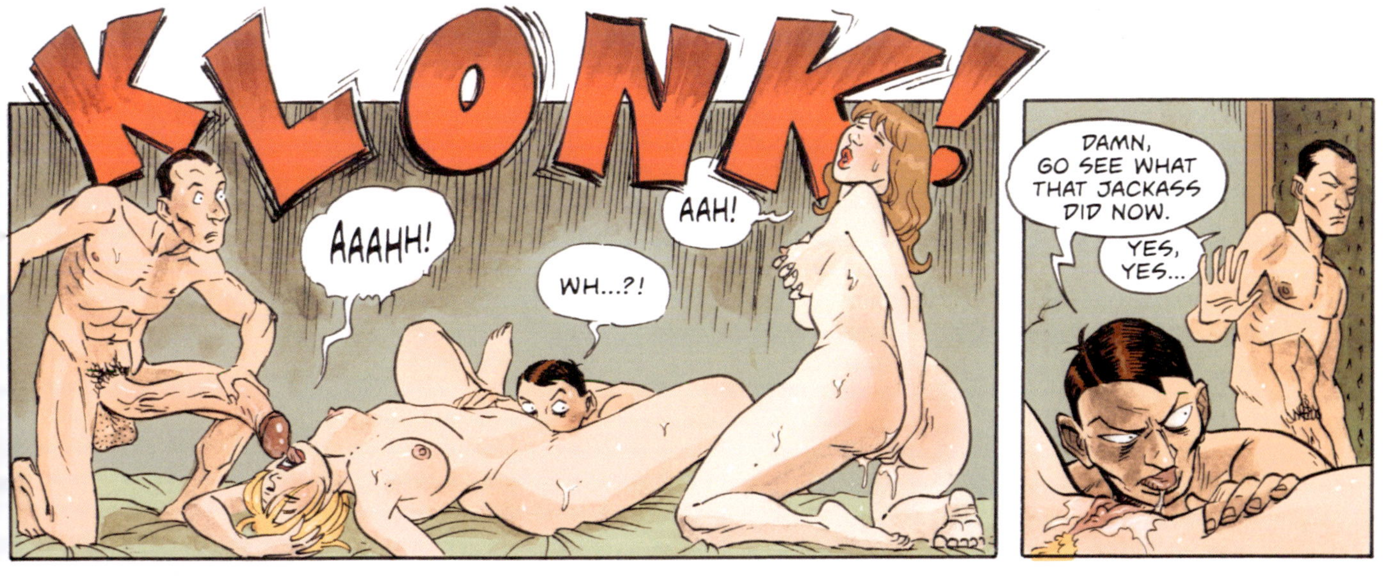

KLONK!
AAAHH!
WH...?!
AAH!
DAMN, GO SEE WHAT THAT JACKASS DID NOW.
YES, YES...

WHAT THE FUCK IS THIS?!
THANK GOODNESS YOU'RE HERE!

AND WHY IS THIS IDIOT IN THE FLOOR WITH HIS COCK OUT?

YOUR BROTHER WAS TORMENTING ME. HE WAS MASSAGING HIS BIG BEAUTIFUL DICK AT THE RHYTHM OF YOUR GASPS BUT HE DIDN'T LET ME TOUCH IT OR LICK IT...
I CAN'T RESIST ANYMORE. I BEG YOU, PLEASE...

WHAT A SURPRISE, DETECTIVE! I BET YOU MISS YOUR VOCATION.
WELL, I AM NOT AS CRUEL AS MY BROTHER.
THANK YOU, THANK YOU...
SLURP!

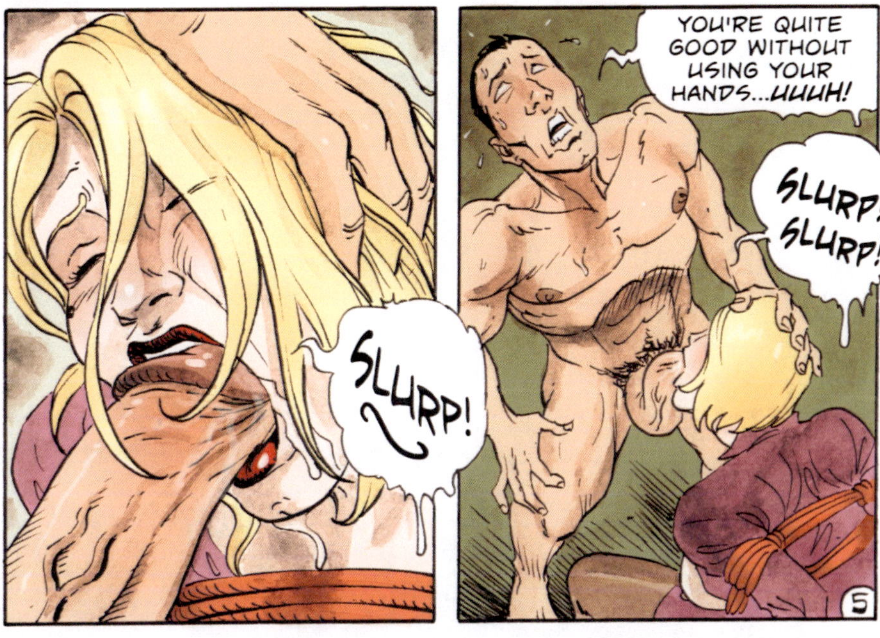

YOU'RE QUITE GOOD WITHOUT USING YOUR HANDS...UUUH!
SLURP! SLURP!

SLAP!
..SLUP!

UUH, DON'T STOP NOW! OOUUH!
SLURP! SLURP!
CHUMP! SLOOPT!

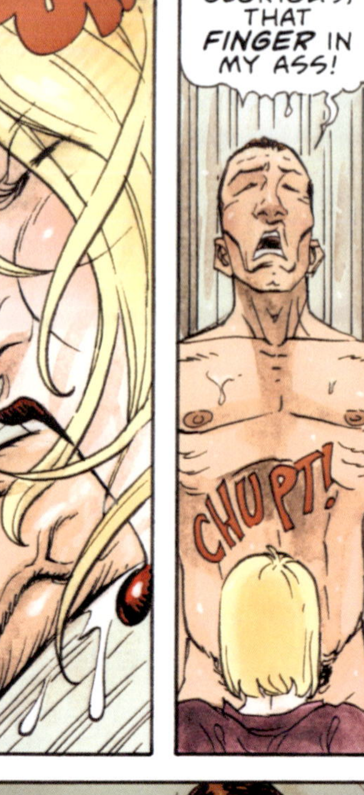

SWOOP!!
OOOH...IT'S GLORIOUS, THAT FINGER IN MY ASS!
CHUP!

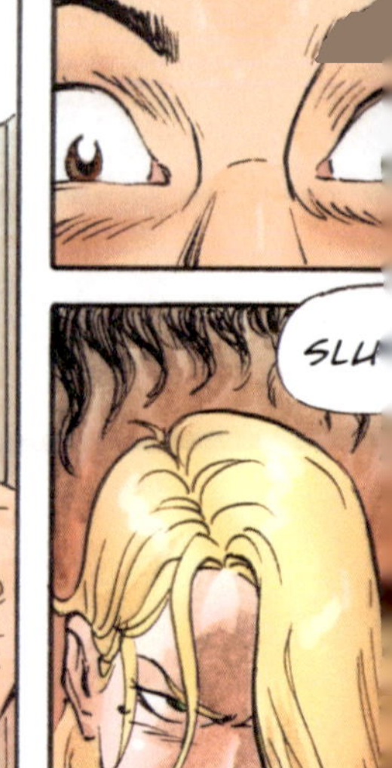

SLU

LICK!
KISS!
WHAT THE FUCK IS THAT IDIOT DOING THAT'S TAKING SO LONG?

GODDAMIT! BECAUSE OF MY TWO RETARDED BROTHERS, I HAVE TO DO EVERYTHING MYSELF.
THEY BETTER HAVE A GOOD EXPLANA- TION...

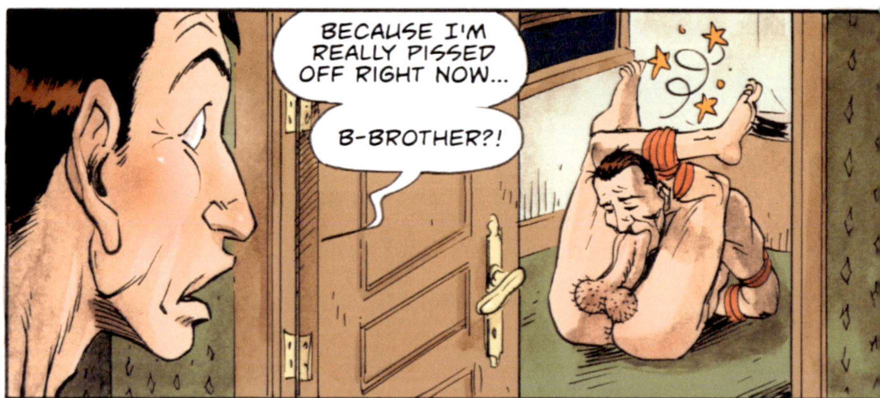

BECAUSE I'M REALLY PISSED OFF RIGHT NOW...
B-BROTHER?!

WHO WOULD DO THAT?
"WONDER WELL DON

HA HA HA! YOU REALLY PUNISHED TO THOSE BASTARDS.
THEY DESERVE IT!
...
COME ON, JOIN THE PARTY. ENJOY YOUR SUCCESS.
AAAH!
OOH! OH!
OOH! FUCK! UH OOH! AH! AAH! OH! AH!

IT WAS A VERY INTERESTING NIGHT...
SEX...

MORE SEX...

...A PROFITABLE MORNING POKER GAME...
...AND EVEN SOME DELIGHTFUL FRIENDSHIPS AMONG THE GUESTS.
THE END.

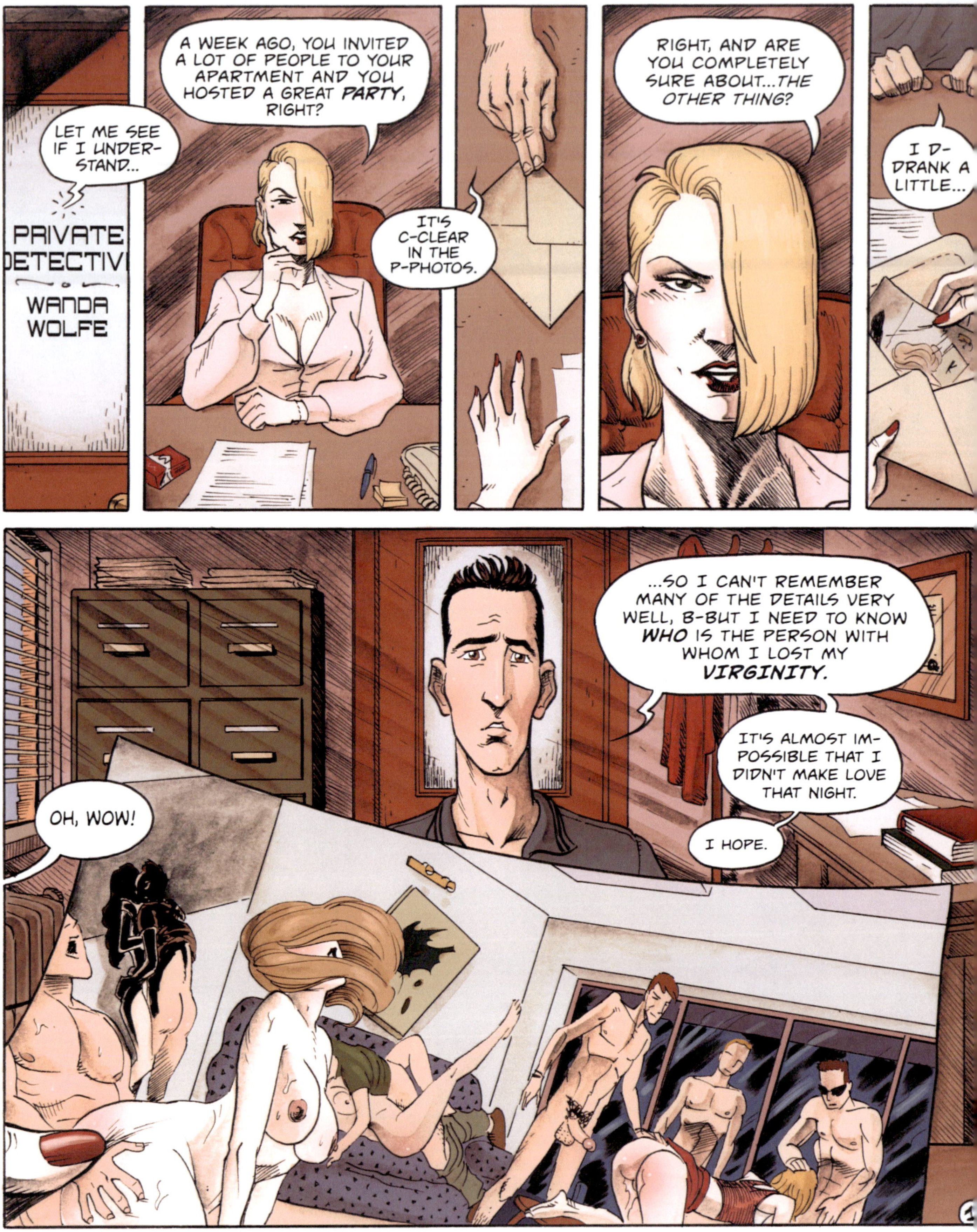

A MATTER OF TASTE

BY ALVARO 2003

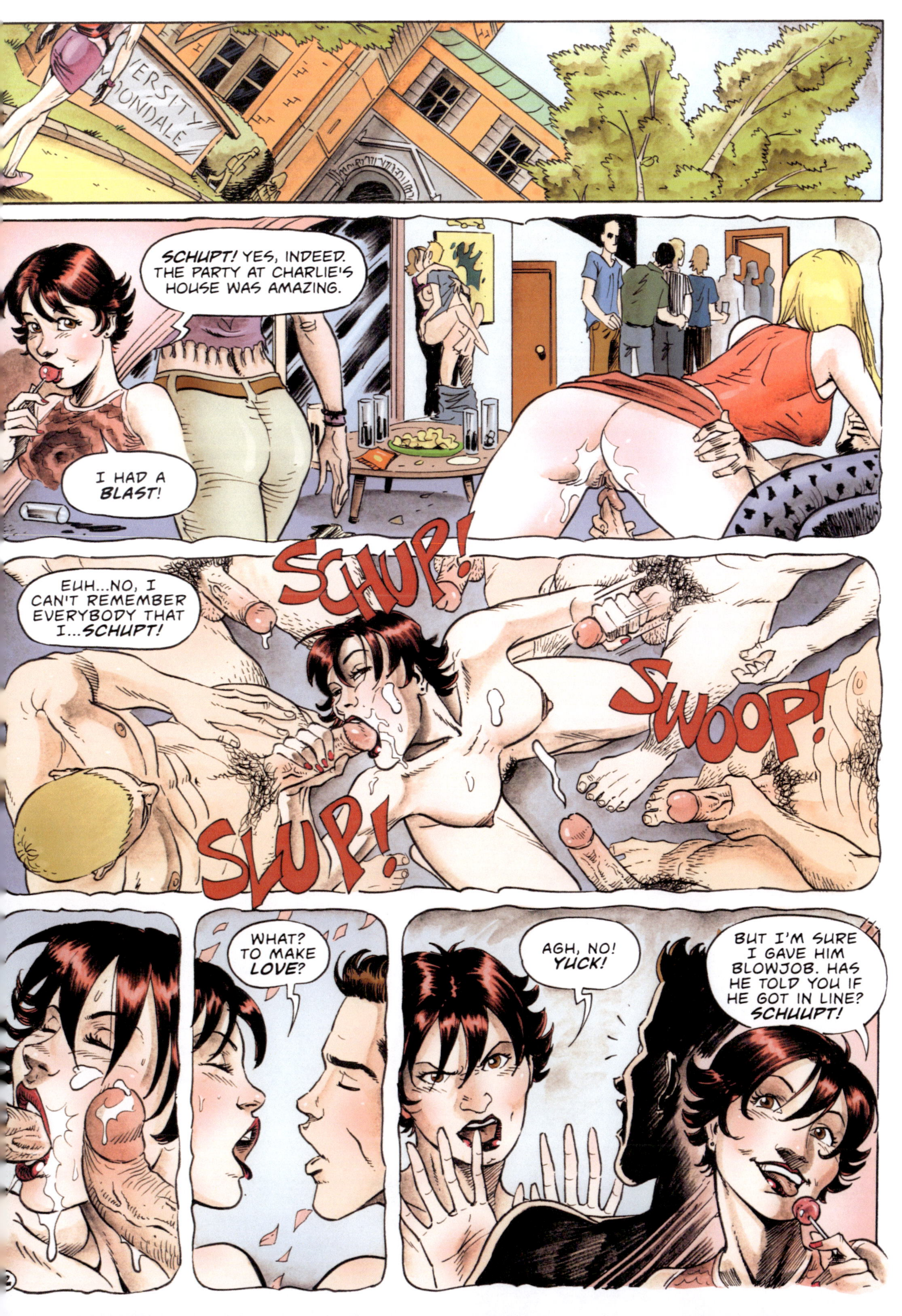
VERSITY
ONDALE
SCHUPT! YES, INDEED. THE PARTY AT CHARLIE'S HOUSE WAS AMAZING.
I HAD A BLAST!
EUH...NO, I CAN'T REMEMBER EVERYBODY THAT I...SCHUPT!
SCHUP!
SWOOP!
SLUP!
WHAT? TO MAKE LOVE?
AGH, NO! YUCK!
BUT I'M SURE I GAVE HIM BLOWJOB. HAS HE TOLD YOU IF HE GOT IN LINE? SCHUUPT!

AYE, I STAYED FOR A WHILE. I HAD HEARD MARK WOULD BE THERE.
YES, I REMEMBER CHARLIE APPROACHING ME.
AH! OH UH
AAH! UH
OH
WHAT THE...!? OF COURSE NOT!
DO YOU THINK I WOULD HAVE AN AFFAIR WITH CHARLIE? I HAVE A REPUTATION!
FOSH!
FOSH!
I DON'T KNOW THE RUMORS OUT THERE, BUT IT'S NOT TRUE!
MORE!
MORE!
OH, WELL, MAYBE JUST A FEW PARTS.

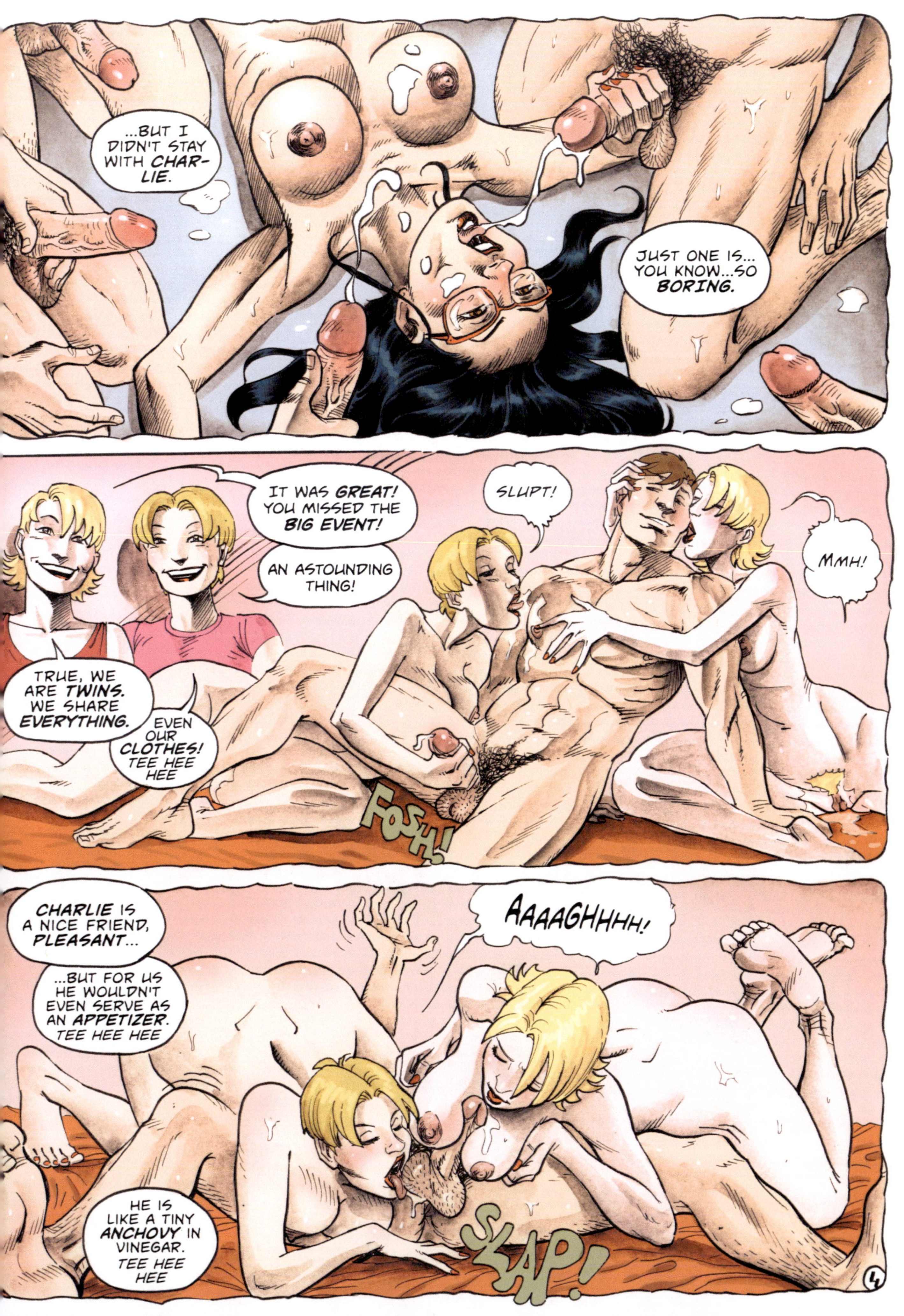

...BUT I DIDN'T STAY WITH CHARLIE.
JUST ONE IS... YOU KNOW...SO BORING.
IT WAS GREAT! YOU MISSED THE BIG EVENT!
AN ASTOUNDING THING!
SLUPT!
MMH!
TRUE, WE ARE TWINS. WE SHARE EVERYTHING.
EVEN OUR CLOTHES! TEE HEE HEE
FOSH!
CHARLIE IS A NICE FRIEND, PLEASANT...
...BUT FOR US HE WOULDN'T EVEN SERVE AS AN APPETIZER. TEE HEE HEE
AAAAGHHHH!
HE IS LIKE A TINY ANCHOVY IN VINEGAR. TEE HEE HEE
SLAP!
4

ME... TOGETHER WITH THAT WEAKLING? HA HA HA HA!! I HAVE TO REMEMBER THIS JOKE!
FUCK!
FUCK!
AH!
AH!
UH
IT WASN'T AN AUSPICIOUS NIGHT, YOU KNOW?
THE CONFLUENCE OF JUPITER WITH SATURN DID NOT FAVOR THE CONSUMMATION OF CARNAL ACTS, BLAH, BLAH, BLAH...

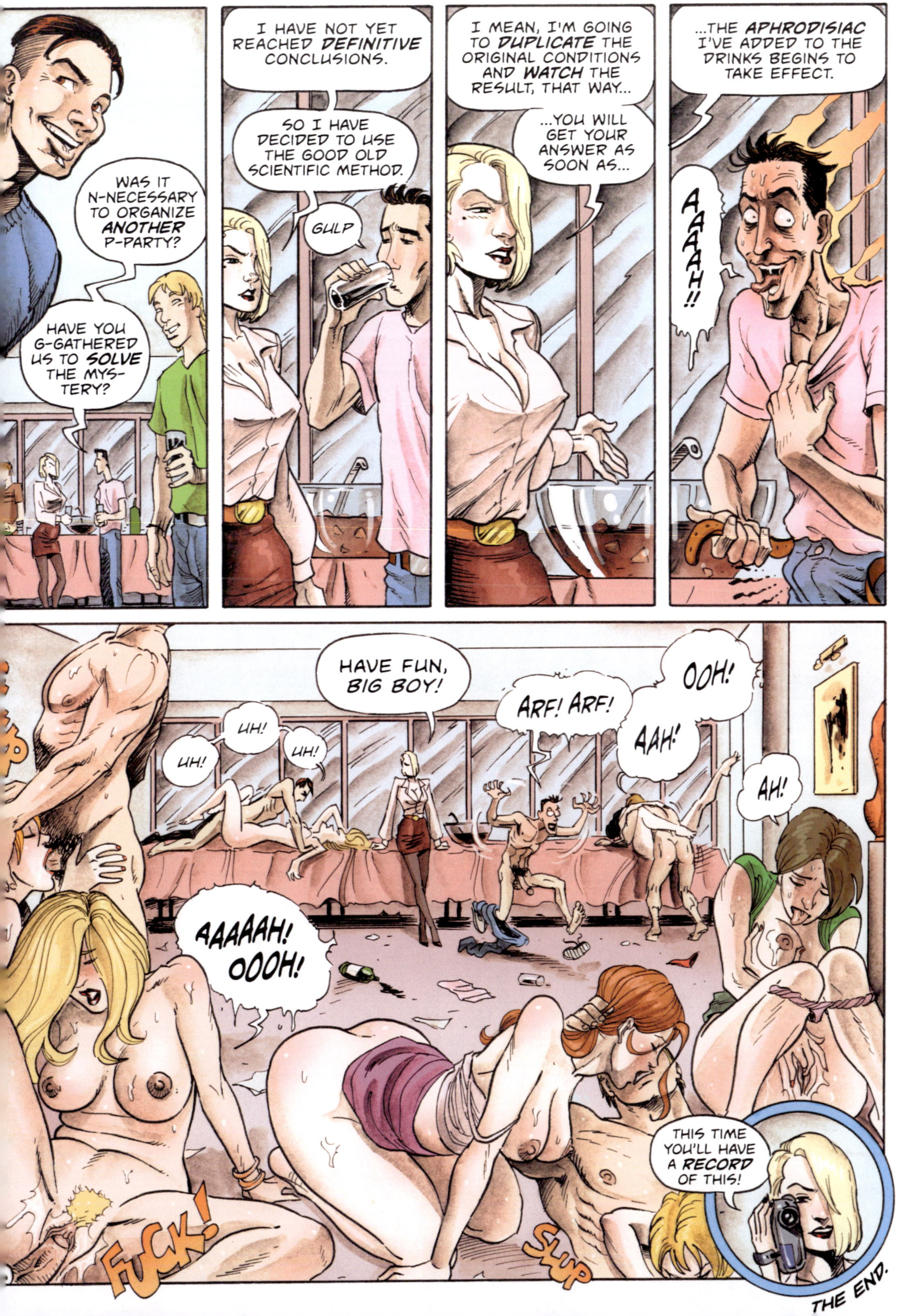

WAS IT N-NECESSARY TO ORGANIZE ANOTHER P-PARTY?
HAVE YOU G-GATHERED US TO SOLVE THE MYS-TERY?

I HAVE NOT YET REACHED DEFINITIVE CONCLUSIONS.
SO I HAVE DECIDED TO USE THE GOOD OLD SCIENTIFIC METHOD.
GULP

I MEAN, I'M GOING TO DUPLICATE THE ORIGINAL CONDITIONS AND WATCH THE RESULT, THAT WAY...
...YOU WILL GET YOUR ANSWER AS SOON AS...

...THE APHRODISIAC I'VE ADDED TO THE DRINKS BEGINS TO TAKE EFFECT.
AAAAH!!

HAVE FUN, BIG BOY!
UH!
UH!
UH!
ARF! ARF!
OOH!
AAH!
AH!
AAAAAH! OOOH!
FUCK!
SLUP
THIS TIME YOU'LL HAVE A RECORD OF THIS!
THE END.

NAUGHTY SPANISH NIGHTS

ALVARO 2003

AND...WHY...NOT... AFTER...THE... MATCH?
MOON, MAGIC, PASSION... PARTY!
YOU DON'T GET IT, BOY! WHEN IS THE STAG PARTY? THE NIGHT BEFORE THE WEDDING!
TONIGHT YOU ARE GOING TO DISCOVER THE TRUE SPANISH SPREE, GUYS.
AND CHRISTMAS EVE? AND NEW YEAR PARTY? IT'S ALWAYS BEFORE!
COME ON. YOU'RE GONNA LOVE IT...
YOU'LL FIND THAT EVERYTHING IS TRADITIONALLY SPANISH.
ONWARDS! THE GIRLS WAITED EAGERLY FOR YOU...
HELLOOO, BOYS.
HELLOOO.

FULL TREATMENT FOR THE GUESTS, LADIES.
HANDSOME... HEARD OF THE SPANISH KISS?
?!?
YOU HAVE TO PROVIDE THEM WITH THE MOST PLEASANT STAY POSSIBLE IN OUR COUNTRY.
RELAX, SWEETHEART
THIS IS TRULY DELICIOSO!
MMM!
GO ON, OOOH! DON'T STOP, BIG MAN!
OOOH! AAH! YES! YES!
SLURP! SLURP!
HEY, DON'T TAKE IT ALL FOR YOURSELF!
FUCK FUCK FUCK
OOH, LAD... BE GOOD... 'CAUSE THIS... 'S WON-DER-FUL!

CLIC
CLIC
INTERESTING... MAYBE I SHOULD PUT THE PHOTOS FOR SALE AND...
CREEK
AH!
OOPS, THAT SOUNDED REALLY BAD.
CREEK!!
MMM...ARE YOU GIRL PART OF THE REINFORCEMENTS?
UH...
SOMMF!!!
SURE, CHAMPION. I'M THE VITAMIN REINFORCEMENT.
4

OOOH!

ISN'T IT BETTER... TO REST NOW...BE- CAUSE...THE MATCH IS TOMORROW?
AH

TOMORROW YOU'RE GOING TO FEEL REAL GOOD, MY SWEETHEART.
COME WITH MUMMY, POPPET!

FUCK ME, DUDE! WRECK MY CUNT WITH YOUR BIG DICK!
YUM!

AAAH! OH!
OOH! MY GOD!
GLÜCKL UUU
C
CALM DOWN, HONEY. SOMEBODY HAS TO PLAY TO- MORROW'S MATCH.

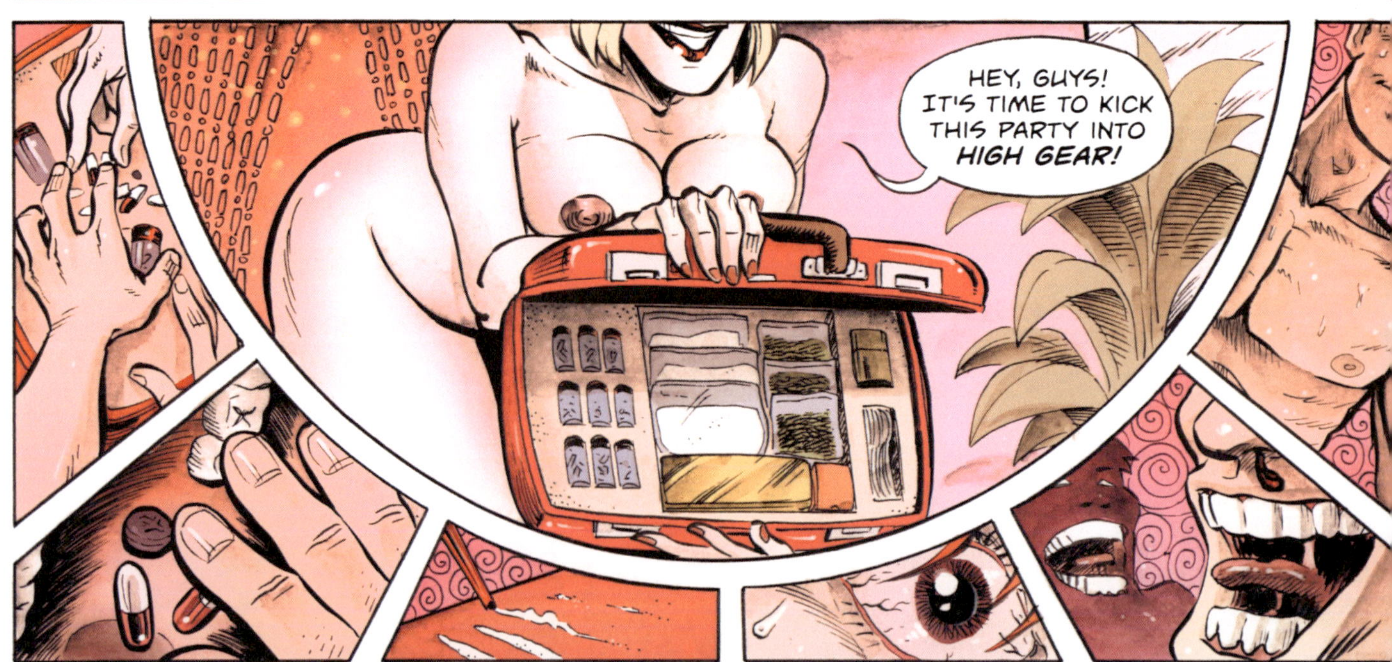

HEY, GUYS! IT'S TIME TO KICK THIS PARTY INTO HIGH GEAR!

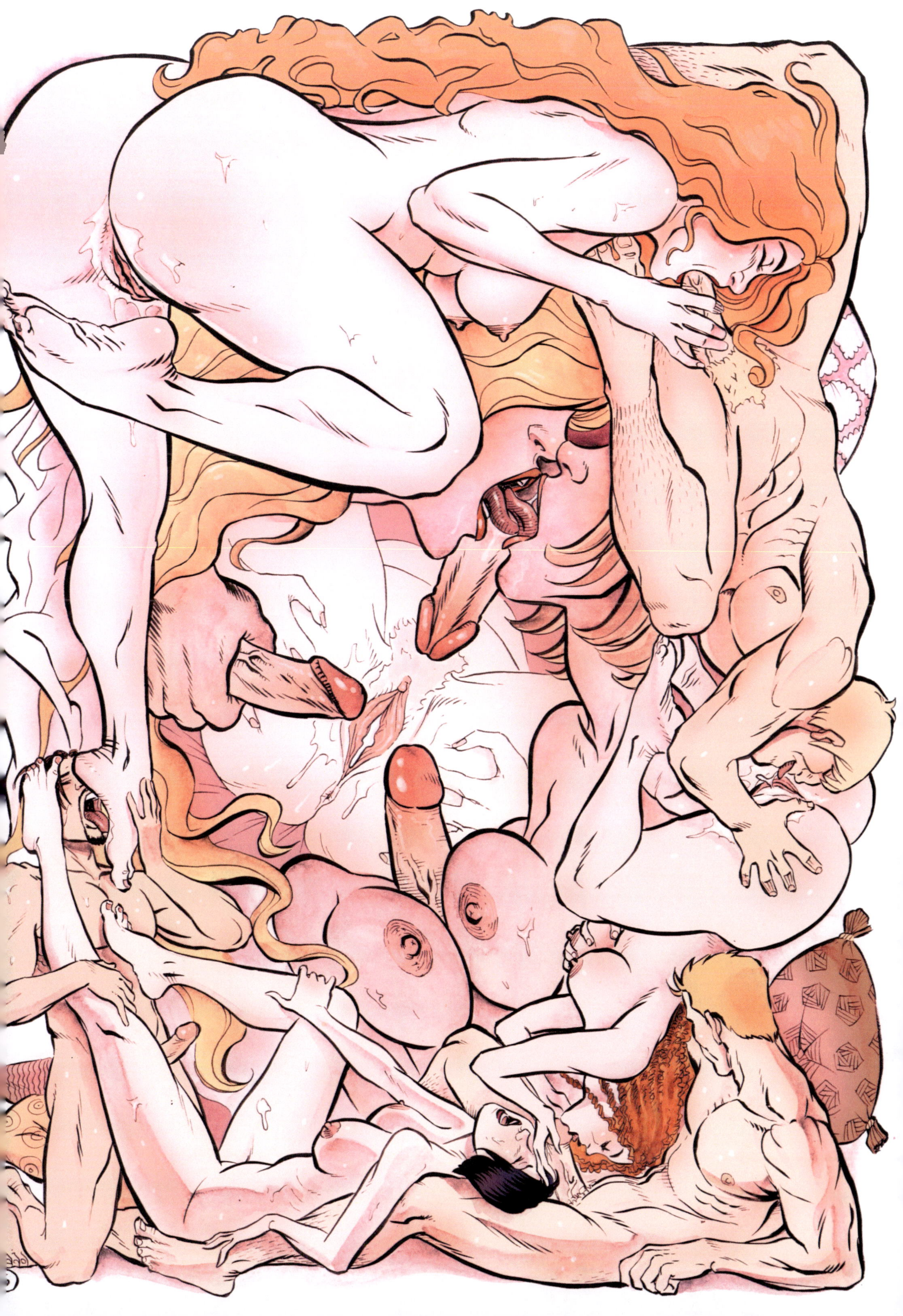

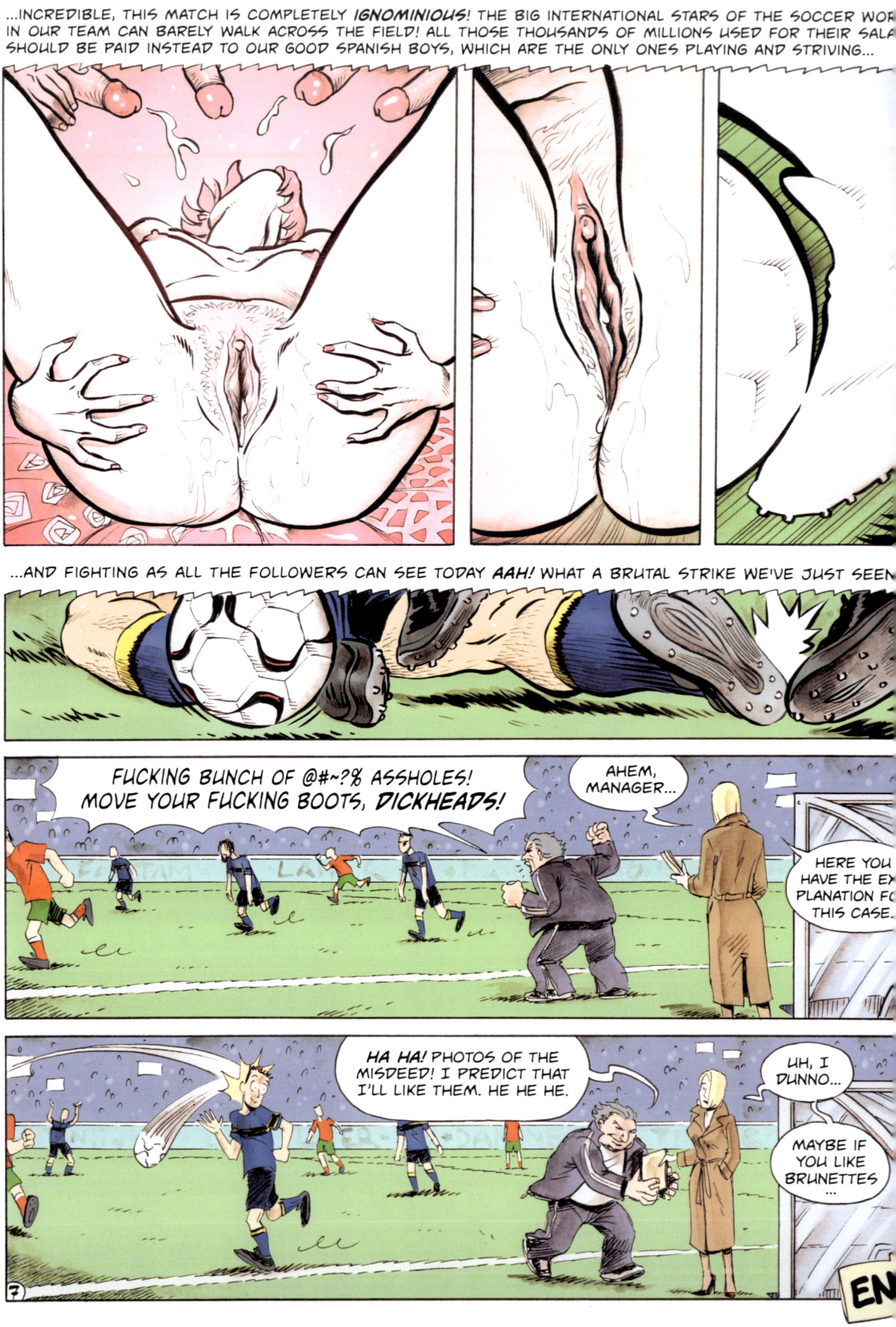

...AND FIGHTING AS ALL THE FOLLOWERS CAN SEE TODAY *AAH!* WHAT A BRUTAL STRIKE WE'VE JUST SEEN

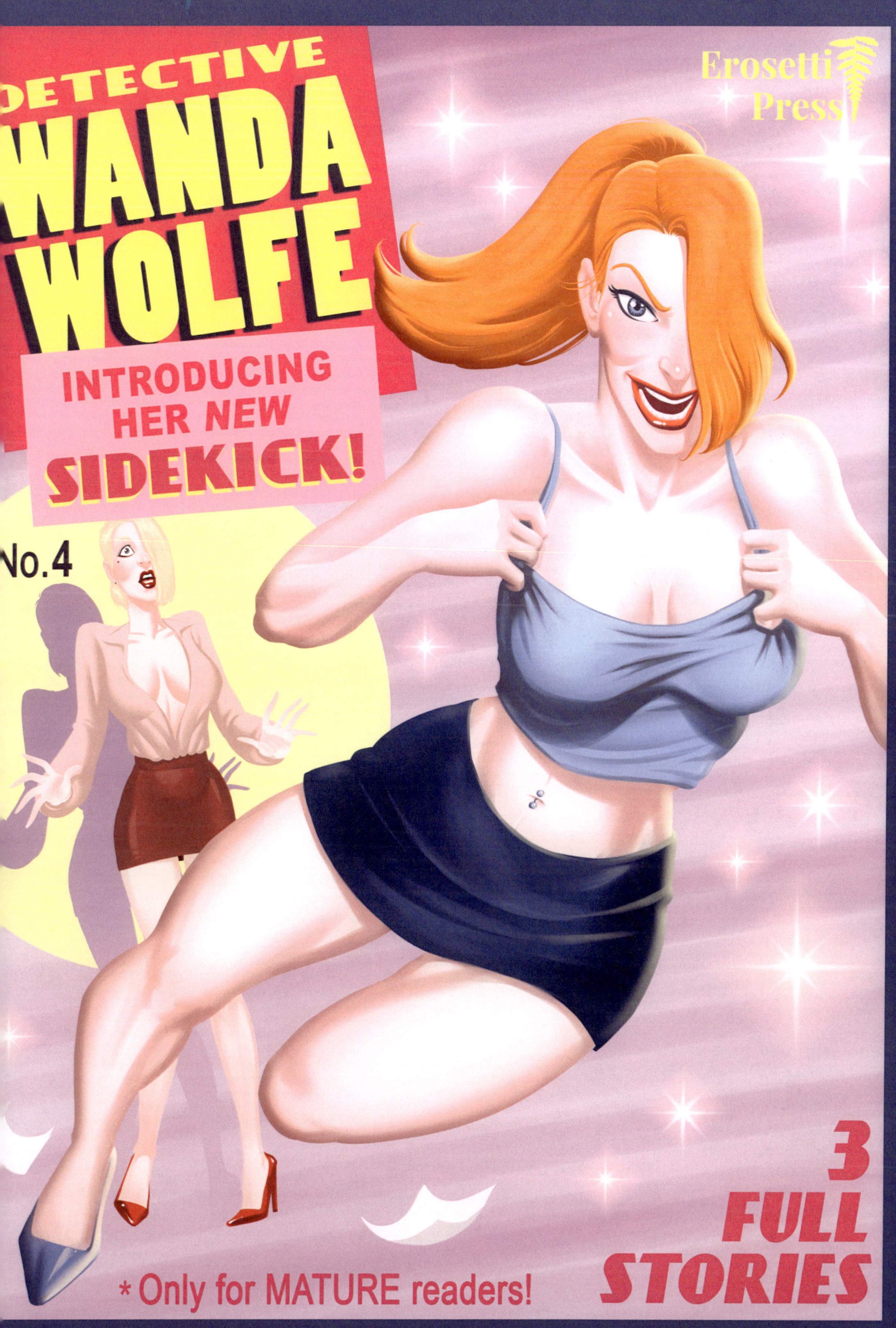

DETECTIVE
WANDA WOLFE
INTRODUCING HER NEW SIDEKICK!
No.4
Erosetti Press
3 FULL STORIES
* Only for MATURE readers!

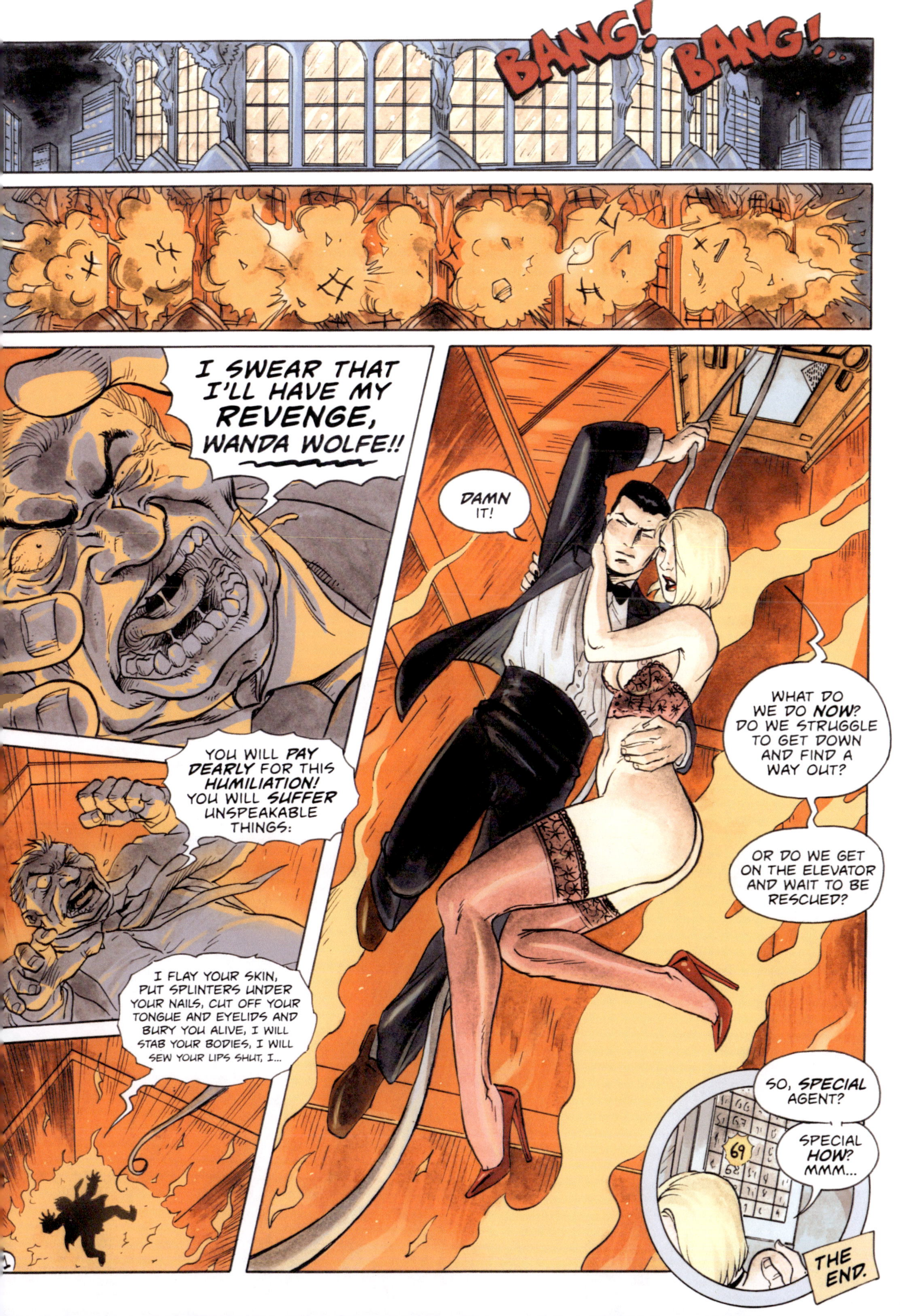

BANG!
BANG!
I SWEAR THAT I'LL HAVE MY REVENGE, WANDA WOLFE!!
DAMN IT!
YOU WILL PAY DEARLY FOR THIS HUMILIATION! YOU WILL SUFFER UNSPEAKABLE THINGS:
I FLAY YOUR SKIN, PUT SPLINTERS UNDER YOUR NAILS, CUT OFF YOUR TONGUE AND EYELIDS AND BURY YOU ALIVE, I WILL STAB YOUR BODIES, I WILL SEW YOUR LIPS SHUT, I...
WHAT DO WE DO NOW? DO WE STRUGGLE TO GET DOWN AND FIND A WAY OUT?
OR DO WE GET ON THE ELEVATOR AND WAIT TO BE RESCUED?
SO, SPECIAL AGENT?
SPECIAL HOW? MMM...
THE END.

Everything you always wanted to know...
...but they never dared to SHOW you after...
THE END.
ANOTHE TORRID ADV TURE FOR T INCOMPARAB DETECTIVE WANDA WOL
AH!
AH!
COME... QUICKLY... OOOH...
ALL THIS GLAMOUR AND VIOLENCE HAS REALLY TURNED ME ON...
ALVARO
SCIENTISTS ARE WRONG, IT'S NOT ADRENALINE PUMPING, BUT RATHER PHERO-MONES.
WAIT...
I HAVE A LITTLE SURPRISE FOR YOU...
YOU'RE GOING T LOVE IT
SLAP!
2

A PEN?! WHAT KIND OF A JOKE IS THIS? A GIFT FROM THE COMPANY FOR MY SERVICES?
CALM DOWN... LOOK!
FLOP!
HA HA A WEIRD CONTRAPTION? WHAT IS IT? A MINI COCKTAIL SHAKER WITH A MULTI-PURPOSE STRAW?
NO...
I HOPE THAT'S NOT A GRENADE YOU'RE SHOVING UP MY ASS!
BRRRRRRR
IT'S ACTUALLY A MULTI-PURPOSE PHONE...
OOHH!!
OOH... YOU'RE QUITE THE EXPERT...
I TRAVEL A LOT, I HAVE LEARNED FROM THE BEST, AND I PRACTICE ALL THE TIME...
I LEARNED THIS TECHNIQUE WHILE I WAS TRAVELING FROM RUSSIA, FROM THIS SPY WHO
SHUT UP BEFORE I GET JEALOUS!
AAH!! OH! AH!
FUCK! FUCK! FUCK!
SHH... DID YOU HEAR THAT? SEEMS LIKE SOMEONE GOT STUCK IN THE ELEVATOR.

OOMPH... DON'T WORRY BUDDY, IN JUST A MOMENT YOU'LL BE...
AAAH!
...OUT OF THERE.
GH.. OOH!
UH, MIKE, DO YOU NEED ANY HELP? ...OH!
WHAT A VIEW!
AH! OH!
AH!
OOH!
AH!
SO, WANT US TO GIVE YOU A HAND?
YES, YES... COME!
SQUAD... TO THE RESCUE!
GHN!
FOSH!

GN!
SLURP!
MMMMM!
OOH!
OOH!
FUCK!
FOSH!
AAHH!
FOSH
ON THE LOWER LEVEL...
COME ON, GUYS! I HEAR SCREAMS FOR HELP!

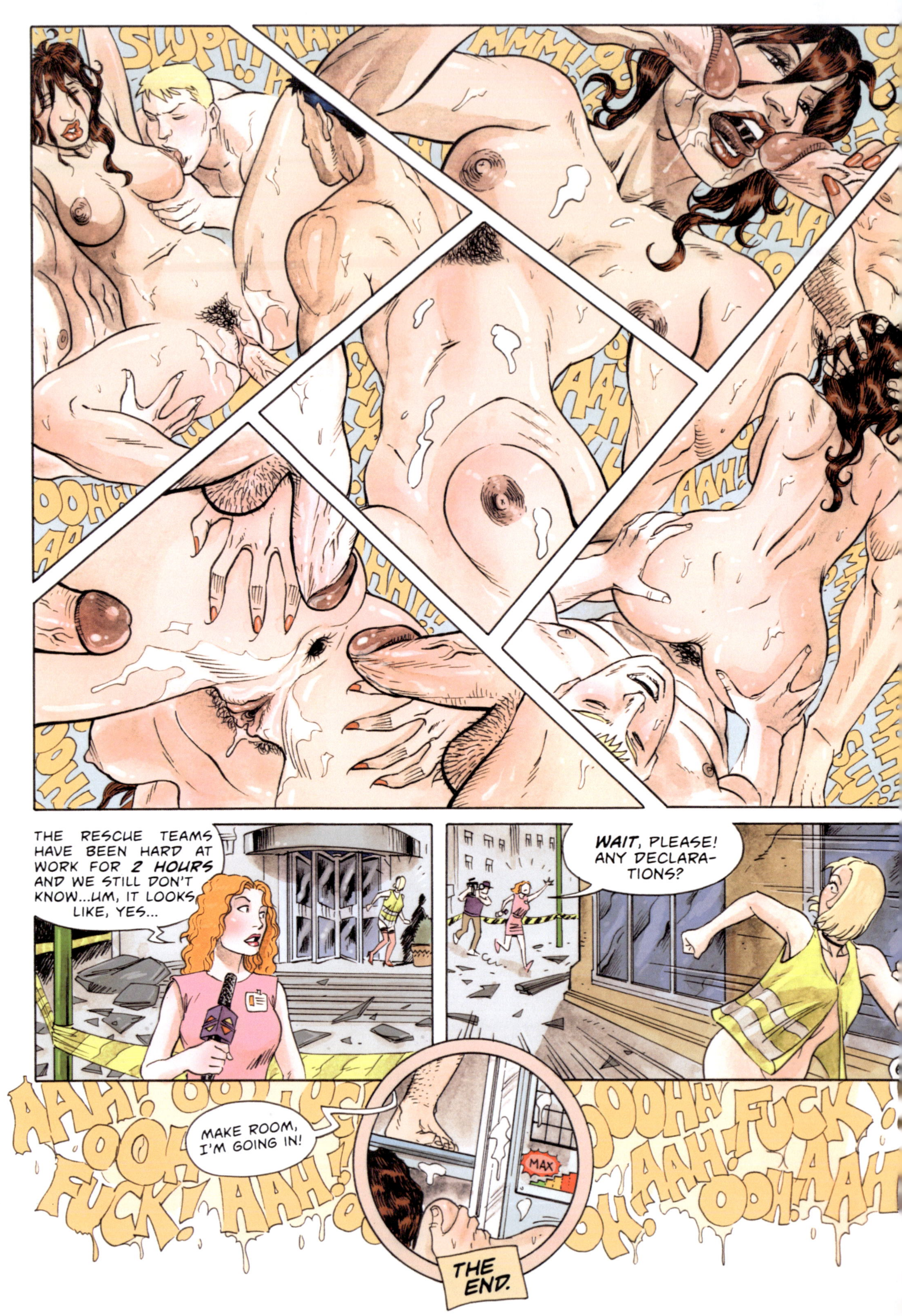
SLURP!!
AAH!
MMM!!
OOH!!
AAH!!
THE RESCUE TEAMS HAVE BEEN HARD AT WORK FOR 2 HOURS AND WE STILL DON'T KNOW...UM, IT LOOKS LIKE, YES...
WAIT, PLEASE! ANY DECLARA-TIONS?
AAH! OOH! OOH! FUCK! AAH! OOHH FUCK! AAH! OOHH
MAKE ROOM, I'M GOING IN!
MAX
THE END.

YOU HAVE TO MAKE AN EFFORT TODAY, WANDA.
WANDA WOLFE

2D

IT'S IMPORTANT TO MAKE A GOOD FIRST IMPRESSION WITH CLIENTS.
COME IN...

IS THIS THE OFFICE OF DETECTIVE...OH!

10 MINUTES LATE!

AND YOU HAVE TO...OOH! RECOVER... THE STOLEN JEWELS... OOOH!
SLUP!

15 MINUTES!
THERE'S SOMETHING STRANGE GOING ON HERE...
WANDA WOLFE
IT ISN'T NORMAL FOR SOMEONE WHO WANTS TO SEE ME TO BE SO LATE!

IT HAS BEEN A PLEASURE, MISS...
1

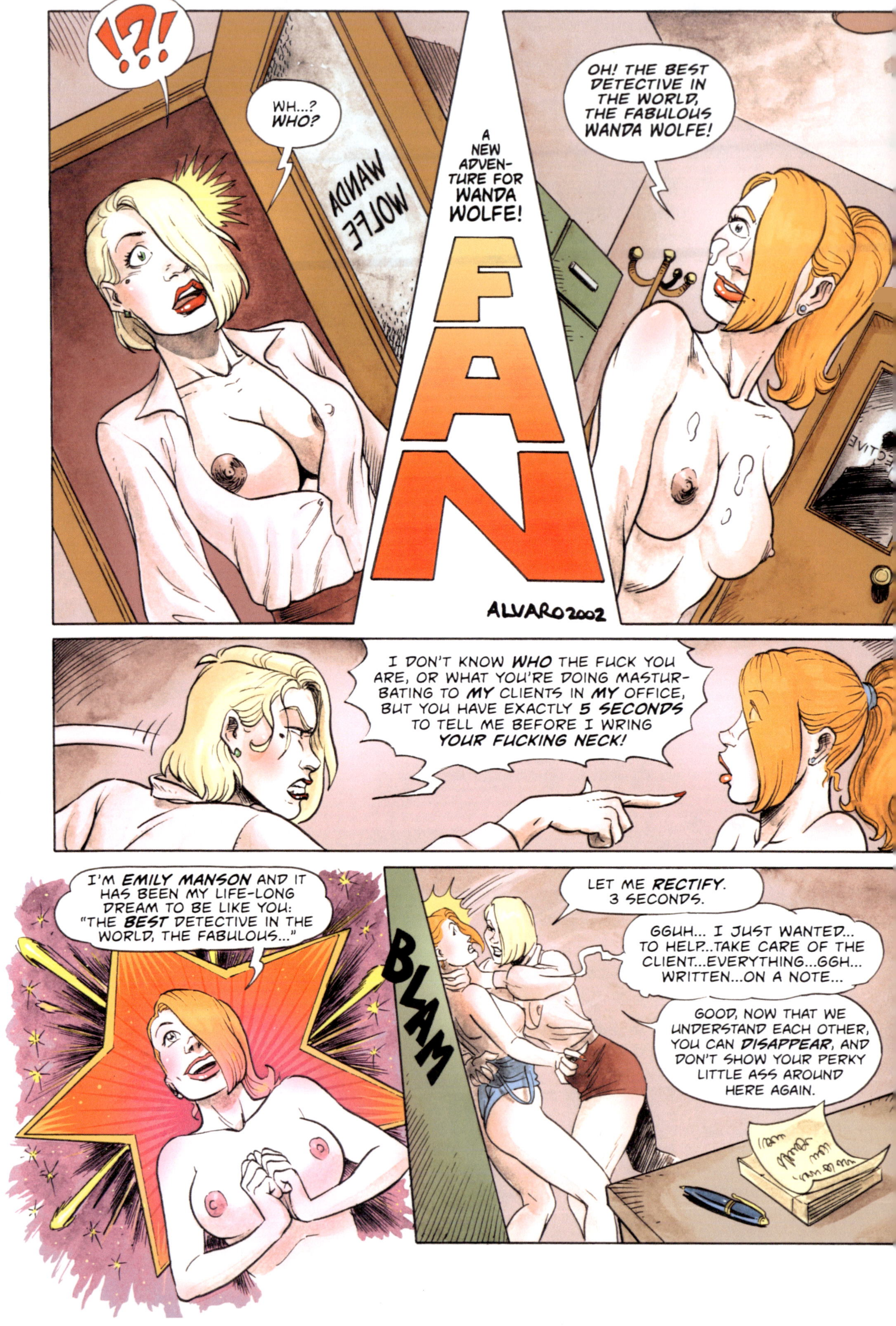
!?!
WH...? WHO?
WANDA WOLFE
A NEW ADVENTURE FOR WANDA WOLFE!
FAN
ALVARO 2002
OH! THE BEST DETECTIVE IN THE WORLD, THE FABULOUS WANDA WOLFE!
I DON'T KNOW WHO THE FUCK YOU ARE, OR WHAT YOU'RE DOING MASTURBATING TO MY CLIENTS IN MY OFFICE, BUT YOU HAVE EXACTLY 5 SECONDS TO TELL ME BEFORE I WRING YOUR FUCKING NECK!
I'M EMILY MANSON AND IT HAS BEEN MY LIFE-LONG DREAM TO BE LIKE YOU: "THE BEST DETECTIVE IN THE WORLD, THE FABULOUS..."
BLAM
LET ME RECTIFY. 3 SECONDS.
GGUH... I JUST WANTED... TO HELP...TAKE CARE OF THE CLIENT...EVERYTHING...GGH... WRITTEN...ON A NOTE...
GOOD, NOW THAT WE UNDERSTAND EACH OTHER, YOU CAN DISAPPEAR, AND DON'T SHOW YOUR PERKY LITTLE ASS AROUND HERE AGAIN.

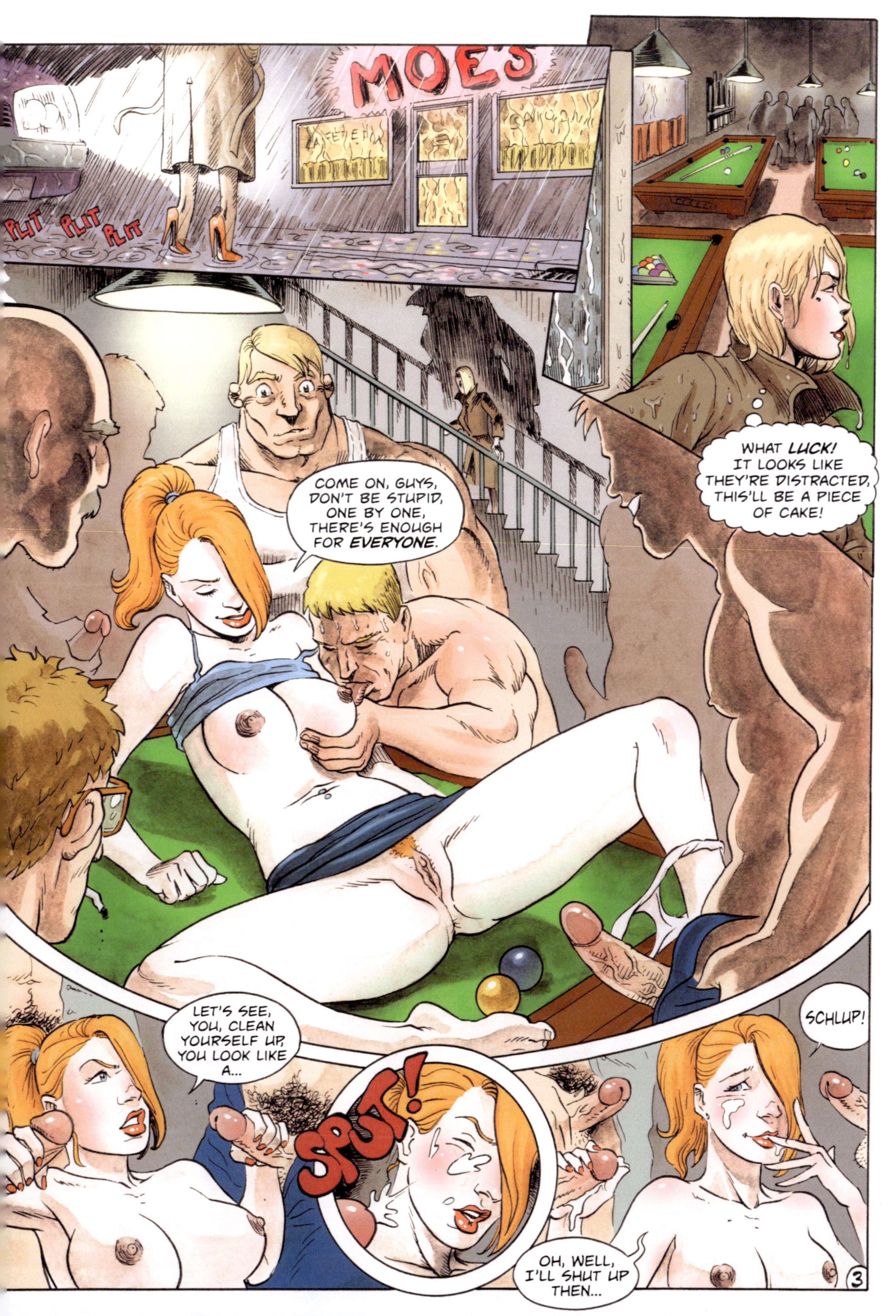

MOE'S
PLIT PLIT PLIT
COME ON, GUYS, DON'T BE STUPID, ONE BY ONE, THERE'S ENOUGH FOR EVERYONE.
WHAT LUCK! IT LOOKS LIKE THEY'RE DISTRACTED, THIS'LL BE A PIECE OF CAKE!
LET'S SEE, YOU, CLEAN YOURSELF UP, YOU LOOK LIKE A...
SPUT!
SCHLUP!
OH, WELL, I'LL SHUT UP THEN...
3

SLAPT!
AHHH! YEEES!
OOH!! AH!AAH!
UM... SO STRANGE THAT THEY WOULD LEAVE ME ALONE THIS WHOLE TIME.
ARE THEY PLOTTING SOMETHING?

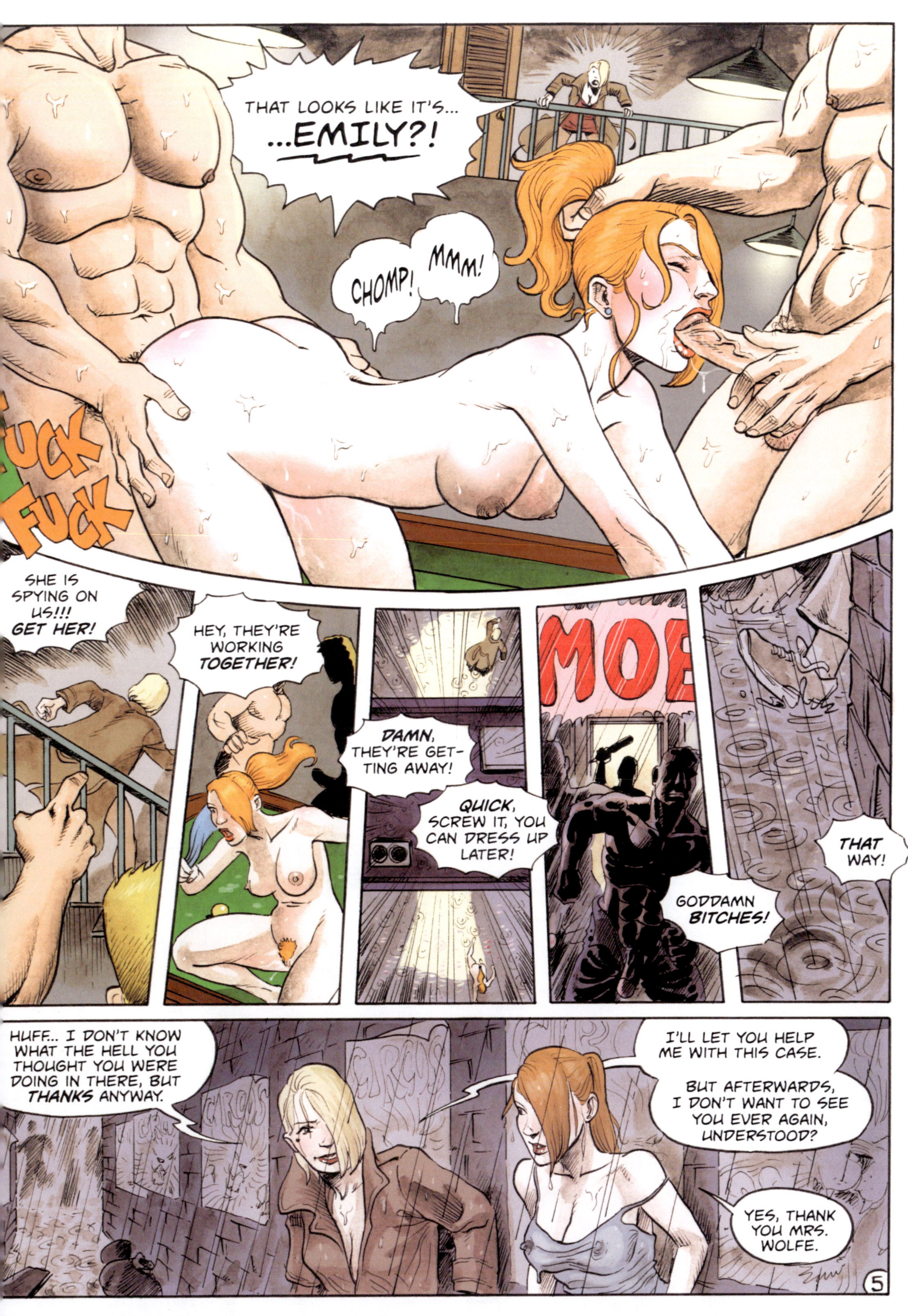

THAT LOOKS LIKE IT'S...
...EMILY?!
CHOMP! MMM!
FUCK FUCK
SHE IS SPYING ON US!!! GET HER!
HEY, THEY'RE WORKING TOGETHER!
DAMN, THEY'RE GETTING AWAY!
QUICK, SCREW IT, YOU CAN DRESS UP LATER!
MOE
THAT WAY!
GODDAMN BITCHES!
HUFF... I DON'T KNOW WHAT THE HELL YOU THOUGHT YOU WERE DOING IN THERE, BUT THANKS ANYWAY.
I'LL LET YOU HELP ME WITH THIS CASE.
BUT AFTERWARDS, I DON'T WANT TO SEE YOU EVER AGAIN, UNDERSTOOD?
YES, THANK YOU MRS. WOLFE.
5

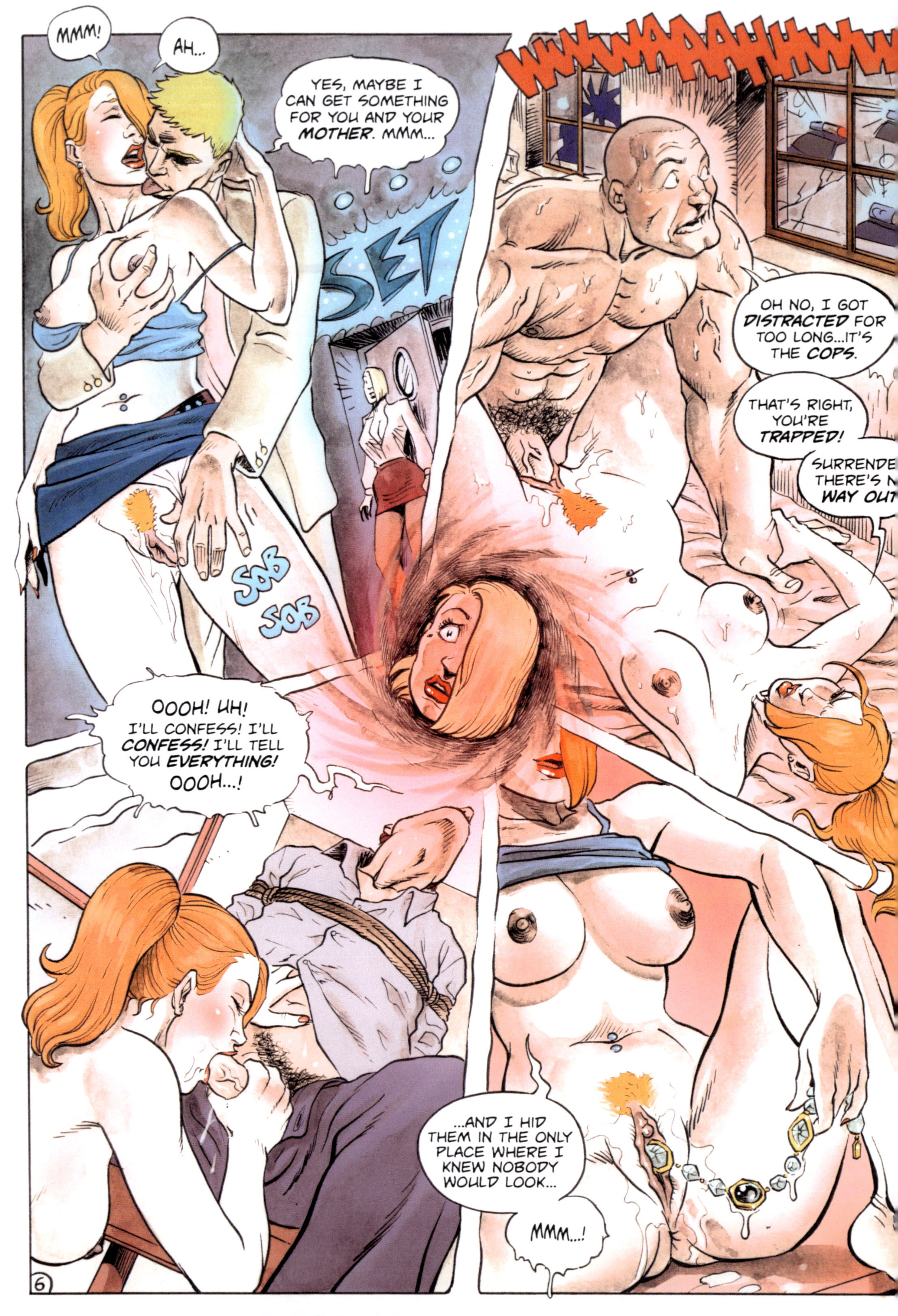

MMM!
AH...
YES, MAYBE I CAN GET SOMETHING FOR YOU AND YOUR MOTHER. MMM...
SET
SOB
SOB
WWWAAAHHH
OH NO, I GOT DISTRACTED FOR TOO LONG...IT'S THE COPS.
THAT'S RIGHT, YOU'RE TRAPPED!
SURRENDER, THERE'S NO WAY OUT!
OOOH! UH! I'LL CONFESS! I'LL CONFESS! I'LL TELL YOU EVERYTHING! OOOH...!
...AND I HID THEM IN THE ONLY PLACE WHERE I KNEW NOBODY WOULD LOOK...
MMM...!

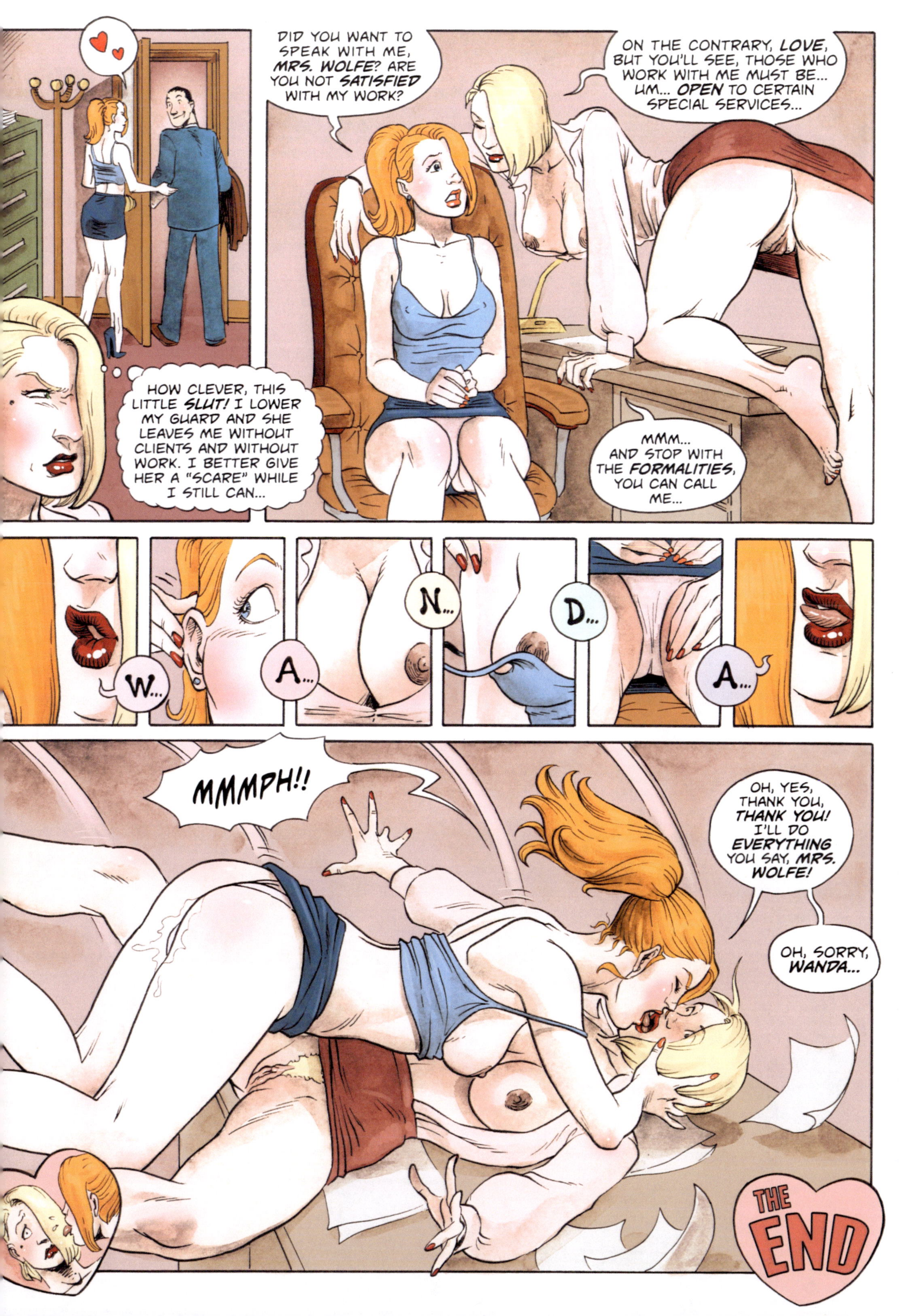

DID YOU WANT TO SPEAK WITH ME, MRS. WOLFE? ARE YOU NOT SATISFIED WITH MY WORK?
ON THE CONTRARY, LOVE, BUT YOU'LL SEE, THOSE WHO WORK WITH ME MUST BE... UM... OPEN TO CERTAIN SPECIAL SERVICES...
HOW CLEVER, THIS LITTLE SLUT! I LOWER MY GUARD AND SHE LEAVES ME WITHOUT CLIENTS AND WITHOUT WORK. I BETTER GIVE HER A "SCARE" WHILE I STILL CAN...
MMM... AND STOP WITH THE FORMALITIES, YOU CAN CALL ME...
W...
A...
N...
D...
A...
MMMPH!!
OH, YES, THANK YOU, THANK YOU! I'LL DO EVERYTHING YOU SAY, MRS. WOLFE!
OH, SORRY, WANDA...
THE END

A CHINESE TALE

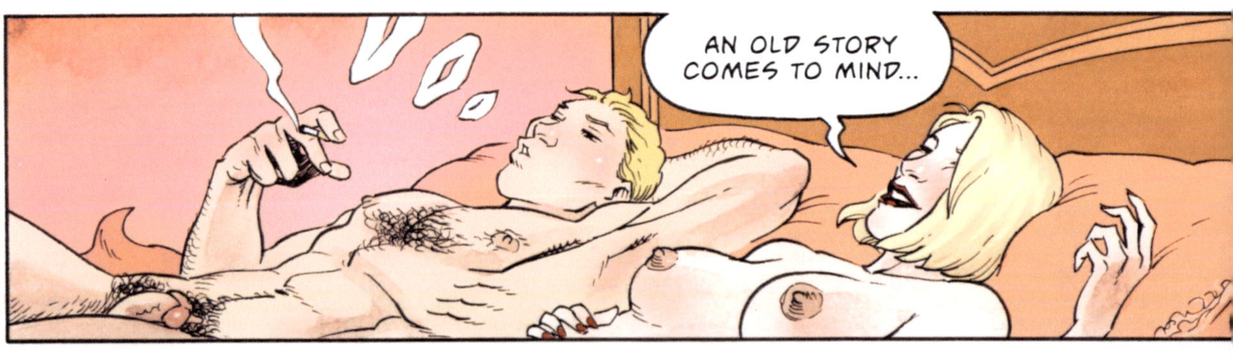

AN OLD STORY
COMES TO MIND...

A LONG TIME AGO, IN A COUNTRY FAR, FAR AWAY, THERE WAS A SMALL CABIN IN THE WOODS WHERE THERE LIVED...

...A YOUNG AND HANDSOME COUNTRY BOY WITH HIS ELDERLY FATHER, WHOM HE CARED FOR AND WHOM HE LOVED AND RESPECTED.

ONE DAY, THE FATHER SAID: "I DON'T HAVE A LOT OF TIME LEFT. SON, IT IS TIME FOR YOU TO FIND A GOOD, BEAUTIFUL WOMAN TO MARRY."

AND EVEN THOUGH HE FATHER'S WORDS WEIGHED HEAVILY UPON HIS HEART, THE COUNTRY BOY WENT OUT TO FIND A WIFE.

TWO DAYS LATER, HE RETURNED, HAVING MARRIED A BEAUTIFUL GIRL. AND IN THAT INSTANT, THE ELDERLY MAN FORGOT ABOUT EVEN DREAMING OF HIS LIFE ENDING SOMEDAY.

WITH MORE AND MORE MOUTHS TO FEED, THE YOUNG COUNTRY BOY WAS FORCED TO WORK RESTLESSLY DAY AND NIGHT.

IN DOING SO, HE LEFT HIS WIFE ALONE AT HOME WITH HIS FATHER, WHO HAD MIRACULOUSLY RECOVERED HIS YOUTHFUL SPIRIT.

ONE MORNING, THE OLD MAN PLUNGED HIMSELF INTO THE SMOLDERING VOLCANOES OF PASSION AND UNLEASHED HIMSELF...

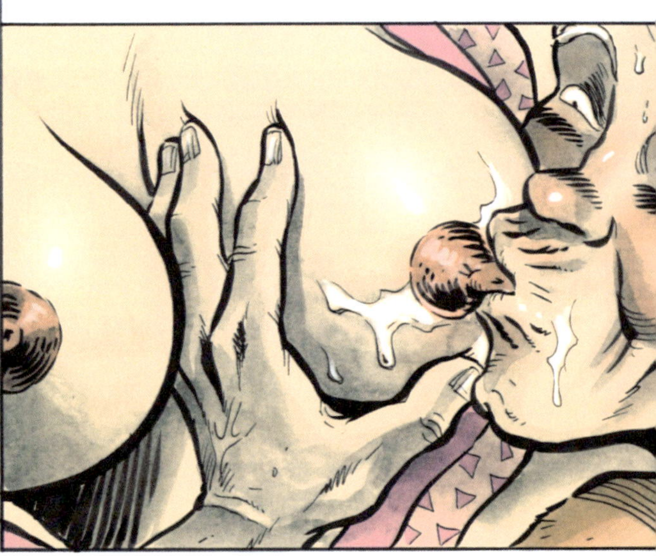
"SLUUUUUUUUUUUUUURP!"

THAT NIGHT, WHEN HER HUSBAND RETURNED HIM, THE GIRL TOLD HIM WHAT HAPPENED WITH HIS ELDERLY AND BELOVED FATHER, BUT THE CLEVER OLD MAN...

...PRETENDED TO BE SICK AND HIS SON DID NOT BELIEVE A SINGLE ONE OF HER ACCUSATIONS, MAKIN HER LOOK LIKE A LIAR IN THE EYES OF HER HUSBAN

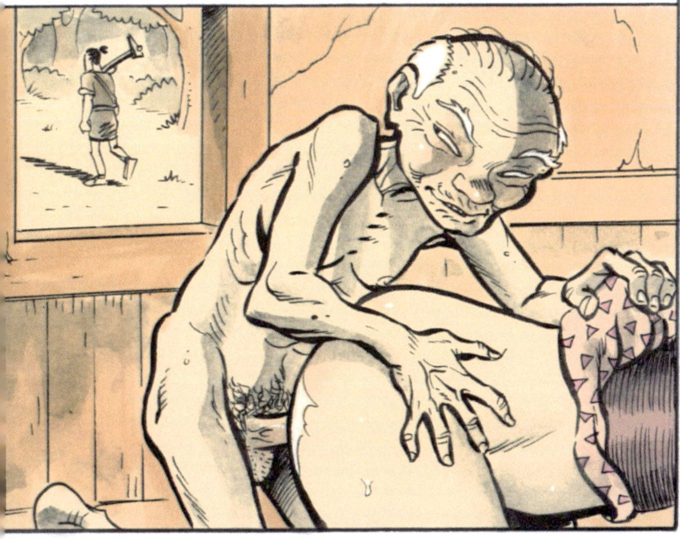
IN THE NEXT FEW DAYS, TAKING ADVANTAGE OF HIS SON'S INCREDULOUSNESS, THE HORNY OLD MAN DID NOT CONTROL HIS IMPULSES...

...AND SHE ENDURED THIS FOR HER HUSBAND. HOPING HE WOULD CATCH THEM AND FINALLY BELIEVE HER ONCE HE HAD SEEN IT WITH HIS OWN EYES.

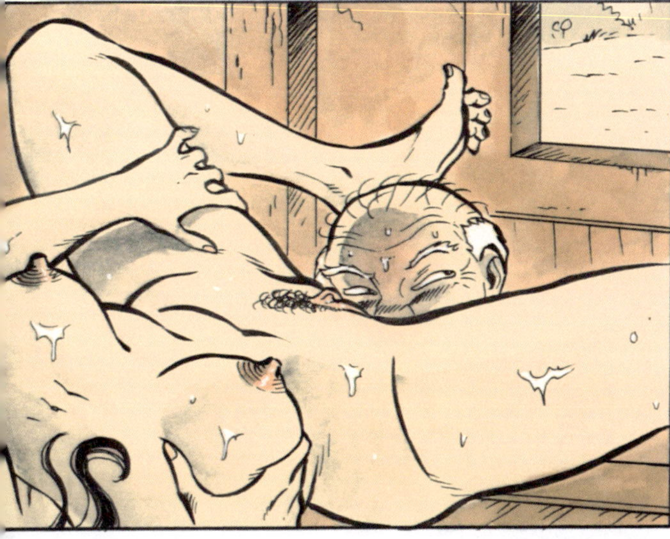
BUT THE OLD MAN, AWARE OF THIS RISK, HATCHED A MALEVOLENT PLAN.

HE CONVINCED THE TOWN DOCTOR TO TELL HIS SON THAT, IN ORDER TO CURE HIM, HE WOULD NEED GIANT CUCUMBERS FROM A DISTANT LAND.

SO, WHILE THE GOOD LAD MARCHED ON IN HIS ARDUOUS SEARCH FOR GIANT CUCUMBERS...

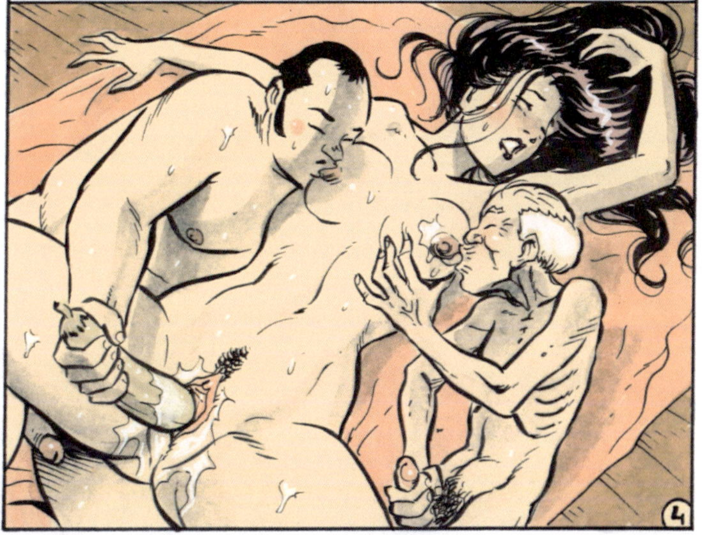
...THE OLD MAN PEACEFULLY ENJOYED THE TENDER VOLUPTUOUSNESS OF THE YOUNG GIRL AT HOME.
4

TIME PASSED, AND THE YOUNG COUNTRY BOY WAS EITHER BUSY WORKING OR ON FUTILE MISSIONS WHILE MORE AND MORE PEOPLE IN TOWN BECAME AWARE OF AND ENJOYED THE TERRIBLE SECRET OF THE OLD MAN AND THE GIRL.

ONE DAY, TERRIBLE NEWS ARRIVED:

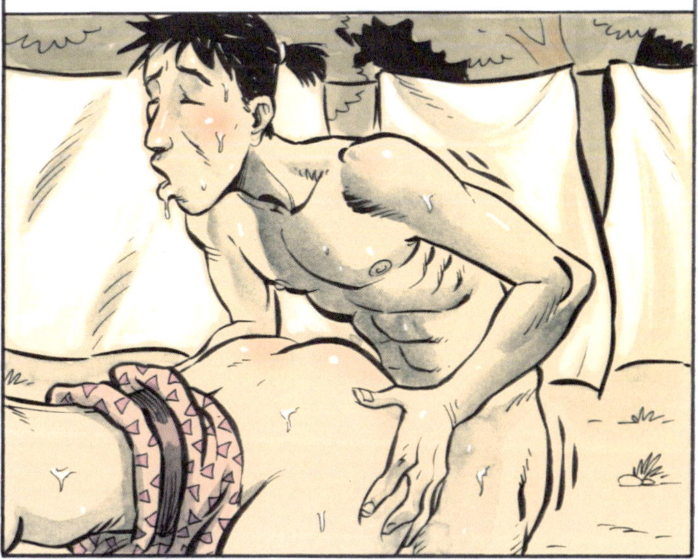
--"THEY FOUND OOH! YOUR SON AAH! FROZEN TO DEATH IN THE MOUNTAINS OOOH!"

THE OLD MAN WAS DEVASTATED... HE HAD KILLED HIS OWN SON BY BEING SO DAMN LECHEROUS!

AS FOR THE YOUNG GIRL... AH! IT WAS FINALLY TIME FOR HER REVENGE!!!

BUT IT HAPPENED IN A WAY THAT TOOK EVERYONE BY SURPRISE. WITH HER HUSBAND DEAD, SHE MARRIED THE OLD MAN, WHO SHE NEVER AGAIN LET TOUCH HER, AND EVERY DAY SHE WOULD MAKE HIM RELIVE HIS CRIME BY MASTURBATING IN FRONT OF HIM WITH THE GIANT CUCUMBERS.

HA HA HA HA HA HA HA!

ARE YOU TELLING ME THAT MY PENIS IS SMALL?
NO, THAT I'M GOING TO BECOME A VEGETARIAN.
THE END

DETECTIVE WANDA WOLFE
BY COAX
No.5
A COAXDREAMS PRODUCTION
3 FULL STORIES
* Only for MATURE readers!
ALTERNATIVE COLOR SCHEME
FIRST SKETCH
BY COAX
FINAL

DETECTIVE
WANDA WOLFE
BY COAX
No.5
3 FULL STORIES
WW
Erosetti Press
* Only for MATURE readers!

THEY FOUND HER NAKED, MASTURBATING LIKE SHE HAD BEEN TAKEN OVER...
...BY AN ACUTE FORM OF NYMPHOMANIA.
WE STILL DON'T KNOW WHO IT IS...

...BUT EVERYTHING POINTS TO THIS BEING THE WORK OF LOMAX.
AND GIVEN YOUR HISTORY WITH HIM...

MENTAL ASYLUM

WE THINK THAT YOU MAY BE ABLE TO HELP US.

WE COULD HAVE EASILY CRUSHED THEM IF THAT USELESS REFEREE HADN'T...OOH?

SSLRPT!
WHAT?

SECOND HALLWAY TO THE RIGHT, SWEETHEART.

WANDA! WAIT!

WE BLINDFOLDED HER, JUST LIKE YOU ASKED...

THERE YOU HAVE HER.
ALL YOURS.

GHN!
WAIT OUTSIDE.
W-WHAT ARE YOU GOING TO DO?

FUCK HER LIKE NOBODY'S FUCKED HER BEFORE!
AND FOR WHAT? YOU MAY BE ASKING...
UH...OF COURSE!
WELL, I'M GOING TO IMITATE LOMAX'S WAY OF FUCKING TO MAKE HER RELIVE THOSE MOMENTS, AND IN DOING SO...
...EXTRACT AS MUCH IN-FORMATION AS POSSIBLE.
GHN!
OOH!
IT'S SURE TO BE VERY EDUCATIONAL.
THE TWO SIDES OF TRUTH
A NEW WET, BIZARRE CASE FOR PARAPHILIAC DETECTIVE WANDA WOLFE
ALVARO 2003
2

AAHH!
MMMM...
WE'RE GONNA HAVE A GOOD TIME...
OPEN THAT PRECIOUS LITTLE MOUTH...
SLUP!!
GHFF! MMFS!
OOHH!
RELAX, DON'T BE SO TENSE.
AAHH!
YOU LIKE THIS, YOU LITTLE SLUT?
OOHH!
FROT!
COME ON NOW, TELL ME YOUR SECRETS...
3

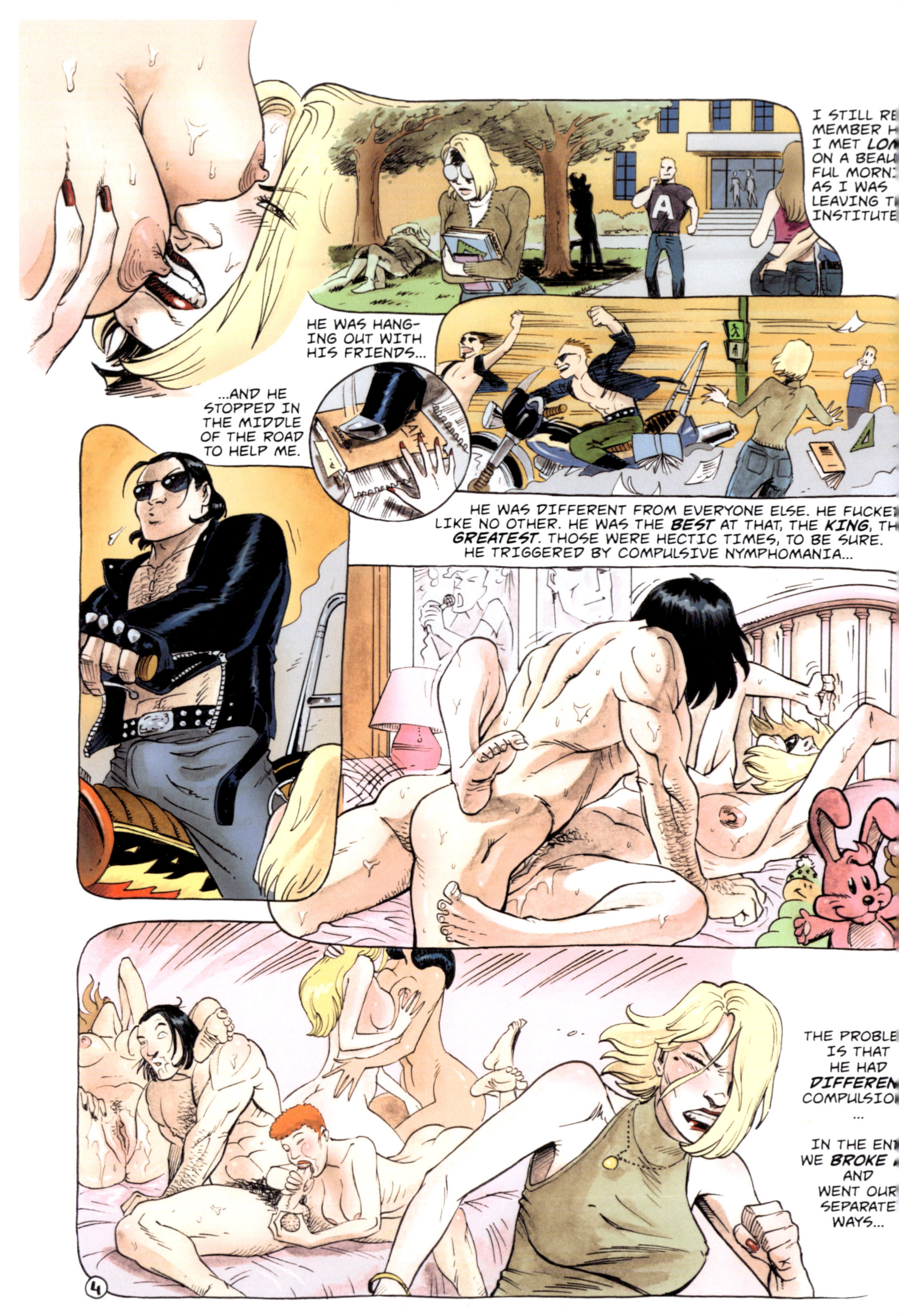

I STILL RE
MEMBER H
I MET LON
ON A BEAU
FUL MORNI
AS I WAS
LEAVING T
INSTITUTE

HE WAS HANG-
ING OUT WITH
HIS FRIENDS...

...AND HE
STOPPED IN
THE MIDDLE
OF THE ROAD
TO HELP ME.

HE WAS DIFFERENT FROM EVERYONE ELSE. HE FUCKE
LIKE NO OTHER. HE WAS THE BEST AT THAT, THE KING, TH
GREATEST. THOSE WERE HECTIC TIMES, TO BE SURE.
HE TRIGGERED BY COMPULSIVE NYMPHOMANIA...

THE PROBLE
IS THAT
HE HAD
DIFFEREN
COMPULSIO
...

IN THE EN
WE BROKE
AND
WENT OUR
SEPARATE
WAYS...

4

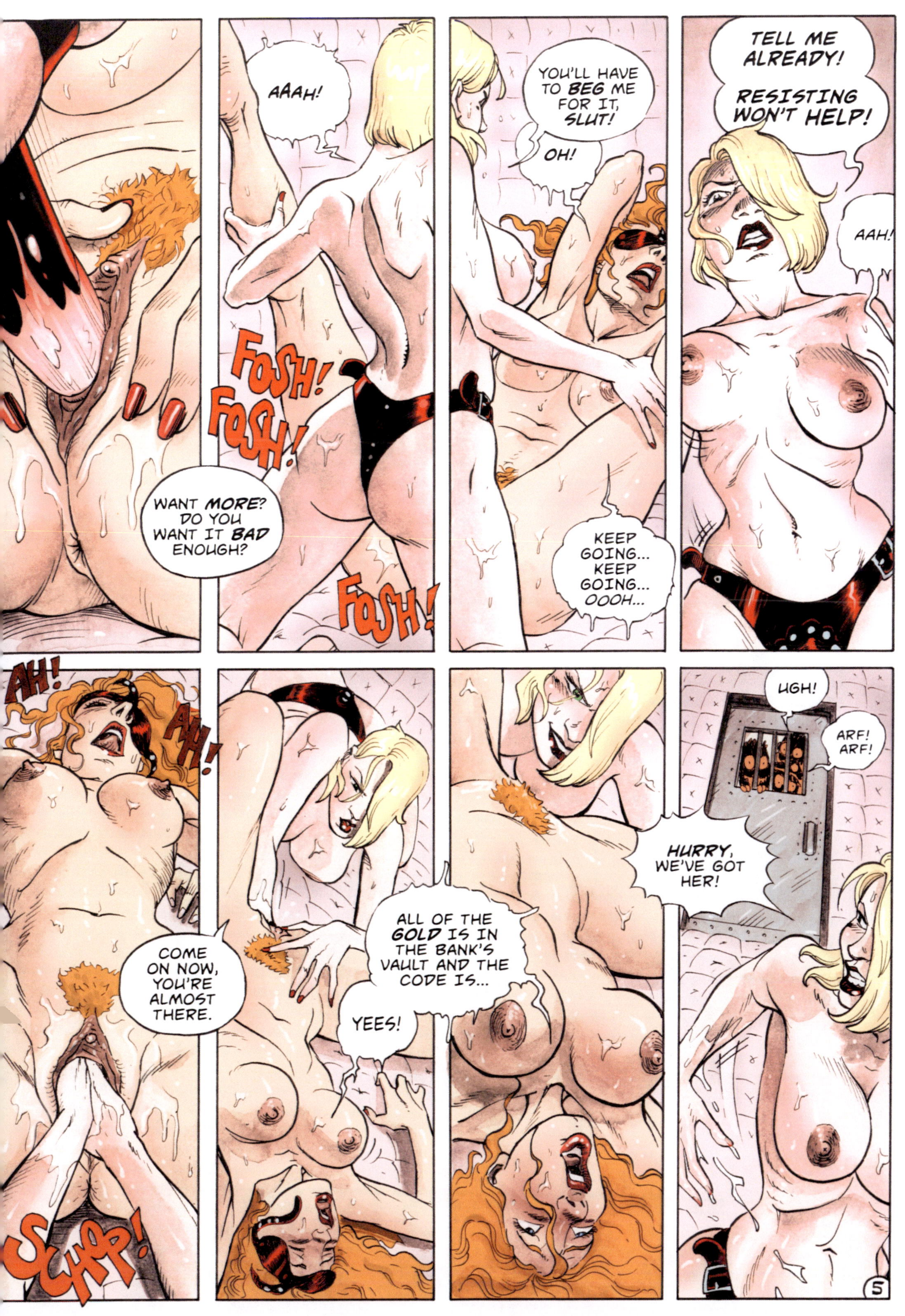
WANT MORE? DO YOU WANT IT BAD ENOUGH?
FOSH! FOSH! FOSH!
AAAH!
YOU'LL HAVE TO BEG ME FOR IT, SLUT!
OH!
KEEP GOING... KEEP GOING... OOOH...
TELL ME ALREADY! RESISTING WON'T HELP!
AAH!
AH! AH!
SCHP!
COME ON NOW, YOU'RE ALMOST THERE.
ALL OF THE GOLD IS IN THE BANK'S VAULT AND THE CODE IS...
YEES!
UGH!
ARF! ARF!
HURRY, WE'VE GOT HER!
5

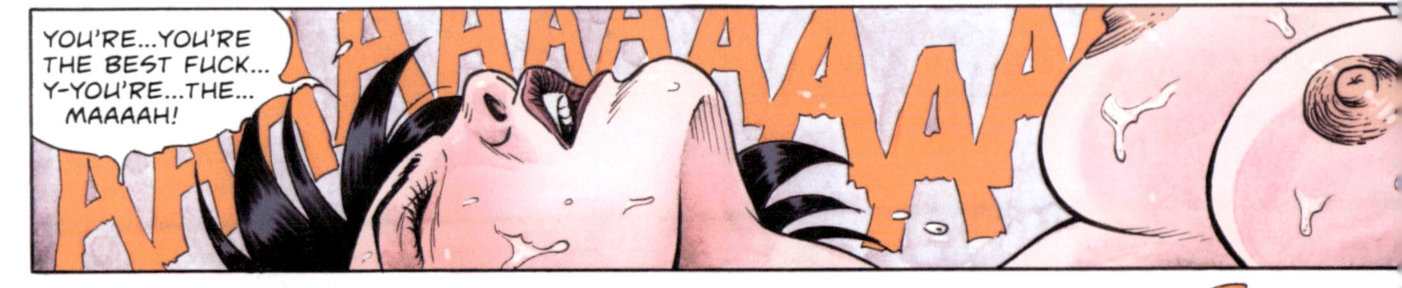

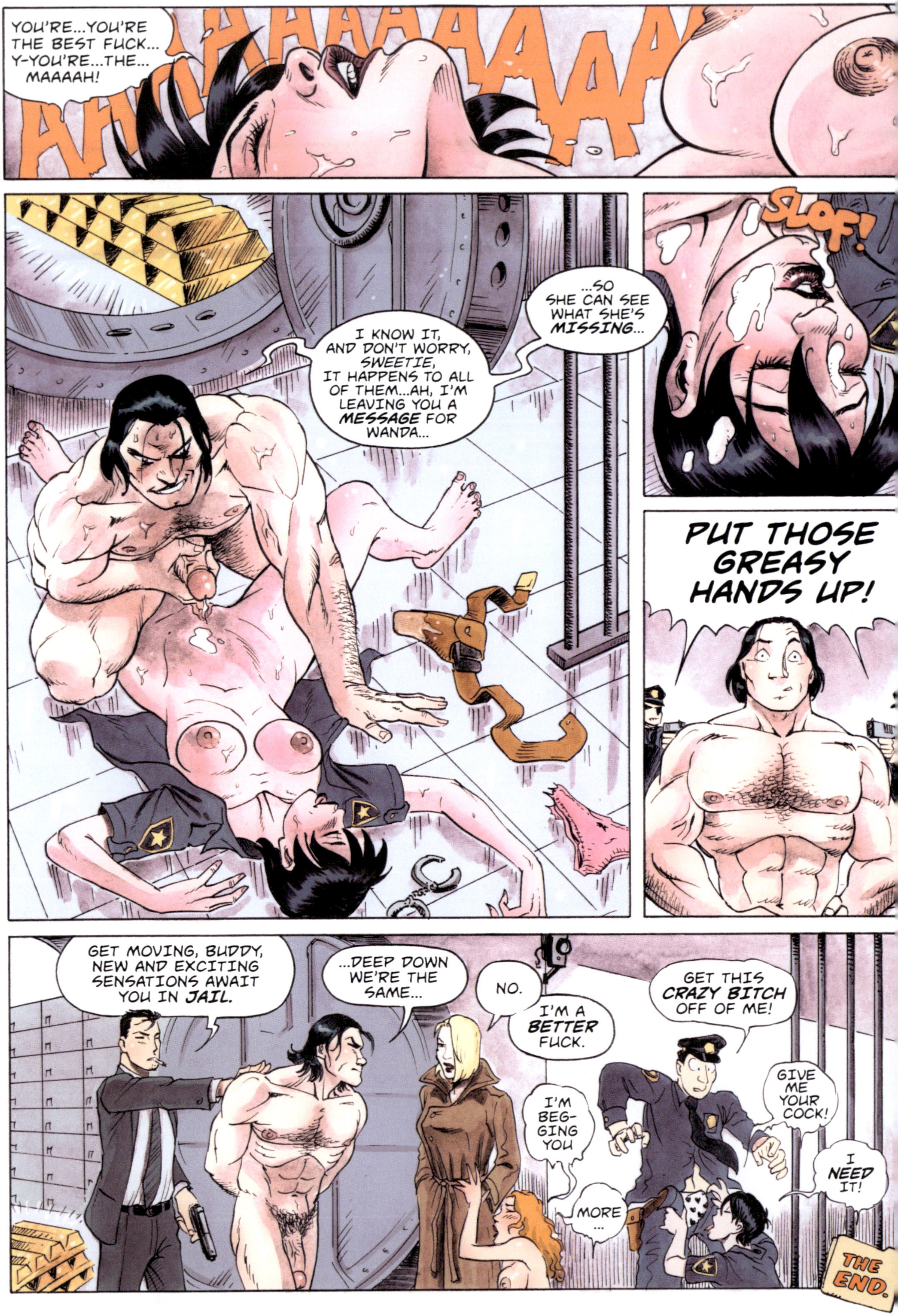

YOU'RE...YOU'RE THE BEST FUCK... Y-YOU'RE...THE... MAAAAH!
AAAAAAAAAAAAAAAH!

I KNOW IT, AND DON'T WORRY, SWEETIE, IT HAPPENS TO ALL OF THEM...AH, I'M LEAVING YOU A MESSAGE FOR WANDA...
...SO SHE CAN SEE WHAT SHE'S MISSING...

SLOF!

PUT THOSE GREASY HANDS UP!

GET MOVING, BUDDY, NEW AND EXCITING SENSATIONS AWAIT YOU IN JAIL.
...DEEP DOWN WE'RE THE SAME...
NO.
I'M A BETTER FUCK.
I'M BEG-GING YOU
MORE...
GET THIS CRAZY BITCH OFF OF ME!
GIVE ME YOUR COCK!
I NEED IT!
THE END.

AND NOW, A BREAKDOWN OF MY FEES:
$800 FOR 3 DAYS OF WORK...
$450 FOR FOOD AND BOARD...
$900 FOR THE REPAIRS TO MY CAR...
YES...
YES... YES...
AH!
OOH, WANDA, YOU DRIVE ME CRAZY...
($40 FOR THE LAMP YOU JUST THREW)
$160 FOR ALL THE GLASS I BROKE AT THE MOTEL...
YEESS!
OUHH!
CRAK!
SLUK!
COME BACK WHENEVER YOU LIKE!
WORKING FOR YOU HAS BEEN A PLEASURE!
WANDA WOLFE
$100, $200, $300...
IT IS IMPRESSIVE, WANDA WOLFE...
EH, WHO?! HOW DID YOU BREAK IN HERE?!
...HOW YOU HANDLE MEN.
AND I'VE COME TO MAKE YOU AN OFFER.

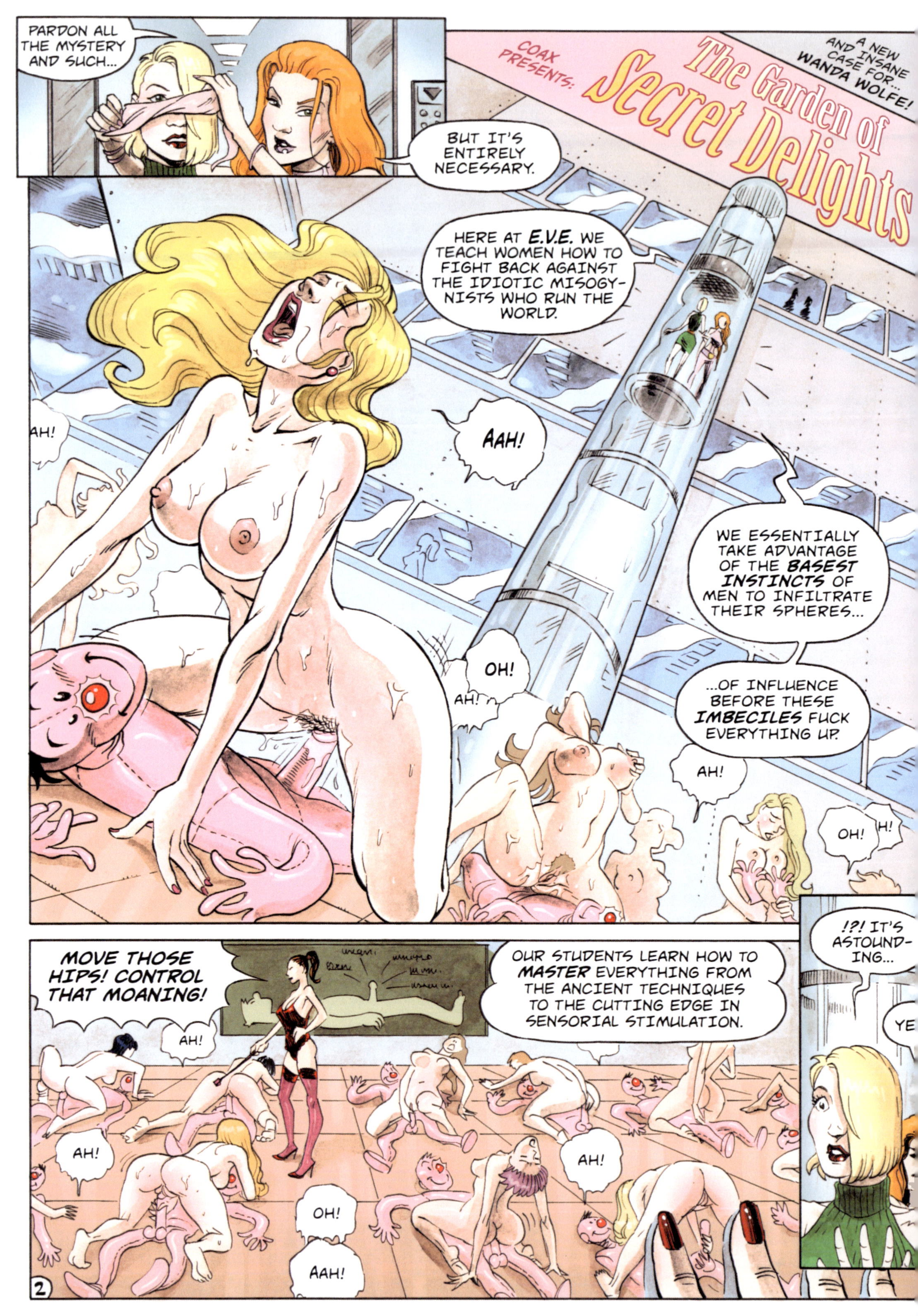

PARDON ALL THE MYSTERY AND SUCH...

COAX PRESENTS:
The Garden of Secret Delights

A NEW AND INSANE CASE FOR... WANDA WOLFE!

BUT IT'S ENTIRELY NECESSARY.

HERE AT E.V.E. WE TEACH WOMEN HOW TO FIGHT BACK AGAINST THE IDIOTIC MISOGYNISTS WHO RUN THE WORLD.

AAH!

AH!

OH!

AH!

WE ESSENTIALLY TAKE ADVANTAGE OF THE BASEST INSTINCTS OF MEN TO INFILTRATE THEIR SPHERES...

...OF INFLUENCE BEFORE THESE IMBECILES FUCK EVERYTHING UP.

AH!

OH!

H!

MOVE THOSE HIPS! CONTROL THAT MOANING!

AH!

AH!

OH!

AAH!

OUR STUDENTS LEARN HOW TO MASTER EVERYTHING FROM THE ANCIENT TECHNIQUES TO THE CUTTING EDGE IN SENSORIAL STIMULATION.

AH!

!?! IT'S ASTOUNDING...

YE

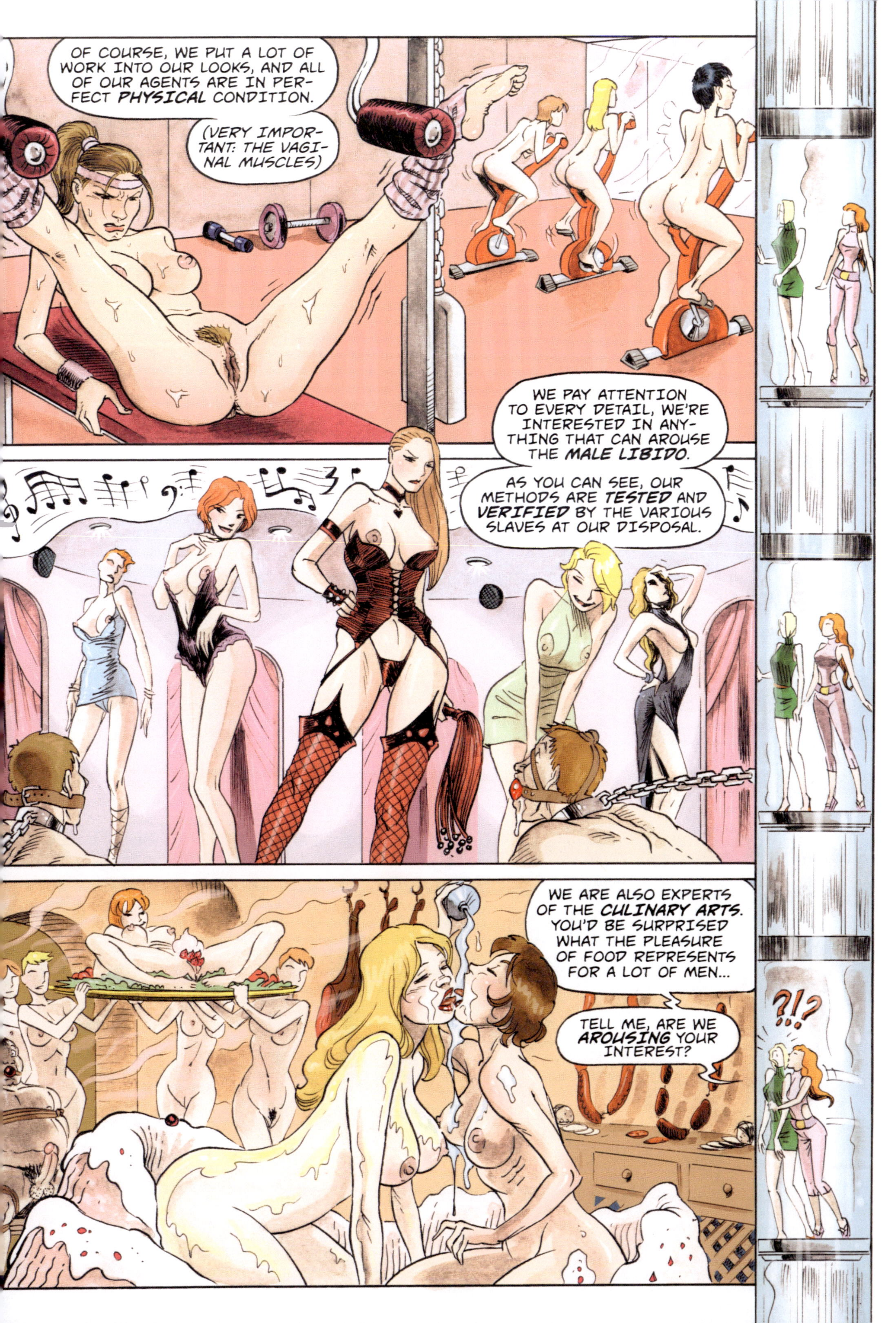

OF COURSE, WE PUT A LOT OF WORK INTO OUR LOOKS, AND ALL OF OUR AGENTS ARE IN PERFECT PHYSICAL CONDITION.
(VERY IMPORTANT: THE VAGINAL MUSCLES)
WE PAY ATTENTION TO EVERY DETAIL, WE'RE INTERESTED IN ANYTHING THAT CAN AROUSE THE MALE LIBIDO.
AS YOU CAN SEE, OUR METHODS ARE TESTED AND VERIFIED BY THE VARIOUS SLAVES AT OUR DISPOSAL.
WE ARE ALSO EXPERTS OF THE CULINARY ARTS. YOU'D BE SURPRISED WHAT THE PLEASURE OF FOOD REPRESENTS FOR A LOT OF MEN...
TELL ME, ARE WE AROUSING YOUR INTEREST?
?!?

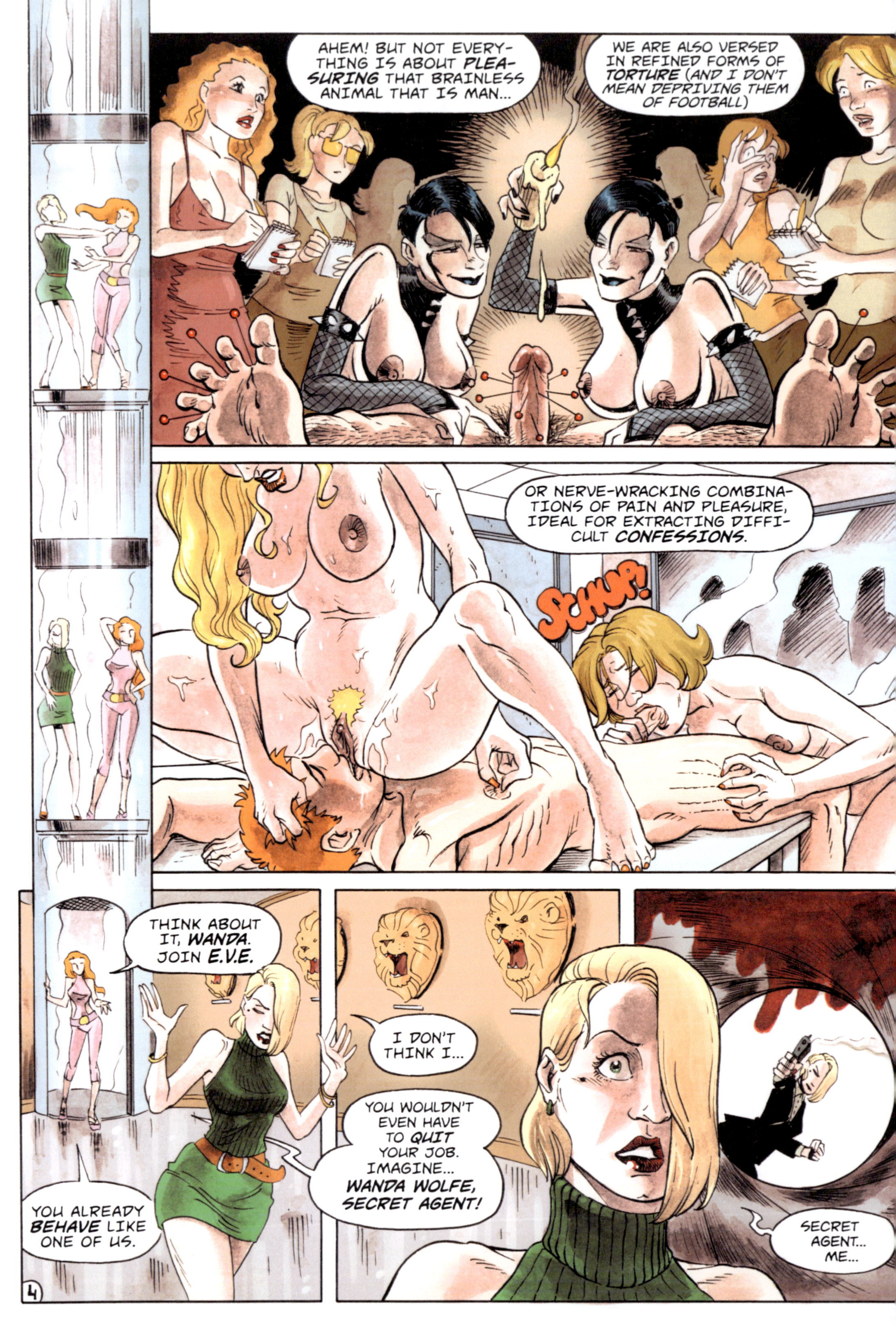

AHEM! BUT NOT EVERY-THING IS ABOUT PLEA-SURING THAT BRAINLESS ANIMAL THAT IS MAN...
WE ARE ALSO VERSED IN REFINED FORMS OF TORTURE (AND I DON'T MEAN DEPRIVING THEM OF FOOTBALL)
OR NERVE-WRACKING COMBINA-TIONS OF PAIN AND PLEASURE, IDEAL FOR EXTRACTING DIFFI-CULT CONFESSIONS.
SCHUP!
THINK ABOUT IT, WANDA. JOIN E.V.E.
I DON'T THINK I...
YOU WOULDN'T EVEN HAVE TO QUIT YOUR JOB. IMAGINE... WANDA WOLFE, SECRET AGENT!
YOU ALREADY BEHAVE LIKE ONE OF US.
SECRET AGENT... ME...
4

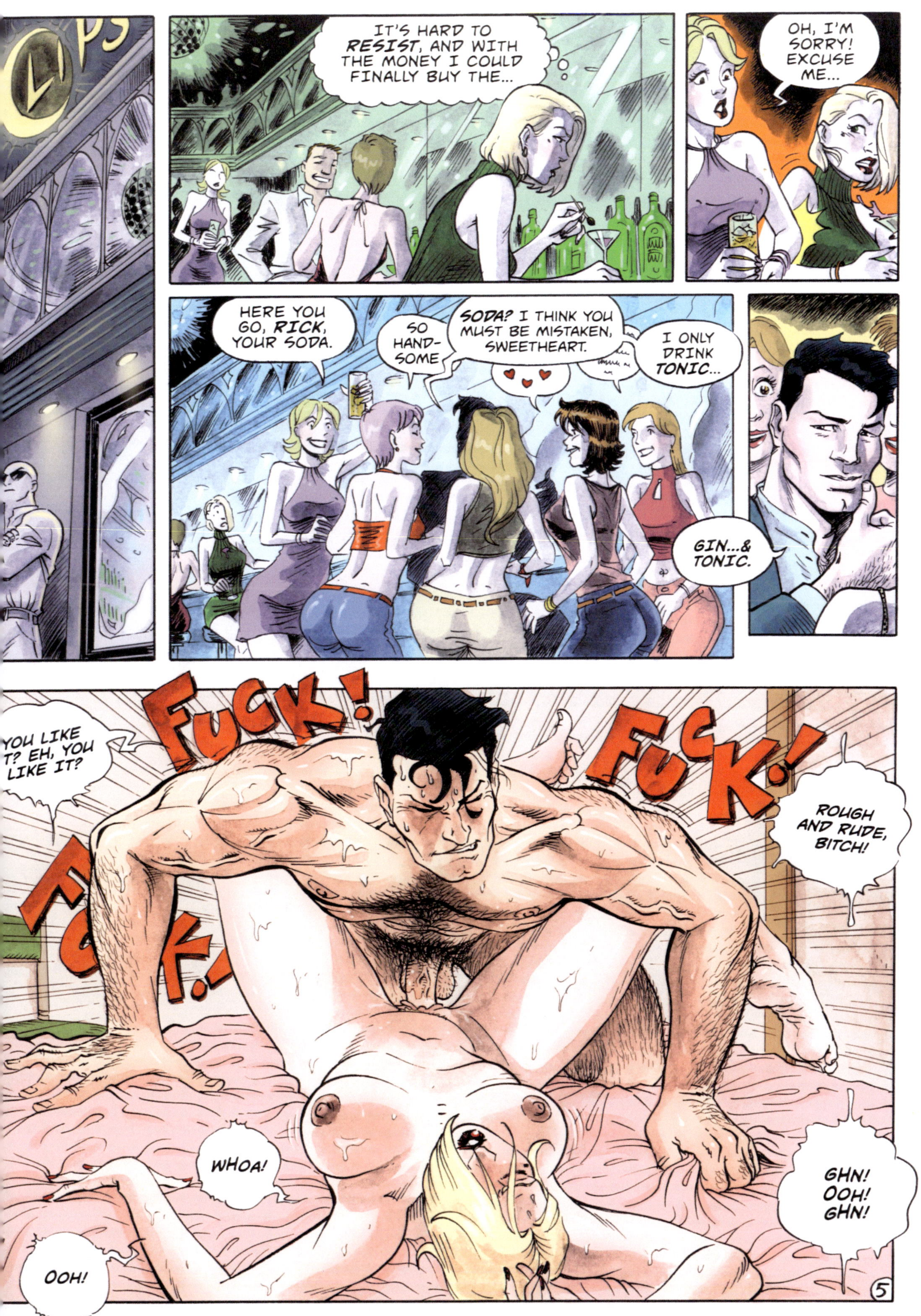

IT'S HARD TO RESIST, AND WITH THE MONEY I COULD FINALLY BUY THE...
OH, I'M SORRY! EXCUSE ME...
HERE YOU GO, RICK, YOUR SODA.
SO HAND-SOME
SODA? I THINK YOU MUST BE MISTAKEN, SWEETHEART.
I ONLY DRINK TONIC...
GIN...& TONIC.
YOU LIKE IT? EH, YOU LIKE IT?
FUCK!
FUCK!
FUCK!
ROUGH AND RUDE, BITCH!
WHOA!
GHN! OOH! GHN!
OOH!

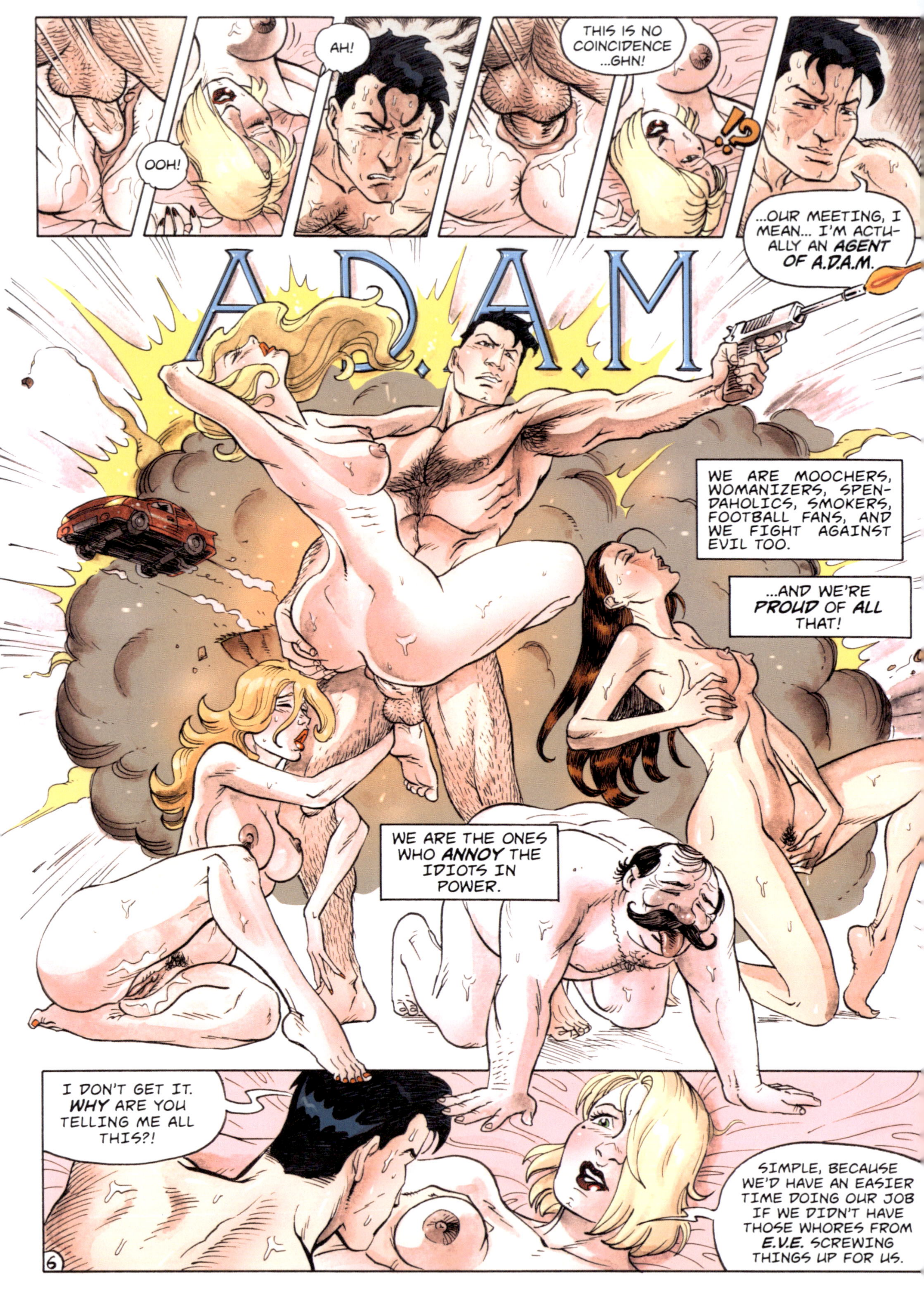

AH!
OOH!
THIS IS NO COINCIDENCE ...GHN!
!?
...OUR MEETING, I MEAN... I'M ACTU- ALLY AN AGENT OF A.D.A.M.
A.D.A.M
WE ARE MOOCHERS, WOMANIZERS, SPEN- DAHOLICS, SMOKERS, FOOTBALL FANS, AND WE FIGHT AGAINST EVIL TOO.
...AND WE'RE PROUD OF ALL THAT!
WE ARE THE ONES WHO ANNOY THE IDIOTS IN POWER.
I DON'T GET IT. WHY ARE YOU TELLING ME ALL THIS?!
SIMPLE, BECAUSE WE'D HAVE AN EASIER TIME DOING OUR JOB IF WE DIDN'T HAVE THOSE WHORES FROM E.V.E. SCREWING THINGS UP FOR US.
6

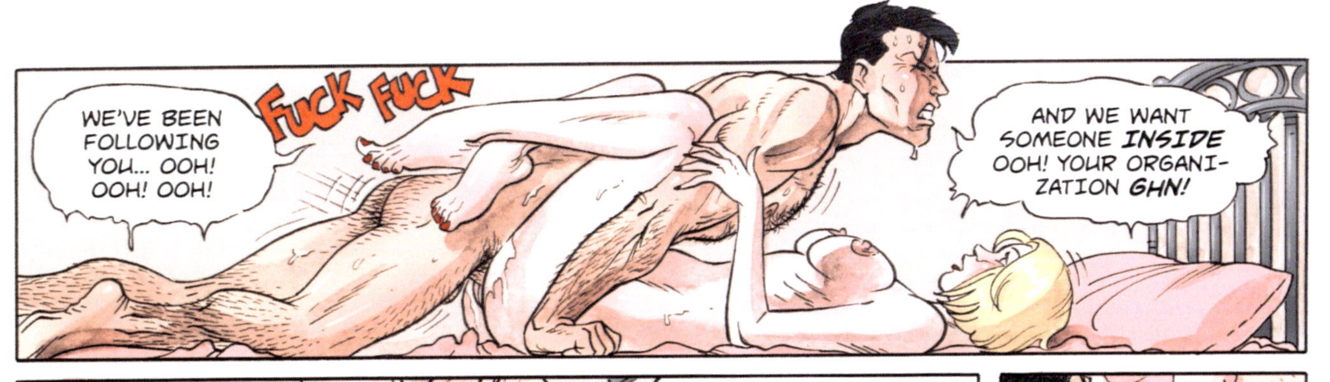

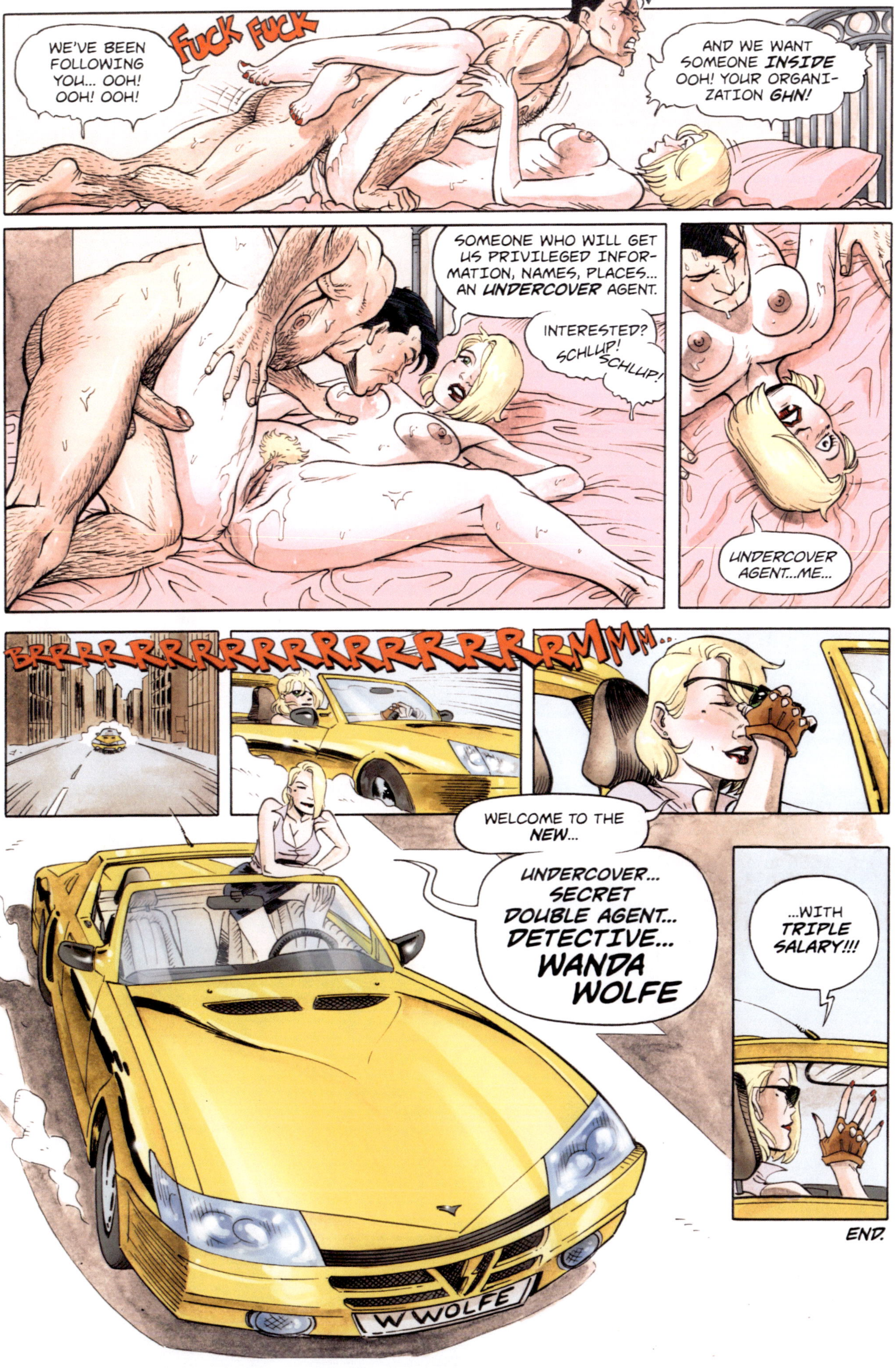

WE'VE BEEN FOLLOWING YOU... OOH! OOH! OOH!
FUCK FUCK
AND WE WANT SOMEONE INSIDE OOH! YOUR ORGANIZATION GHN!

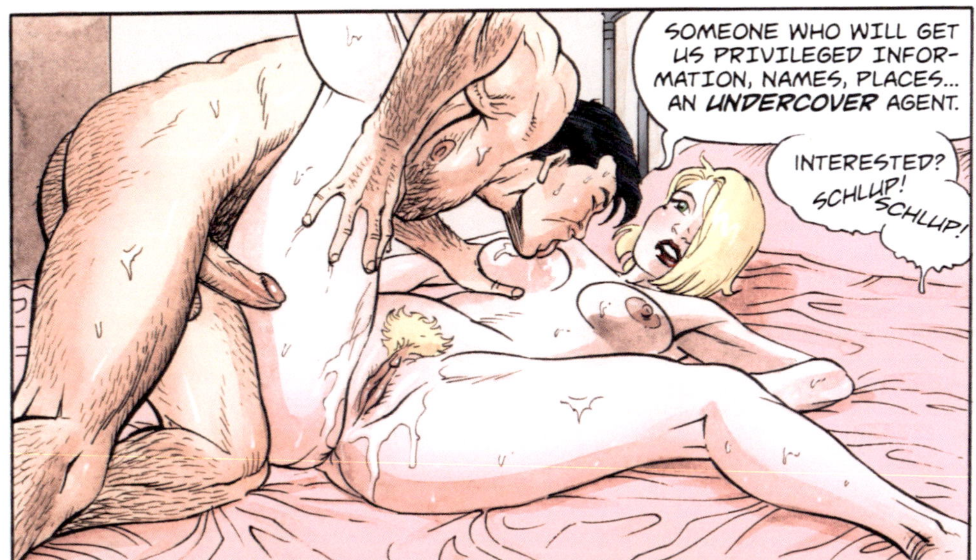

SOMEONE WHO WILL GET US PRIVILEGED INFORMATION, NAMES, PLACES... AN UNDERCOVER AGENT.
INTERESTED? SCHLUP! SCHLUP!

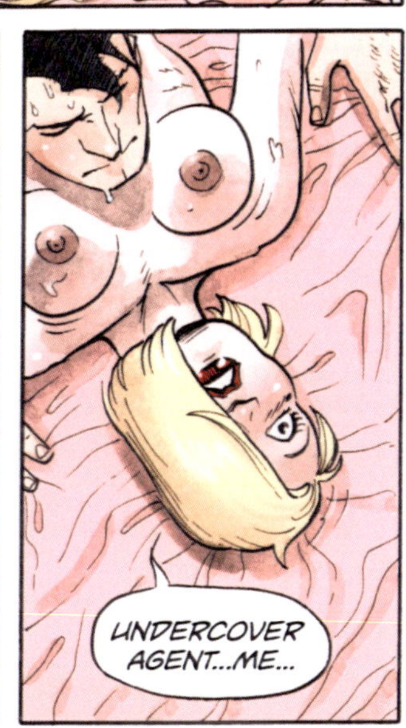

UNDERCOVER AGENT...ME...

BRRRRRRRRRRRRRRRRRRRRMMM...
WELCOME TO THE NEW...
UNDERCOVER... SECRET DOUBLE AGENT... DETECTIVE... WANDA WOLFE
...WITH TRIPLE SALARY!!!
W WOLFE
END.

A NEW CASE FOR DETECTIVE WANDA WOLFE
BY ALVARO
WELL I'M CHARGING THEM FOR A NEW BLOUSE AND SKIRT FOR...
YOU WON'T GET ANYTHING PLAYING THOSE LITTLE GAMES.
EH?
THE BITCH IS GOING TO SING LIKE A CANARY.
AN EASY MISSION, THEY SAID, JUST RECOVER SOME SECRET DOCUMENTS, THEY SAID...
OH, SHIT!!
THOSE IDIOTS!
THEY CAPTURED LUCY. HANG IN THERE, PARTNER, I'LL SAVE YOU!
IT'S A SLOW AND BORING ART. GO ON, LEAVE IT TO ME.
THIS IS A DELICATE ART.
COME NOW, TELL US WHERE WANDA WOLFE IS HIDING, GHN!
TEAM WORK
1

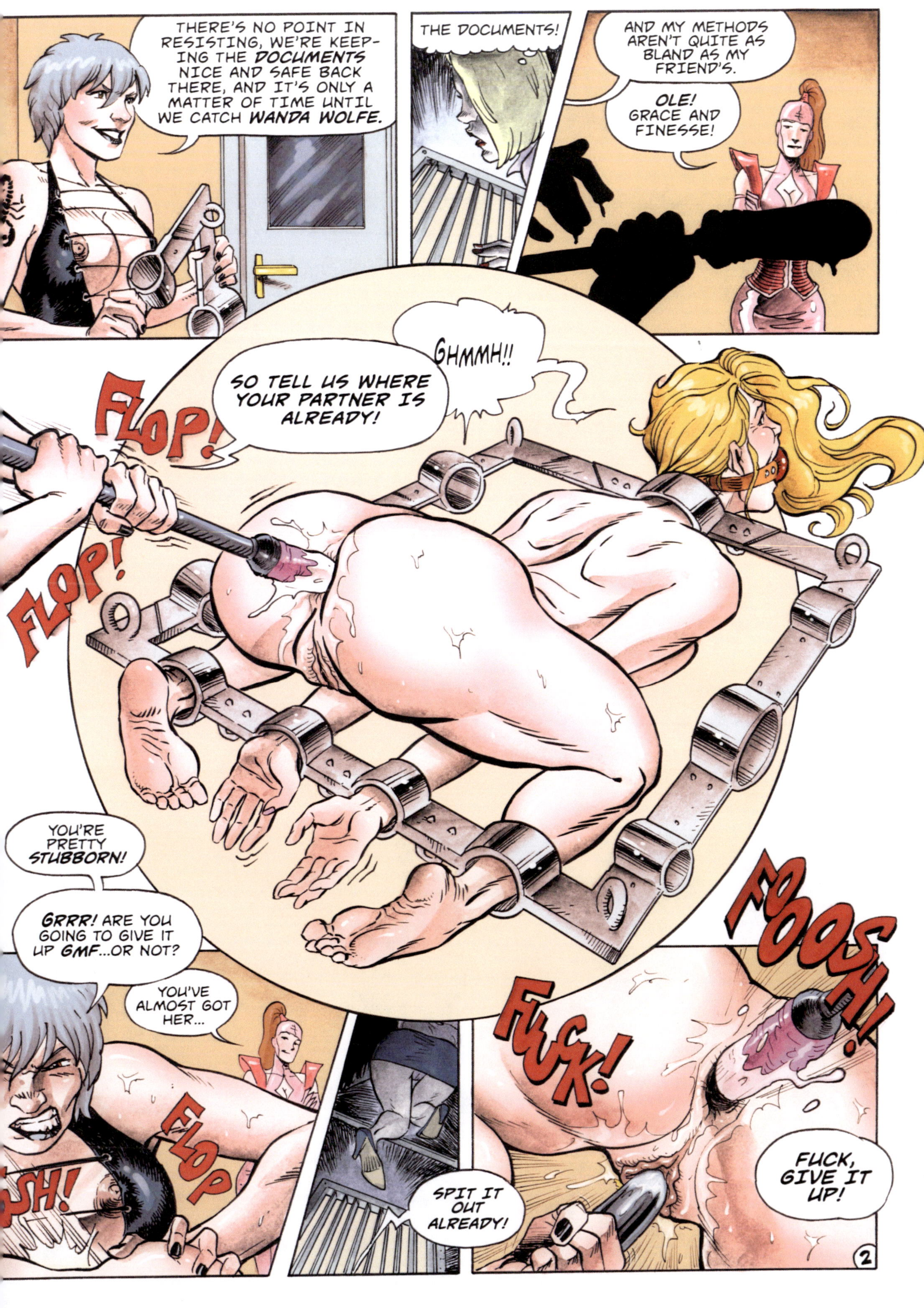

THERE'S NO POINT IN RESISTING, WE'RE KEEPING THE DOCUMENTS NICE AND SAFE BACK THERE, AND IT'S ONLY A MATTER OF TIME UNTIL WE CATCH WANDA WOLFE.
THE DOCUMENTS!
AND MY METHODS AREN'T QUITE AS BLAND AS MY FRIEND'S.
OLE! GRACE AND FINESSE!
FLOP!
FLOP!
GHMMH!!
SO TELL US WHERE YOUR PARTNER IS ALREADY!
YOU'RE PRETTY STUBBORN!
GRRR! ARE YOU GOING TO GIVE IT UP GMF...OR NOT?
YOU'VE ALMOST GOT HER...
FLOP!
OSH!
SPIT IT OUT ALREADY!
FUUCK!
FOOSH!
FUCK, GIVE IT UP!

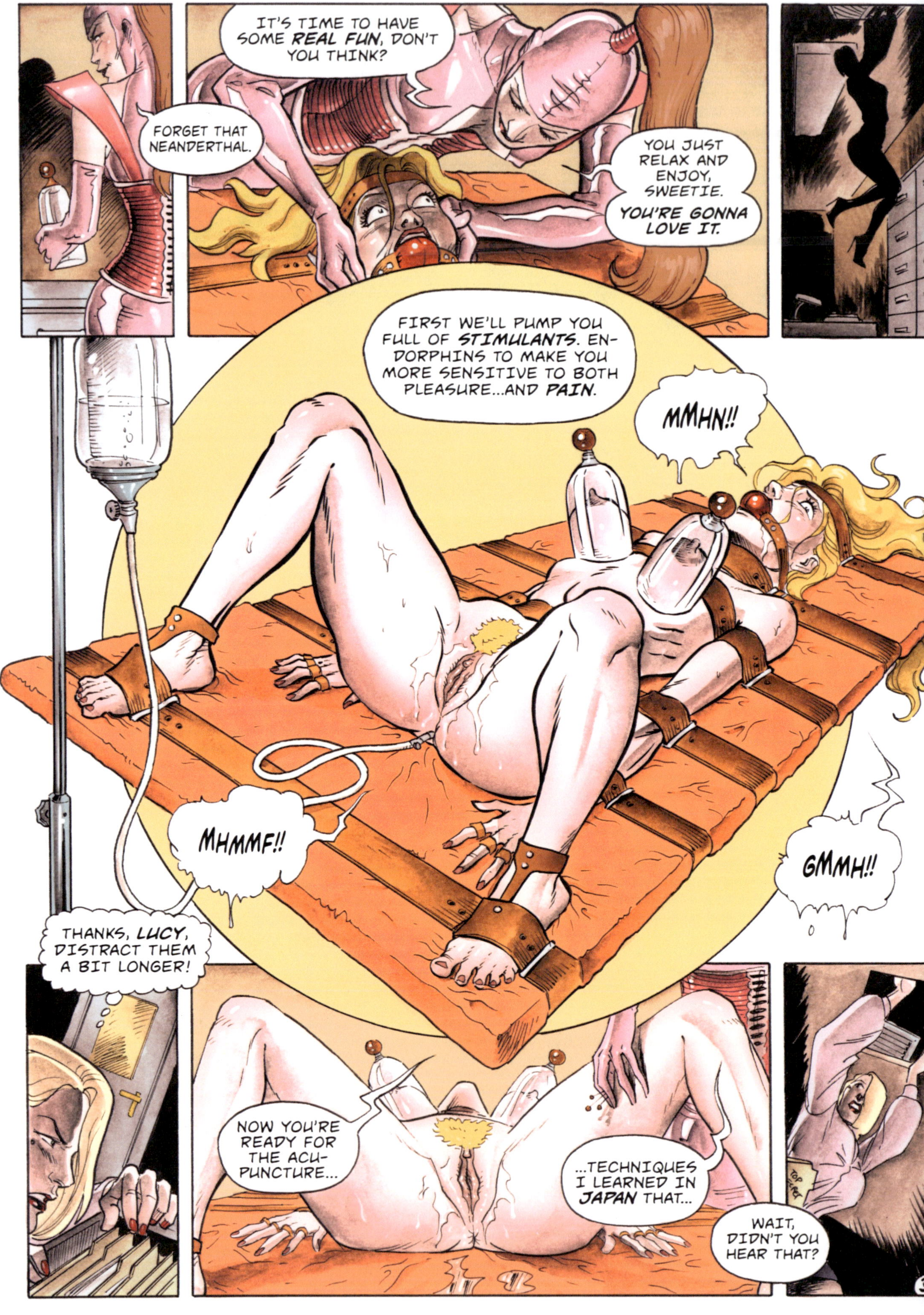

IT'S TIME TO HAVE SOME REAL FUN, DON'T YOU THINK?
FORGET THAT NEANDERTHAL.
YOU JUST RELAX AND ENJOY, SWEETIE. YOU'RE GONNA LOVE IT.
FIRST WE'LL PUMP YOU FULL OF STIMULANTS. EN-DORPHINS TO MAKE YOU MORE SENSITIVE TO BOTH PLEASURE...AND PAIN.
MMHN!!
MHMMF!!
GMMH!!
THANKS, LUCY, DISTRACT THEM A BIT LONGER!
NOW YOU'RE READY FOR THE ACU-PUNCTURE...
...TECHNIQUES I LEARNED IN JAPAN THAT...
WAIT, DIDN'T YOU HEAR THAT?

TAP
TAP
TAP
THE DARK LADY!
WELL?
SHE STILL HASN'T TALKED?
RRRMMMM!
MIND TELLING ME WHAT YOU'RE WAITING FOR?
AND WHAT THE HELL HAVE YOU BEEN DOING THIS WHOLE TIME?
IT'S HER, SHE'S AN IDIOT WHO ONLY KNOWS HOW TO... HELLBENT USING CHINESE TORTURE TECHNIQUES THAT DON'T...
THAT'S ENOUGH OF YOUR NONSENSE!

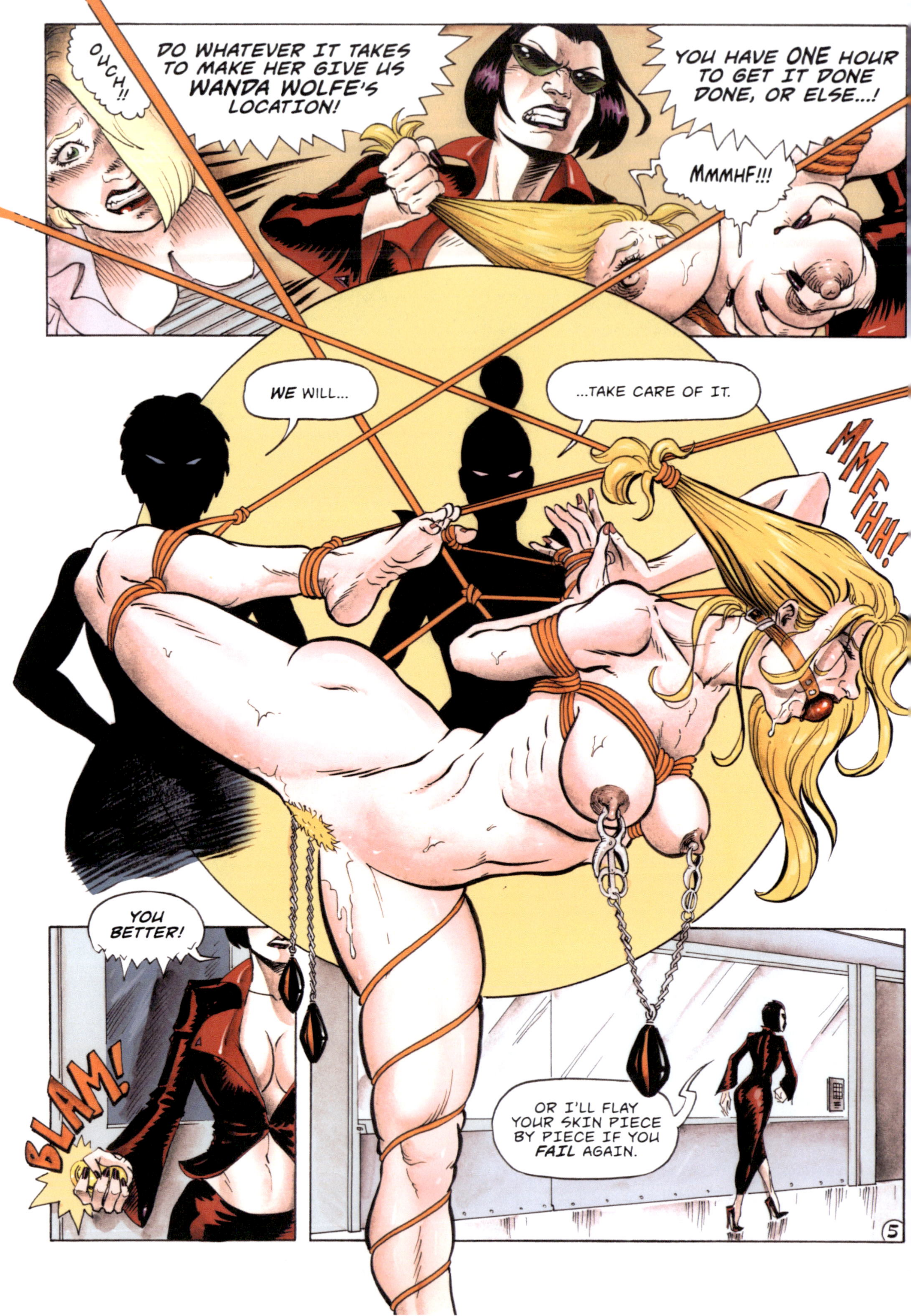

OUCH!!
DO WHATEVER IT TAKES TO MAKE HER GIVE US WANDA WOLFE'S LOCATION!
YOU HAVE ONE HOUR TO GET IT DONE DONE, OR ELSE...!
MMMHF!!!
WE WILL...
...TAKE CARE OF IT.
MMFHH!
YOU BETTER!
BLAM!
OR I'LL FLAY YOUR SKIN PIECE BY PIECE IF YOU FAIL AGAIN.

YOU'RE MINE!
CLANG!
EH!? WHO?
YOUR WORST NIGHTMARE!!
UGH!
ZAS
ZAS
ZAS
ZAS
COME ON, SPIT IT OUT AL-READY!
YOU ASKED FOR IT! TAKE THIS!
WHAT A STROKE OF LUCK.
I'VE RECOVERED THE DOCUMENTS AND HAVE THE DARK LADY WITHIN MY GRASP...
BE BRAVE, LUCY, I'LL BRING REINFORCEMENTS!
TOP SECRET
HEY, WHAT IF WE TAKE THE GAG OFF?
...
THE END

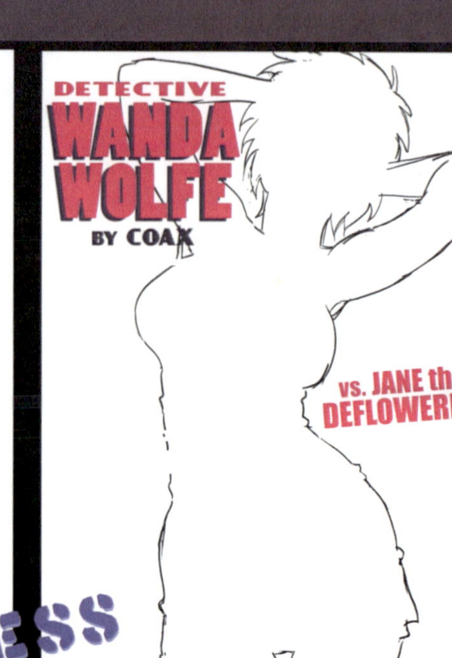

WORK IN PROCESS

DETECTIVE
WANDA
WOLFE
BY COAX
VS. JANE the DEFLOWERER!
3 FULL STORIES
Erosetti Press
No.6

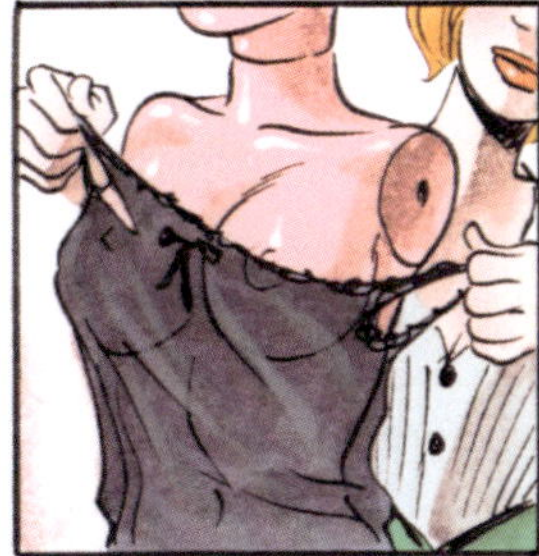

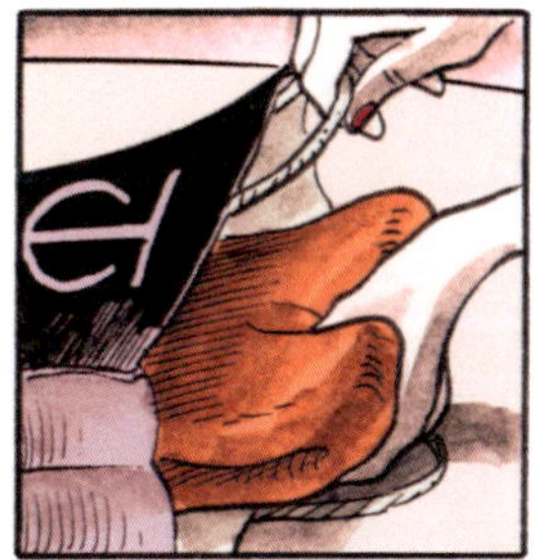

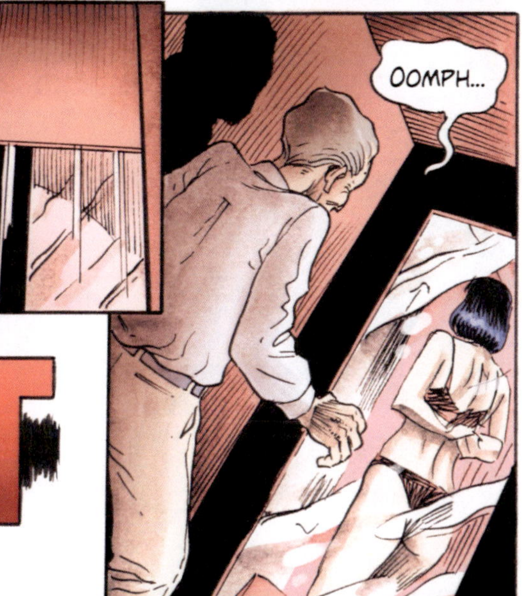

INDISCREET

ANOTHER CASE FOR DETECTIVE WANDA WOLFE.

BY ALVARO 2003

1

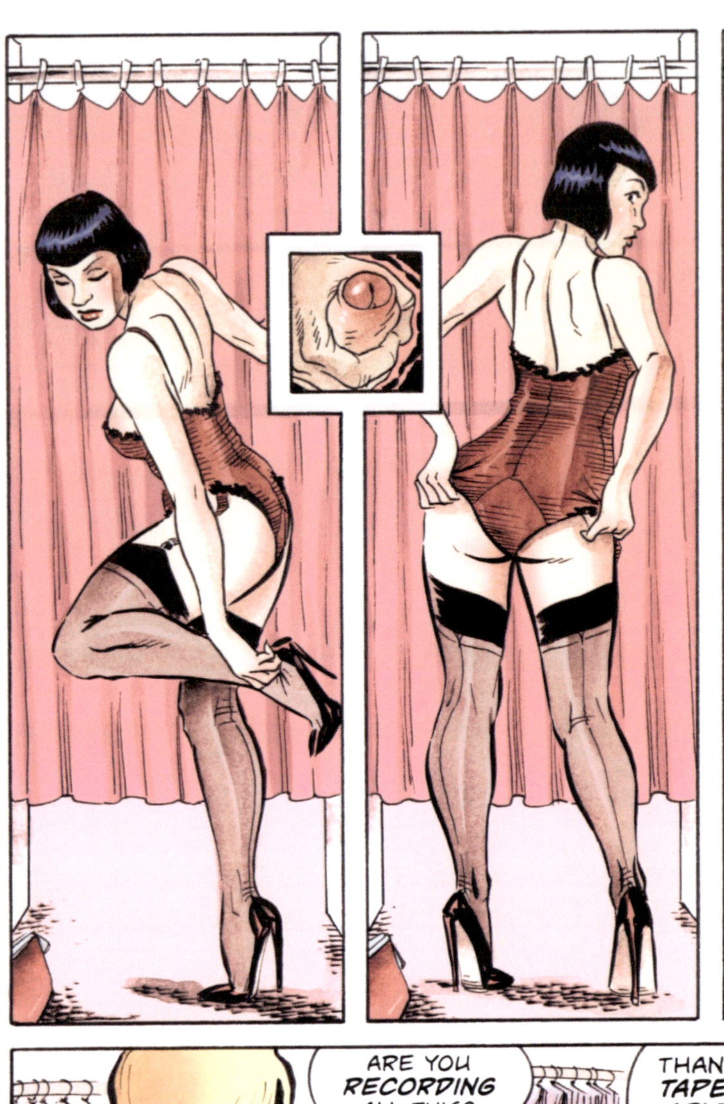
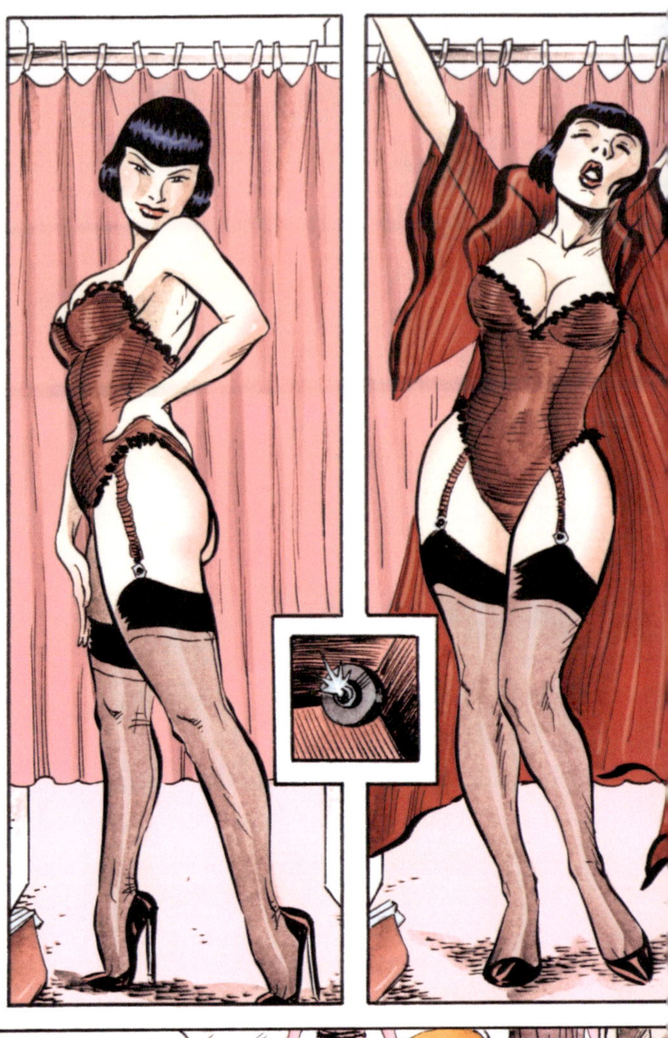

ARE YOU RECORDING ALL THIS?
WE HAVE THAT FILTHY PIG ON TECHNICOLOR.
THANKS TO THIS TAPE, WE'LL BE ABLE TO MAKE HIM STOP.
AND HE WON'T BE ABLE TO FIRE US!
HAH, HE MIGHT EVEN GIVE US A RAISE.

IS FEDORA READY?
READY AND MORE THAN WILLING.
-GASP-
THAT HORNY OLD MAN IS GOING TO LEARN HIS LESSON.
LET THE SHOW BEGIN!

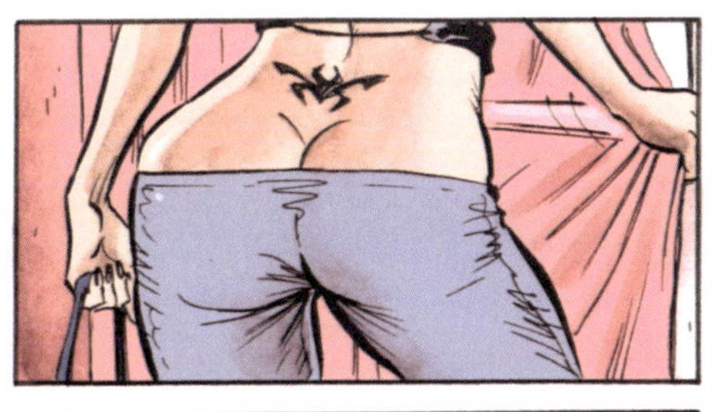
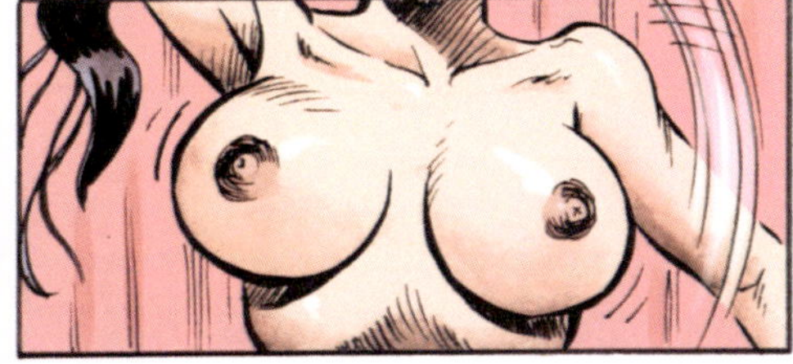
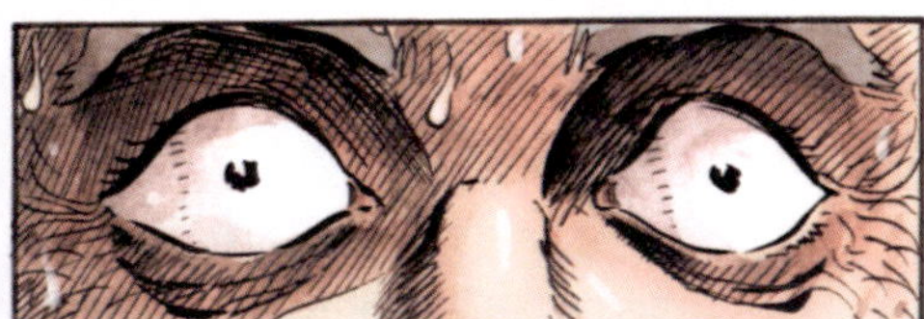
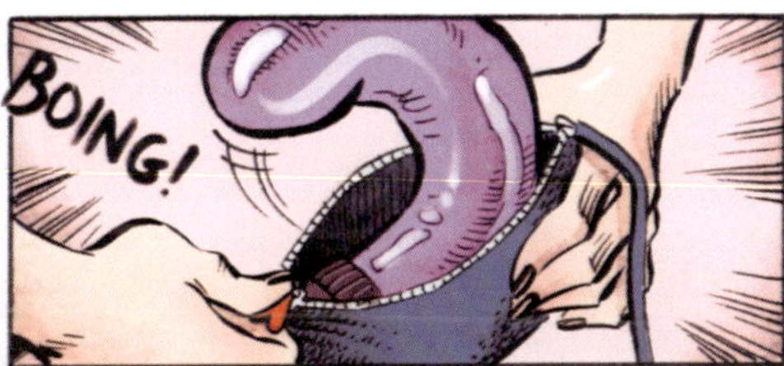

BOING!

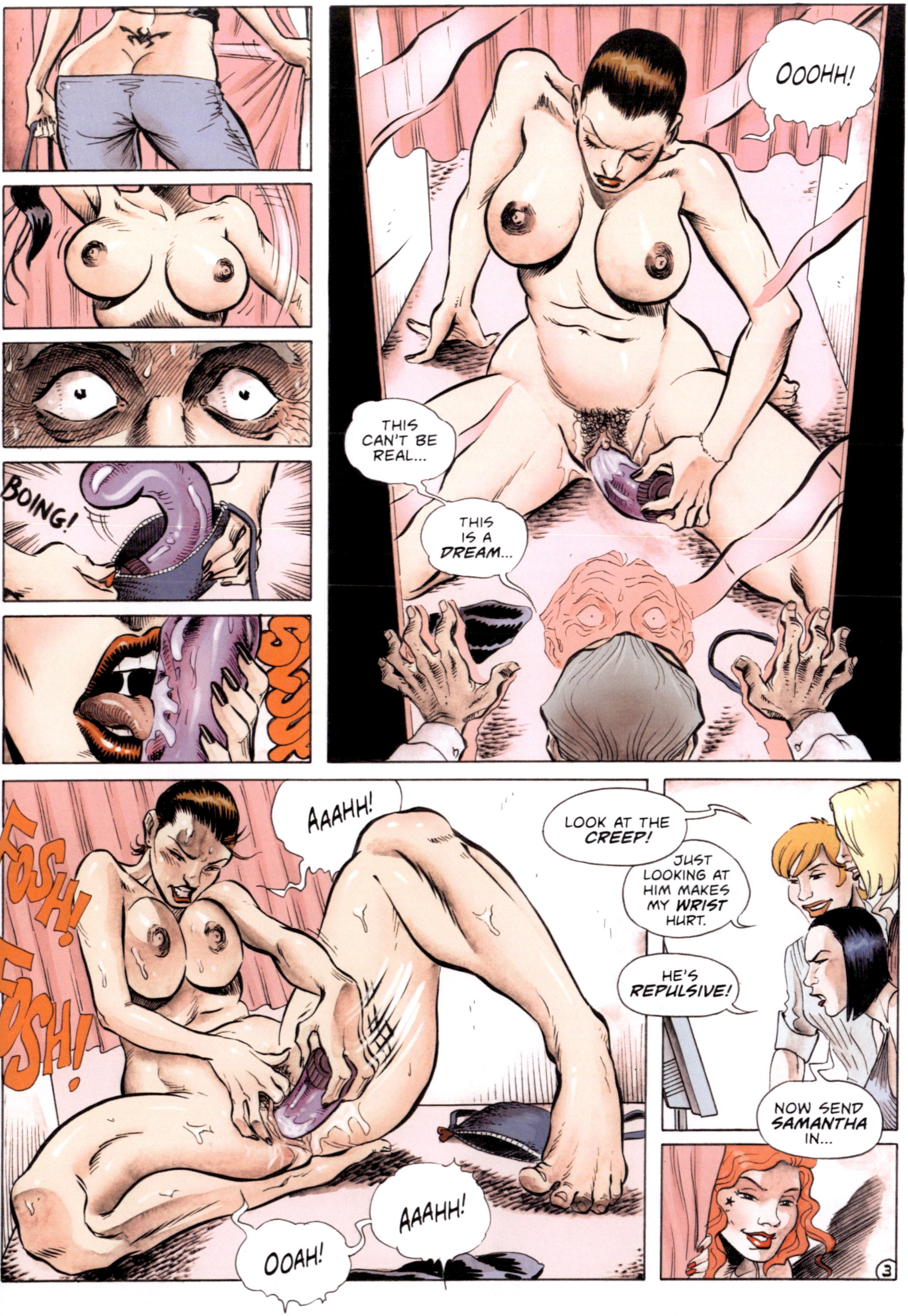

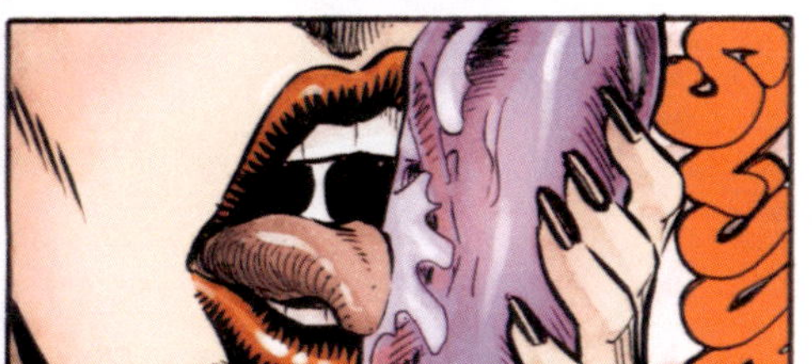

SNURF

OOOHH!
THIS CAN'T BE REAL...
THIS IS A DREAM...

FOSH!
FOSH!
AAAHH!
LOOK AT THE CREEP!
JUST LOOKING AT HIM MAKES MY WRIST HURT.
HE'S REPULSIVE!
NOW SEND SAMANTHA IN...
OOAH!
AAAHH!

③

HELLO ♥
MMMM...
PLOP
AAAHH!
SPP!!
WE SHOULD SEND THIS TO ANIMAL PLANET.
AND MR.WHITE TO COMEDY CENTRAL! HAHAHA
UH!
UH!

OOHH...
YOU LIKE THIS, HUH?
SCHLUP!
SLURP!
HAHAHAHA HAHA
OOOOH! OOH! AAAAH!
FDSH!
FDSH!
SWOP!
SWOP!
UH! UH!
SCHLUP!
RRASSH!!

SO YOU DON'T KNOW ANYTHING... AND HOW DID YOU ASSIST HIM SO QUICKLY?
SEE, IT'S JUST THAT OUR BOSS IS A PAIN THE ASS AND HE CALLS US OVER EVERY 5 MINUTES, AND WE COME IN EVEN WHEN HE DOESN'T CALL US...
WHAT IS IT, THEN? ARE YOU A DETECTIVE, OR ARE YOU AN EMPLOYEE HERE?
TIMES ARE TOUGH, MR. AGENT.
POSSIBLE VIAGRA OVERDOSE!
QUICK, MANUAL ERECTION RELIEF!
AAH! AAAAH! OOH! OOOH!
SCHLUP! SCHLAP!
MMMM
I'M TALKING TO YOU, GARCIA!
THE END

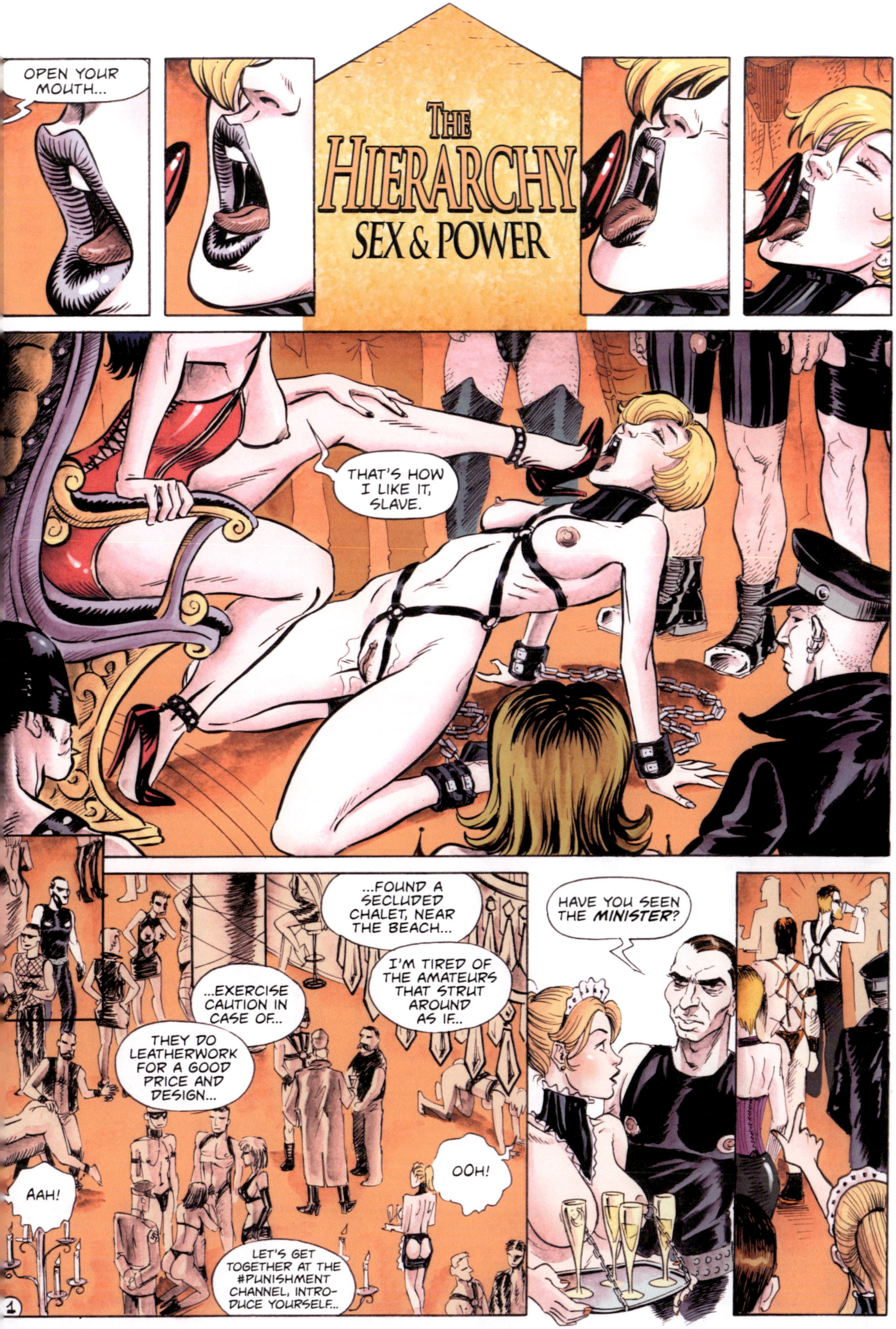

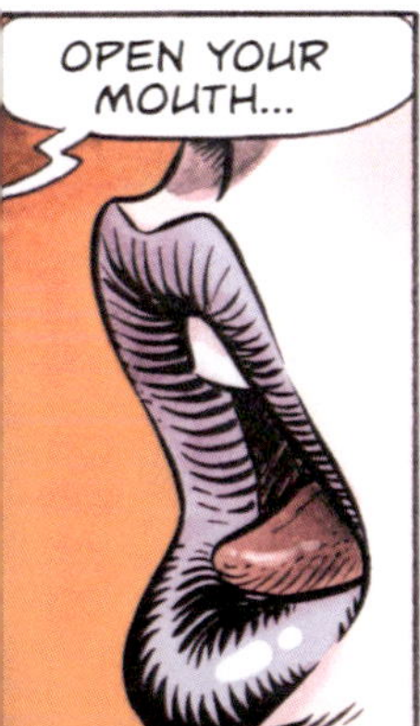

THE HIERARCHY
SEX & POWER

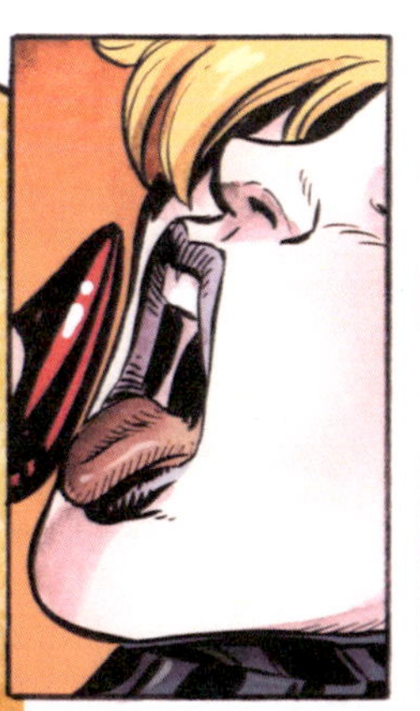

CAN WE TALK?
SHH! NOT HERE.
SHOW EVERYONE YOUR DEVOTION TODAY.
MAKE ME PROUD.
TELL ME, HAVE YOU BEEN ABLE TO ARRANGE THE RECLASSIFICATION OF THE PLOTS?
OOH!
I CAN'T HEAR YOU! HARDER!
AND HAVE YOU ALREADY SPOKEN WITH EVERYONE?
MAKE THE DEPOSIT TONIGHT...
IT'LL BE VOTED ON TOMORROW...
OOHH... THANK YOU, MISTRESS!
SHH... VERY GOOD, LITTLE ONE...
JUST A BIT MORE...
WILL YOU LET ME ENJOY THE PARTY NOW?

THEREFORE, WE, WENSOR & NONSER, WILL TAKE CARE OF...
HELLO

...PRODUCTION AND DISTRIBUTION OF...
YES, YES... I KNOW THE DEAL!
...THE EXCLUSIVE NATION-WIDE...

WE'VE TALKED ABOUT THIS BEFORE, RIGHT? BUT I CAME HERE TO HAVE A GOOD TIME.
??
LAY OFF IT ALREADY. RELAX.

GULP!
YOU DON'T WANT ANYTHING, SWEETIE?
LET'S SEE, GIRLS...

...THE LUCKY ONE IS...
OOH!
AAAH!
YES, I LOVE IIIT! OOOOH!

OHH, GOD. YOU DRIVE ME CRAZY, DID YOU KNOW THAT?
SCHLURP!

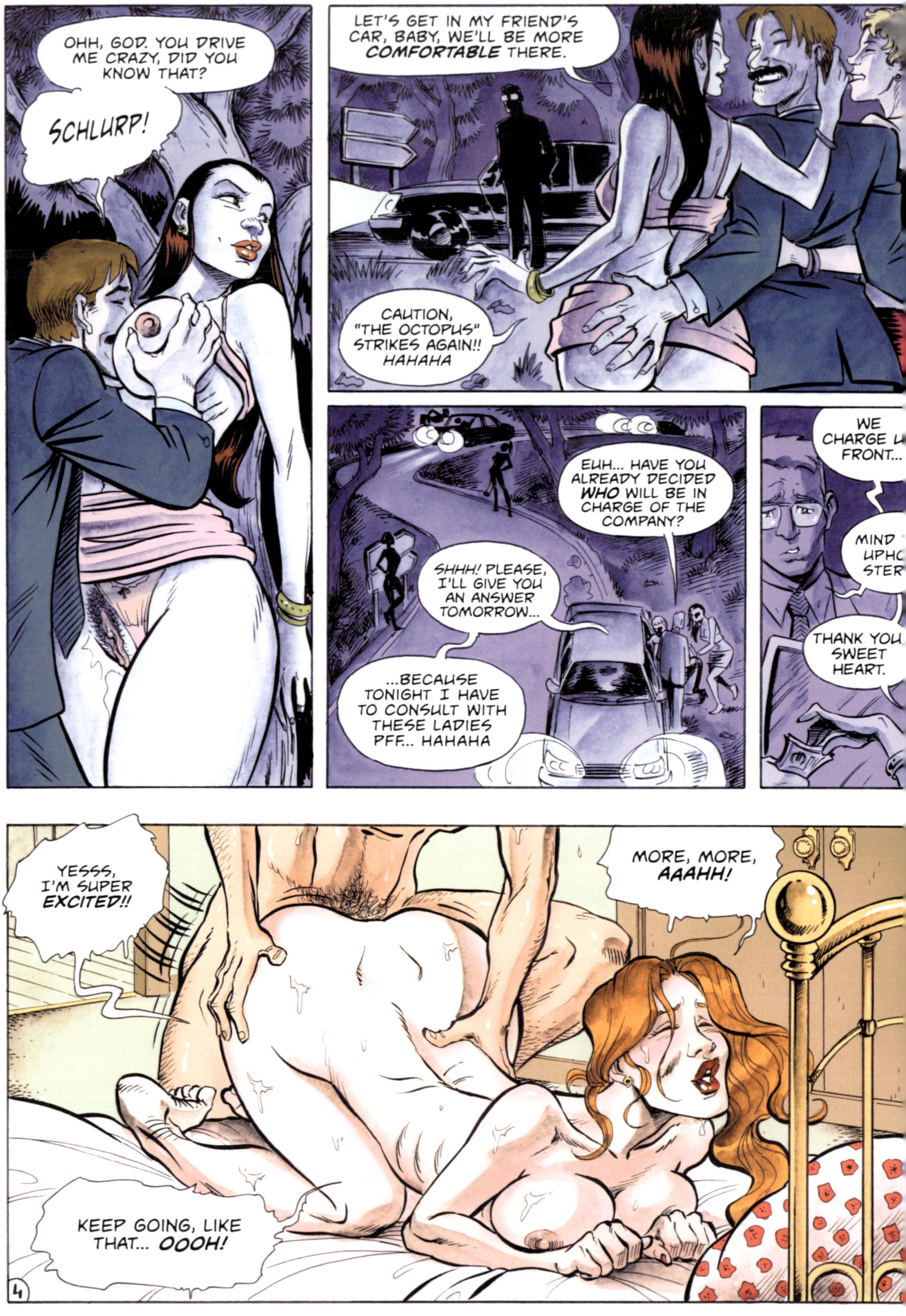

LET'S GET IN MY FRIEND'S CAR, BABY, WE'LL BE MORE COMFORTABLE THERE.
CAUTION, "THE OCTOPUS" STRIKES AGAIN!! HAHAHA

EUH... HAVE YOU ALREADY DECIDED WHO WILL BE IN CHARGE OF THE COMPANY?
SHHH! PLEASE, I'LL GIVE YOU AN ANSWER TOMORROW...
...BECAUSE TONIGHT I HAVE TO CONSULT WITH THESE LADIES PFF... HAHAHA

WE CHARGE U FRONT...
MIND UPHO STER
THANK YOU SWEET HEART.

YESSS, I'M SUPER EXCITED!!
KEEP GOING, LIKE THAT... OOOH!
MORE, MORE, AAAHH!

4

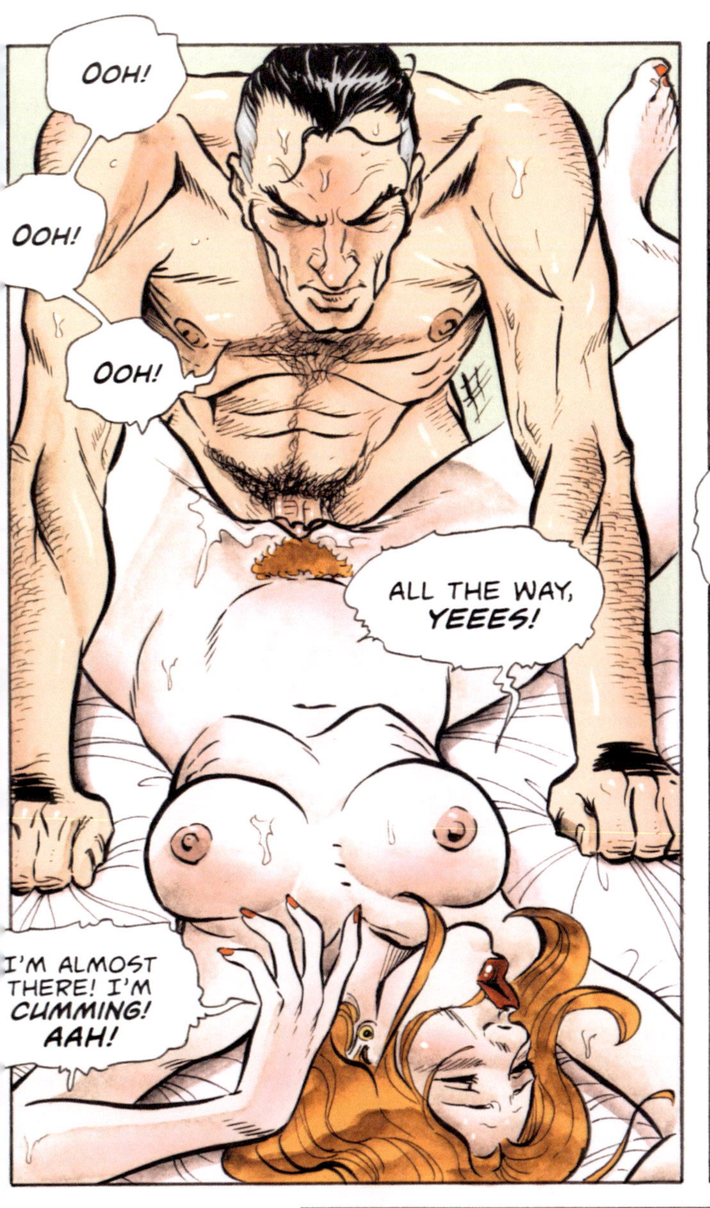

OOH!
OOH!
OOH!
ALL THE WAY, YEEES!
I'M ALMOST THERE! I'M CUMMING! AAH!

OOH!
I WANT ALL OF IT, MMMH!
OOOH! IT'S DELICIOUS!

HAS EVERY-THING BEEN TO YOUR LIKING?
WOULD YOU LIKE ANYTHING ELSE?

HM, GOT ANYTHING DECENT TO DRINK?
A WHISKEY ON THE ROCKS FOR THE DIRECTOR!
COMING RIGHT UP, HONEY!

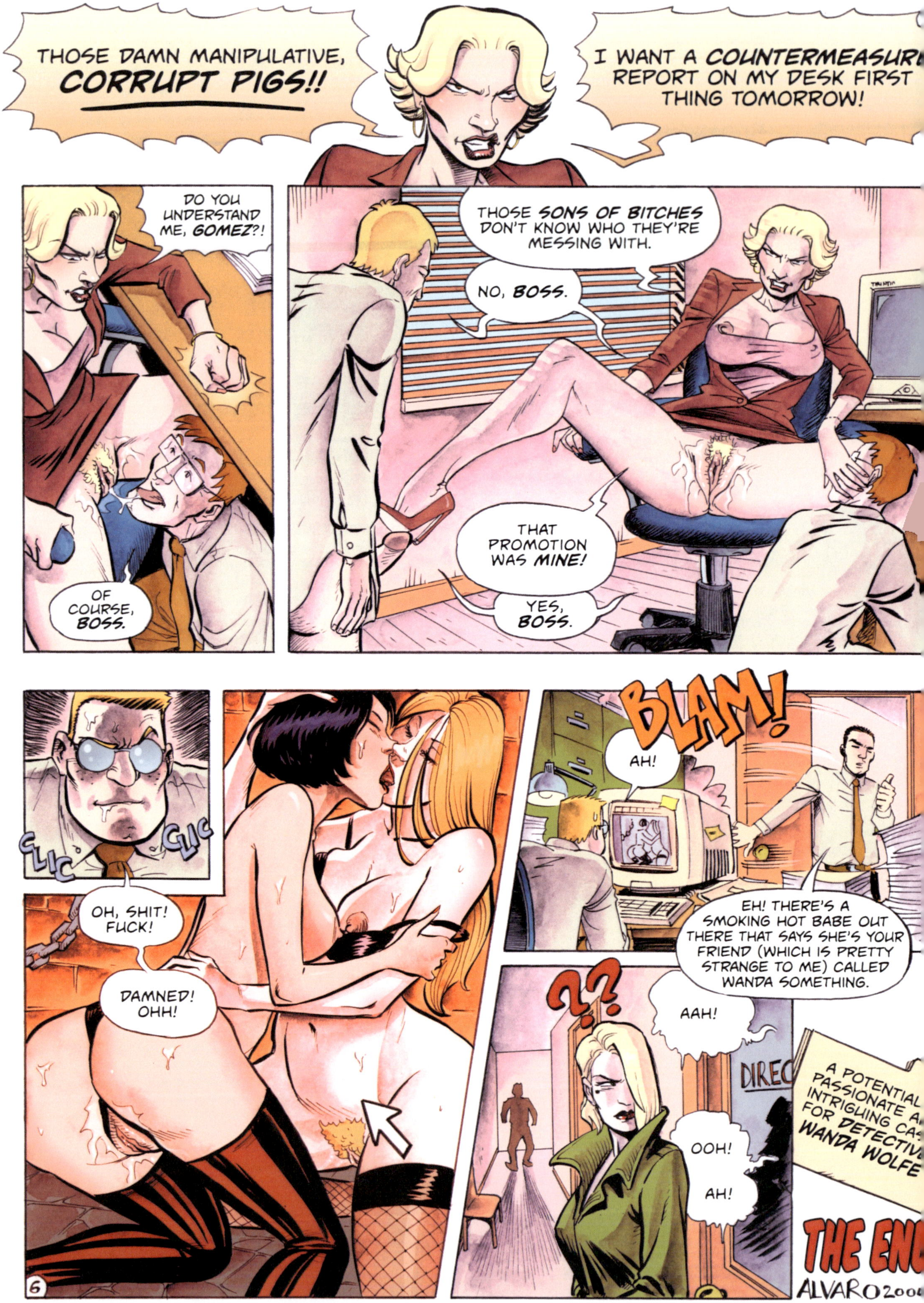

THOSE DAMN MANIPULATIVE, CORRUPT PIGS!!
I WANT A COUNTERMEASURE REPORT ON MY DESK FIRST THING TOMORROW!

DO YOU UNDERSTAND ME, GOMEZ?!
OF COURSE, BOSS.

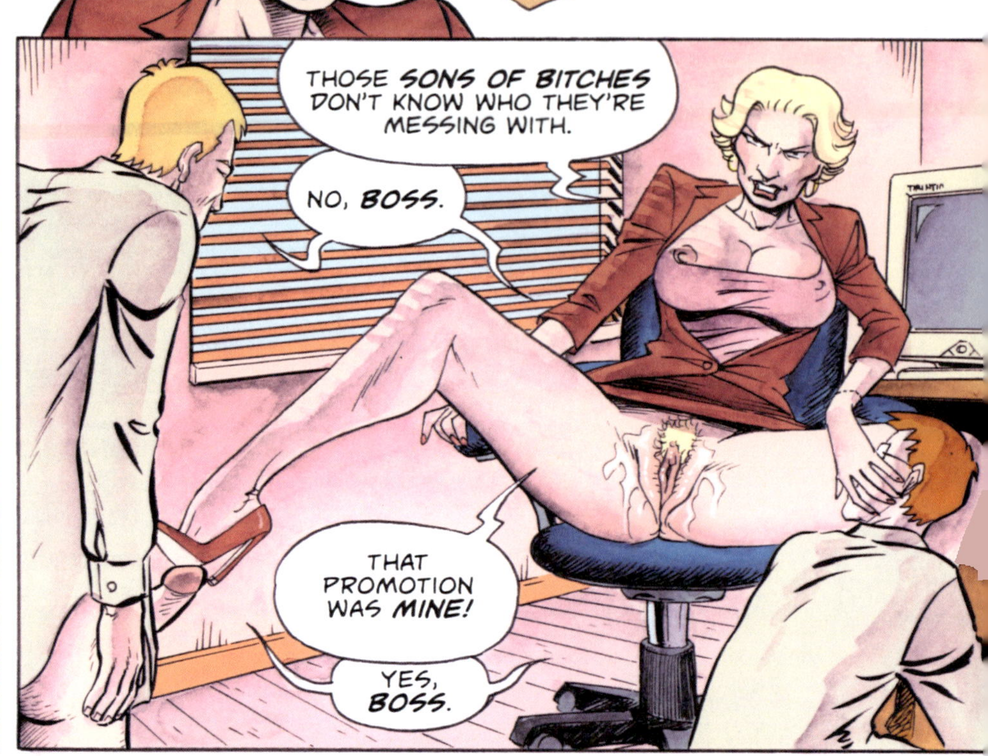

THOSE SONS OF BITCHES DON'T KNOW WHO THEY'RE MESSING WITH.
NO, BOSS.
THAT PROMOTION WAS MINE!
YES, BOSS.

CLIC
CLIC
OH, SHIT! FUCK!
DAMNED! OHH!
BLAM!
AH!
EH! THERE'S A SMOKING HOT BABE OUT THERE THAT SAYS SHE'S YOUR FRIEND (WHICH IS PRETTY STRANGE TO ME) CALLED WANDA SOMETHING.
??
AAH!
OOH!
AH!
DIREC
A POTENTIAL PASSIONATE A... INTRIGUING CAS... FOR DETECTIV... WANDA WOLFE
THE EN...
ALVARO 2006
6

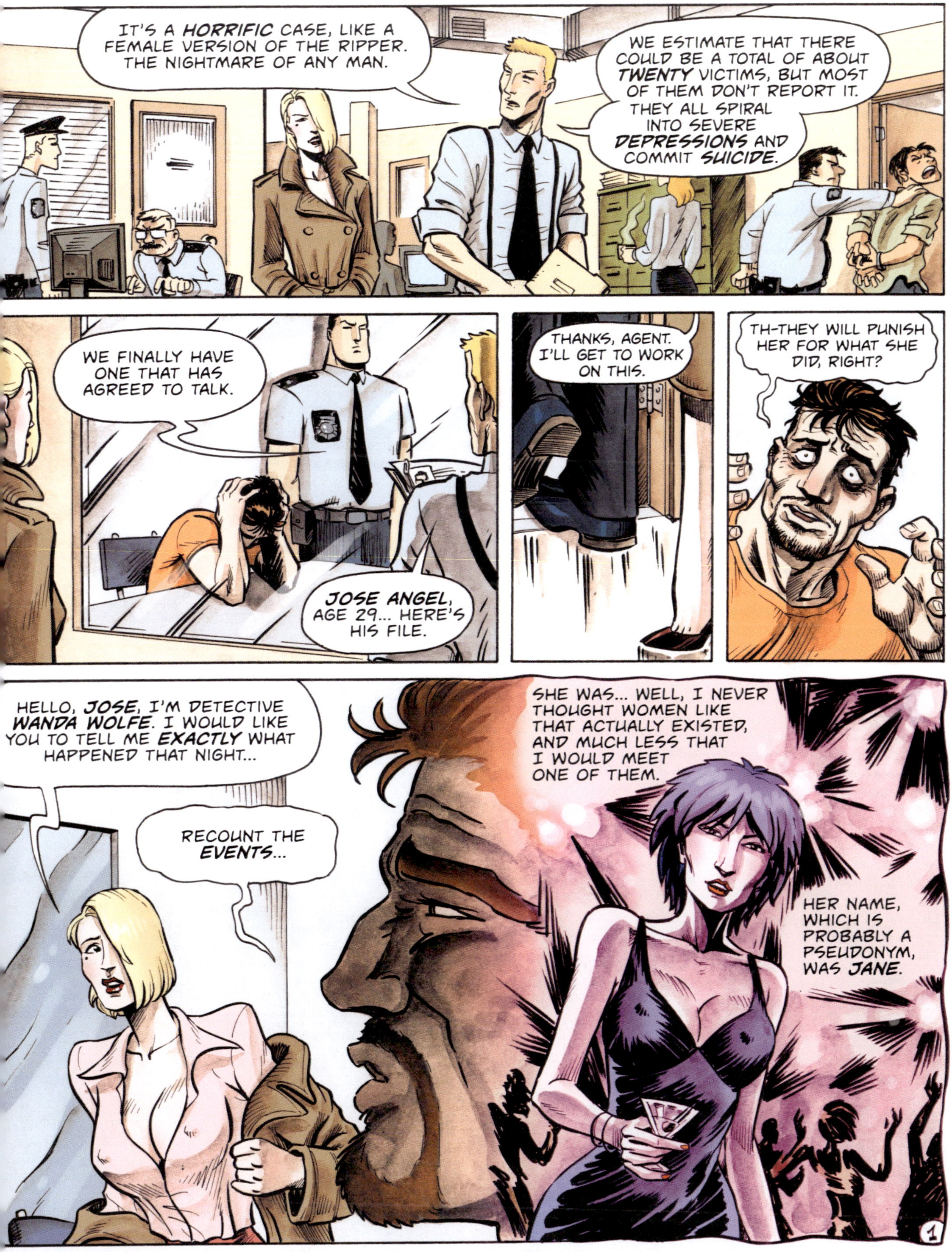

JANE "THE DEFLOWERER"

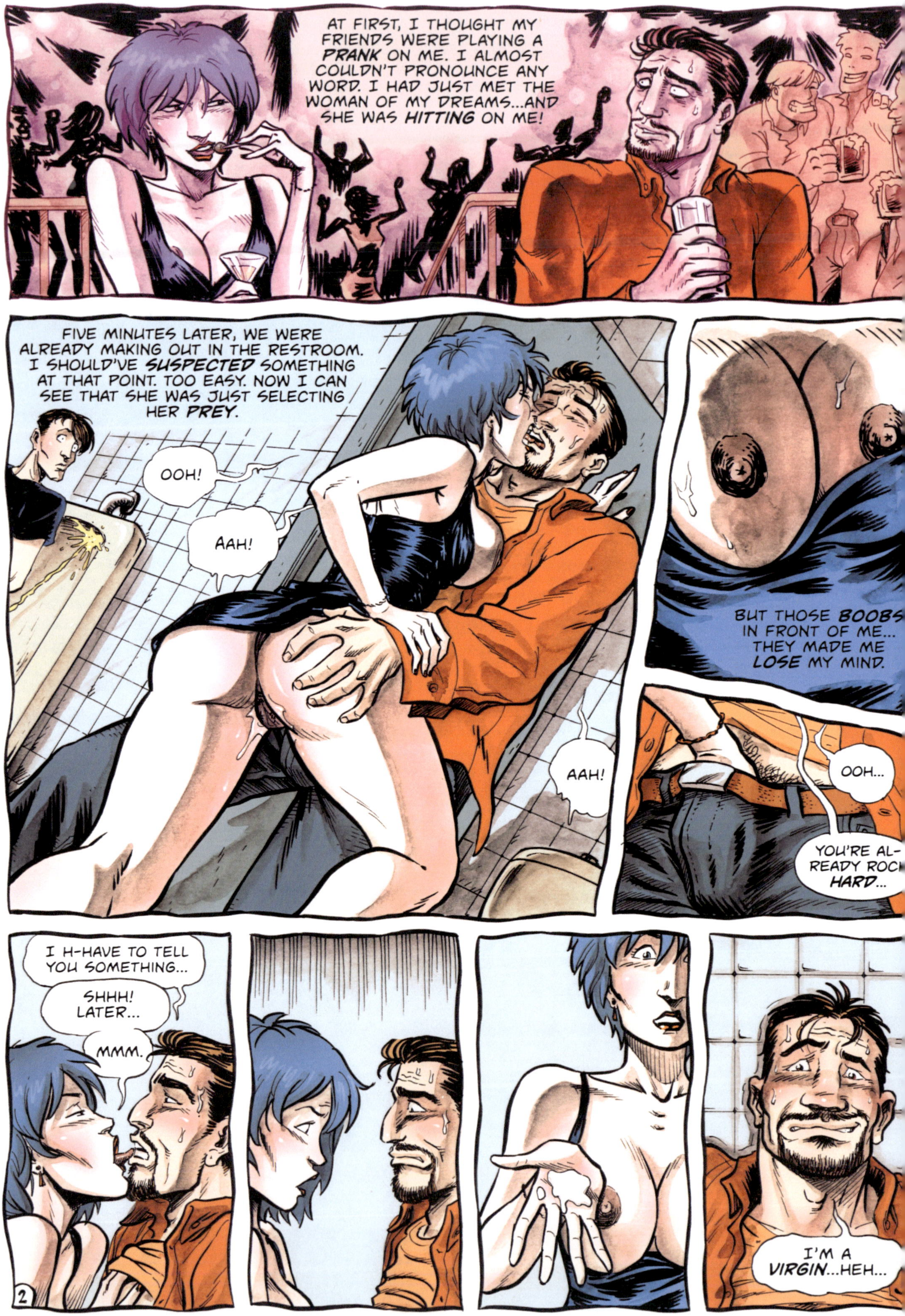

AT FIRST, I THOUGHT MY FRIENDS WERE PLAYING A PRANK ON ME. I ALMOST COULDN'T PRONOUNCE ANY WORD. I HAD JUST MET THE WOMAN OF MY DREAMS...AND SHE WAS HITTING ON ME!

FIVE MINUTES LATER, WE WERE ALREADY MAKING OUT IN THE RESTROOM. I SHOULD'VE SUSPECTED SOMETHING AT THAT POINT. TOO EASY. NOW I CAN SEE THAT SHE WAS JUST SELECTING HER PREY.
OOH!
AAH!
AAH!
BUT THOSE BOOBS IN FRONT OF ME... THEY MADE ME LOSE MY MIND.
OOH...
YOU'RE AL-READY ROC HARD...

I H-HAVE TO TELL YOU SOMETHING...
SHHH! LATER...
MMM.

I'M A VIRGIN...HEH...

WE WENT UP TO MY FLOOR. I COULDN'T BELIEVE IT WAS FINALLY GOING TO HAPPEN FOR ME.
I'M ABOUT TO BUST A NUT!
GODDAMN...!
MMFSSMP
EASY, BIG BOY, I'M NOT A DAIRY COW.
THEN SHE WENT TO GET SOMETHING TO DRINK.
WE SHOULD TOAST TO OUR WONDERFUL MEETING, DON'T YOU THINK?
...OR FOR PASSIONATE, SINCERE MEN... WITH HUGE, JUICY COCKS!
I PROMISE THIS WILL BE AN UNFORGETTABLE EVENING...
3

THE BITCH *RAPED YOU* AND VICIOUSLY *USED YOU* AS HER *SEX SLAVE!*

...
NO. IF ONLY...
WOULD YOU LET ME *CONTINUE* ?!

THERE I WAS, IT WAS BETTER THAN MY *SWEETEST FANTASIES.*

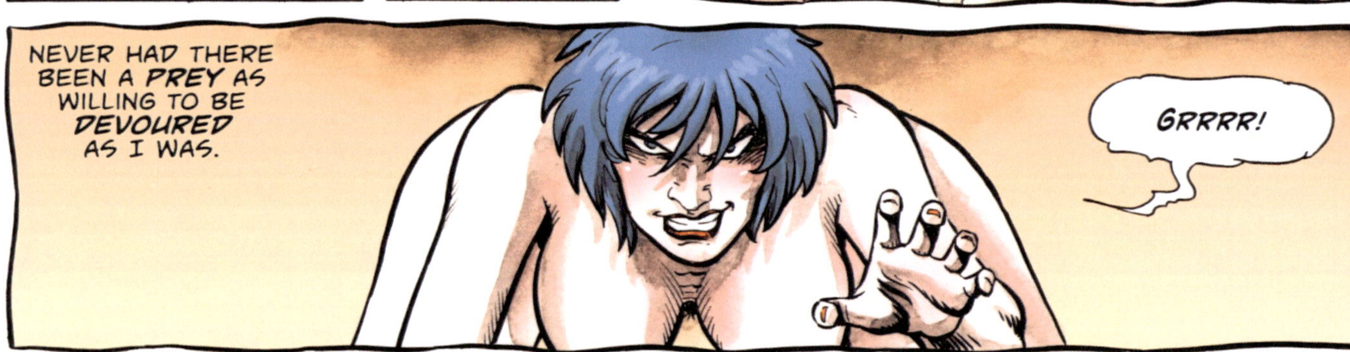

NEVER HAD THERE BEEN A *PREY* AS WILLING TO BE *DEVOURED* AS I WAS.
GRRRR!

SLUR!
SCHLUPT!
SHE WAS FULL OF FIRE AND PASSION, PERHAPS BORN IN THE FLAMES OF *REVENGE.*

IMPALED UPON ME, HER PRECISE MOVEMENTS... IT LOOKED LIKE A SCENE FROM SOME EXOTIC INITIATION RITUAL...
AH!
AH!
AH!
FUCK! FUCK! FUCK!
OH!
NNNG!
WE BROKE TABOOS... WE TRIED... EVERYTHING...
5

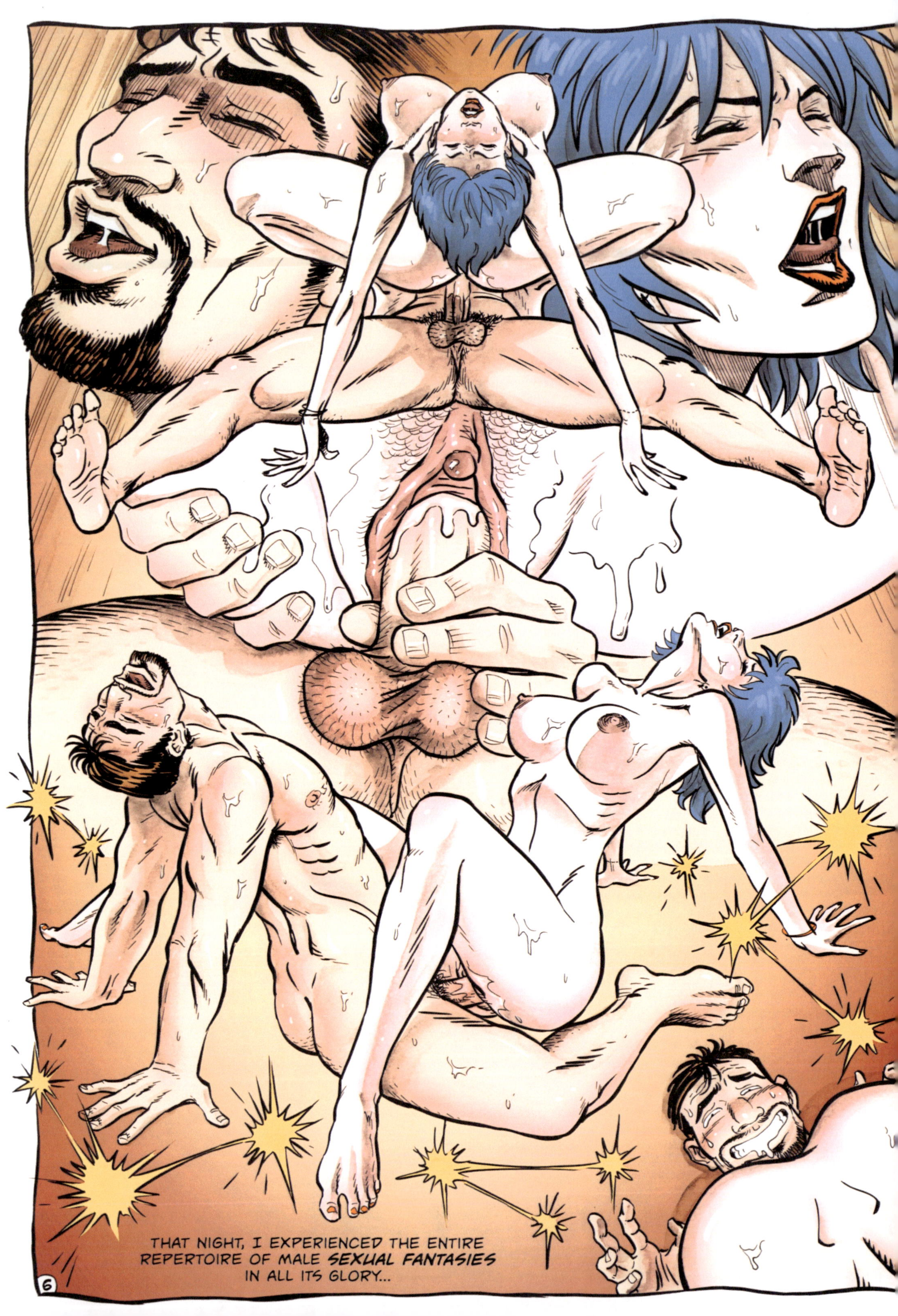
THAT NIGHT, I EXPERIENCED THE ENTIRE
REPERTOIRE OF MALE *SEXUAL FANTASIES*
IN ALL ITS GLORY...

THE NEXT MORNING, SHE WAS GONE. NO PHONE. NO ADDRESS.

BUT SHE LEFT ME PHOTOS AND VIDEOS AND ALL SORTS OF EVIDENCE OF "OUR WONDERFUL NIGHT".

SHE ALSO SENT COPIES TO MY FRIENDS, WHO HAVE NOT STOPPED CONGRATULATING AND ENVYING ME SINCE.
AND I'M ALREADY FAMOUS IN MY NEIGHBORHOOD FOR MY "FEAT".

I DON'T UNDERSTAND ANY OF THIS. JUDGING FROM YOUR STORY, IT SEEMS LIKE IT WAS A PERFECT NIGHT WITH A MYSTERIOUS LADY?!?

PERFECT, EXCEPT FOR THE FACT THAT THE TRAITOR MUST HAVE PUT SOMETHING IN MY DRINK...

...AND TO BE HONEST... I DON'T REMEMBER ANYTHING!!!
I WANT TO DIE!!!
END

DETECTIVE
WANDA
WOLFE
No.7
BY COAX
3 FULL STORIES
Erosetti Press

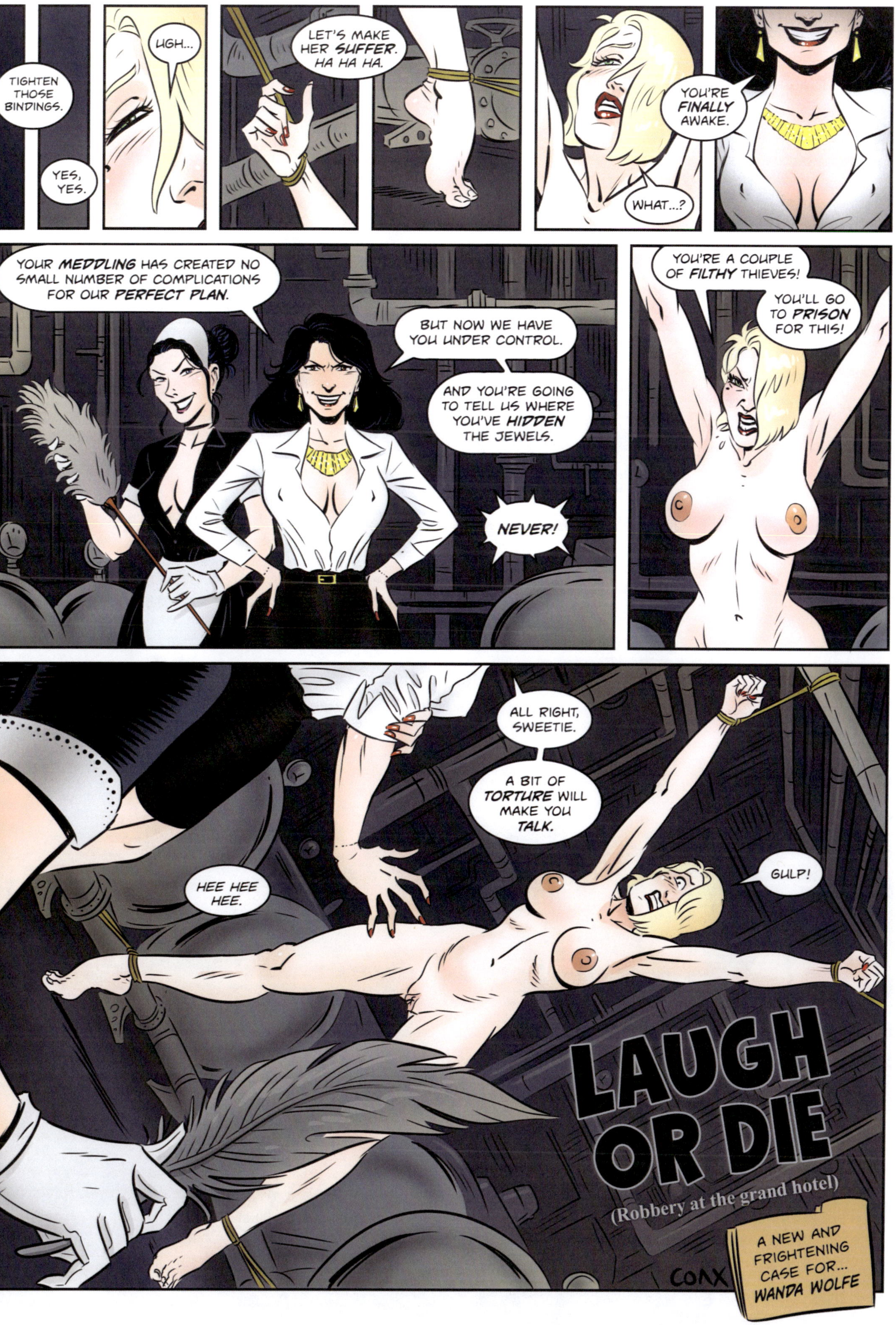

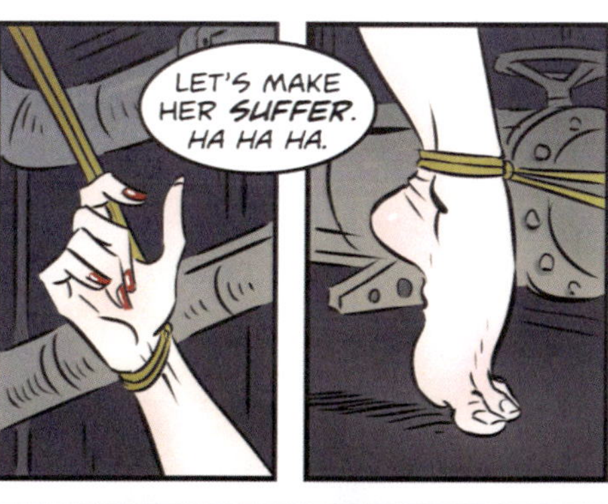

LAUGH OR DIE

(Robbery at the grand hotel)

CONX

A NEW AND FRIGHTENING CASE FOR... WANDA WOLFE

OH MY GOD!

WE KNOW YOU'RE MULTIORGASMIC. AND THAT YOU ARE SENSITIVE TO TICKLING.
AS SOON AS YOU START LAUGHING, YOU WON'T BE ABLE TO STOP.
AND THEN THE ORGASMS WILL COME.
ONE AFTER THE OTHER...
ON AND ON...
UNTIL YOU TURN INTO A DEFENSELESS LITTLE GIRL, CRYING AND WHIMPERING.
I WON'T TALK!
AND I WON'T LAUGH!

WE'LL SEE!

MMHH!

DON'T BE STUBBORN! TALK!

I WON'T GIVE YOU THE SATISFACTION, YOU BASTARDS!

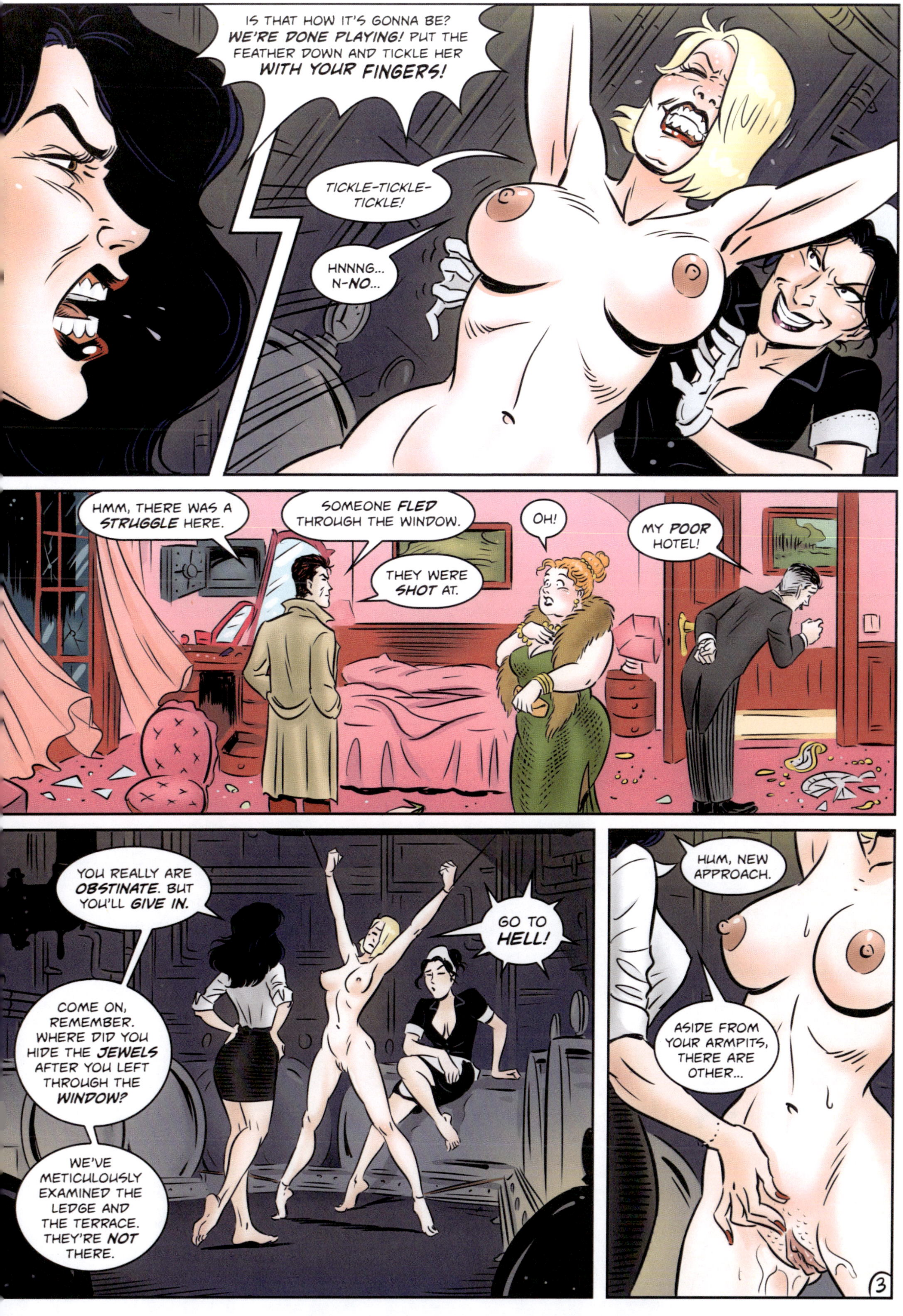

IS THAT HOW IT'S GONNA BE? WE'RE DONE PLAYING! PUT THE FEATHER DOWN AND TICKLE HER WITH YOUR FINGERS!
TICKLE-TICKLE-TICKLE!
HNNNG... N-NO...

HMM, THERE WAS A STRUGGLE HERE.
SOMEONE FLED THROUGH THE WINDOW.
THEY WERE SHOT AT.
OH!
MY POOR HOTEL!
YOU REALLY ARE OBSTINATE. BUT YOU'LL GIVE IN.
GO TO HELL!
COME ON, REMEMBER. WHERE DID YOU HIDE THE JEWELS AFTER YOU LEFT THROUGH THE WINDOW?
WE'VE METICULOUSLY EXAMINED THE LEDGE AND THE TERRACE. THEY'RE NOT THERE.

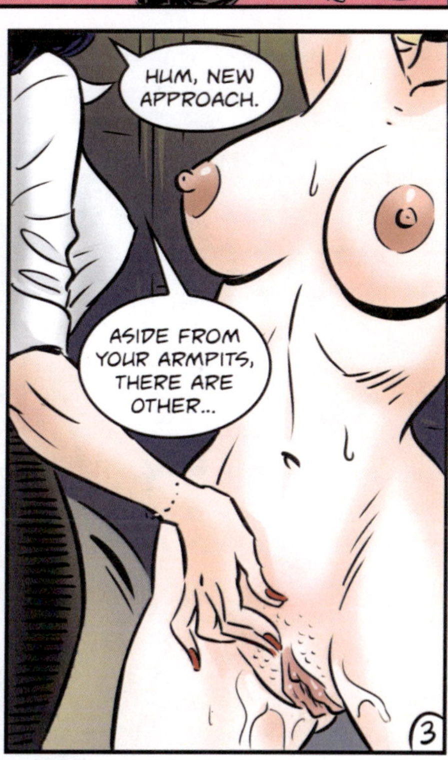

HUM, NEW APPROACH.
ASIDE FROM YOUR ARMPITS, THERE ARE OTHER...
③

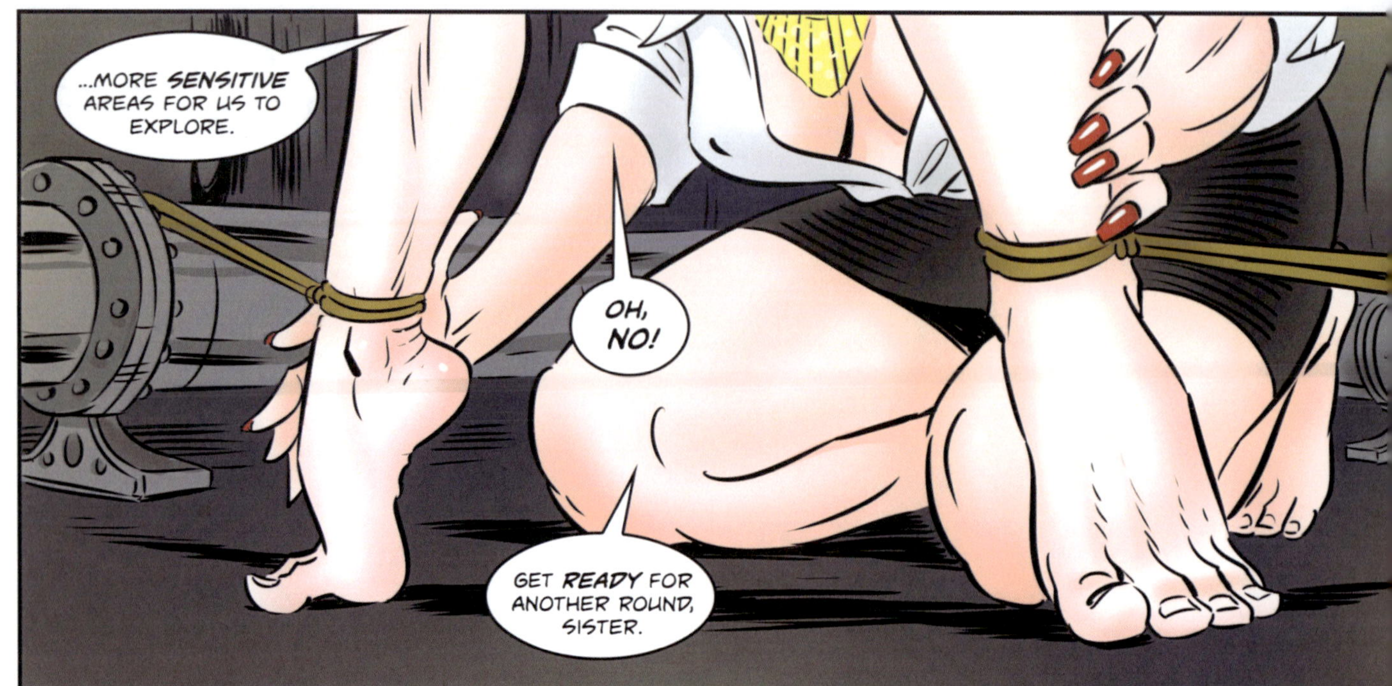

...MORE SENSITIVE AREAS FOR US TO EXPLORE.
OH, NO!
GET READY FOR ANOTHER ROUND, SISTER.

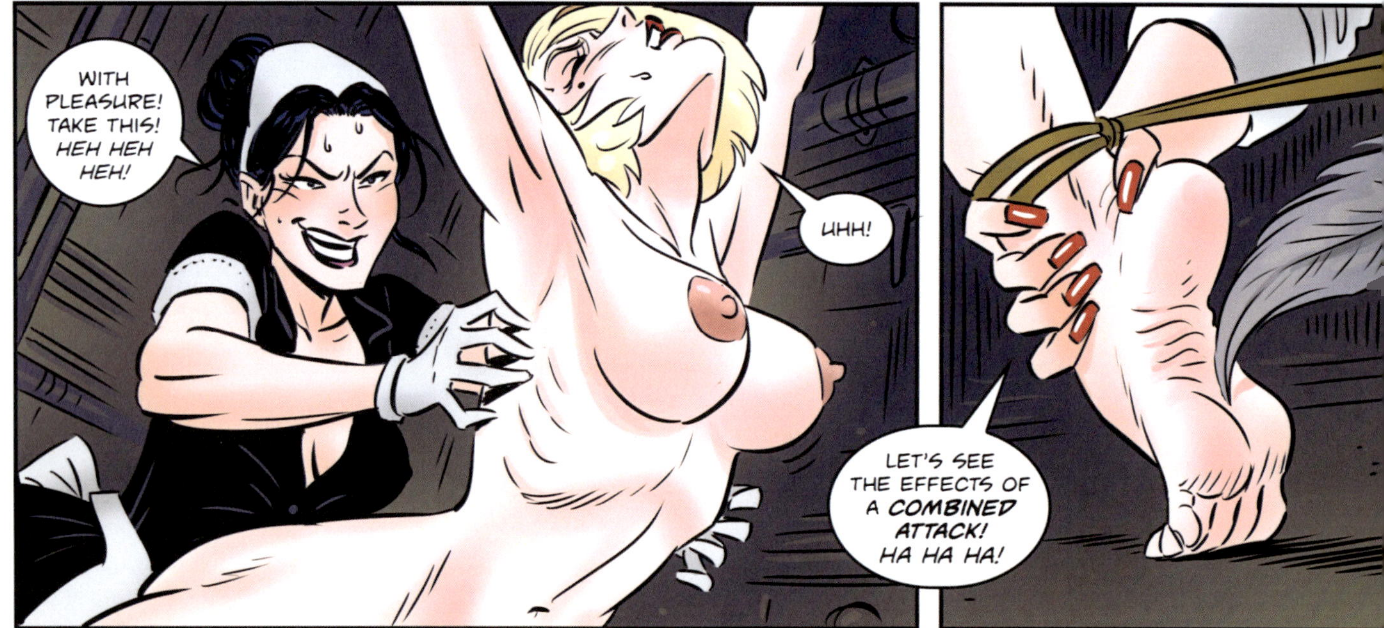

WITH PLEASURE! TAKE THIS! HEH HEH HEH!
UHH!
LET'S SEE THE EFFECTS OF A COMBINED ATTACK! HA HA HA!

UGH... I W-WON'T BE ABLE TO TAKE MUCH MORE...

IS WATER LEAKING FROM THE CEILING?
HMM, COINCIDENCE? WE'LL HAVE TO INVESTIGATE.
MY REPUTATION WILL SINK!
OH!

YOU'LL CUM VERY SOON. AND AFTER THE FIRST ORGASM, YOUR TICKLISHNESS WILL BE SO INTENSE THAT YOU'LL TELL ME EVERYTHING I WANT TO KNOW.
I'LL HOLD OUT UNTIL MY LAST BREATH!
AAAAH! WHAT A DISASTER!
WE HAVE TO TELL OTILIO, GO TO THE BASEMENT, CUT THE WATER OFF!
I HAVE JUST THE RIGHT TORTURE IMPLEMENT FOR SOMEONE AS STUBBORN AS YOU...
...A CHINESE BRUSH!
SOFT, ISN'T IT?
I W-WON'T... SAY... A-ANY-THING...
YES, THIS IS WORKING!
LOOK AT THE WAY SHE WRITHES AROUND!
GGRRRHHSS!
HAVE SOME MORE TICKLING!

EXIT
AY, CARAMBA!
I CAN'T TAKE IT ANYMORE... AAAAH!
UH!
FWOOSH!
OH!
CRASH!
I'VE GOT YOU!
AH!

THESE TWO THIEVES WERE ABOUT TO SWIPE SOME VALUABLE JEWELS. I JUST HAPPENED TO NOTICE THEM FORCING THE DOOR TO THE ROOM OPEN. I FOLLOWED THEM, SAW THE THEFT, WE FOUGHT.
I ESCAPED TO THE UPPER FLOOR WITH THE JEWELS...
I THREW THEM INTO THE TOILET INSIDE A BAG. SHORTLY AFTERWARDS THEY CAPTURED AND TORTURED ME.
NOW THEY'LL GET WHAT THEY DESERVE.
WOW!
OH!

THE EN

PAMELA LAUREN HAD DISAPPEARED.
SHE HAD REACHED THAT AGE WHEN YOU WANT TO DISCOVER THE WORLD AND HAD VANISHED.

HER PARENTS WERE WORRIED.
IT'S HARD TO FIND SOMEONE WHO'S TRAVELLING AROUND...
...FUCKING HER FRIENDS MADE IT EASIER.
THE TRAIL STOPS HERE.

AT THE LAST DAMN REFUGE FOR THE MALADJUSTED.
DAMN MY LUCK.
WELCOME TO TWIN HILLS
NUDIST CAMPING
-W.WOLFE-

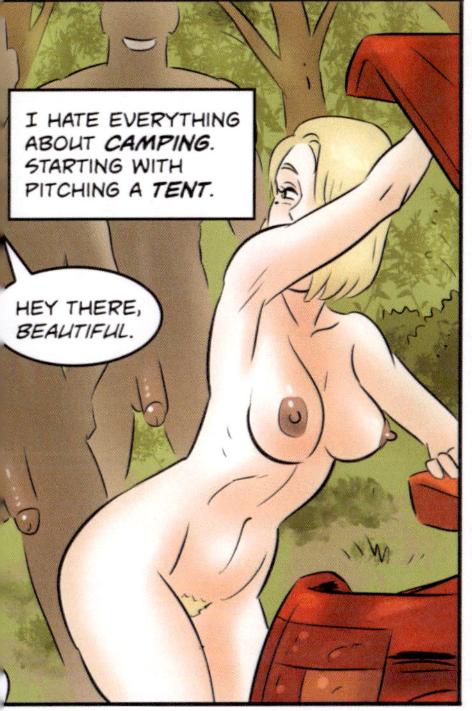

I HATE EVERYTHING ABOUT CAMPING. STARTING WITH PITCHING A TENT.
HEY THERE, BEAUTIFUL.

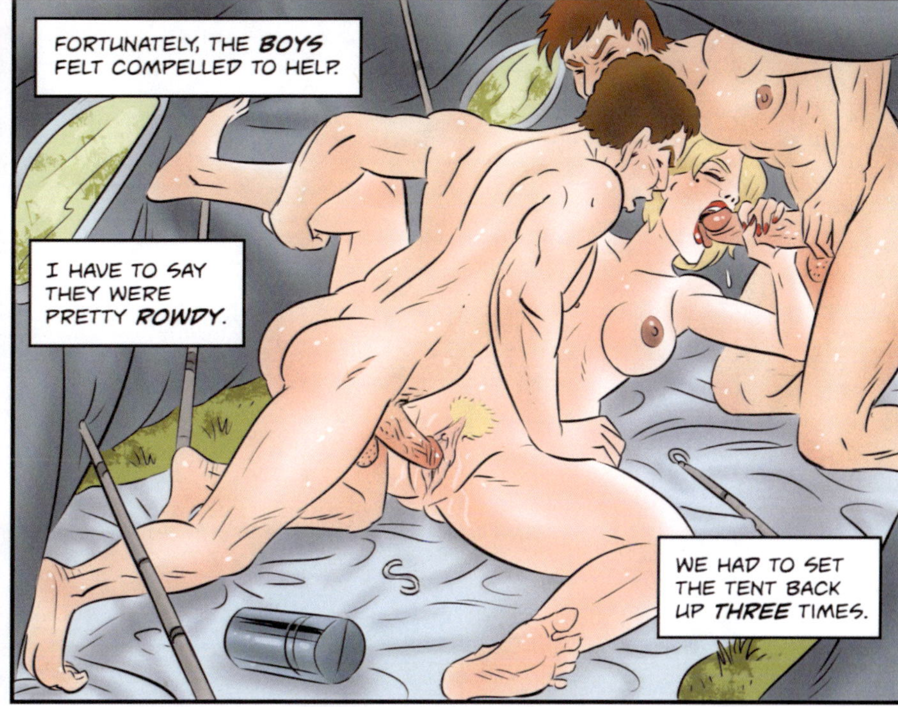

FORTUNATELY, THE BOYS FELT COMPELLED TO HELP.
I HAVE TO SAY THEY WERE PRETTY ROWDY.
WE HAD TO SET THE TENT BACK UP THREE TIMES.

ONCE I GOT MYSELF SETTLED IN, I WENT OUT TO SCOUT THE AREA.
I NEEDED TO STRETCH MY LEGS TOO.
I SOON STUMBLED UPON A GROUP OF NATURISTS IN THE MIDDLE OF A BANQUET.
THEY WERE ALL VERY OPEN AND FRIENDLY.

THEY HAD COVERED A GIRL IN HONEY AND TIED HER TO A TREE TO KEEP THE MOSQUITOES AWAY.
WHERE DO THESE PEOPLE GET AN IDEA LIKE THAT?
I ACTED CASUALLY AND DIDN'T SAY ANYTHING, OF COURSE.
THAT MADE ME EVEN MORE SUSPICIOUS.

I SAW A LOT OF STRANGE THINGS THERE THAT I DON'T THINK I NEED TO MENTION.

I RAN INTO A GUY AT A BEND WHO WAS BUSY MAKING ART PIECES (OR SOMETHING LIKE THAT) WITH ROPES, OBJECTS, AND PEOPLE.
COAX
THERE WAS A PIECE OF PAMELA'S CLOTHING HANGING THERE!

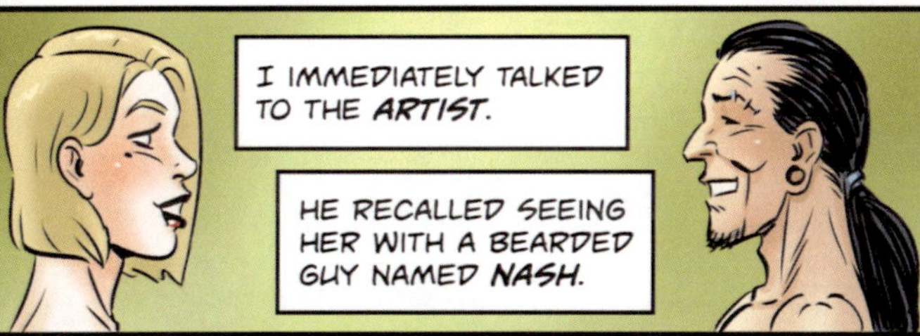
I IMMEDIATELY TALKED TO THE ARTIST.
HE RECALLED SEEING HER WITH A BEARDED GUY NAMED NASH.

HE DIDN'T MIND GIVING ME THE SHIRT AND EVEN MADE ME A CUTE HANDMADE BRA.
HOW NICE!

THEY STARTED A BONFIRE THAT NIGHT.
I DIDN'T FIND ANY NEW INFORMATION.
THEY GOT CAUGHT UP IN HIPPIE THINGS LIKE FREE LOVE AND DRUGS AND I WENT TO BED RIGHT AWAY.

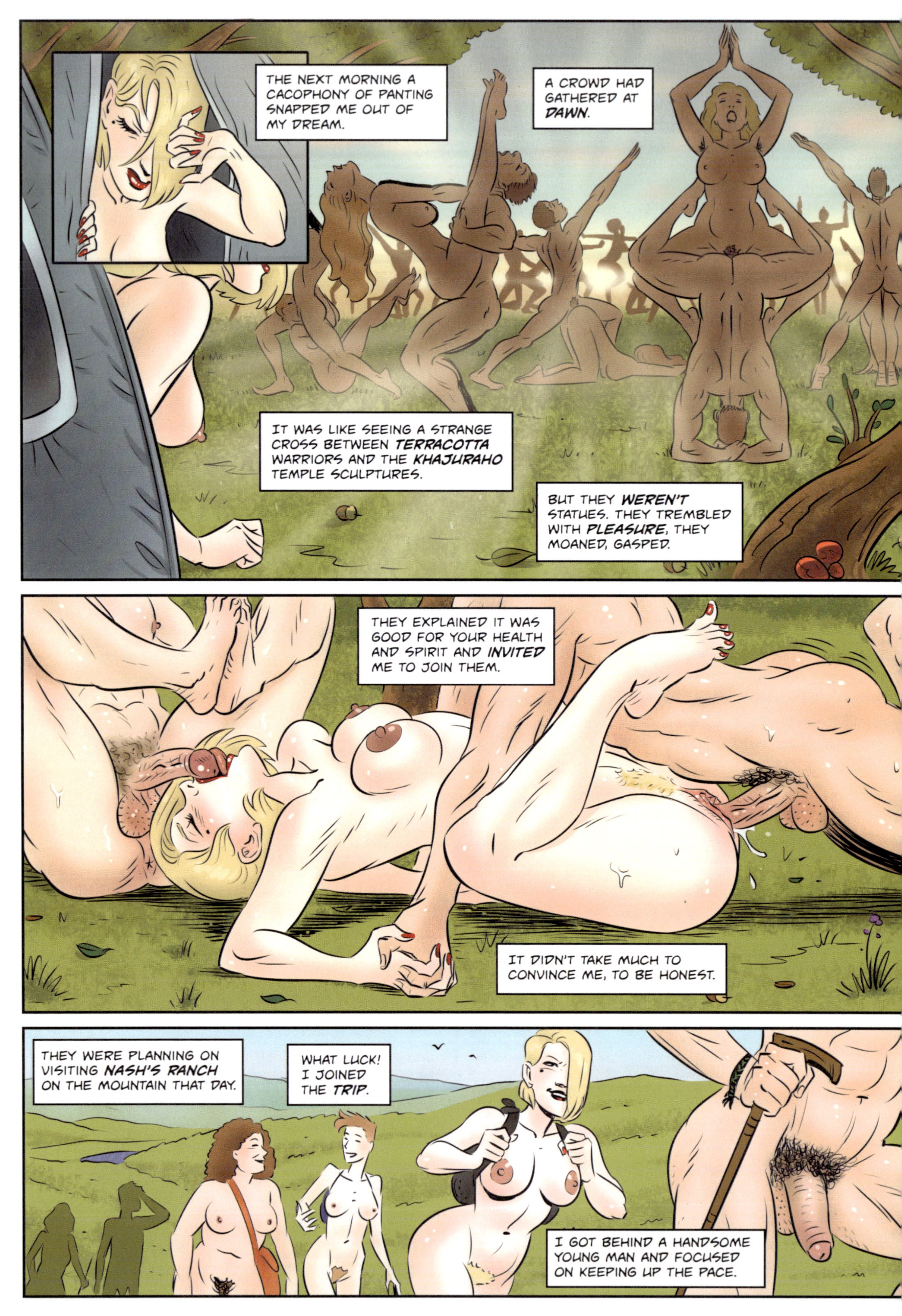

THE NEXT MORNING A CACOPHONY OF PANTING SNAPPED ME OUT OF MY DREAM.
A CROWD HAD GATHERED AT DAWN.
IT WAS LIKE SEEING A STRANGE CROSS BETWEEN TERRACOTTA WARRIORS AND THE KHAJURAHO TEMPLE SCULPTURES.
BUT THEY WEREN'T STATUES. THEY TREMBLED WITH PLEASURE, THEY MOANED, GASPED.
THEY EXPLAINED IT WAS GOOD FOR YOUR HEALTH AND SPIRIT AND INVITED ME TO JOIN THEM.
IT DIDN'T TAKE MUCH TO CONVINCE ME, TO BE HONEST.
THEY WERE PLANNING ON VISITING NASH'S RANCH ON THE MOUNTAIN THAT DAY.
WHAT LUCK! I JOINED THE TRIP.
I GOT BEHIND A HANDSOME YOUNG MAN AND FOCUSED ON KEEPING UP THE PACE.

DURING THE HIKE, I GOT CLOSE TO A VERY UPBEAT, CHUBBY GIRL.
SHE HAD PINEAPPLES HANGING FROM HER NIPPLES, SO SHE WOULDN'T "FALL ASLEEP," SHE SAID.

KATHLEEN, OR KATHY AS HER FRIENDS CALLED HER, WAS UP FOR ANYTHING.
SHE TOOK A GOOD PLUNGE INTO THE STREAM ALONG THE PATH.
FFFF

THEN, TO WARM THEM-SELVES BACK UP, THEY CAME UP WITH A GAME.

LIKE BLIND MAN'S BLUFF BUT TRYING TO CATCH A CARROT WITH YOUR MOUTH.
HANDS WERE TIED BEHIND THEIR BACKS.
AND WHIPPING.
LOTS OF WHIPPING.

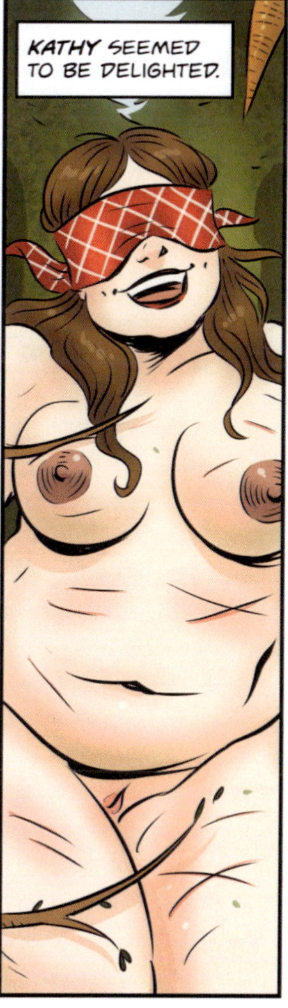

KATHY SEEMED TO BE DELIGHTED.

AFTER WE ATE, WE WENT TO NASH'S RANCH.
HE WAS A GUY WHO TRAINED PONYGIRLS. HE HAS QUITE A REPUTATION.
PONYFARM
GIRLS FROM ALL OVER THE COUNTRY WOULD COME TO HIM.
THEY DID A SMALL DEMONSTRATION FOR US.
I ASKED NASH ABOUT PAMELA.
HE REMEMBERED HER PERFECTLY. "AN INDOMITABLE SPIRIT", HE ADMITTED.
SHE WAS THERE FOR A SHORT WHILE, THEN LEFT. A FEW DAYS AGO.
KATHY DIDN'T MISS HER CHANCE TO GET IN ON THE RODEO.

AFTER THAT EXHAUSTING DAY, WE HEADED BACK TO CAMP.
DAMN, WHERE COULD THIS GIRL BE HIDING?

I HAD STRANGE DREAMS THAT NIGHT.
I THINK CITY FOLK LIKE ME AREN'T REALLY USED TO THE FREEDOM AND WILDNESS THAT ARE SO INTRINSIC TO NATURE.
WE NEED LIMITS, RULES.
WE'RE CONDITIONED TO KEEP UP A FAÇADE OF CIVILITY BUT DEEP DOWN WE'RE ANIMALS DRIVEN BY BASE INSTINCTS.
I DON'T KNOW. MAYBE IT WAS JUST THE SMELLS --OR HOW UNCOMFORTABLE THE SLEEPING BAG WAS.

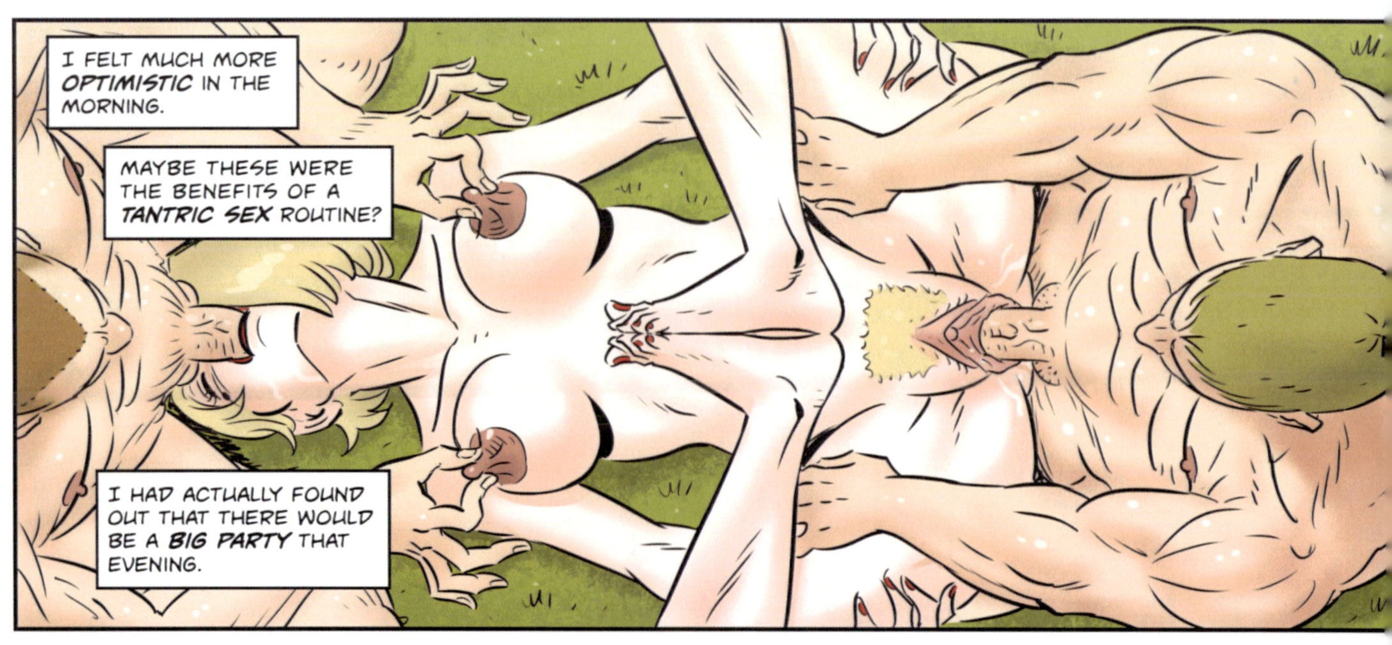

I FELT MUCH MORE OPTIMISTIC IN THE MORNING.
MAYBE THESE WERE THE BENEFITS OF A TANTRIC SEX ROUTINE?
I HAD ACTUALLY FOUND OUT THAT THERE WOULD BE A BIG PARTY THAT EVENING.

A GRAND CELEBRATION OF THE SUMMER SOLSTICE.
IF PAMELA WAS STILL AROUND, SHE WOULD UNDOUBTEDLY BE THERE.
EVERYONE IN THE CAMP WAS CHEERFULLY WORKING ON THE PREPARATIONS.

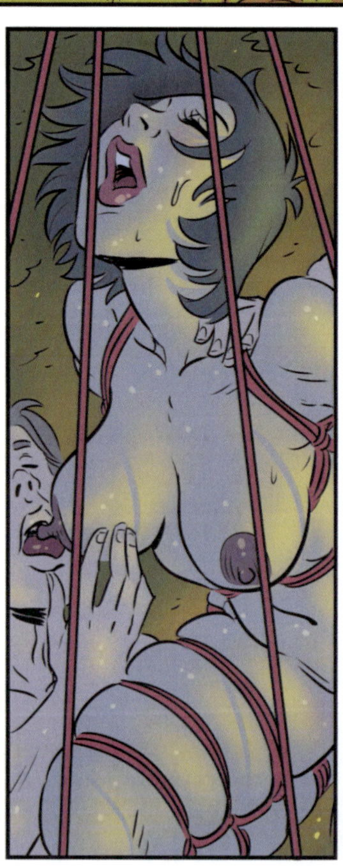

A LOT OF PEOPLE HAD COME.
THERE WERE BONFIRES AND DANCING AND QUITE A RUCKUS.
I HAD TO FOCUS IF I WAS GOING TO FIND PAMELA IN THE CROWD.
THERE WAS ALSO SOMETHING STRANGE IN THE AIR... OR IN THE DRINKS...
OH, SHIT.
THE COLORS... THE SHAPES... THEY WERE UNRAVELING.
SOME OF THE GIRLS WERE CALLING OUT TO THE GUYS FROM AN ISLET IN THE LAKE LIKE SIRENS.
AND THERE WAS KATHY... A GODDESS EMERGING FROM THE DEPTHS.
KA'THAL'HEEN...
WRITHING MOBS OF SUBMISSIVE ACOLYTES WANTING TO RECEIVE HER NECTAR.
I COULD HAVE SWORN THEY WERE WHISPERING HER NAME IN A LITANY...
KA'THAL'HEEN...

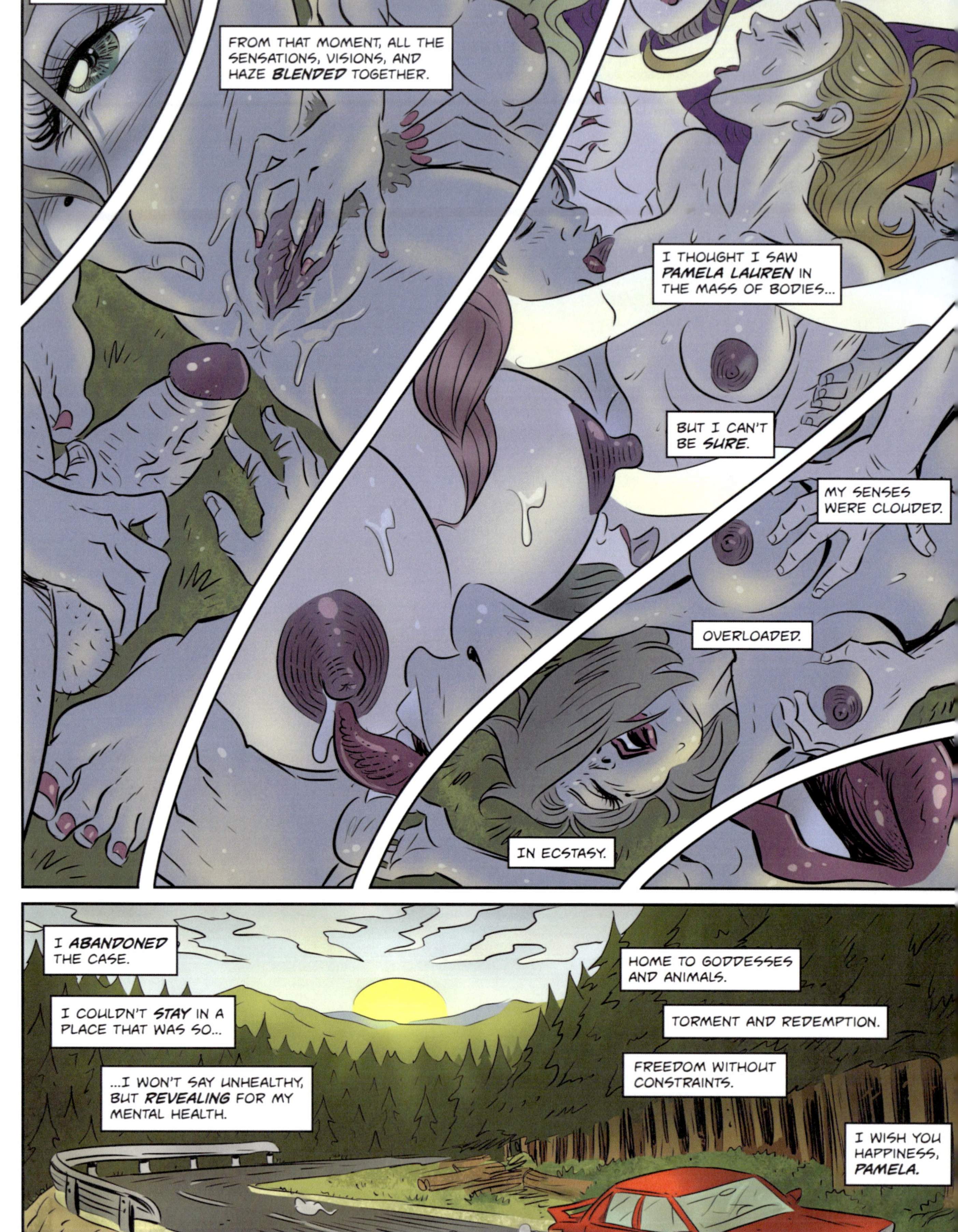

I DON'T RECALL MUCH ELSE.
FROM THAT MOMENT, ALL THE SENSATIONS, VISIONS, AND HAZE BLENDED TOGETHER.
I THOUGHT I SAW PAMELA LAUREN IN THE MASS OF BODIES...
BUT I CAN'T BE SURE.
MY SENSES WERE CLOUDED.
OVERLOADED.
IN ECSTASY.
I ABANDONED THE CASE.
I COULDN'T STAY IN A PLACE THAT WAS SO...
...I WON'T SAY UNHEALTHY, BUT REVEALING FOR MY MENTAL HEALTH.
HOME TO GODDESSES AND ANIMALS.
TORMENT AND REDEMPTION.
FREEDOM WITHOUT CONSTRAINTS.
I WISH YOU HAPPINESS, PAMELA.
THE EN

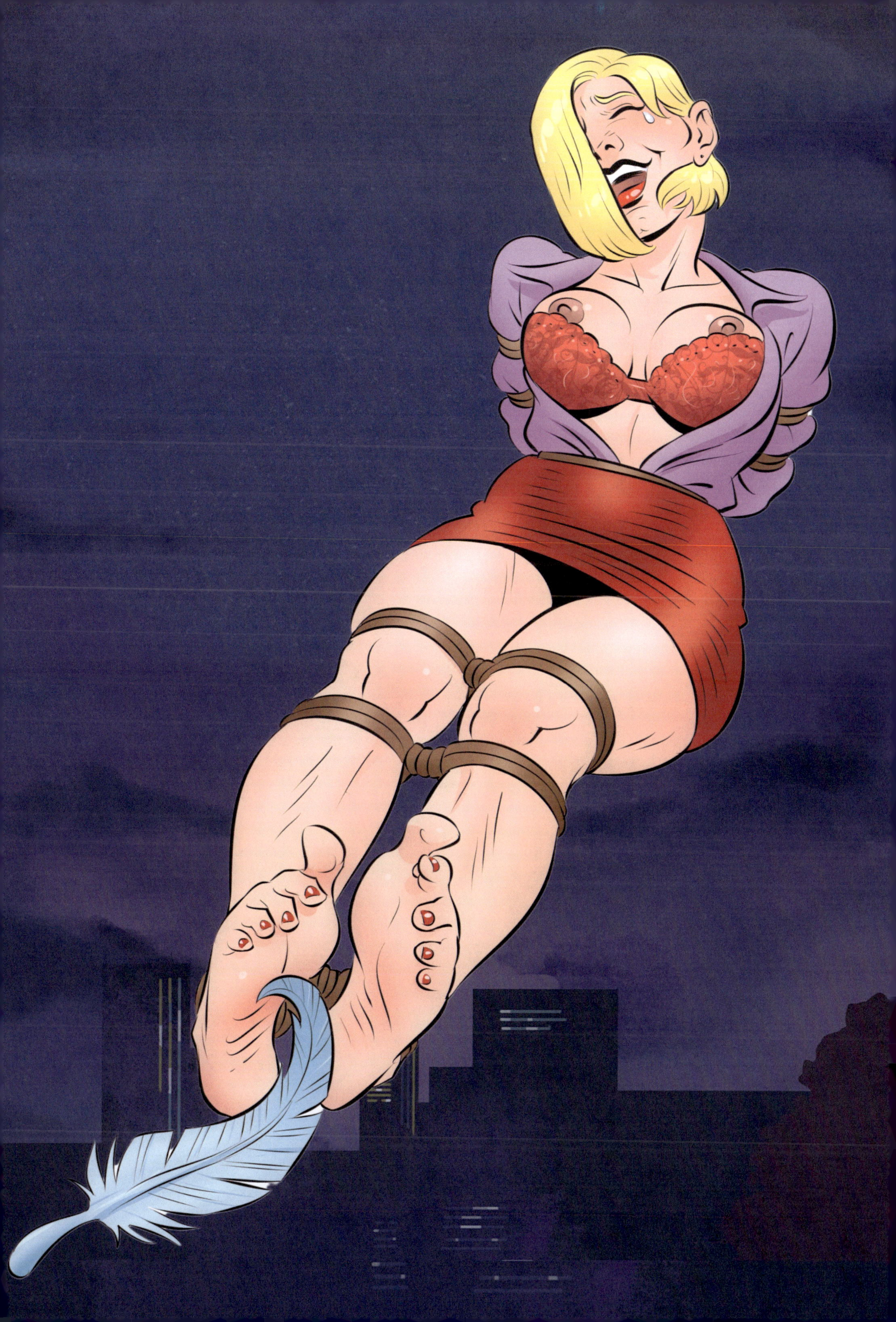

CONXA.

5 HOURS WITH WANDA

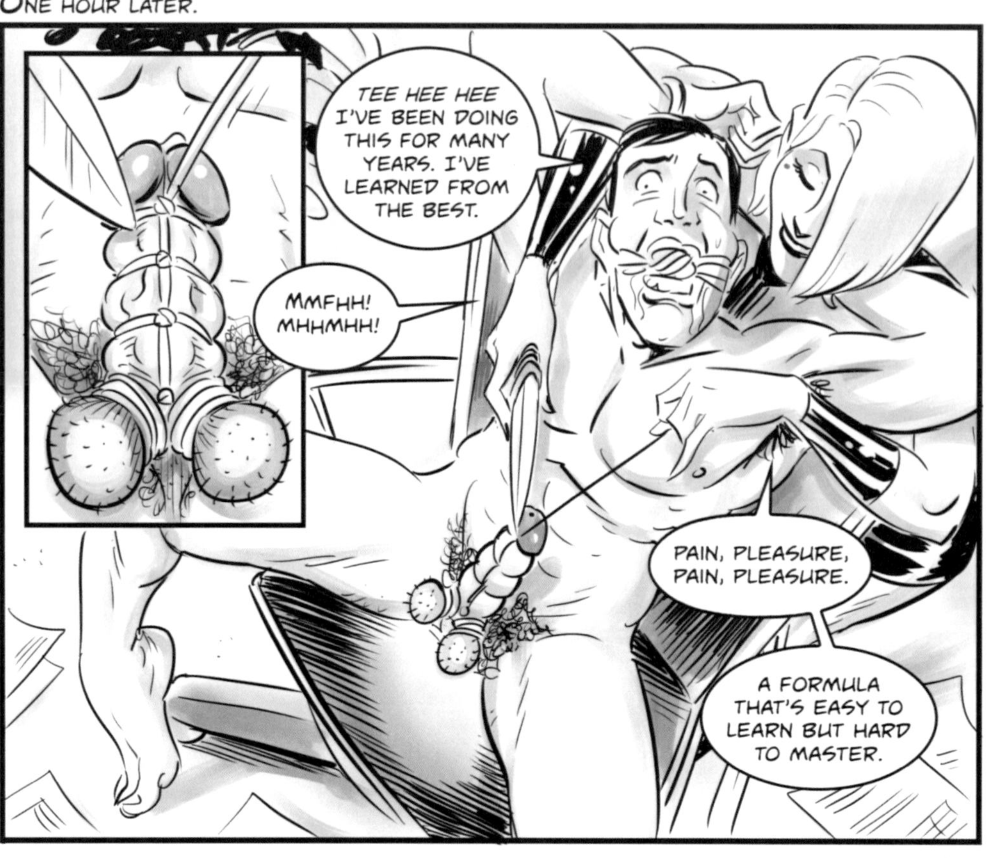
TEE HEE HEE I'VE BEEN DOING THIS FOR MANY YEARS. I'VE LEARNED FROM THE BEST.
MMFHH! MHHMHH!
PAIN, PLEASURE, PAIN, PLEASURE.
A FORMULA THAT'S EASY TO LEARN BUT HARD TO MASTER.

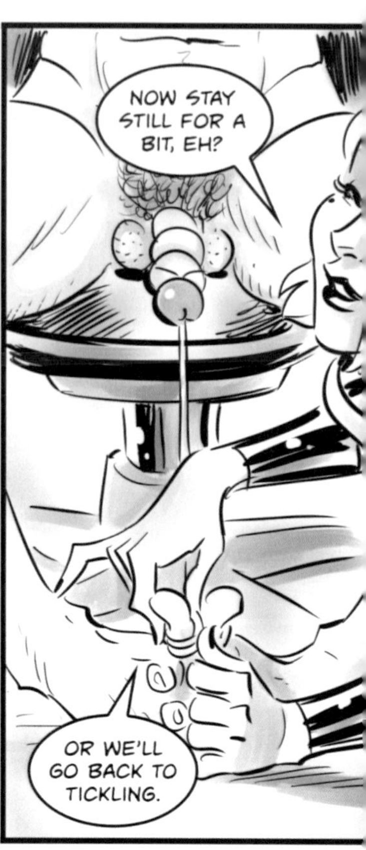
NOW STAY STILL FOR A BIT, EH?
OR WE'LL GO BACK TO TICKLING.

LET'S REVIEW. YOU'VE GIVEN ME YOUR SECRET SWISS BANK ACCOUNTS...
...ACCESS TO THE COMPUTER...
...YOUR MASSEUSE'S PHONE NUMBER...
...THE CODE FOR YOUR SAFE...
...LEWD PHOTOS OF YOUR EX-GIRL-FRIENDS...
...AND YOUR BEST CIGARS.

WHAT'S LEFT?
NOTHING.
SO THEN LET'S START WITH THE PLEASURABLE PART.

FAMILIAR WITH URETHRAL DILATORS?
!!!

YOU'LL LOVE THEM.

TWO HOURS LATER.
...WORK, WORK, AND MORE WORK.
DON'T GET ME WRONG, I LIKE IT, BUT IN THE END YOU HAVE NO LIFE.
NOR FRIENDS, JUST COLLEAGUES. IN MY CASE, FUCK-COLLEAGUES.
ZING!
ZING!
ZING!
AND I HAVE A GOOD TIME. I AM CONSTANTLY MEETING NEW PEOPLE, I HAVE ADVENTURES, I'VE HAD SEX IN EXOTIC PLACES, AND SO ON.
ZING!
SURELY YOU, WITH YOUR MILLIONS AND YOUR LUXURIOUS LIFE, SHOULD KNOW WHAT I MEAN.
ZING!
BUT DON'T YOU SOMETIMES WONDER IF THERE SHOULD BE MORE THAN JUST FUN AND PLEASURE?
DOESN'T IT ALL SEEM A TAD POINTLESS?
ZING!
ZING!

...MOTHERS ARE LIKE THAT. ALWAYS WANTING YOU TO SETTLE DOWN.
DID YOU KNOW I HAD A FLING WITH A SECRET AGENT IN HER MAJESTY'S SERVICE?
WELL, COUNTERAGENT OR DOUBLE AGENT OR WHATEVER.
OH, IT'S DAWN! TIME TO LEAVE!

THE CLEANING LADY SHOULD BE ALMOST HERE. LET'S MAKE YOU PRESENTABLE.

I HOPE YOU TRUST HER. TEE HEE HEE

SHOULD I LEAVE THE ANAL PLUG VIBRATING?
COME ON, DON'T BE SHY, IT DOESN'T MATTER TO ME.

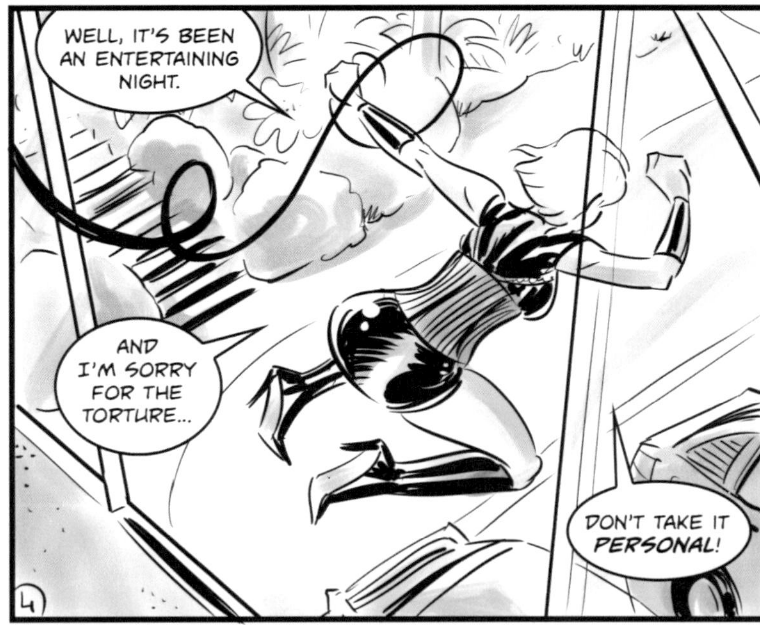
WELL, IT'S BEEN AN ENTERTAINING NIGHT.
AND I'M SORRY FOR THE TORTURE...
DON'T TAKE IT PERSONAL!

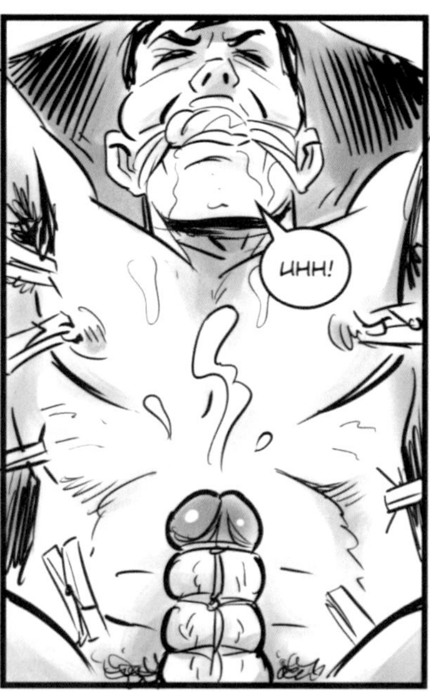
UHH!

THE E

Ink
Flats
Cover step by step
Volume
Final FX

SPECIAL ISSUE
DETECTIVE
WANDA WOLFE
BY COAX
THE WORLD HAS GONE CRAZY ...FOR LOVE!
Erosetti Press

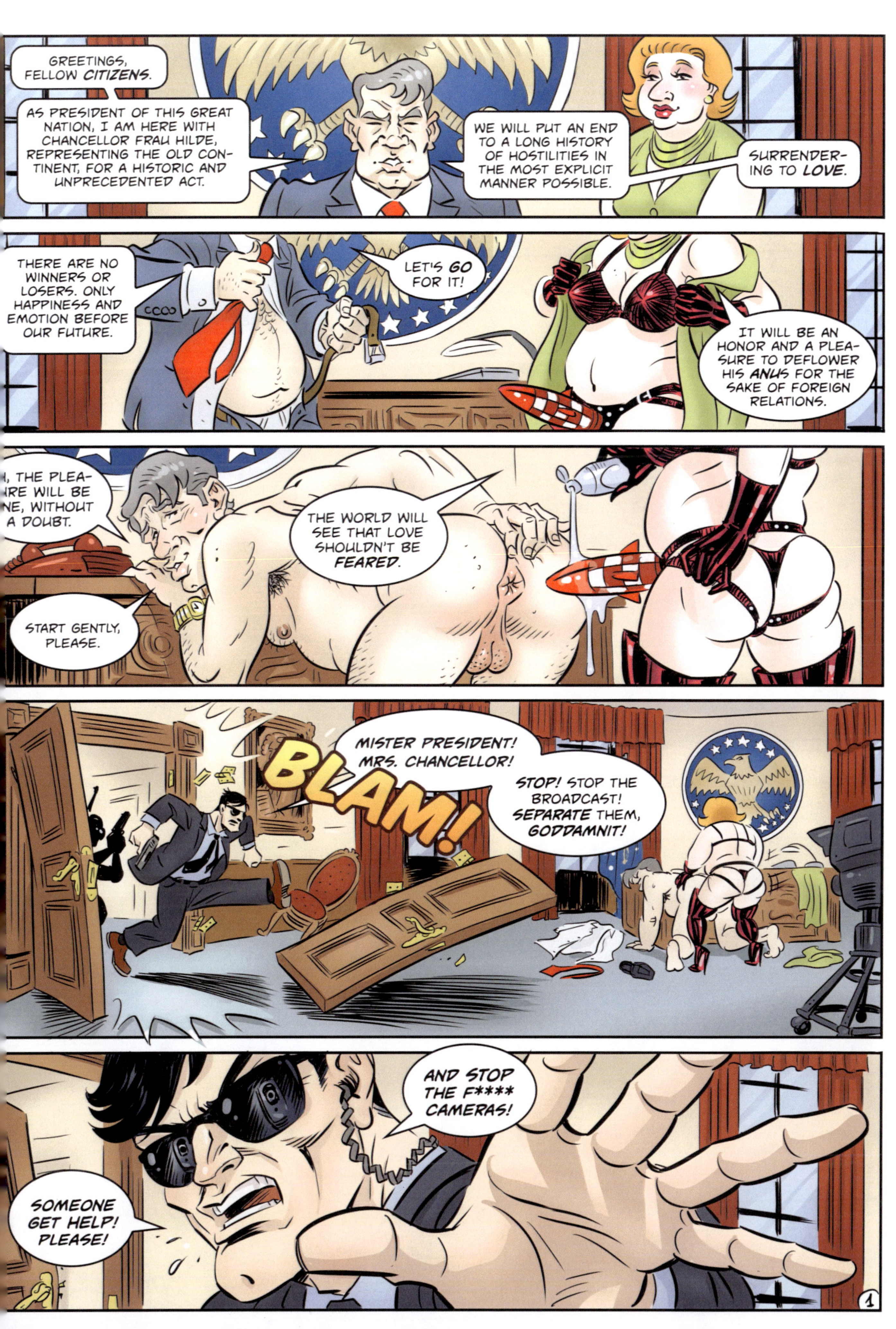

GREETINGS, FELLOW CITIZENS.
AS PRESIDENT OF THIS GREAT NATION, I AM HERE WITH CHANCELLOR FRAU HILDE, REPRESENTING THE OLD CONTINENT, FOR A HISTORIC AND UNPRECEDENTED ACT.
WE WILL PUT AN END TO A LONG HISTORY OF HOSTILITIES IN THE MOST EXPLICIT MANNER POSSIBLE.
SURRENDERING TO LOVE.
THERE ARE NO WINNERS OR LOSERS. ONLY HAPPINESS AND EMOTION BEFORE OUR FUTURE.
LET'S GO FOR IT!
IT WILL BE AN HONOR AND A PLEASURE TO DEFLOWER HIS ANUS FOR THE SAKE OF FOREIGN RELATIONS.
..M, THE PLEA-..RE WILL BE ..NE, WITHOUT .. DOUBT.
THE WORLD WILL SEE THAT LOVE SHOULDN'T BE FEARED.
START GENTLY, PLEASE.
MISTER PRESIDENT! MRS. CHANCELLOR!
BLAM!
STOP! STOP THE BROADCAST! SEPARATE THEM, GODDAMNIT!
AND STOP THE F**** CAMERAS!
SOMEONE GET HELP! PLEASE!
1

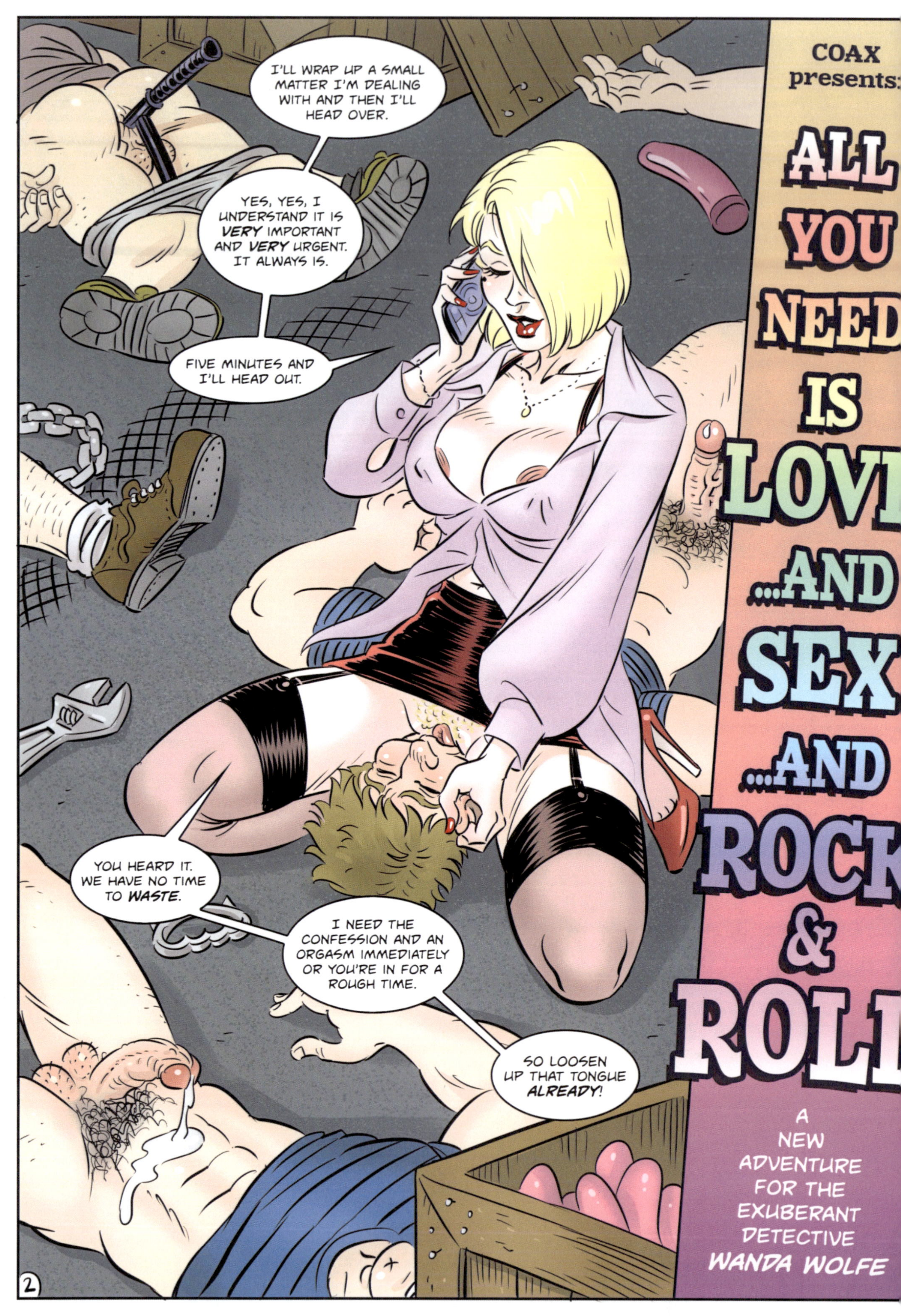

COAX
presents:

ALL
YOU
NEED
IS
LOVE
...AND
SEX
...AND
ROCK
&
ROLL

A
NEW
ADVENTURE
FOR THE
EXUBERANT
DETECTIVE
WANDA WOLFE

I'LL WRAP UP A SMALL MATTER I'M DEALING WITH AND THEN I'LL HEAD OVER.

YES, YES, I UNDERSTAND IT IS VERY IMPORTANT AND VERY URGENT. IT ALWAYS IS.

FIVE MINUTES AND I'LL HEAD OUT.

YOU HEARD IT. WE HAVE NO TIME TO WASTE.

I NEED THE CONFESSION AND AN ORGASM IMMEDIATELY OR YOU'RE IN FOR A ROUGH TIME.

SO LOOSEN UP THAT TONGUE ALREADY!

LITARY
EADQUARTERS.
SINCE TWO DAYS AGO, THE ENTIRE WORLD POPULATION'S LIBIDO HAS GOTTEN OUT OF CONTROL.
PEOPLE HAVE STOPPED WORKING AND DONE NOTHING BUT FUCK WHENEVER AND WHEREVER.
THERE'S NO PRODUCTION. THERE'S NO CONSUMPTION. THE ECONOMY IS GOING UNDER. THE MARKETS ARE FALLING APART. THE CHAOS!
WE THINK WE'RE DEALING WITH A TERRORIST ATTACK... ON A WORLDWIDE SCALE!
IT SOMEHOW AFFECTS BRAIN SYNAPSES. IT CAUSES AN AFFECTIONATE OPENNESS.
IT REDUCES EMOTIONAL INHIBITIONS AND CREATES SENSORY STIMULATION LIKE DRUGS AND ALCOHOL DO, BUT IN A PERMANENT AND UNCONTROLLABLE MANNER.
WE DON'T KNOW HOW IT'S PRODUCED OR WHERE IT COMES FROM. NOBODY HAS TAKEN CREDIT FOR THE ATTACK.
THE BASTARDS MUST BE WAITING FOR THIS REIGN OF TERROR TO EXPAND.
THE EVIL!
IN SHORT, IT MAKES THEM AS HORNY AS CATS IN HEAT.
HE HE HE
3

LEADERS FROM THE WORLD'S GREAT POWERS MET TO DISCUSS THIS TRAGEDY AND ENDED UP IN AN ORGY BROADCASTED ON TV.
AND WHAT'S THIS GOT TO DO WITH ME?
AHEM, WE CALLED YOU BECAUSE YOU HAVE A REPUTATION OF BEING PROFICIENT WITH... CASES OF A SEXUAL NATURE.
RECORD VIEWERSHIP IN OVER 20 COUNTRIES!
AND APPARENTLY YOU ARE IMMUNE TO THIS EPIDEMIC.
WHAT AN EMBARRASSMENT!
WELL, I'M USED TO LIVING WITH A HIGH LIBIDO. I ALSO TAKE REFUGE IN MY WORK, HEH.
BUT IF IT AFFECTS EVERYONE WITHOUT EXCEPTION...
HOW HAVE YOU RESISTED IT?

I SERVE GOD AS WELL AS SERVING IN THE MILITARY, MISS.
OUR DUTY TO OUR COUNTRY COMES BEFORE OUR LUST!

THE LORD PROTECTS ME FROM TEMPTATION!

OUR SCIENTISTS HAVE DESIGNED THESE DEVICES THAT PRODUCE A SHOCK WITH THE SLIGHTEST SLIP-UP. HEHEHEH
THREE CASES O ATROPHIE PLEASUR RECEPTOR IN SHOR ...

FIND OUT WHO IS RESPONSIBLE FOR THIS PANDEMIC AND HOW WE CAN REVERSE ITS EFFECTS, WANDA.
ALRIGHT, ALRIGHT.
THE WORLD IS IN YOUR HANDS! YOU HAVE OUR FULL SUPPORT!
SEE YOU LATER, BOYS. I'LL KEEP YOU INFORMED.
AND OUR BLESSINGS!

4

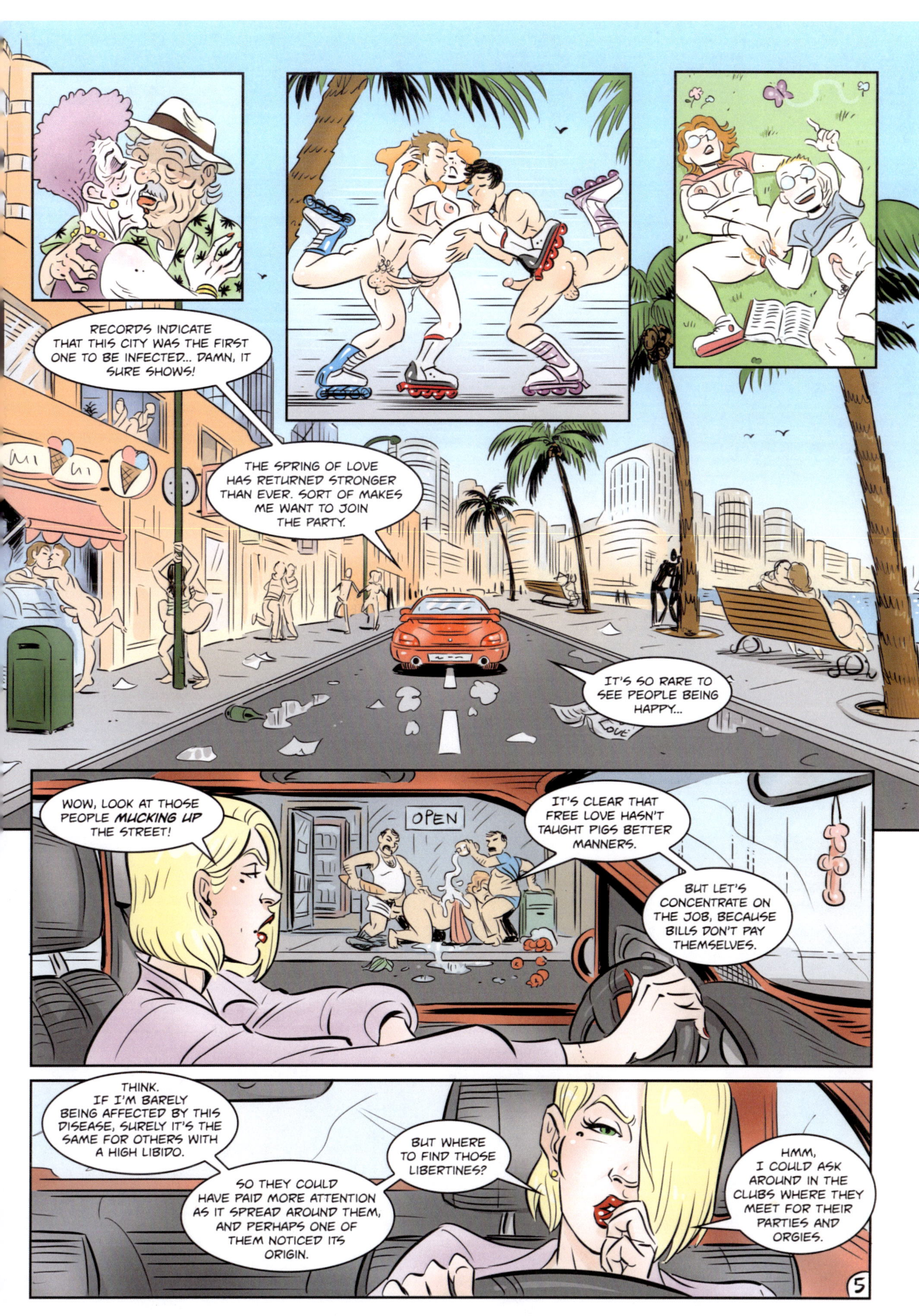

RECORDS INDICATE THAT THIS CITY WAS THE FIRST ONE TO BE INFECTED... DAMN, IT SURE SHOWS!
THE SPRING OF LOVE HAS RETURNED STRONGER THAN EVER. SORT OF MAKES ME WANT TO JOIN THE PARTY.
IT'S SO RARE TO SEE PEOPLE BEING HAPPY...
WOW, LOOK AT THOSE PEOPLE MUCKING UP THE STREET!
OPEN
IT'S CLEAR THAT FREE LOVE HASN'T TAUGHT PIGS BETTER MANNERS.
BUT LET'S CONCENTRATE ON THE JOB, BECAUSE BILLS DON'T PAY THEMSELVES.
THINK. IF I'M BARELY BEING AFFECTED BY THIS DISEASE, SURELY IT'S THE SAME FOR OTHERS WITH A HIGH LIBIDO.
SO THEY COULD HAVE PAID MORE ATTENTION AS IT SPREAD AROUND THEM, AND PERHAPS ONE OF THEM NOTICED ITS ORIGIN.
BUT WHERE TO FIND THOSE LIBERTINES?
HMM, I COULD ASK AROUND IN THE CLUBS WHERE THEY MEET FOR THEIR PARTIES AND ORGIES.
5

OH, WOW!
BY SODOM AND GOMORRAH! TO THINK IT LOOKED LIKE THE PARTY WAS OUTSIDE!
MMH!
UH
EXCUSE ME, WHO'S IN CHARGE?
SORRY, WHO'S IN CHARGE?
ARE YOU IN CHARGE?
I THINK HE'S OVER THERE AT THE BOTTOOOH
IT'S THE GUY WITH THE -OOH- BLUE HAIR LICKING FEET -AAH-
MMM, YES... WHO'S ASKING?
OOH!
SLURP!
UHH!

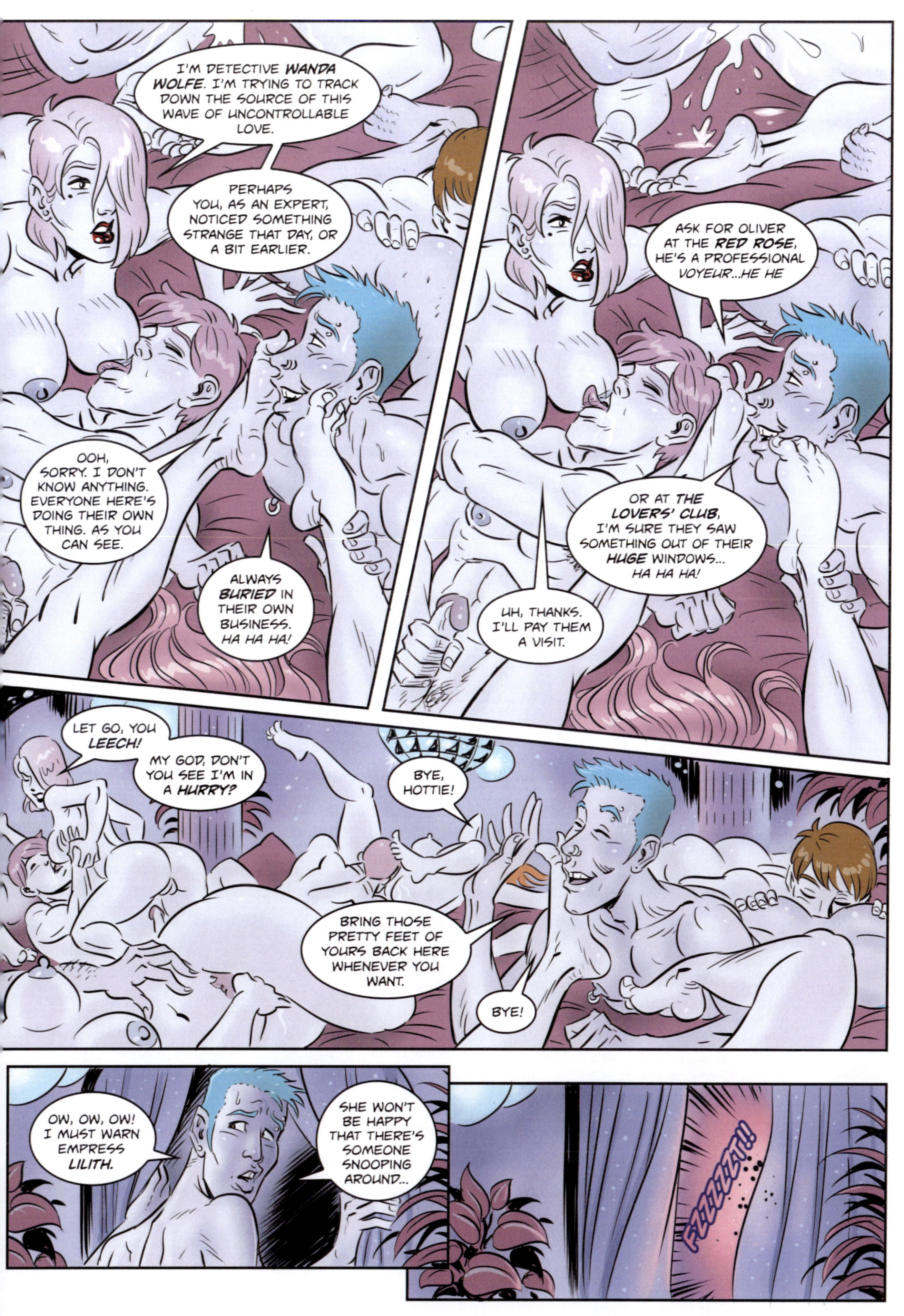

I'M DETECTIVE WANDA WOLFE. I'M TRYING TO TRACK DOWN THE SOURCE OF THIS WAVE OF UNCONTROLLABLE LOVE.
PERHAPS YOU, AS AN EXPERT, NOTICED SOMETHING STRANGE THAT DAY, OR A BIT EARLIER.
OOH, SORRY. I DON'T KNOW ANYTHING. EVERYONE HERE'S DOING THEIR OWN THING. AS YOU CAN SEE.
ALWAYS BURIED IN THEIR OWN BUSINESS. HA HA HA!
ASK FOR OLIVER AT THE RED ROSE, HE'S A PROFESSIONAL VOYEUR...HE HE
OR AT THE LOVERS' CLUB, I'M SURE THEY SAW SOMETHING OUT OF THEIR HUGE WINDOWS... HA HA HA!
UH, THANKS. I'LL PAY THEM A VISIT.
LET GO, YOU LEECH!
MY GOD, DON'T YOU SEE I'M IN A HURRY?
BYE, HOTTIE!
BRING THOSE PRETTY FEET OF YOURS BACK HERE WHENEVER YOU WANT.
BYE!
OW, OW, OW! I MUST WARN EMPRESS LILITH.
SHE WON'T BE HAPPY THAT THERE'S SOMEONE SNOOPING AROUND...
FLLLLLT!!

RED ROSE AND LOVERS' CLUB...
I'M GOING TO WRITE DOWN THE ADDRESSES HE GAVE ME, CAN'T TRUST MY TERRIBLE MEMORY...
DID HE SAY OLIVIA OR OSWALD?
?
BOOOOOM!!
OOMPH!!
UUH!?
HE HE HE
I WOULDN'T NORMALLY RUN AWAY FROM TWO WELL ENDOWED HUNKS, BUT I HAVE A FEELING THEY'RE TRYING TO KILL ME.
YAAAAARGGHHH!

BLAM!
BLAM!
BLAM!
OOPH! OOPH! I SHOULD TRY OTHER SPORTS BESIDES SEX.

8

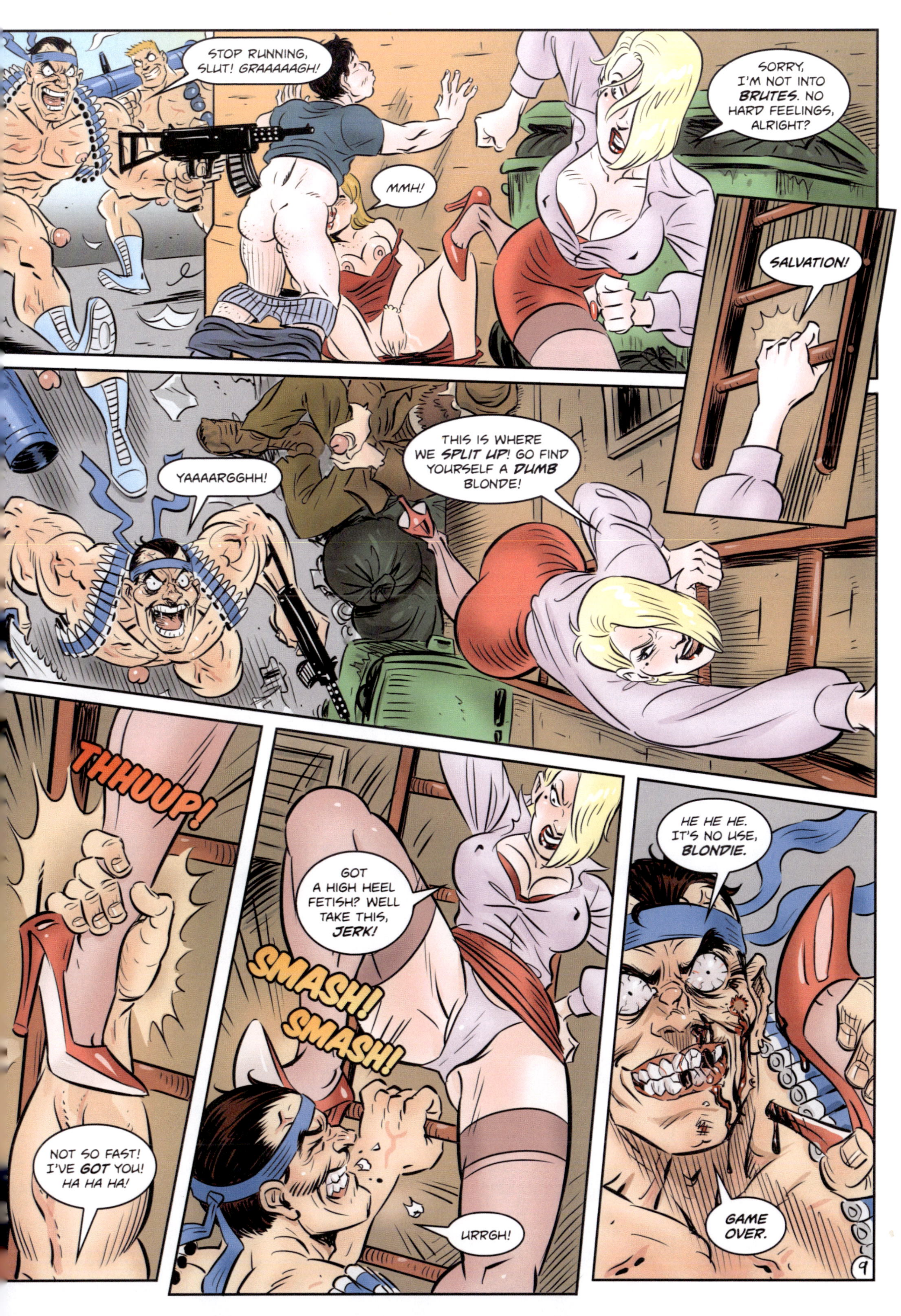

STOP RUNNING, SLUT! GRAAAAAGH!
MMH!
SORRY, I'M NOT INTO BRUTES. NO HARD FEELINGS, ALRIGHT?
SALVATION!
YAAAARGGHH!
THIS IS WHERE WE SPLIT UP! GO FIND YOURSELF A DUMB BLONDE!
THHUUP!
GOT A HIGH HEEL FETISH? WELL TAKE THIS, JERK!
SMASH!
SMASH!
HE HE HE. IT'S NO USE, BLONDIE.
NOT SO FAST! I'VE GOT YOU! HA HA HA!
URRGH!
GAME OVER.

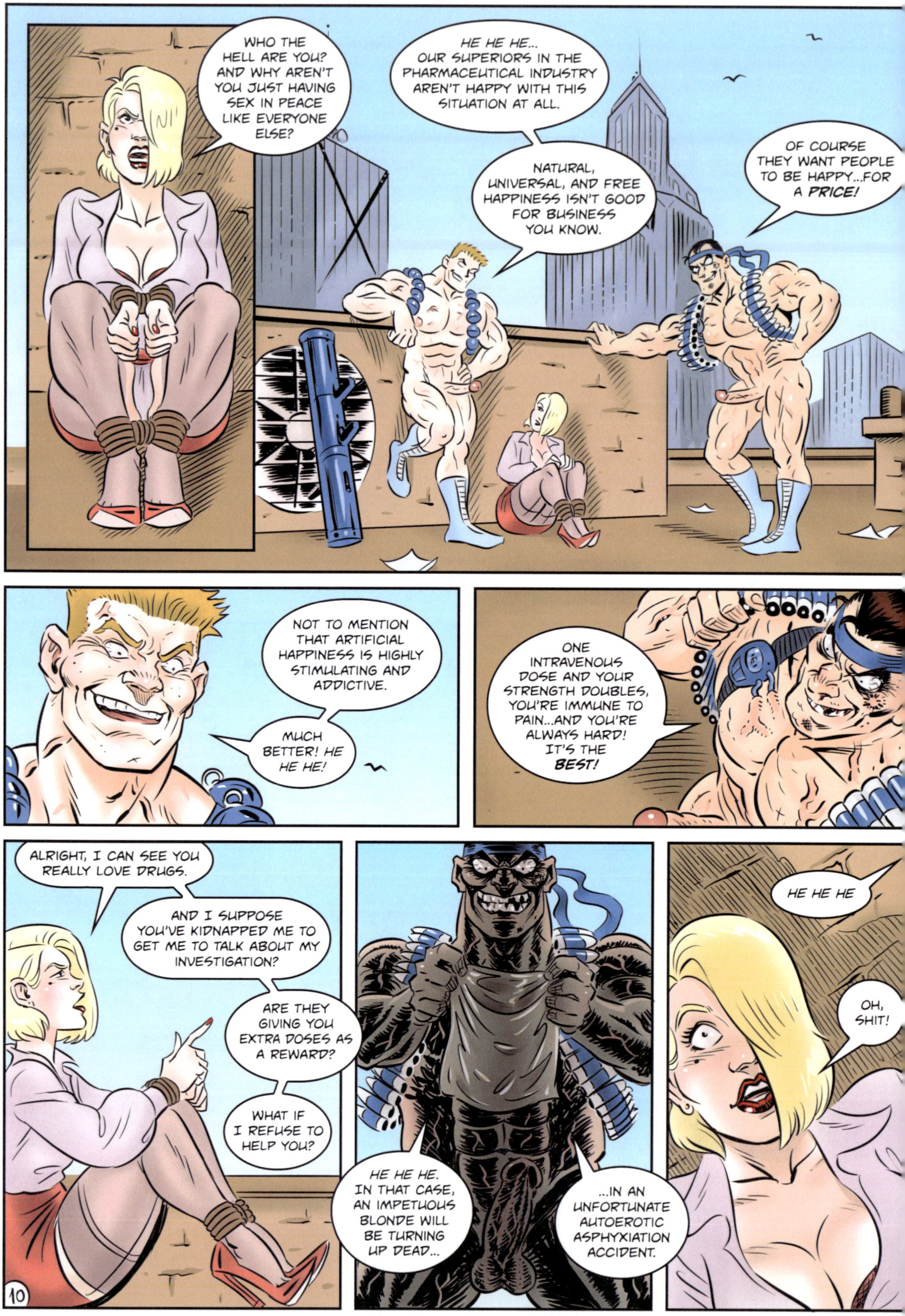

WHO THE HELL ARE YOU? AND WHY AREN'T YOU JUST HAVING SEX IN PEACE LIKE EVERYONE ELSE?
HE HE HE... OUR SUPERIORS IN THE PHARMACEUTICAL INDUSTRY AREN'T HAPPY WITH THIS SITUATION AT ALL.
NATURAL, UNIVERSAL, AND FREE HAPPINESS ISN'T GOOD FOR BUSINESS YOU KNOW.
OF COURSE THEY WANT PEOPLE TO BE HAPPY...FOR A *PRICE*!

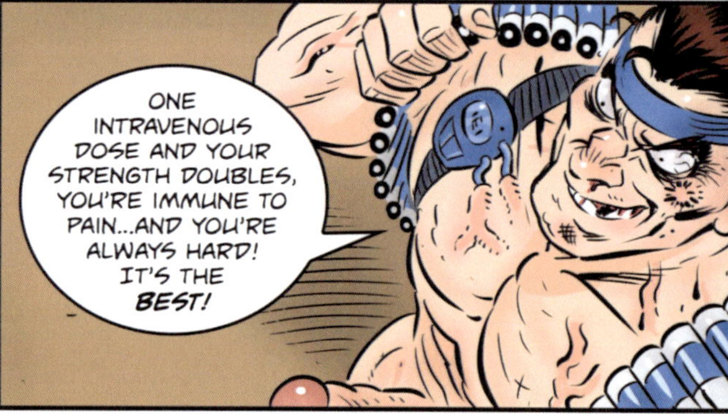

NOT TO MENTION THAT ARTIFICIAL HAPPINESS IS HIGHLY STIMULATING AND ADDICTIVE.
MUCH BETTER! *HE HE HE!*
ONE INTRAVENOUS DOSE AND YOUR STRENGTH DOUBLES, YOU'RE IMMUNE TO PAIN...AND YOU'RE ALWAYS HARD! IT'S THE *BEST*!

ALRIGHT, I CAN SEE YOU REALLY LOVE DRUGS.
AND I SUPPOSE YOU'VE KIDNAPPED ME TO GET ME TO TALK ABOUT MY INVESTIGATION?
ARE THEY GIVING YOU EXTRA DOSES AS A REWARD?
WHAT IF I REFUSE TO HELP YOU?
HE HE HE. IN THAT CASE, AN IMPETUOUS BLONDE WILL BE TURNING UP DEAD...
...IN AN UNFORTUNATE AUTOEROTIC ASPHYXIATION ACCIDENT.
HE HE HE
OH, SHIT!

LET'S LEAVE THE ASPHYXIATION PLAY FOR SOME OTHER TIME! WE'RE KICKING FACES TODAY!
HOLD ONTO ME IF YOU WANT TO LIVE!
?!
CRUSH!
DAMN! THEY'RE GETTING AWAY!
BLAM!
BLAM!
BLAM!
BLAM!
GRAAAAAAGGGHHH!
11

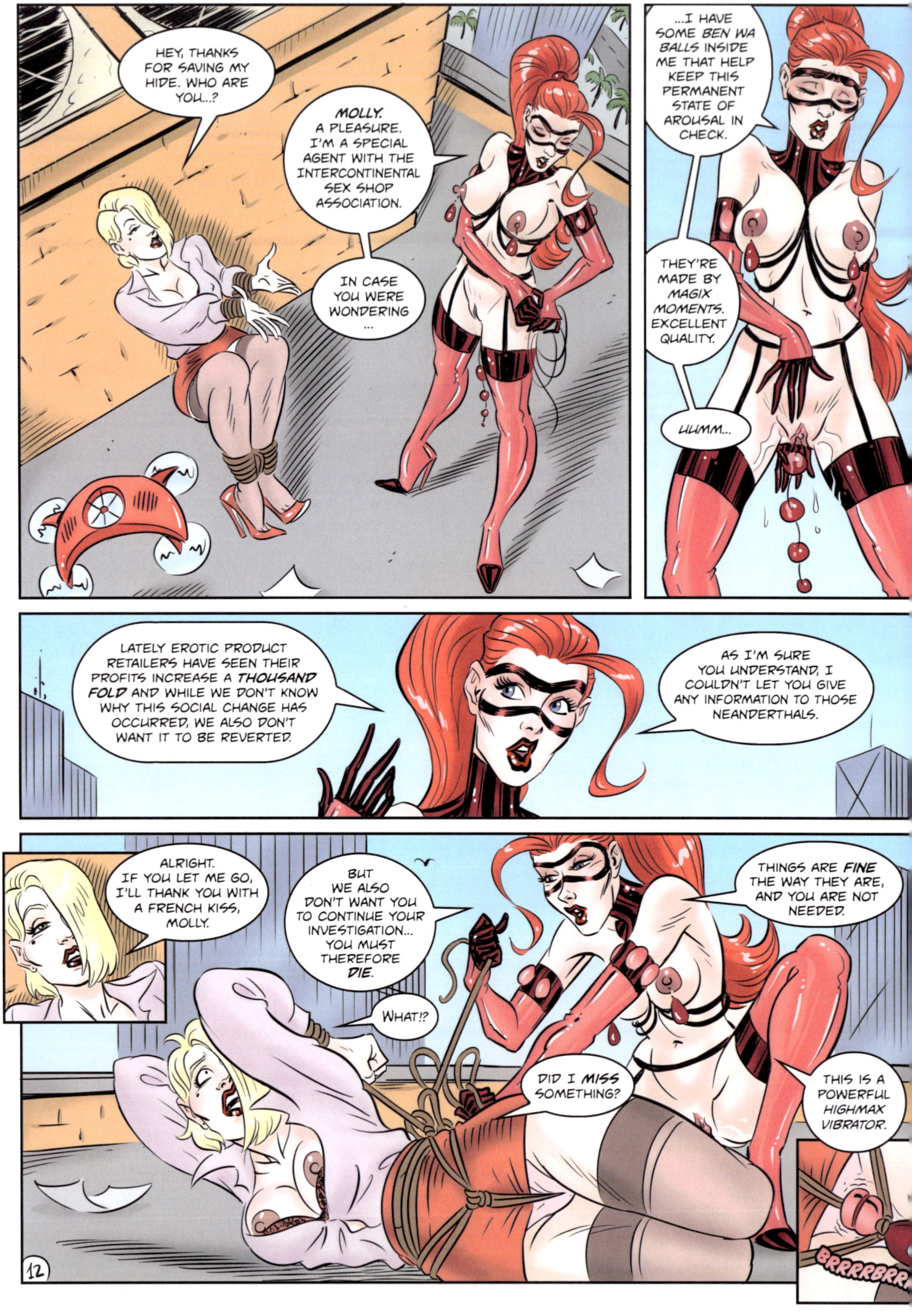

HEY, THANKS FOR SAVING MY HIDE. WHO ARE YOU...?
MOLLY. A PLEASURE. I'M A SPECIAL AGENT WITH THE INTERCONTINENTAL SEX SHOP ASSOCIATION.
IN CASE YOU WERE WONDERING ...
...I HAVE SOME BEN WA BALLS INSIDE ME THAT HELP KEEP THIS PERMANENT STATE OF AROUSAL IN CHECK.
THEY'RE MADE BY MAGIX MOMENTS. EXCELLENT QUALITY.
UUMM...
LATELY EROTIC PRODUCT RETAILERS HAVE SEEN THEIR PROFITS INCREASE A THOUSAND FOLD AND WHILE WE DON'T KNOW WHY THIS SOCIAL CHANGE HAS OCCURRED, WE ALSO DON'T WANT IT TO BE REVERTED.
AS I'M SURE YOU UNDERSTAND, I COULDN'T LET YOU GIVE ANY INFORMATION TO THOSE NEANDERTHALS.
ALRIGHT. IF YOU LET ME GO, I'LL THANK YOU WITH A FRENCH KISS, MOLLY.
BUT WE ALSO DON'T WANT YOU TO CONTINUE YOUR INVESTIGATION... YOU MUST THEREFORE DIE.
WHAT!?
THINGS ARE FINE THE WAY THEY ARE, AND YOU ARE NOT NEEDED.
DID I MISS SOMETHING?
THIS IS A POWERFUL HIGHMAX VIBRATOR.
BRRRRBRR

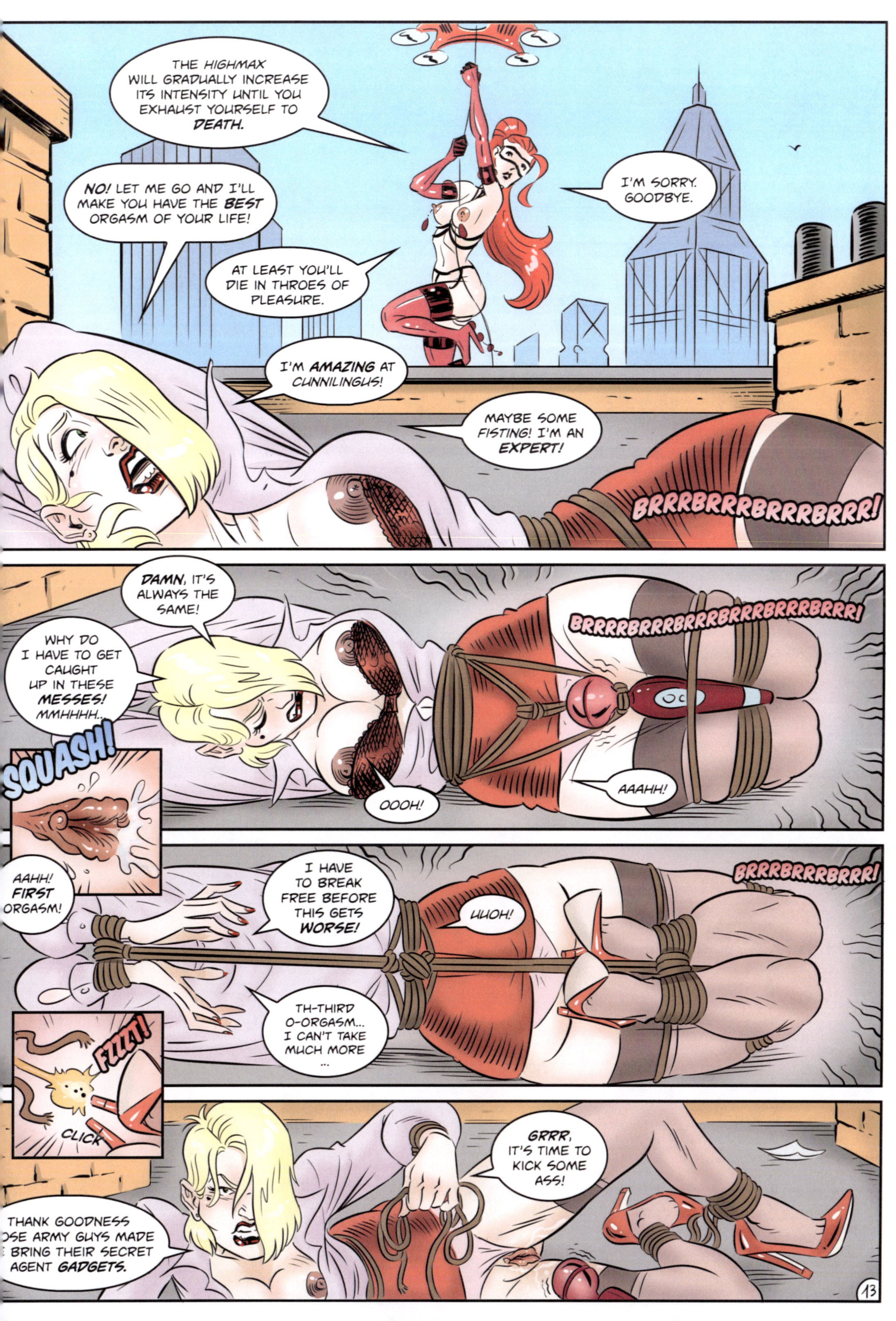

THE HIGHMAX WILL GRADUALLY INCREASE ITS INTENSITY UNTIL YOU EXHAUST YOURSELF TO DEATH.
NO! LET ME GO AND I'LL MAKE YOU HAVE THE BEST ORGASM OF YOUR LIFE!
I'M SORRY. GOODBYE.
AT LEAST YOU'LL DIE IN THROES OF PLEASURE.
I'M AMAZING AT CUNNILINGUS!
MAYBE SOME FISTING! I'M AN EXPERT!
BRRRBRRRBRRRBRRR!
DAMN, IT'S ALWAYS THE SAME!
WHY DO I HAVE TO GET CAUGHT UP IN THESE MESSES! MMHHHH...
BRRRRBRRRRBRRRRBRRRRBRRRRBRRR!
SQUASH!
OOOH!
AAAHH!
AAHH! FIRST ORGASM!
I HAVE TO BREAK FREE BEFORE THIS GETS WORSE!
UUOH!
BRRRBRRRBRRR!
TH-THIRD O-ORGASM... I CAN'T TAKE MUCH MORE ...
FZZZT!
CLICK
GRRR, IT'S TIME TO KICK SOME ASS!
THANK GOODNESS OSE ARMY GUYS MADE BRING THEIR SECRET AGENT GADGETS.
13

THAT SLUT'S ABOUT TO FIND OUT HOW WANDA WOLFE ROLLS!
AAH!
I'LL ASK THE GUY AT THE CLUB. HE PROBABLY KNOWS HER OR KNOWS HOW TO FIND HER SINCE THEY RUN IN THE SAME CIRCLES.
AAH!
OOH!

-MUTTERING-
...HER DAMN BEN WA BALLS HAVEN'T PREPARED HER FOR WHAT I'LL RAM INTO HER!
LISTEN, I'M LOOKING FOR SOMEONE AND I'M NOT IN THE MOOD FOR NONSENSE!

AAAH! THE DETECTIVE'S CAUGHT US! RUN!
TELL EMPRESS LILITH!
HUH?
RUN!

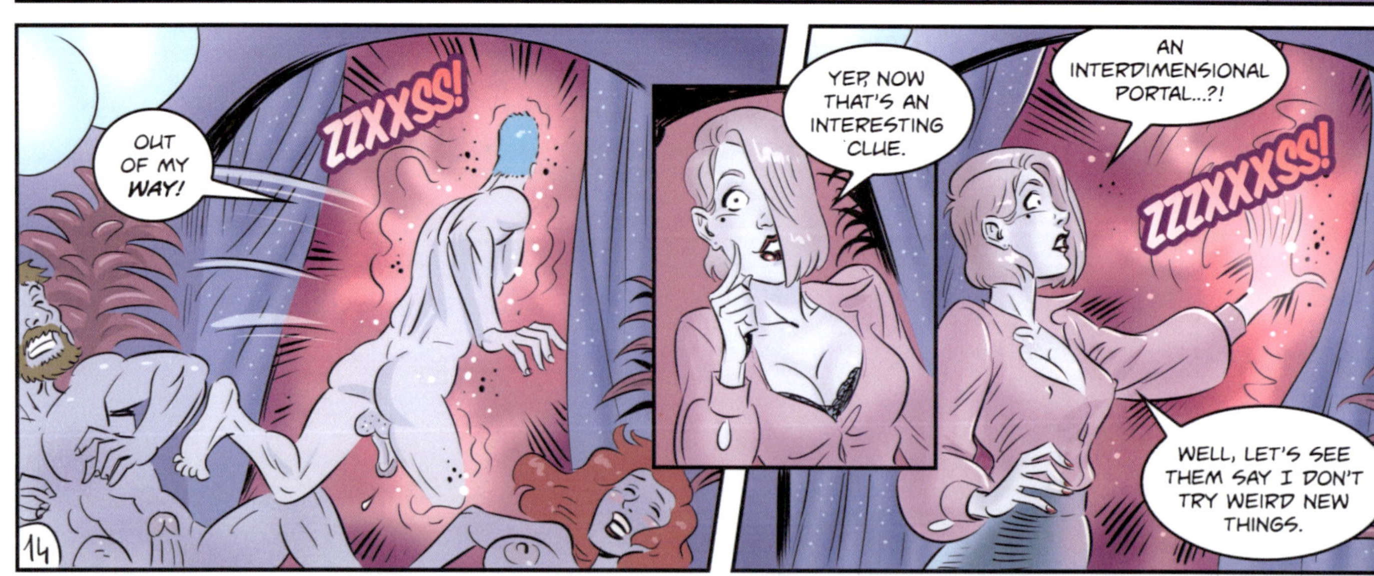

OUT OF MY WAY!
ZZXXSS!
YEP, NOW THAT'S AN INTERESTING CLUE.
AN INTERDIMENSIONAL PORTAL...?!
ZZZXXXSS!
WELL, LET'S SEE THEM SAY I DON'T TRY WEIRD NEW THINGS.

ZZZXXXSSS!
UH... EMPRESS LILITH I PRESUME.
I AM A MISERABLE WORM! I'VE FAILED YOU! I DESERVE TO BE PUNISHED! BOOOO!
DAMN, FEEDING ON HUMANS REALLY FATTENS THESE ALIENS UP.
LICK
LICK
LICK
LICK
LICK
15

WHAT ARE YOU TALKING ABOUT? MORE LIKE EATING HAMBURGERS AND ICE CREAM.
RELAX, YOU HAVE NOTHING TO FEAR.
YOU CAN CALL ME ELISABETH OR LIA. THAT EMPRESS LILITH THING IS FOR MY TRUSTED SLAVES.
OH, WAIT UNTIL I OPEN THIS.
THESE ARE ROB, JOHN, AND TIM.
NICE TO MEET YOU!
HELLOOOO!
BEFORE YOU ASK, YES, THIS PORTAL WAS NOT MADE WITH HUMAN TECHNOLOGY.
NEITHER ARE OUR OUTFITS.
NOR ARE THE DECORATIONS.
WHAT'S UP?
HI!
PLANET EARTH HAS FINALLY MADE CONTACT WITH SUPERIOR LIFE-FORMS AND AN ERA OF PEACE AND PROSPERITY OPENS ITSELF UP TO US.
LET ME START FROM THE BEGINNING...

ABOUT A WEEK AGO, WE WERE TOGETHER AT OUR ORG...AHEM, I MEAN, AT ONE OF OUR REGULAR PARTIES WHEN SUDDENLY...
GREETINGS, EARTHLINGS.
UPON PASSING BY THIS SYSTEM, WE NOTICED HOW PRIMITIVE YOUR SPECIES IS...
...AND WE HAVE DECIDED TO MAKE A QUICK STOP TO GIVE YOU A HAND.
THE PROBLEM SEEMS TO STEM FROM YOUR ARCHAIC REPTILIAN AND PRIMATE BRAINS, WHICH FLOOD YOU WITH FEAR AND DISTRUST AT THE UNKNOWN.
THAT IS PREVENTING YOU FROM REACHING THE SERENITY AND SPIRITUAL WELLBEING NECESSARY TO MAKE AN EVOLUTIONARY LEAP.
OUR PSYCHOSENSORS INDICATE THAT THIS SMALL COMMUNITY OF YOURS IS OPEN AND TOLERANT, AND IS THEREFORE THE MOST ADEQUATE FOR ESTABLISHING CONTACT AND HELPING THE REST.
WE'RE LEAVING YOU SOME TOOLS THAT WILL FACILITATE THE TASK OF SPREADING HAPPINESS THROUGHOUT YOUR WORLD.
A PLANETARY DISINHIBITOR TO GET RID OF YOUR RIDICULOUS COMPLEXES. ALSO SOME DIMENSIONAL PORTALS, A CLOTHING GENERATOR, A UNIVERSAL MULTISPECIES TRANSLATOR...
17

THE LATEX MACHINE IS GREAT!
IT'S LIKE A VACUUM BED!
DON'T WORRY, EVERYTHING WE'VE LEFT YOU IS SAFE TECHNOLOGY.
SUCH RESPONSIBILITY! THANK YOU SO MUCH.
PRACTICALLY TOYS WE GIVE TO OUR INFANTS.
MORE FOOD!
THERE IS NO DANGER OF ACCIDENTALLY DESTROYING ANYTHING.
UNIVERSAL PEACE AND LOVE!
HAVE FUN!
BYE!
TALKING TO BIRDS IS AWESOME!
WE REGRET NOT BEING ABLE TO STAY, BUT WE'RE LATE FOR THE MULTIORGY FESTIVAL IN THE ORION NEBULA.
OH WOW...
AND SO, THANKS TO THE SELFLESS AID OF OUR ALIEN FRIENDS, WE HAVE BEGUN OUR MISSION OF GUIDING HUMANITY TOWARDS A NEW ERA OF UNIVERSAL PEACE AND LOVE.
FINALLY A HOPEFUL FUTURE FOR OUR CIVILIZATION...
SPLURR!
HIT 'EM HARD AND IN THE HEAD, BOYS!
RATATATATATAT!
DON'T LET ANY ESCAPE! DIE, YOU DAMN FREAKS!
BANG!
BANG!
AAAH!

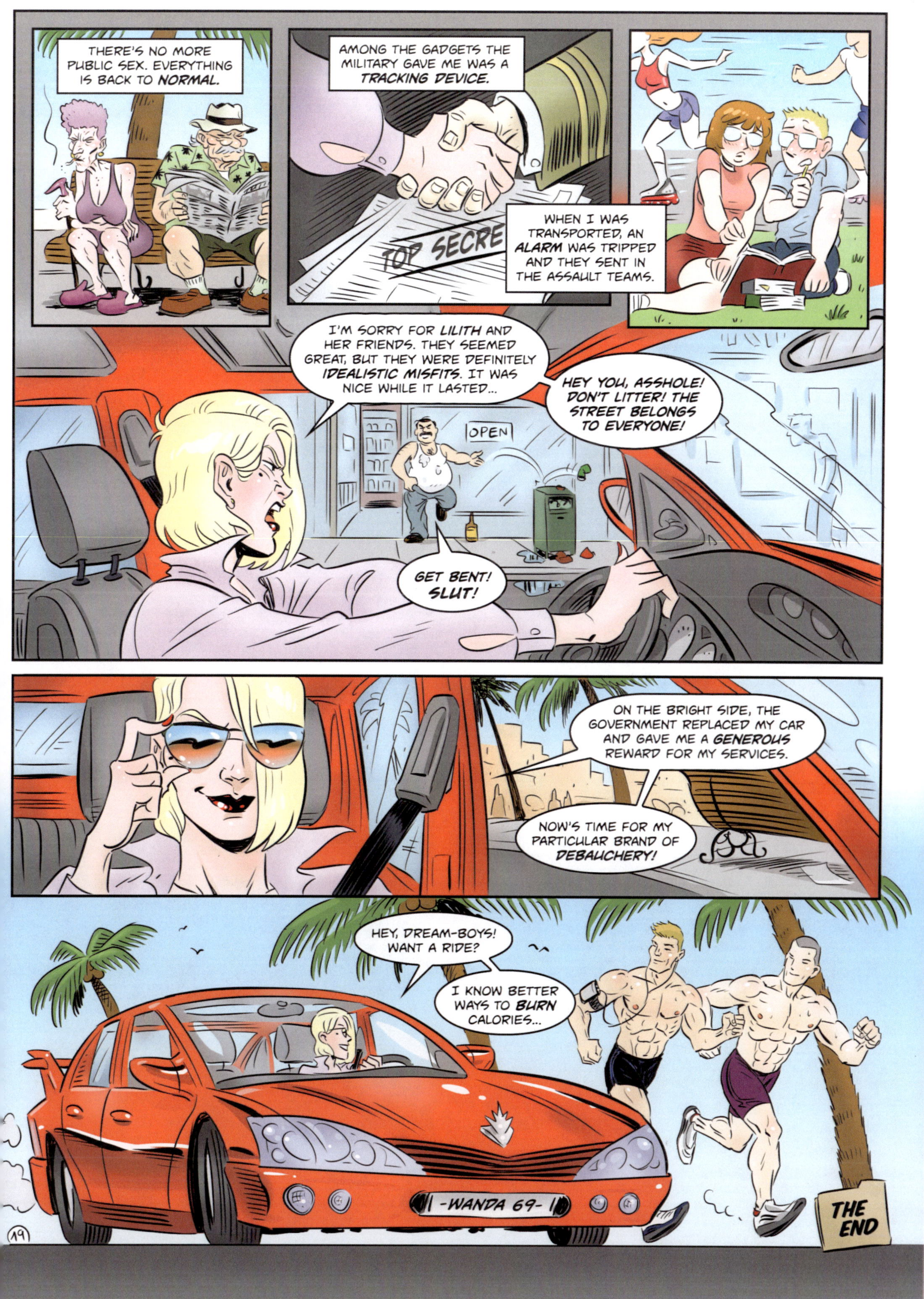

THERE'S NO MORE PUBLIC SEX. EVERYTHING IS BACK TO NORMAL.
AMONG THE GADGETS THE MILITARY GAVE ME WAS A TRACKING DEVICE.
TOP SECRE
WHEN I WAS TRANSPORTED, AN ALARM WAS TRIPPED AND THEY SENT IN THE ASSAULT TEAMS.
I'M SORRY FOR LILITH AND HER FRIENDS. THEY SEEMED GREAT, BUT THEY WERE DEFINITELY IDEALISTIC MISFITS. IT WAS NICE WHILE IT LASTED...
HEY YOU, ASSHOLE! DON'T LITTER! THE STREET BELONGS TO EVERYONE!
OPEN
GET BENT! SLUT!
ON THE BRIGHT SIDE, THE GOVERNMENT REPLACED MY CAR AND GAVE ME A GENEROUS REWARD FOR MY SERVICES.
NOW'S TIME FOR MY PARTICULAR BRAND OF DEBAUCHERY!
HEY, DREAM-BOYS! WANT A RIDE?
I KNOW BETTER WAYS TO BURN CALORIES...
-WANDA 69-
THE END

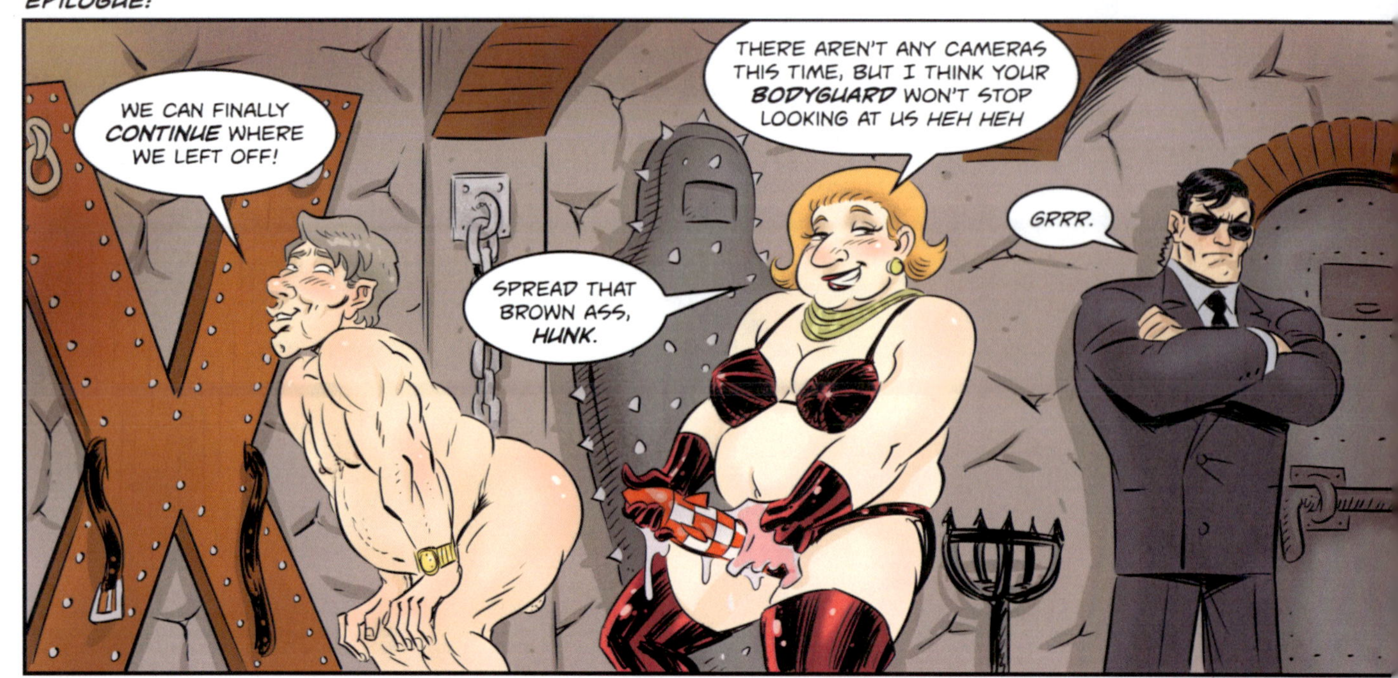

EPILOGUE:
WE CAN FINALLY CONTINUE WHERE WE LEFT OFF!
THERE AREN'T ANY CAMERAS THIS TIME, BUT I THINK YOUR BODYGUARD WON'T STOP LOOKING AT US HEH HEH
SPREAD THAT BROWN ASS, HUNK.
GRRR.

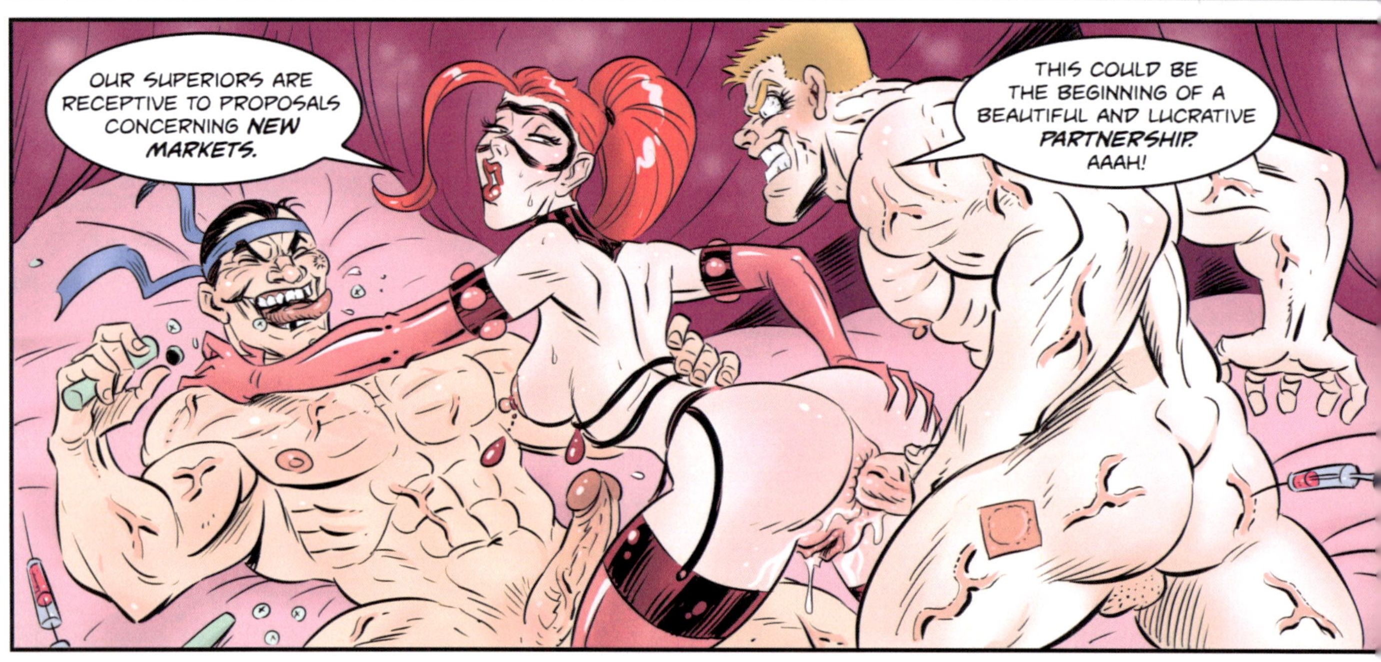

OUR SUPERIORS ARE RECEPTIVE TO PROPOSALS CONCERNING NEW MARKETS.
THIS COULD BE THE BEGINNING OF A BEAUTIFUL AND LUCRATIVE PARTNERSHIP. AAAH!

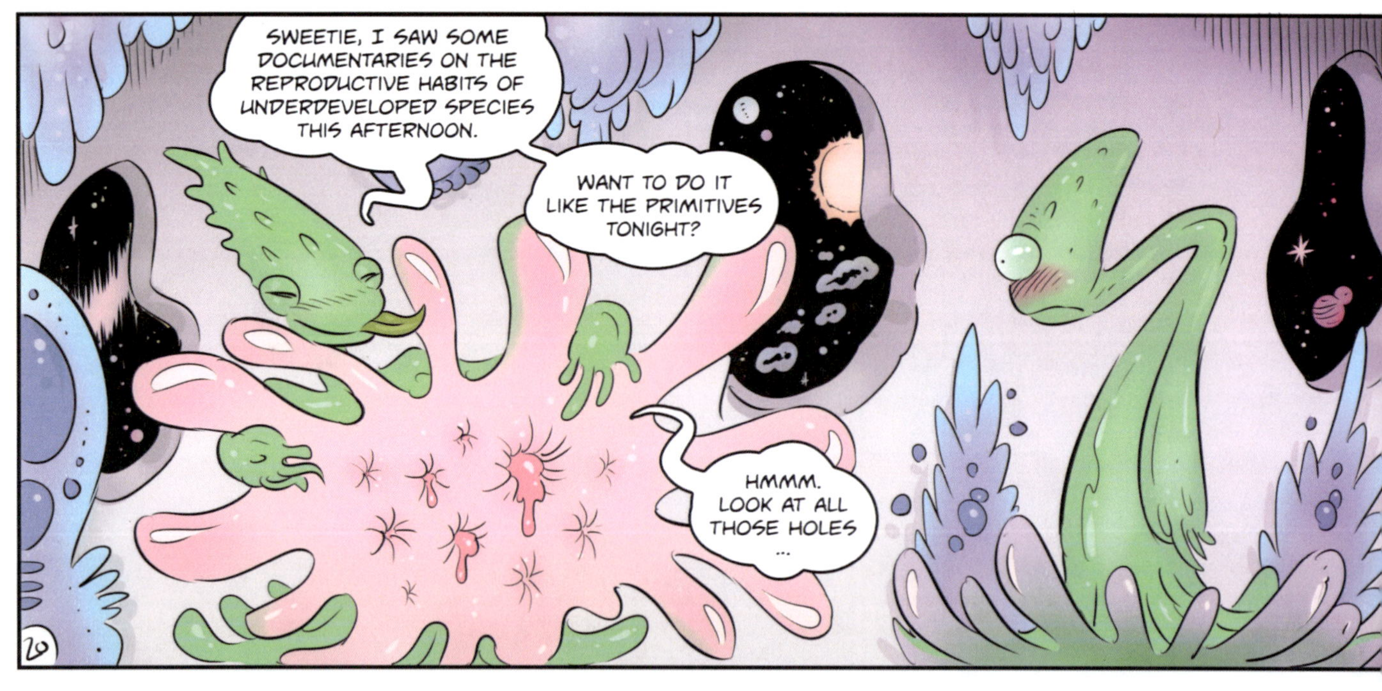

SWEETIE, I SAW SOME DOCUMENTARIES ON THE REPRODUCTIVE HABITS OF UNDERDEVELOPED SPECIES THIS AFTERNOON.
WANT TO DO IT LIKE THE PRIMITIVES TONIGHT?
HMMM. LOOK AT ALL THOSE HOLES ...

ESCAPOLOGY HOMEWORK (A ONE-PAGE WANDA CAMEO, 2025)

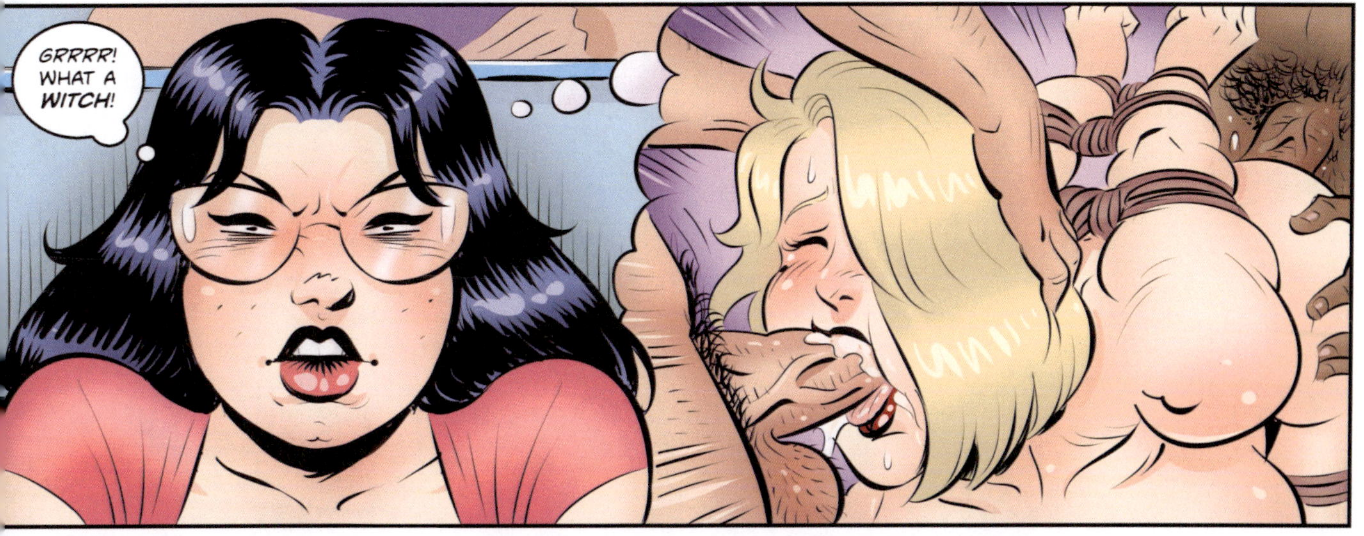

HISTORICAL INDEX OF WANDA IN PRINT

Detective Wanda Wolfe first appeared in the Spanish magazine *Kiss Comix* as individu
stories in black & white and grays during the years 2002-2005. Kiss Comix, published by I
Cupula Editorial, also had similar editions in other countries, mainly in France as *Poud.
Aux Reves*, and in USA as *French Kiss*. The first independently published Wanda comics k
Coax were recolored by hand and published as issues 1-6 in 2014-2015. Comic issue 7 ar
the Special issue 8 were created a few years later and their creative process (ink ar
coloring) done In digital. The story Laugh of Die" in issue 7 was a commission from a tickl
fan. The following index lists the *Kiss Comix* issue number or year where the *Detectiv
Wanda Wolfe* story first appeared and the Spanish and English story titles

Kiss Issue	Spanish Title	English Title
119	Estampitas	The Mystery of the Trading Cards
121	Lazos	Bonds
125	Una orgía de muerte	Orgy & Death
127	Calor Humano	Human Heat
129	¿Apuestas?	Gamblers
131	Misión Increible	Mission: Incredible
133	Fan	Fan
135	Todo lo que siempre supo y nunca se atrevieron a mostrarle después del FIN	Everything You Always Wanted To Know, But They Never Dared To Show You After... "THE END"
136	Tres eran Tres	Three Filthy Pigs
138	El jardín de las tentaciones	The Garden of Secret Delights
139	Las dos caras de la moneda	The Two Sides of Truth
141	Un cuento chino	A Chinese Tale
143	Trabajo en equipo	Teamwork
144	Cuestión de gustos	A Matter of Taste
147	Indiscreto	Indiscreet
149	El que no corre, vuela	Naughty Spanish Nights
151	La pirámide del poder	The Hierarchy of Sex and Power
159	Mercado competitivo	This story never appeared in English.
165	Jane "La Desvirgadora"	Jane "The Deflowerer"

Independently Published Only:

2017	All you need is Love ...and Sex ...and Rock & Roll
2018	Laugh or Die (Robbery at the Grand Hotel)
2018	Welcome to Twin Hills
2018	5 Hours with Wanda

Wanda made a one-page cameo in the story "Mercado Competitivo" in Spanish *Kiss Comix* number 159. This story never appeared in English.

ABOUT THE ARTIST

Coax is Alvaro Muñoz, a celebrated Spanish artist, illustrator, and author specializing in fetish story and art. His first fetish works appeared during the year 2000 in the Spanish bdsm magazine *Sumissa*. The next year, he formally launched his professional career in the comics world publishing with the international company La Cupula in their world-famous magazine *Kiss Comix* (also known as *La Podre au Reves* in France and *French Kiss* in the United States). *The Wanda Wolfe Detective* series first appeared in black & white and grays in *Kiss comix*. Since 2011, he has published all his fetish works under the name Coax. His French editions have been published by La Musardine and Murano Publishing. *The Collar and Other Fetish Stories* and *Secret Domination League, The Complete Series Edition*, are exclusive English-language publications from Erosetti Press. Explore his art and comics on his website coaxdreams.com and at ErosettiPress.com.